At the End of the Storm

At the End of the Storm

by

Marleen Pasch

This is a work of fiction whose characters and events are products of the author's imagination or used fictionally. Any similarities with people or actual events are coincidental.

Dedication

To Ruth, who knew the writer in me before I set a word on paper.

Acknowledgments

Thank you, Michael James and Penmore Press, for bringing *Storm* to light. Thanks also to Christine Horner for her telling cover design, Chris Kuell for inspired developmental editing, and Haley Hampton for insightful copy editing.

Without Glenn Sanislo's comments on early drafts, Daria's story might still be tucked in a dark drawer. B.J., Dee, Gail, Joe, Kelly, Lorrie, Mary, Phil, Richard, Sandy, Stephanie, Susan, Victor—always interested, always encouraging.

The librarians in Darien, Connecticut and Boca Raton, Florida provided research expertise and friendship. What remarkable minds and spirits.

And then there's Cindy, who provides me with a room of my own, and somehow still allows me my quirks and foibles. I wish Donna were here too.

Arise, my darling,
My beautiful one,
Come with me.
See! The winter is past;
The rains are over and gone.
— Song of Solomon, 2:10-11

Chapter One
August 1988

The two of them are alone. Wrapped in warm light and protected by possibility. The young woman's eyes on the days-old child in her arms, adoring her creation, clenching fists and eyes, determined to make her way in the world, but uncertain how.

The mother leans down. Her long brown hair drapes close to the child's tossed-about curls. The same color.

Those nine months of hard-boiled certainty, knowing how she would feel at this moment rather than how she wouldn't feel. All those weeks of preparing to let the child go as easily and unintentionally as she was conceived. All that fear and dread, now washed away by light and promise and, yes, wholly unexpected and consuming joy.

Close enough to feel the child's breath, the young mother opens her mouth to whisper her daughter's name. Instead, she gasps. What is her child's name?

Shadow crosses the infant's face, belly, arms, legs, feet. Then darkness swallows her. Laumės, the Lithuanian field fairies, gather. "Čiūčia liūlia," they chant. "Forgotten child."

The girl is gone.

Where?

At the End of the Storm

The young woman looks down at her belly, just days ago ripe and full, now flaccid. Empty. She screams into the dark.

Against her will, Daria Demarest's eyes fluttered open. Her heart pounded. Her breath ran short and quick in her chest.

She looked around the room, dimly lit by the half-moon shining over nearby Long Island Sound. Everything—antique armoire, tufted chaise, ginger jar lamps—in its place. No coal dust or sulfur smell from Mount Laurel, Pennsylvania's mines.

She reached for one of the overstuffed pillows on her bed, all linen and white. She pulled it close and wrapped herself around it. Folly to think its lifeless feathers could calm her. Still, she clung to it until her heart slowed, until she could take a proper breath, until she could return to the life she had made for herself. The life she created to shake off Mount Laurel's residue and the nightmare that constantly pestered her. The dream that reminded her of how she gave up her child—no, *how her child was taken from her*. Which was it? How many years ago now? Twenty. Twenty years this past December.

But now, her masterfully crafted life had fissured. It was being filched from her, just like her child had been.

She glanced toward the clock. 3:19 a.m. No surprise. Even without those diabolical red digits glowering at her, she would have known it was between three and four. The hour when, until only weeks ago, she would have been riding down I-95 from Connecticut to Manhattan so that, by seven, studio lights would forgive any fatigue or regret, and audience adoration would reassure and complete her. For an hour, at least.

No more, though. Daria closed her eyes, trying to snuff out the memory of the Friday she filed for divorce, the day her job, maybe her career, had derailed, sending her down a precipitous embankment on which she hadn't yet found footing.

******

Her driver was idling at the studio's Fifty-Second Street entrance, ready to get a jump on the weekend exodus from Manhattan. But inspiration struck Daria on her way out the revolving front door. What if she interviewed Rudy *and* his wife the following week? It was old news that U.S. Attorney Giuliani was angling to become New York's next mayor. But if she could convince Donna Hanover to join them to talk about life as both anchorwoman and candidate Rudy's wife, that would reel in *Wake Up*'s mostly female audience at least as much as his contentious cleanup of organized crime as a federal prosecutor. She circled back into the building and took the studio's private elevator to the nineteenth floor.

"Gavin," she called, careening into her co-host's office. "I think . . ."

But Gavin McGee—his green eyes fixed on general manager Vince Foster, fists supporting him on his desk as he leaned across it—was absorbed in his diatribe. He couldn't stop himself before Daria heard the words "aging divorcé" and "ratings disaster."

When he caught sight of her, though, Gavin forced a smile. He straightened his tie and stood as tall as his five-foot-eight frame would allow. "Daria, honey," he cooed. "Aren't you supposed to be halfway to Greenvale by now?"

Daria didn't allow her face to betray what she had already begun to suspect. Her days at *Wake Up* were nearing an end. She needed this job. Not just for the money. Or the ballast it would provide while she navigated through the divorce. She needed the stage. Without one, where would she shine? Where would she hide?

She might not live up to the standards she had set for herself as a mother and certainly not as a wife; but when the lights went up, her limitations, her regrets? They drifted away like leaves on a swift-flowing stream. She had known that since her college musical theatre days, followed by two years of practice and precision—five, six, seven, eight—as a Radio City Rockette. A Rockette.

So that afternoon, when her eyes shifted from Gavin to Vince as Vince tossed out two-word locutions about changes in *Wake Up*'s format—fresh faces, new approaches—his voice faded as she steadied herself against Gavin's credenza. *Lawsuit?* The possibility crossed her mind. Probably not. As best she knew, Vince had the right to renew or not. *Hot. It's getting so hot in here.*

"*Wake Up*," he continued, "needs a facelift."

Daria's hand migrated to her neck, to the poultry-like fold of skin that had begun draping from her throat only months ago. Why hadn't she had it taken care of? She eased away from the credenza so she could stand straight and tall. She pulled in her stomach, taut and flat. And, yes, she raised her chin, just a bit, to minimize the sagging.

"Research shows," Vince was saying, "that our advertisers get the biggest bang for their buck with the twenty-five- to thirty-nine-year-olds."

Daria counted the months to herself—August, September, October—until she would turn forty. She would be out of the coveted market segment just in time for trick-or-treating.

"Viewers who tune in from eight thirty to ten, they're busy moms, most of them. They've just shuttled the older kids off to school while they're corralling the toddlers into playpens or strollers. And they're doing it all alone." Vince leaned against the wall, waved his hand as if he, and certainly not Gavin, would ever abandon his wife that way. "They're lucky to get a peck or a kiss before their husbands run off for a train or a cab. And these gals . . ."

Gals? Why did he insist on using that hideous four-letter word?

"They want to think a little less, laugh a little more. But most of all, they want to start their day with at least a little attention from a man." He nodded to Gavin. "That's what Gavin gives 'em."

"So, what you're saying . . ." Daria felt heat rising to her face. "What you're saying," she repeated, "is that once these women had kids, their brains shrunk?" She heard her voice go shrill and paused. If there was any possibility of salvaging the situation, she wouldn't change Vince's mind by barking like a fishwife. She summoned her on-camera voice, honed over the years to betray just enough edge during a hard-hitting interview and just enough warmth to keep from appearing overly syrupy when she was forced to do fluff.

"It's just that, if you want to talk demographics," she continued, "those same stroller-pushers are college educated. Seventy-six percent of them anyway. And about a third have done at least some graduate work."

"And," Gavin piped in as he leaned across the front of his desk, "they're tired. They—"

But when Vince signaled to him, Gavin sank into his chair, looked out the window onto Fifty-Second Street, chewed on his manicured thumbnail, and shut up.

Daria's eyes shifted from Vince to Gavin. Why me and not that ruddy little weasel? She had done her best to maintain a sense of intelligence and dignity on the show, while he . . . he —what was that word, she couldn't think of it—*pandered* to the audience. He treated women like babymakers, more interested in Hollywood breakups and make ups than making the City a better place to raise their children. But she knew the truth. *Wake Up* had been losing market share to startup shows even more insistent on turning women's brains to Cream of Wheat. What were these women thinking?

"There's no good time to have to say this, Daria."

Daria reeled herself back to Vince's monologue.

"I had hoped we could discuss it in a different place at a different time."

"But?"

"But we won't be renewing your contract. We have to let you go."

Let me go? Lightheaded. Hot. It was so damned hot. "Let me go?" Did that weak-willed little squeal actually emanate from her throat? *You got ice water in those veins 'a yers, and that's all you need in life, Dairee Darlin'.* That's what her father taught her. I've. Got. Ice. Water. In. My. Veins.

"It's not personal." Vince screwed up his face in what Daria could only guess was attempted empathy. "It's just that . . ."

His disingenuousness stirred her up enough that she could recover her voice. "I don't suppose Ted's heat-seeking penis has anything to do with this . . . this facelift," she interrupted. "That his tryst with, what's her name, Juliette influenced your thinking?"

A name partner at one of the City's premiere marketing firms, Daria's soon-to-be-former husband, Ted Demarest, counseled several of WNYY's most lucrative accounts on media buys. He worked closely with the station's senior media specialist—most recently that was Juliette Ramsey. But when Juliette spurned him for a venture capitalist making three times Ted's salary, Ted started steering clients to *City Morning*, which aired opposite *Wake Up.*

"No, no." Vince grimaced. He shook his head as if her insinuation was hysterical imagining. "Of course not." But he had hesitated just long enough to confirm Daria's suspicion. Ted was at least partly to blame. "Why don't you stop by my office on Monday first thing? We can chat, wrap up a few loose ends."

Loose ends? Daria bit the inside of her cheek. She wouldn't grant them another word, another minute of her time. She left the office, took the elevator back to Fifty-Second Street, and stepped into the black car waiting to drive her home.

Chapter Two
September 1988

Daria looked into the oversized mirror above the family room fireplace. "You made it out of coal mining country to New York, then Connecticut," she reminded herself. "You can find a way. You *will* find a way." She was due a year's severance. Plenty of time to reestablish herself, *re-create* herself. Again. But as what? That was the question. And though she bristled at the thought of any continued tether to Ted, he had, after all, *done well* in Fairfield County parlance. He had risen to the top at Werner, McCall, Demarest, with a mid-six-figure salary, plus bonus. She even managed a laugh when her friend Frankie reminded her there would be a handsome divorce settlement. As if a six-foot, slick-haired "settlement" would arrive on her doorstep wearing a tux, a red rose in his lapel, proffering a silver platter heaped with T-bills and stock options in one hand, a martini—extra dry, two olives—in the other.

When the phone rang, she took one more look at her confident, assured reflection, even though, inside, she felt empty and afraid.

"You're sitting down?" In the fifteen years she had known Gil Hodges, he had never begun a conversation with words other than "Hi, Daria. How are you?" He was that predictable, that CPA-steady.

"Should I be?" She made her way toward the sofa. "Why do I feel I should be pouring a double Dewar's, neat?"

"I can wait."

"It's that bad?"

When Gil said nothing, Daria approached the bar. *Ted's bar.*

"Okay," she said. "I'm pouring as we speak." But instead of reaching for the Scotch, she filled a tumbler full of seltzer. This was no time to lose control. She had to stay clearheaded and focused.

As she sank into the couch, Gil advised her that, over the last months, Ted had methodically drained their joint accounts: savings, brokerage, checking. He had tapped the life out of their home equity line of credit. He had even convinced his mother to allow him to raid the trusts she had set up for the children's college tuition.

Ted's first love, it turned out, wasn't Juliette the media specialist. Or the bare-breasted executive assistant Daria had caught him with in his office two years earlier. Or the travel agent who called the house two, three times a week to advise of last-minute flight changes, though her voice sounded suspiciously like Sassy Connors from the Greenvale Club. No, Ted's favorite mistress was Lady Luck, who persistently eluded him, despite his attempts to seduce her over blackjack tables. So much for those Vegas "trade shows" he flew to every month.

Why, Daria berated herself, hadn't she stayed on top of their finances? If her childhood had taught her anything, it was that trusting anyone to take care of her was not just foolish but unsafe.

******

By the time Ted's U-Haul carted off his Eames chair and his Bose sound system and his two-thousand-dollar suits and his squash racket to the SoHo loft he would be sharing with an as-yet-unnamed roommate, Daria had formulated a temporary Band-Aid of a survival plan.

First, she sold the Greenvale house. With what she salvaged from the sale, she paid the help their back salaries and Jack's tuition at Saint Gregory's Prep. Then she put down twenty percent on a weatherworn little Cape Cod in a funky, up-and-coming section of Greenvale's Sound Shore.

There were other adjustments. Twelve-year-old Lizzy would finish the year at Greenvale Country Day, but after that, she would transfer to Sound Shore schools. And until Daria found work, there would be no dance or figure skating classes for Lizzy, no cheerleading camps.

Without a fuss, Jack found a summer job running the launch at the Sound Shore Yacht Club. So what if he had to give up his J24 and his junior membership at the Greenvale Club? "I can still crew on Rick Reardon's Hinckley," he told Daria. How she and Ted had brought as amenable a soul as Jack into the world, she would never know. If she hadn't felt the labor pains herself, she might have run a DNA test on him. Lizzy, though, had thrown a princess-sized fit. It wouldn't take a tarot reader to predict that girl's future: Lizzy was a royal handful in the making.

******

Silent. At least it was silent. Daria's dreams and memories might have intruded once again on her sleep, as they had for almost twenty years. But at least there wasn't yet any bird-chirping, any trash truck grinding and heaving. And Lizzy wasn't up and about, whining because she couldn't find her backpack or math homework.

Daria let go of the pillow she had been clenching and extricated herself from the duvet that had insinuated itself around her legs. She reached to her bedside chair for her well-worn terry robe—the only remotely raggedy piece of clothing she allowed herself—wrapped herself in its familiarity, then made her way from the master suite to the kitchen. With one fluid move—even at a sleep-deprived thirty-nine, even in the middle of the night, all those years of dance wouldn't allow her body to betray anything out of order—she turned on the stove, filled the tea kettle with water, and set it on the burner.

She opened the cupboard and pulled out the little paper sack Frankie had bought at that place called Remedies. In the week or so since she had been drinking it, the chamomile and lavender Insomnia Blend hadn't fulfilled the label's promise of "more restful sleep and peace-filled dreams." A shot of Dewar's wouldn't have hurt, but Frankie had warned her that, in the end, alcohol aggravated rather than relieved sleeplessness.

Daria wasn't altogether convinced Frankie had her facts straight. After all, following a good toot, Frankie could, and usually did, sleep like the dead. But in the weeks since Frankie had started going to AA, she had become even bossier and more pedantic than when she drank. The one good thing about her newfound *program*, as Frankie called it, was that she had taken to preaching to Lizzy about the hazards of drinking. And with Lizzy, Daria could use all the help she could get.

When Daria opened the fridge, the glare inside slapped her and dashed any hope of falling back asleep. She pulled out the milk and honey, loaded the infuser with tea, and placed it in a mug. She poured the boiling water over the tea. Then, mug in hand, like a soul wandering in search of release from perpetual sleepless purgatory, Daria made her way to the laundry room and opened the supply cabinet.

After the first few nights of sleepless pillow-clenching, Daria decided it was better to accomplish something rather than trying to wrestle her worries into submission. She had hauled out mops and brooms—things she hadn't gone near in years, thanks to the help she used to be able to afford—and those toxic orange and green chemicals ominously labeled "eye irritant," the ones that made her sneeze. She opened the windows, pulled on bubble-gum-pink rubber gloves, and scrubbed. She erased scuff marks, lifted dirt off the floors, shined the refrigerator and stove and sinks. Clean. She got things clean. When she saw results, she felt better, for a little bit anyway.

Her job-hunting hadn't produced results, though. She had made the rounds of the Manhattan studios but struck out. She had been identified so long with *Wake Up* that the networks wouldn't touch her. At least that was the reason they gave. The truth, though, she couldn't know for sure. Was it her age? The trend toward insipidness? Ted? The louder the questions clamored in her head, the harder she scrubbed.

For the next few weeks, her task was to get herself and the kids moved and resettled. The cleanup she was doing was good training, boot camp, for the little place they would be moving to up the coast a bit in Sound Shore. Its vintage forties bathrooms, with rust-stained tubs and sinks, its grimy little kitchen, the size of her current walk-in closet—only layered with what looked and smelled like decades of accumulated bacon grease—would call for all-out janitorial warfare. And when she fell into wallowing, she barked the same order to herself as she did when Lizzy whined because she couldn't go to cheerleading camp: snap out of it.

This morning's mission, Daria decided as she reached for a box of nefarious black trash bags, was to tackle her office. Tea and bags in hand, she passed through the great room with its vaulted ceiling, the dining room that could seat twelve comfortably, eighteen with a little finesse, and the living room with French doors leading to the now untended perennial garden.

When she opened the office door, she allowed herself one mournful moment. She would miss this room the most, done in cream and taupe, with its silky Bokhara on the floor, the Tiffany lamp on the antique mahogany desk. It was her refuge, where, whatever was going on outside the room or inside her head, she could enter, close the shantung drapes, turn on *Sleeping Beauty* or *The Girl with the Flaxen Hair,* and dance.

But this morning Daria was all business. Most of the room's contents wouldn't fit in her new Cape. And most of what might make it through the door would feel too imposing, as if stealing the air from the place. Her new "office" would be a postage-stamp-sized breakfast area off the kitchen.

Snap out of it.

She put her tea on her desk and set her objective: weed out half a dozen file cartons before sunrise, the rest after breakfast.

One by one, she went through drawers, salvaging a few files, tossing others into the black bags. Until she came across a blue Werner, McCall, Demarest binder. Ted's. How it had landed in her office, she didn't know. She opened it and leafed through. *Identifying and Penetrating Marketing Opportunities Among Baby-Boomer Women.* Ted had certainly penetrated that market segment, and plenty of others too.

She stopped at the section titled "The Spiritual Quest: Transforming Women's Search for Meaning into Profit." Only Ted and his fellow Rumpelstiltskins could spin gold from a spiritual quest, whatever that was. But, Daria conceded, Ted knew how to make money, and she needed money. She sank into the sofa, sipping her Insomnia Blend and skimming the executive summary.

Pollster Craig Cunningham reports the number of women born between 1946 and 1964 seeking spiritual growth climbed eight points in the last two years. Projections are for that number to increase annually by at least five percent through 1992.

Baby boom women want access to every possible tool—fitness products, cosmetics, surgery, supplements—to ward off the aging process.

For many women, physical fitness is connected to emotional and spiritual wellbeing, which, in turn, is facilitated by meditation, prayer, or other life-affirming practices.

Daria's mind started working through its gears. She leapt from the sofa, sat at her desk, and rooted through the top drawer for a highlighter.

While some are becoming more involved in traditional religions, many are drawn to non-traditional disciplines, such as yoga, meditation, and other Eastern and Western traditions.

She skimmed the rest, highlighting in yellow:

No contradiction between self-improvement and spirituality . . . increasingly single by choice . . . value friendship as much as family . . . view healing as a mission, not just a casual pursuit . . . coming to terms with the past, resolving issues . . .

Daria tried to ignore the stab in her chest when she read those last phrases. For two decades, she had done her best to avoid "coming to terms" with her past. She had skirted around "resolving issues" by creating an outwardly enviable life. She had married well. (At least she thought she had.) She had made a name for herself. (At least she thought she had.) But *healing?* She wasn't quite sure what that meant, but she knew she hadn't experienced it. Just a few hours ago, despite all she had to distract her, all she had to accomplish,

Daria's first-born daughter had winnowed into her dreams. Again. Where was she? Who had she become?

As for spirituality, she wasn't sure what that meant either. But she knew it didn't mean her childhood Catholicism. She had shed that part of her upbringing as decisively and intentionally as she had her central Pennsylvania twang.

She focused on the report's executive summary, skipping to the section headed "The Bottom Line."

Boomer women have dollars to spend, and they like to spend them. Their new affinity for spiritual health represents a largely untapped but potentially lucrative opportunity.

Daria pushed back her chair and swiveled to face the room's center. She stood and paced. She considered her reflection in the gilt floor mirror next to her bookcase. She didn't have alimony or a 401(k) to loot for spa treatments or yoga classes. Not now, anyway. But she looked as if she might. And if she looked the part, she could play the part. She may not be on any spiritual quest, but if there were money to be made by convincing other women—and some studio exec—she was, so be it.

She pulled a yellow pad and a black felt-tip pen from the desk drawer. TO DO, she scrawled across the top. Then, flipping through Ted's binder, she started her list.

1. *Go to Remedies; talk to owner.*

What was the name of that yoga center in the Berkshires, the one Frankie had been urging her to go to for hazy-sounding courses like Inner Peace: Anywhere, Anytime?

2. Ask Frankie about yoga center.

Speaking of Frankie, what was that phrase she and her fellow AA cult members were always yapping about? Spiritual awakening? She jotted it down.

Maybe she could even do something with what Nana had taught her about all those Lithuanian gods and goddesses, the ones she journaled about when . . . She didn't want to think about that time in her life. Still, they were spiritual. Or were they?

3. Find Nana's stories.

As the sun rose, Daria reread the proposal she had roughed out: *Awakenings: A Talk Show for Women with Money to Spend.* She edited with a firm grip on her pen, scratching out a paragraph here, fleshing out a sentence there. When she set down her pen and pushed back her chair, she ran toward the window, flung open the drapes. For the first time in weeks, she didn't curse the maniacal sparrows that announced another dreaded day.

******

Daria perched on a tweed-upholstered chair in the Connecticut Channel 77 offices in downtown Norford. A sad and spartan little place, with its jarring fluorescent lighting, worn cadet-blue carpeting, and the enlarged, but somewhat faded, photos of the station's local news anchors, weatherman, and traffic commentator on the walls. This place was a world, not an hour, away from WNYY's Manhattan studios. But she had made the rounds in the City, Westchester, even Newark, and *Awakenings* hadn't found a home. This might be her last shot.

The nameplate on the station manager's door read *John Fisher*. When the receptionist showed her into his office, he stood, shook her hand a little too firmly, and smiled a little too eagerly. In his forties, he was average height, or would have been if he didn't slouch. When his eyes lingered, first on her breasts, then longer on her legs, Daria put a choke hold on the temptation to turn and run.

Don't you know who I am, she wanted to scream. *Or at least who I was?* Instead, she smiled and took the plastic chair opposite John's desk.

"Your target skews a little older than our advertisers typically want to reach," he said, once he reviewed the executive summary in the folder Daria had handed him. He took off his tortoiseshell glasses and tapped them on his desk.

"And that," Daria countered, "is exactly why this idea has such potential." Breezing by the fact that John was looking at her rather than the data in the report, she pressed on. "If you turn to Exhibit D—that's page seven—you'll see that as the women in this cohort age, they'll actually spend more than younger women. At least on products and services to keep them looking, acting, and feeling youthful. That's not exactly new news. But," she said, "*Awakenings*' point of difference is that it focuses on these women's desires to satisfy unfulfilled spiritual needs."

John's eyes narrowed. "You mean like religion? I don't think . . ."

"Not exactly." Daria uncrossed her legs, crossed them again. She had anticipated this question and rehearsed an answer, though she herself was still fuzzy on the distinction. "Not," she said, "religion *per se*." She rattled off how the show would focus on practices like yoga, tai chi, and meditation and explore other traditions from Native American and Eastern cultures.

John looked even more perplexed than Daria felt until she led him back to the proposal and the dollars baby boomer women had to spend in Connecticut alone. "If you don't jump on this, John, someone else will," Daria said, her foot tapping her chair. "Wouldn't you rather be ahead of the curve than behind it?"

He closed the folder, pushing it forward on his desk. Then he clasped his hands behind his head and leaned back, his eyes shut for a moment. When he opened them, he smiled, a little too eagerly. "It's about time we shook things up around here. When can you start?"

******

Okay, Daria thought as she got in the Volvo wagon the former nanny had used to haul Lizzy from cheerleading practice to slumber parties. She wasn't sure whether it was her legs or her proposal that had convinced John Fisher to take a shot on *Awakenings*. Right now she didn't care. It's local. It's cable. And it's sure as hell not *Wake Up*. "But, damn it," she muttered as she jammed the key in the ignition, "it's a start."

Chapter Three
March 1992

"I'm pregnant."

Daria's eyes sliced across her Lexus and fixed on sixteen-year-old Lizzy, who stared straight ahead. A horn blared when her car veered left, and Daria snapped her attention back to the ice-glazed intersection.

Never, her father taught her when she'd learned to drive central Pennsylvania's circuitous back roads in the sixties, *but never take your eyes off the road, Dairee Girl. Not if a dog or a deer or a baboon darts in front of you. You just sit tight, with your hands on the wheel, eyes on the road. Like you got ice water in those pretty little veins 'a yers.*

Daria's ice-water veins had kept her cool through her divorce, her professional plunge, the financial detritus that followed. But Lizzy? Pregnant? At sixteen? Daria tightened her grip on the wheel.

"I'm pregnant," Lizzy said again, dismissively this time. "How can you listen to this stuff?" Without waiting for her mother to respond, Lizzy reached to the radio tuner and jabbed at it until Michael Jackson came on.

Daria nimbly avoided an oncoming Pathfinder as she navigated through Greenvale's main intersection. Lizzy had been at a cheerleading conference at the high school, and

20

Daria had picked her up. When she checked her rearview mirror, Daria saw the SUV fishtailing on the pavement, left slick and treacherous by a late-winter storm. She stole another glance at her daughter. "You're *pregnant*?"

"For the third time, Mom, yes." Lizzy released her ponytail from the scrunchie that held it, her shiny black hair roiling around her perfect, pouty face. "That's what they said."

"They? Who's they?"

"The clinic. The one on the Post Road. By Toys 'R' Us."

"The *clinic*?" Daria responded as if Lizzy had gotten the news from someone who operated out of a hut with no running water. She glanced at the mirror again, this time checking her own deftly layered chestnut hair that just grazed her shoulders, her tidily made-up brown eyes, her impeccably applied apricot blush and lipstick. She had just taped a show and still looked camera-ready. And, she reminded herself, if she *appeared* okay, she *was* okay.

Yet her heart hammered, her stomach constricted, lurched, then constricted again. Her chest burned. Ice water, she reminded herself. I've got ice water in my veins. Why is she telling me this now, in the middle of a rush-hour storm?

There could never be a perfect time—not even a good time—for news like this. Daria knew that. If Lizzy really was pregnant, this was one of those "where were you when Kennedy was shot" moments. One that signaled life-altering, irreversible change.

Daria guided the car from the Boston Post Road into the library parking lot. She needed to get off the treacherous surface onto solid ground, somewhere she could get traction. The library was closed because of the weather. The lot was empty except for the big lime-green Bookmobile that looked like a bloated caterpillar. Still, Daria steered the car between two faint yellow lines that marked a proper parking space. *If I can just stay between the lines, everything will be okay.* Daria's thoughts swirled as haphazardly as the flakes that taunted the car—no two alike, no single one overwhelming, but taken together, one monstrous mess.

Daria slipped the gearshift into park and turned off the radio. She fumbled for words. "When . . . I mean . . . how pregnant?" Without waiting for an answer, she fired another question. "Who?"

"A couple months." Lizzy still looked away. "I think, anyway." Then she wriggled in her seat. "Danny Fitzgerald."

"That son of a—" Of all Lizzy's friends, Daria liked Danny least and distrusted him most. He was a 1990s Eddie Haskell suck-up with deliciously slicked back blondish hair, a Brad Pitt smile, and a fire-engine-red BMW convertible. Though only seventeen, Danny already followed his surgeon father's lead, lining his trophy shelf with sailing accolades and notching his belt with conquests.

"Are you sure?" Daria shouted.

"What do you mean, am I *sure*?"

There was that disdain Lizzy and her friends reserved for all things parental. Daria refrained from responding.

"And don't yell at me."

"What about birth control?" Daria's restraint had exceeded its limits. "I'm not stupid. I know girls your age have sex. Didn't we talk about birth control? Look at me, Lizzy."

Begrudgingly, Lizzy turned her head, gunmetal-gray eyes meeting Daria's. Her father's eyes, her father's hair. Ever since Lizzy kicked and screamed her way into the world sixteen years earlier, Daria couldn't look at her without seeing Ted. Blame someone, anyone else. That was Ted's motto.

"For God's sake, Lizzy," Daria snapped. "Don't hold *me* responsible."

"Well, maybe if you had been around more." Lizzy glared. But then her eyes fluttered to hold back tears. "Do you hate me?" she whimpered.

"No, honey." When the jungle cat shapeshifted into wounded kitten, Daria unfastened her seatbelt. She leaned over to hug Lizzy, who allowed herself to be pulled into her mother's arms. "I don't know exactly what I feel. But I don't hate you."

Daria closed her eyes and stroked her daughter's hair, still as silky-smooth as it had been when she was a toddler. With Lizzy, there always had been some mess to clean up, whether she had terrorized a fellow first grader during recess, faced middle school suspension for smoking pot under the school bleachers, or because her freshman grades threatened to keep her back a year. They had gotten through those crises, and they would get through this one.

But as she held Lizzy, another memory insisted on Daria's attention. A long-untended phoenix rising from the past. No. She couldn't think about that. Not now.

Daria opened her eyes. The ice was beginning to coat the car. "We better get going," she said, kissing Lizzy's hair, then letting her go. She buckled her seatbelt, turned on the defroster and windshield wipers to high, then put the car in reverse. The car's wheels spun, got purchase, and Daria eased onto the Post Road. Turning north onto I-95, she broke into the traffic column that was creeping along. But when a fenderless old Mustang up ahead slid across two lanes, traffic stopped altogether for almost ten minutes, and Daria drummed her shiny manicured fingertips on the wood steering wheel.

"Mo-om. That's so annoying."

The disdain again. Truce broken, Daria looked to Lizzy, ready to snap. Instead, she turned on the radio again, slammed the car in neutral, propped her elbow on her armrest, and massaged her throbbing temple. The best she could do was settle into the fact that she—and Lizzy—had a long, slow haul ahead of them.

******

Close to an hour later, after a drive that took fifteen minutes in reasonable weather, Daria drove through the stone pillars marking the entrance to Sound Shore. *At least we're home.* When she bought her little Cape on Authors Street after the divorce, she felt she had been banished from back country Greenvale to a developing country. But in the years since, both she and Sound Shore had come a long way.

The village's meandering streets had once been lined with mismatched but charming homes where, in the twenties, men with seats on the Exchange or partnerships in white-shoe Park Avenue firms brought their families on weekends or sent them for summers. The fifty-minute train ride from Grand Central got them out of the City, but kept them tethered to their identities, prospects, and fortunes via Manhattan's steel and glass skyline, visible across Long Island Sound.

Until the post-crash thirties, when many of those scions, fortunes lost, were forced to sell their Sound Shore properties. When they were eventually bought up, delicate old Victorians were parceled into apartments, leased out to masons and carpenters and domestics and women who sewed at the dress factory in nearby Tyler Hill. Absentee landlords ignored rotting gingerbread trim. Broken six-over-six windows on Craftsman bungalows were boarded, and picket fences peeled and went unpainted.

Then came the eighties, when even the most ramshackle properties doubled or tripled in value. Sound Shore had gentrified, in realtor-speak. Many homes on Sound Shore's most prized parcels—those closest to the water—had been refurbished thanks to bulging stock portfolios and Wall Street bonuses. Hundred-year-old Victorians, previously pale from neglect, were now dolled up in pinks and lavenders and outfitted with enough too-precious gingerbread trim to induce a sugar high. Others were guarded by stone walls Robert Frost might have deemed suitable for making good neighbors. French doors led to decks with views of Manhattan's Twin Towers across the Sound.

Daria's little place wasn't in a prime Sound Shore location. Not when she bought it, anyway. Her realtor, Simon Danson, had to coax her out of the car to see it.

"Now, keep an open mind," he said when he rounded the corner from Sound Shore Avenue and parked in front of what was then a powder-blue Cape, the front storm door decorated with a scrolling aluminum letter *Z* in its center. "It's the best buy on the Sound Shore market. Besides," he whispered, "it's an estate sale. They're dying to get rid of it. Pun intended."

Worn down from weeks of searching for something she could both tolerate and afford, Daria disregarded Simon's pattering. When he unlocked the back door, she took three steps inside the kitchen and stopped. The walls were papered in a fifties era, grease-stained print of barnyard roosters and chicks. A baited mousetrap peeked out from under a cabinet.

Daria turned to leave, but her eyes gravitated above the sink. She saw a metal plaque of the Asvieniai twin horses, like the one her Nana had hung in their kitchen in Mount Laurel. For protection, Nana said. The day after Nana's funeral, Daria's mother, Helena, had hauled out her stepstool. "Pagan idols." She reached above the sink and yanked the plaque from the wall.

"You'll need to update." Simon continued with a breezy wave toward the avocado-green, vintage sixties appliances. "But,"—he rapped his fist on a solid plaster wall—"it's got good bones."

Daria's eyes turned again to the Asvieniai twins. "I'll take it."

For two years, Daria, Jack, and Lizzy made do in their cramped, dingy quarters. But when Daria won her first Emmy, and *Awakenings* was syndicated, she invited Frankie, Simon, and his contractor friend Andres over for ideas on how to expand and add some personality to her nondescript little house. For nine long months after that, she, Jack, and Lizzy suffered the rootless, disorienting existence of renovation nomads, setting up camp in whatever rooms were clear of table saws and wood shavings. In retrospect, her new kitchen, the expanded master suite, her new office, and the finished basement were worth it. As for the Asvieniai twins, Daria took them down and tucked them into the back of a kitchen drawer.

******

This place, Daria recalled as she drove up to the house, was supposed to represent a new beginning. A chance to start over. But Lizzy's news didn't mesh with the future Daria had imagined. She's sixteen. And I'll be a grandmother. At forty-four.

Lizzy bolted from the car and leapt up the steps despite the icy film that covered them. She tore into the house, leaving the front door open, her backpack on the entryway table, her parka flung toward the coat rack, and ran upstairs to change.

It won't be long, Daria thought as she followed, before Lizzy wouldn't fit into that skimpy red-and-white cheerleading skirt anymore. And she certainly wouldn't be doing cartwheels at that competition she and Megan had been practicing for.

Daria set down her briefcase, purse, and grocery bag. She resisted the temptation to yell out for Lizzy to come pick up her jacket, which lay crumpled on the hardwood floor. This wasn't the time to try to teach her domestic responsibility.

"Dinner's in fifteen," she called upstairs. "Lizzy? Did you hear me?"

When she got no answer, Daria shook off her Burberry and hung it up. Then she picked up Lizzy's jacket and held the furry hood to her face before placing it on the rack. She looked through the hallway to the kitchen clock. It was three when she had shopped for the dinner she was about to serve.

It was only five thirty now—two and a half hours later—but it felt like a millennium had passed.

After changing into her cashmere drawstring pants and a turtleneck, Daria made a salad, heated the pasta, and set the table. "Lizzy?" Daria called upstairs.

"All *right*."

While Lizzy slithered into her chair at the table, Daria picked up the linen napkin from the matching placemat. She unfolded it, spread it on her lap, poured a glass of water from the pitcher, hoping Lizzy would talk first. Or at least look at her. Then, unable to wait longer, she asked the questions she needed to. "How are you feeling?"

"Fine."

"What did the doctor say?"

"Everything's fine."

"Have you told your father?"

"No."

"Your brother?"

"Yes."

It didn't surprise Daria that Lizzy had confided in her brother. Jack was a rule-abiding A student, and Lizzy was anything but. Yet they had always been more than brother and sister; they were friends.

Other questions, unspoken, roiled inside her like trapped squirrels. *Why didn't you tell* me? *And what are we going to do with the baby?*

Lizzy dallied with her food, shoving the vegetables aside but forcing small bites of penne. After ten minutes of dawdling, unbearable for each of them, Lizzy backed away from the table. "I've got a history paper to write."

Daria suspected there was no paper due, that Lizzy would be on the phone to Megan as soon as her bedroom door closed. "Go ahead, then."

Out of the corner of her eye, Daria caught Lizzy glancing back at her, expecting more from her mother. Daria was already whisking away their plates, scraping them and loading them into the dishwasher. She wanted the questions to be over as much as Lizzy did. For tonight anyway. So, as Lizzy made herself a glass of chocolate milk and took off upstairs, Daria leaned against the counter, grateful for a temporary reprieve.

She heard the snowplow rumble down the street, its blade scraping the road with the same force that was abrading her memories and her fears. She splashed her face with water, wiped her hands on the kitchen towel, then went to the living room window and pulled back its gauzy curtain. The snow and sleet had slowed, but when her gaze drifted through the street's skeletal trees to the shore, where the waves slap-Slap-SLAPPED the beach, she knew the storm inside her was far from over.

"Mom?"

From upstairs, Lizzy's voice reeled Daria back from the past. "What?"

"Where are you?"

"In the living room. Why?"

"Nothing. I just wanted to know where you were."

"Here, honey. I'm right here."

******

Daria reached for the kitchen phone and dialed. "I need to talk," she spit out, even before Frankie finished saying "Women's Crisis Center."

"Daria darlin'." Frankie drew out the syllables in her New Orleans way that, depending on her mood, Daria found either utterly charming or overwhelmingly irritating. "Talk to me."

"Not now." Phone tucked between her shoulder and ear, Daria paced, opening and closing cupboards and drawers, stowing the plates, glasses, and utensils that littered the countertops. "I mean not on the phone. Do you have time for coffee?"

"Sugar, you're either gonna have to talk slower and louder or tone down that racket. You redoin' that kitchen again?"

"Sorry." Daria forced herself to stand still and enunciate her words. "Can you stop for coffee on your way home?"

"Sure can. I could use a good ole heart-to-heart. How about I come 'round seven, seven thirty?"

"No," Daria snapped. She couldn't risk alienating Frankie, so she sweetened her tone. "Not here, I mean. Silverman's maybe?"

"I don't mind, but the girls've been sayin' the roads are a little slick. Lemme look and see what it's doin' out there." Daria tapped her foot, waiting. "Traffic's slower than syrup. I swear, days like this I wonder why I ever left the Big Easy."

"I don't mind the roads." Daria jumped in. Frankie was an excellent listener, once she stopped talking. The challenge was to keep her from sliding onto one of her favorite conversational side roads, like unfounded nostalgia for her hometown, where she had been tossed around, first by her father, then her first husband. "So, Silverman's? Seven?"

"Sure."

"Okay. See you then." Daria started to hang up, but Frankie was still talking.

"Dar?"

Daria held the phone to her ear again. "Um-hmm."

"You gonna be all right till then, sugar?"

"You mean without downing a pint of Scotch?"

"A pint of Scotch. A fistful of valium." Frankie's tone shifted from concerned to bossy. "Don't sass me. I'm serious. You'll be okay? If not, I'm comin' right over."

Daria met Frankie back in their Greenvale Club days, when they became partners in the business of living up to, then raising, social expectations. They co-hosted kick-ass, dusk-to-dawn dinner parties. Stole away to Lake Como or Vail to escape the burden of needing to be "on all the time," whether at the studio for Daria or a fundraiser for Frankie. But after Frankie stopped drinking—four years ago now— Daria still didn't know what to make of what Frankie called her new, improved version of herself.

She no longer subsisted on lettuce and crudités. She threw out her bathroom scale and put on a good twenty-five, thirty pounds, took up with Andres, the contractor, and grew her hair into a tempestuous gray froth around her rounder but still arresting face. Instead of black or taupe—Fairfield County mainstays—she took to wearing peacock- and parrot-colored clothes. Daria admitted they brought out Frankie's blue eyes, clearer now that she didn't have to sleep half the day to ameliorate the effects of her late-night rendezvous with her "good ole pal Johnny Red." And her New Orleans accent no longer bubbled up only when she was angry. She "y'all-ed" this and "honey-ed" that all the time now. She still talked fondly, but no longer incessantly, of her second husband—who had died in a car accident five years earlier—but she removed the photos of him from every end table, bureau top, or mantel in her Sound Shore beach house.

Most unsettling to Daria, though, Frankie had taken the wraps off her childhood and first marriage. She opened up about her father's bourbon-fueled brutality against Frankie and her mother. And how her first husband, Clay, though charming during their courtship, morphed into a carbon copy of "Daddy," James Lee Buxton.

Not knowing about Frankie's past had been easier for Daria. It didn't stir up the feeling that, without reciprocating with equal amounts of truth, she might lose the undemanding friendship she and Frankie had shared. When Frankie became a counselor at the crisis center for battered women, Daria felt that even more of her co-conspirator had slipped away.

Equally unsettling—downright annoying—Frankie had grown fond of rambling on about her "Higher Power," whatever that was. When Daria asked, "What exactly is this Higher Power?" Frankie's mouth curled, her eyes softened. "It's not really somethin' I can put into words, sugar. It's like someone's always lookin' out for me. Knowin' what's better for me than I know for myself."

"After thirteen years of therapy? Hundreds of fifty-five-minute sessions at two fifty a pop to get to know your inner child, speak your truth? Now you're going to let someone or something else tell you right from wrong?"

Frankie only smiled. "Well, I"—which came out ahhh —"guess I am."

"Well, if 'ahhh' were you," Daria mimicked, "ahhh'd ask for a refund. You could retire to Tahiti on all the cash you spent on shrinks. Hell, you could *buy* Tahiti."

Despite Daria's peevishness, Frankie was there when Daria lost her job on *Wake Up,* there when Ted strayed. And, best of all, she was there for Lizzy. Whenever Daria came close to drawing a line in the sand that would send either her or Lizzy permanently abroad, Frankie drove over in her little white Mercedes and whisked Lizzy from her mother's wrath. When they returned hours later, each wearing Isadora Duncan scarves or Jackie O sunglasses or bougainvillea blossoms in their hair, Lizzy would be smiling. The Frankie Effect, Daria called it.

"Do I have a choice," Daria asked as she pulled herself back to her conversation.

"Well, sugar, as a matter of fact you do."

"Okay," Daria said, unable to warm the chill in her voice. "I'll see you at Silverman's. And, yes, I can hang on until then."

Once she set down the phone, Daria rinsed her glass in the sink. So this is what it's like to be the mother and not the little girl. To stand still and not run away. "I'm here," she whispered again, as if Lizzy were close enough to hear.

Chapter Four
June 1968

Daria's stomach lurched when she downshifted the mushroom-colored Beetle into second and turned onto Foundation Street. The engine sputtered and slowed, but her thoughts raced. The half-hour drive from MacMillan University's campus had been torturously uneventful and short. No construction to delay her arrival. No lane-closing accidents to force her to turn around and head back to school. The car she had borrowed from T.J.—always present T.J.—turned out to be just as reliable as its owner.

If she backed up and jumped onto Route 84 West, she could be in Chicago by midnight. Or, better yet, Haight-Ashbury in three or four days. She would blend right in at The Haight, what with her new bell-bottom jeans, tie-dyed tank, and blue bandana. Flower power and all that. Not that she gave a damn about that anymore. Like just about everything else, the Peace Movement—thanks to Stefan Janaczek, *Father* Stefan Janaczek—had proven to be laced with false promise and disappointment.

When a black-and-gray tabby darted in front of her, she hit the brakes and steered hard right to avoid the cat, bringing her back to Mount Laurel, Pennsylvania. Home. Or at least the house, the street, the town where she was raised.

The cat, Daria's Nana would have counseled, meant that Gabija, Old Country goddess of home, was near. And while Gabija provided protection, it paid to be wary—and respectful—when she appeared. Her favors could fade as quickly as they arrived. That's why Nana had always kept the little blue-and-white dish on the kitchen counter, filled with water. In case Gabija stopped by, it was important to please her with an offering.

Even more haunting was the memory of Daria's father, Zack, who had left town three years earlier. No note. No call. Thirty-six dollars and change left in the credit union savings account. And a state trooper at the door two years later, hat tucked under his arm—"I'm sorry to have to tell you this"—extending condolences when Zack and his friend Janette were found dead in Black Valley Ravine, just outside Johnstown, an empty Popov bottle rattling out from under the seat of Zack's red F-100.

Maybe Mount Laurel's fading prospects had chased him away. Or her mother's moods. Or Daria's needing him too much. Daria never asked, and Zack never told her. It was better to not know than to risk the certainty that his departure had been her fault.

When the mine shut down the same year Zack disappeared, a lot of others with hope and prospects did the same. Most of those who remained looked as desolate as the thin layer of coal dust that still coated the houses, the schools, the shuttered stores that lined downtown streets.

Still, as Daria drove up to number sixty-four, a sliver of hope brought a thin smile to her face. Maybe her mother would open her arms, hug her, kiss her, welcome her. Like she used to when Daria was small, before the tension with

Zack tightened around Helena's throat. Before she went dark and distant. If Nana were still alive, sitting at the kitchen table, putting her thick, fleshy arms into the dough she was kneading or the potatoes she was grating, Daria could count on a protectress. Nana would assure her granddaughter that Gabija and the other goddesses would shield Daria from the petulant barbs Helena aimed at anyone who dared cross her when the darkness, as Nana called it, crept up on her.

Nana could soothe the hurt, then salvage the good, even in the most irascible, least contrite offender. Like Zack, when he rolled in after a two-day bender, smelling of Camels and vodka and Evening in Paris, his pockets empty after another losing streak. Or when Helena breathed fire because a light bulb burned out or a cake refused to rise. "Not so bad, Helena. We make new cake."

Darinnina, Nana called her. Little Daria. When Daria was small enough, Nana rocked her in her lap, singing to her, "Ahhh, aahhh, ahhh, aahhh, Darinnina," her round belly providing a soft pillow, her cradling arms offering safe haven from any threat. When Daria was older, Nana interceded when Helena's wrath spilled out. "Taste babka," she would say as she held out a slice of the warm egg bread. "Tell Nana. She needs more sugar, Darinnina?"

For sure, Daria used to imagine, Nana was Zemyna, goddess of the earth. Why offer rye bread or pour ale into the springtime garden to please Zemyna, like tradition suggested, when it was Nana who should be praised and reverenced? Why burn candles in front of the Madonna icon that Helena hung in the living room, when it was Nana who soothed every hurt, who filled every loss, who embroidered red and orange and black full-sleeved peasant blouses and billowy skirts for Daria to wear as Nana taught her the dances of her Lithuanian homeland? "Darinnina," she would say, "dance for Nana. Sing stars and moon song and Nana tells Ausrine story, morning star." After Daria performed Nana would tell her how, when Menulis, the moon, divorced Saule, the sun, he wanted to marry Ausrine. But on her wedding day, Ausrine's father, Perkunas, ruler of the sky, struck an oak tree with lightning, splashing her white dress with oak's blood. "You see why must you obey father, Daria? No matter he has faults?"

Eager to share her newfound wisdom with her classmates, Daria—smiling and proud—sang Ausrine's story to her second-grade class at Holy Redeemer, the day the principal, Sister Domenica, came to visit. But not even halfway through, Sister Domenica nodded to Sister Agatha Rose. Sister Agatha Rose—so much fun, especially when she jumped rope with the girls at recess—stood from her desk and shepherded Daria to her seat. "Boys and girls," she said as she looked back toward Sister Domenica, her amorphous black habit swishing along the floor, "witchcraft is a sin. And when Daria makes her first confession next month, she'll tell Father Frank how she sinned by telling this story. Right?"

"Yes, Sister," the class, hands folded on their desks, replied in unison. Except for perfect little Jasia Bronkowsky. Daughter of perfect father, Stan, and perfect mother, Anna, who dressed Jasia in frothy ruffled dresses for Sunday Mass, sent her to summer sleepaway camp in the Poconos, and threw her birthday parties with pony rides and chocolate sheet cakes with buttercream-frosting roses. No, when Sister's gaze settled on her Catechism, Jasia turned to Daria. She grinned and shook her head. *Bad Daria.*

"Now turn to page six," Sister said. "The unity and trinity of God. Is there only one God?"

"Yes," the class repeated, "there is only one God."

"Let's pray that in His infinite mercy, God will forgive Daria her sin as we repeat the lesson of the Blessed Trinity."

"There is only one God," the class recited. "In God there are three Divine Persons—the Father, the Son, and the Holy Ghost."

Daria glared at Sister Agatha Rose. Hadn't Daria been her favorite, always getting *As* on spelling tests? Hadn't Sister pasted gold stars on her report card for good behavior? Didn't Daria have that photo, standing next to Sister, who smiled down at her as Daria held up that sign—PERFECT ATTENDANCE—because Daria wouldn't think of missing a day of school, not when she could sit in the first row, right in front of Sister?

And what did Sister mean when she said Nana was a witch? No, it was Sister Agatha Rose who wore that black witch's outfit. Daria's eyes shot fire at the Witch in the Wimple, as she thereafter called Sister. And in the confessional, she would never tell Father Frank what happened in class that day. How could she? Father Frank always spoke a kind word in a soft voice. It was all right to tell him she snitched that Baby Ruth from Switzer's candy store. But she couldn't tell him Nana was a witch. No, she couldn't disappoint Father—or betray Nana—not like that.

From then on, Daria never spoke of Ausrine, except to Nana. But on nights she wakened to hear Helena screeching as Zack stumbled in the door—"You stink like drugstore perfume"—Daria pulled back the curtains on her bedroom window, searching, waiting for Ausrine, the morning star.

******

On a Thursday afternoon shortly after her twelfth birthday, Daria walked in the back door after school. Nana, as always, was seated at the table, a wooden spoon propped in her aproned lap. "Nana?" She walked around to find Nana's loose chins pressed into her chest, her yellowed hair still tidily coiled into a braided bun, a blue crockery bowl, fallen to the floor, creamy batter spreading across the linoleum. "Nana?" Daria laid her head in Nana's lap and sang and rocked. "Ah-ah-ah-ah, Na-a-na."

Weeks later, without Nana to soothe the tension between Helena and Zack, he left the house. Where exactly he went, Daria wasn't sure. Jasia told her he had taken up with one of the Rotolo sisters and was living in their trailer outside Mount Laurel, until they kicked him out. Then she reported that Zack had moved on to a place in Duncansville with a cocktail waitress named Gloria. Jasia's revelations earned her a good shove from Daria. Right to the ground. "Blackboards for a week," Sister said. But Daria smiled. Such a small price to pay for those imperfect red scrapes on Jasia's perfect little knees.

Jasia was wrong anyway. She had to be. Still, when Zack met Daria after school to take her out for a drive, or to the Laurel Diner where Janette served her sundaes with extra whipped cream, he always smelled like Janette's perfume. Evening in Paris, she later learned it was called.

******

Daria parked curbside. The houses on Foundation Street were only a couple arm lengths apart, leaving no room for driveways. Just space enough so that when windows were open wide on Central Pennsylvania's suffocating summer nights, neighbors could hear couples' Saturday night rows and Sunday reconciliations before ten o'clock Mass.

The house, a narrow, two-story farmhouse, looked much like the others on the street. A couple aluminum chairs with yellow webbing sat, unoccupied and lonely, on the front porch, a few gangly red geraniums in clay pots straining to give the place some sign of color and life. The house, like the rest on the street, was gray. Like the sky.

Just get it over with. Daria grabbed her macramé bag and rummaged inside it for her pale pink lipstick. She stroked the tube across her mouth and checked the mirror. Her hair, thick and rambunctious in the late-spring humidity, hung past her shoulders, bare except for the straps of her tie-dyed magenta tank top. She got out of the car, locked it, and went into the house.

"Ma?" When Daria closed the front door behind her, she stood in the living room and looked around. The pullout sofa was still strewn with the tan-and-aqua afghan Nana had crocheted years earlier. Two dark brown plaid chairs still bookended the cherry coffee table. The smell of Pine-Sol hung in the air, but from the looks of the place, Helena hadn't been putting the stuff to good use. *Clean enough to eat off the floors* is how the neighbors used to talk about Helena's housekeeping. But, from the dirt ground into the tan rugs, which turned them as gray as the house paint, to the sticky film on the kitchen counters, those days appeared to be over. Helena now preferred cleaning the Holy Redeemer rectory, where she worked as housekeeper.

"Ma?" The floorboards voiced their displeasure as Daria made her way past the Madonna beside the kitchen door. In the kitchen, she looked out the back window and saw Helena twisting the tops off dill plants. For a moment, when Daria saw how her mother bent down, carefully tending her garden, a little voice whimpered inside her. *Mommy.* But when Helena began walking toward the house, Daria's momentary grief changed back to dread. She tore a paper towel from the holder above the sink, then ran it along the Formica counter. She sat at the table, took her bag from her shoulder, and set it on the chair next to her.

Daria's eyes lifted to the scalloped maple molding above the stainless sink. The faint outline remained where Nana had tacked the Asvieniai twin equines, betrotheds of Saule, the sun, protectors of house and home, almost, but not totally, covered by the crucifix Helena had nailed there.

Daria thought better of meeting Helena outside. Her news was better delivered in the kitchen, with less risk of being overheard by Mrs. Como next door. She could at least save Helena that shame. And ashamed, Helena would be. When Daria heard footsteps on the back porch and the screen door slapping its frame, she looked up as Helena entered, a clump of dill in one hand, a Mason jar full of pink and fuchsia peonies in the other. Helena would, Daria supposed, take the flowers to Nana's grave. Or the rectory. Why set them out in the house, where they might bring her a little hope, a little joy?

"What's wrong?" Helena and Daria shared the same insistent cheekbones, nose, and eyes. Now an inch or so shorter than her daughter, she still seemed taller to Daria, and imperious, almost regal, even in her flowered housedress. Even if Helena had tried to soften her tone, Daria would still see judgment in her mother's eyes.

"Nothing. I just . . . wanted to come home."

"It's Tuesday." Helena's eyes locked on her daughter's, searching out whatever problem had brought her to Mount Laurel. She glanced at Daria's braless breasts, then her untamed hair and silver hoop earrings.

Daria smoothed the front of her tank top to try to feel less tawdry. "That's right." She glanced at her purse. If she picked it up and walked out, she could just pretend she had come to get something from her room. Helena set the herbs and flowers on the counter.

"You didn't flunk out?"

"Flunk out? Ma, no. Of course not."

"Of course not. Of course not. Only people who learn to be something—teachers, doctors—only they flunk out. Not dancers."

There was no point in delay. All she needed was to spit out three little syllables. I'm-preg-nant. Her eyes fixed on her mother's, but the words caught in her throat. For a moment, she indulged the possibility that maybe Helena would reach for her and hold her close. "Hurry upstairs to Nana's trunk and get the crib sheets she brought from the old country. We need to lay them out so the Laumė spirits shower you and the baby with good fortune."

But no, Helena would never say those things. And she certainly wouldn't hold her daughter.

"You didn't get yourself in trouble, I hope." Helena reached inside her skirt pocket for her rosary beads, fingering them. "More shame we don't need."

A hole opened in Daria's chest and out whooshed the thin little possibility of comfort.

"No." Daria stood and headed down the hall, reaching to the walls to balance herself. "I just need a book from my room."

"Thank God for small favors." Then Helena called down the hallway. "You know, that's how tramps wear their hair."

"Yeah, Ma," Daria muttered. "I know."

"There's borscht in the refrigerator."

A peace offering. But Daria wasn't hungry. Not for food anyway.

"I'm going to church now."

"Okay, Ma."

When Daria heard her mother's old Fairlane start up and drive off, she returned to the kitchen and gathered her purse and car keys. On her way out, she emptied the bowl she had set out for Gabija, then blew out the candle in the glass holder by the Madonna. So much for the kindness of women, on earth or in heaven.

Chapter Five
March 1992

Daria pulled herself back to the present and called up the staircase. "I'm going out, Lizzy." No response. "Liz? You okay?"

Lizzy's bedroom door opened, and she ran out. "Where you going?" She was dressed in a Victoria's Secret floral number Daria had seen in a catalog, but not on Lizzy.

Apparently, Lizzy needed to be reminded—again—of the spending moratorium Daria had imposed a month earlier. Daria walked up two stairs so she wouldn't need to crane her neck when she spoke. "To meet Aunt Frank. Is that a new nighty?"

"No, Mom. Geez."

"Look, Lizzy, I thought we agreed—"

"At Silverman's?" Ever since Frankie had stopped drinking, Lizzy was used to her mother and Aunt Frankie spending evenings at diners and coffee shops.

"Yeah, why?"

"Bring me a piece of strawberry cheesecake?"

Cheesecake? That's what she's thinking about? Then Daria noticed that, in addition to her negligee, Lizzy was wearing her years-old slippers, the big fuzzy ones that looked like Babe the pink pig. *One-part woman, one-part little girl.*

Now wasn't the time to talk fiscal responsibility. "Okay. But I might be a while."

"How long?"

Was that fear in Lizzy's voice? Was Fearless Liz, as she was known to her friends, really capable of being afraid?

"An hour," she said. "Maybe two."

"Okay. Don't forget, though." Lizzy skittered back to her room.

"Forget," Daria muttered as she closed the door behind her. Then, protecting her hair with her scarf, she hurried to the car. "How in the hell could I forget?"

******

"Table for one?"

"No." Daria brushed past as the hostess proffered a plastic-coated menu. "I'm meeting someone." Daria looked beyond the chrome hostess station, past the rotating glass dessert case filled with mile-high layer cakes, lemon meringue, and chocolate cream pies. *Cheesecake,* she reminded herself.

"Over here, darlin'," Frankie called from a booth in back, waving with a flourish, her multitudinous silver bracelets tinkling. Daria threaded her way through the aisles to the turquoise leatherette booth. Without returning Frankie's smile, she tossed down her purse and slid into the seat.

"I'd say 'good evenin'," Frankie said, "but from the look on your face, somethin' tells me it's not so good."

Without responding, Daria shrugged off her coat, then waved to catch the waitress's attention. "Miss?"

The young woman, serving an elderly couple two tables away, smiled. "Be right there, ma'am."

"Ma'am," Daria groaned. "I hate that word."

"You're shakin', honey," Frankie said.

When Daria saw that Frankie's eyes had focused on her trembling hands, she stowed them under the table on her lap.

"And," Frankie continued, "you look like you just got spooked by the Ghost of Christmas Past."

"Very perceptive. About the ghost, I mean." She brought her hands back onto the table and ran her fingers through her wind-tussled hair to try to tame it. "As for the holiday, it's more like Halloween.

"You know my Nana used to set out food for dead relatives on Halloween? She called it All Soul's Day Eve, when the line between the otherworld and this one blurred and you never knew who might stop by." She paused, looking again for the waitress. "Well, the otherworld is here."

Frankie wrapped her hands around the coffee mug in front of her. She leaned forward, focusing on Daria in a way that excluded the Supremes background music and the bantering from the table across the aisle. "Okay, darlin'. What do you say we dismiss the generalities and get down to the nitty gritty?"

"It's Lizzy," Daria said. "She's pregnant." She reached for the water glass in front of her, drank from it, hoping that speaking the words would loosen the knot in her chest, slow her pounding heart. But speaking only gave the truth a harder edge.

"She says she is, anyway. She's only been to the clinic. I guess the first thing I've got to do is get her to a real doctor."

As Daria's thoughts spun, the waitress sauntered up, brandishing a coffee pot and mug.

"Coffee?"

Daria stared at the young woman, not much older than Lizzy, the way her red baseball cap sat jauntily on her head, her thick ponytail swinging out the back. The words ROCK STAR were spelled out in rhinestones on her pink tee shirt. She looked so happy, so free. So un-pregnant.

"Yes," Frankie said. "She'll have coffee."

The woman poured the coffee, then reached into the apron that skirted her hip-hugging jeans, pulled out two plastic containers of cream and set them near Daria's cup. "My name's Carla," she said, smiling. "Can I get you anything else?"

When Daria stared but didn't speak, Frankie jumped in. "Give us a couple minutes, okay, hon?"

Carla winked. "Just wave when you're ready."

Frankie stirred more sugar into her coffee, then looked up. "Talk to me."

Daria added cream to her coffee while she spilled the few details Lizzy had provided. Then she lifted her mug, expecting, *hoping* Frankie would whip herself into hurricane-force judgment. Outrage at Danny, maybe. Pity for Lizzy. Or at least anger toward Daria for not having been a better mother. For any verdict that would incite an emotion in Daria stronger than the excoriating blame she was heaping on herself. But Frankie said nothing, her disarming eyes fixed on Daria.

"Say something, will you?"

"Well," Frankie said, leaning back, diverting her eyes, "in my line of work I hear things like this—and plenty worse— every day of the week." She hesitated.

"And?" Daria prompted. Frankie was calm. More of that serenity stuff she'd been espousing since she got sober. "What aren't you telling me?"

"I already knew about Lizzy," Frankie said.

Daria leaned across the table. Even if Frankie was unwilling to overreact, Daria wasn't. "Then why didn't you tell me?" Daria reached for a napkin, wadded and unwadded it, then tossed it on the table.

"When?" Daria's eyes bore into Frankie's.

"When what?"

"When did she tell you?"

"Honey, can you take the volume down a notch. People are startin' to stare."

While Daria seethed, Frankie continued. "Thursday."

"She told you almost a week ago, and you didn't tell me?" Daria's voice was louder, sharper than it was before Frankie suggested she tone it down. "*She's* known almost a week, and *she* didn't tell me?"

"Yes."

"Why the hell—"

"Because I thought it was Lizzy's place to do that. And she didn't tell you because she was afraid."

"Afraid? Why would she be afraid?"

"Well, darlin', I can't be one hundred percent sure, but it might have somethin' to do with the way you're actin' now."

"That's ridiculous." Daria finished her coffee and leaned back.

"Go ahead. Work yourself up somethin' good. Just don't take it out on Lizzy."

"Why not?"

"Because she's a child who's gonna grow up real quick now, and she's gonna need her mama. And, Dar?"

"What?"

"I hate to tell you this, but worse things could happen."

Daria refused to respond with words. Instead, she looked away.

"You know," Frankie said, "you're actin' like a brat. Like Lizzy went out and did this *to you*."

Frankie leaned across the table, reached for Daria's hands, and gave them a squeeze. "You're talkin' to someone who doesn't have kids, remember? I would have given the world to have at least one daughter. Preferably three or four. And if one of 'em came home and told me she was gonna have a baby, even if she was still in high school, well, I don't know. It might not be the best news in the world, but it doesn't have to be the worst either."

Daria tried to withdraw her hands from Frankie's, but Frankie squeezed tighter. "Maybe," Frankie continued, "I'm not the right one to discuss this with." She let go and sat back.

"Oh, Frank." Daria brought her eyes back to Frankie's. For a moment, she released the feeling, the certainty, that life had done her dirty. Again. "I didn't mean to make you feel bad."

"Honey," Frankie said, "I'm just gonna say this once. You don't have to go through this alone. And you don't have to go through it feelin' like a victim."

"Victim?" Daria's anger resurfaced as quickly as it had retreated. "What are you talking about?"

Frankie closed her eyes, took a deep breath.

Here it comes, Daria thought. The judgment. The condemnation she felt she deserved.

"Dar," Frankie said, her voice measured now. "You're still blamin' Ted for forcin' you to stand up on your own two feet, still blamin' your mother for I don't know what exactly. You never mention her much, but when you do, it's not pretty.

"And, hell." Frankie's resolve to remain calm had apparently flown away. Her voice became more insistent. "Even though *Awakenings* is goin' great guns, you're still blamin' Gavin McGee and *Wake Up Manhattan* for lettin' you go. I guess because you don't feel you're livin' up to some perfect idea in your head of how famous you should be, how much money you should be makin'. But, sugar, if you felt good enough about yourself, none of that would matter. Or at least it wouldn't eat at you the way it does.

"All I'm sayin'," she said, leaning forward, "is maybe it's time you had your own awakening." As soon as the words were out, Frankie bit her lower lip. "Well . . ." Frankie smiled again. "Listen to me, actin' all high and mighty, tellin' you what to do, like I know what's best."

But Daria had turned her attention away from the table as soon as Frankie said the word *perfect*. She was looking at the large mirror covering the back wall, and all the diners' reflections. Some were eating, laughing, reading newspapers, carrying on conversations. Normal. That's how they looked. And normal, Daria knew, was something she would never, *could* never be. Perfectly manicured nails? Tidily coifed hair? An impressive resume? They were her insurance that no one, not even Frankie, was going to see her for who and what she really was.

"I called you," Daria said, glaring when she turned back to Frankie, "for help with Lizzy. Not Ted or Gavin or anybody else. So, save the psychobabble, will you?"

"Okay, I tried," Frankie said, raising her hands in surrender, her bracelets clinking again. "Tomorrow, if you want, I'll call around and arrange for you and Lizzy to talk with an agency or two."

"An adoption agency?"

Frankie nodded. "It's too late for an abortion, I gather?"

"God, I hope so. I mean, she's just a kid. And we're Catholic. Sort of. Jack is, anyway. On the other hand, maybe that's the easiest thing." Daria shrugged. "I don't know what's right here. But whatever happens is going to stick with Lizzy the rest of her life."

"That's sure as spring rain." Frankie motioned to Carla across the aisle, where she was serving a couple of high school boys.

When Carla reached their table, she pulled a pencil and pad from her apron pocket. "What can I get you ladies?"

"I'll have the Greek salad," Frankie said, smiling as she handed over the menu.

"I'll stick with coffee," Daria said.

"No mud pie or bread pudding to go with that?"

Daria suddenly wanted to slap the wide, genuine smile off the girl's face. "No." Daria didn't need to look across the table to see that Frankie's eyes were signaling, *get a grip.* "Just the coffee," she said, softening her voice. "Thanks."

"Coffee it is." Carla, still smiling, gathered the menus then left, ponytail swinging saucily after her.

Daria's eyes filled. She reached for the chrome dispenser, pulled out a napkin. "You're right," she said, blotting away the mascara that had trickled under her eyes. "About the agency, I mean. I'm just, I don't know, overloaded, I guess."

"Sounds normal under the circumstances." Frankie picked up a slice of banana bread from the basket on the table, slapping it with a pat of butter. "Who actually uses only one of these little bitty things?" She reached for more butter, then returned her attention to Daria. "This isn't your average, everyday suburban-Mom dilemma about whether to make brownies or double chocolate chip cookies for a bake sale. On the other hand," she said as she swallowed a bite of bread, "damn, this is good. Lizzy's not the first cheerleader to get swept away by a dreamy lookin' quarterback."

Daria bristled again at the thought that Lizzy had confided in Frankie before her. She said nothing.

"So," Frankie continued, "how about Thursday afternoon? Are you and Lizzy free to talk with someone who can walk her through the options and help her decide what's best?"

"Help *her* decide? I'm her mother, Frank." As soon as the words came out, Daria wondered just how much weight they carried. What kind of a mother had she been, after all?

"That's true, sugar, but this isn't all about you. Lizzy's sixteen, not six. It's her baby. And her life."

Daria tried to shake off the memory that kept insinuating itself into her thoughts. Maybe Lizzy's situation wasn't about her, but her own first pregnancy was. She nodded like one of those cheap Kewpie dolls that boys with big-finned cars used to glue to their dashboards in the fifties. All she felt capable of doing was bobbing her head up, down, left, right. Yes. No. I think so. "Maybe you're right," she said. "I'm just not there yet."

Carla returned with an oval salad platter, heaped with glistening greens, Kalamata olives, and feta for Frankie. "There you go. How about a refill?" she asked Daria, aiming the coffee pot toward her. Daria nodded and Carla poured. "Just holler if you need anything," she said, then moved on to a table across the room.

"I don't specialize in adoption," Frankie said, fork in hand, ready to dig into her salad. "But I know things are a helluva lot easier now for teen moms than when we were young." Frankie went on, oblivious to Daria's lapse into her past. "Not that it still doesn't hurt to give up a child. It's just that now most girls don't have to crawl under a bushel basket for nine months or run off to Nebraska or some other foreign country, pretendin' to nurse their sick Aunt Margaret. With support, Lizzy'll move on. God knows she's a survivor. Just like you."

Daria's lower lip trembled. Tears ran down her cheeks.

"That's not the reaction my pep talk was supposed to inspire," Frankie said softly. She set down her fork, waiting. When Daria didn't respond, Frankie leaned forward, bracing her forearms on the table. "Honey, what aren't you tellin' me?"

"Back off, Frank." Daria tossed her mascara-stained napkin onto the table and reached for her water glass. "Can't I have any privacy?" After she took a healthy slug, she set down the glass, splashing the table. A renegade ice cube skittered across the Formica, landing in Frankie's lap.

Without speaking, Frankie extricated the ice and placed it on her bread plate. She sat back and pushed away her unfinished salad. "I know you're in a tough spot here." She took a final sip of coffee, dabbed at her lips with a napkin, reached for her purse. "And you know I love you. Lizzy too." She fished through her wallet and pulled out a ten. "But when you slap me around like a hockey puck, I'm just not sure how much I like you." She tucked the bill under her coffee cup. "I'll start lookin' into agencies for Lizzy tomorrow. And as far as privacy goes,"—she stood and wrapped herself in her periwinkle coat—"you can have all you want." She nestled her silver fox fur hat on her head, blew Daria a kiss, and left.

Daria's face tightened. If Frankie hadn't pressed so hard, she rationalized, she wouldn't have had to fight her off. She looked around for Carla, who was already on her way to the table.

"You're all set?" she asked, wiping down the table and gathering Frankie's plate.

Daria nodded. "Except for a piece of strawberry cheesecake. To go."

"No problem." Carla made her way to the dessert carousel.

Daria pulled her makeup bag from her purse. She opened her compact and swept blush across her cheeks while checking her eyes for puffiness. She had a show to do tomorrow. The only thing worse than going through what she was going through was letting it show. Keeping her job was tough enough at her age, what with all the thirty-year-old assistant producers salivating for Daria to exhibit some fatal—human—flaw. Like crow's feet or thinning lips or memory lapse. Anything that signaled the chance to fill Daria's slot as *Awakenings'* host.

Carla returned and placed a square Styrofoam container in front of Daria. She hesitated before setting down the check. "You're the lady from Channel 77, right? On *Awakenings* I mean."

Daria's on-camera smile returned. "Yes," she said. "Yes, I am."

"Must be fun, being a celebrity and all."

Here we go. Daria summoned her standard response to the many young women who approached her for advice on how to jumpstart their television careers. But Carla took a different tack.

"That program last month? The one where that yogi showed how to breathe when you're stressed to the max? Eight counts in, eight counts out?"

Daria shook her head slowly, trying to recollect the man. "A week, two weeks ago?"

"More like a month. Let me tell you," Carla said with a wink, "it works.

"Anyway," she continued, "I'm writing a paper for my psychology class at Greenvale Community. Do you think I could maybe interview you?"

"I'll let the producer know." Daria cut her off. "Perhaps she can set something up."

"You know," Carla lifted her eyes from her pad as she tore Daria's check from it. "Maybe you should try it. The breathing I mean." She put down the check. "*Namaste.*" She headed past the counter and through the swinging kitchen doors.

That little bitch. Daria stroked her lipstick across her lips, tossed it and her mirror back in her purse, then snatched the check.

******

When Daria arrived home, she opened the dishwasher, took out a clean fork, then went upstairs and knocked on Lizzy's door. "Honey?" she called. "I've got the cheesecake." When she got no response, she cracked the door open. Light from the nearly full moon filtered through the blinds. Curled up under her lavender quilt, Lizzy didn't look much different than she had a month or even six months ago. But six months from now, both her body and her life would take a whole new shape.

Daria shut the door, went back downstairs, and put the cheesecake in the refrigerator. Then she went to her room, changed into her robe, and propped herself up on her bed pillows. She took out her notes for the following day's program. For the first time since Lizzy's announcement that afternoon, Daria escaped both the past and present that had set her mind and stomach churning. *Work. What would I do without work?*

In the years since she developed *Awakenings*, Daria had interviewed a panoply of Tibetan monks, yogis, Reiki practitioners, and Peruvian shamans. Each had a different spin on how to access The Answer to whatever ailed Daria's audience. The good news, for Daria and *Awakenings* anyway, was that the peace and self-acceptance her audience said they wanted required discipline. Without reinforcement, without practice, they couldn't hang on to it. So, when they tired of walking down one path, or drifted from it, they returned, looking for another. It was the search, not the achievement of what they said they wanted, that kept them coming back. And that was good for ratings.

Besides, in addition to feeling good inside, they also reported they wanted to look as good as Daria. They wanted to be thinner than their adolescent daughters. They wanted their triceps and abductors as trimmed and toned as their personal trainers promised. If meditation would help them lose weight, then they would meditate. If practicing *oujai* yoga breath would keep them from snapping when someone snuck into the grocery express line with more than eight items, they might hear Daria coaching them to pull their shoulders back and down, elevate their chins slightly, breathe deeply, and smile a Buddha half-smile. "Why expend precious energy unwisely," Daria might counsel. "Why allow someone or something else to control you?"

What Daria's audience didn't see—what she would never let them see—was the way she too frequently clashed with people like Carla, or even Frankie. No, Daria allowed them to see exactly what she wanted them to see. No more, no less.

Daria set her alarm for five and turned on her reading light before arranging her bastion of pillows against her headboard. Careful to sit with knees bent to the height that would allow her to read without slumping, she reached for the studio mail piled on her bedside table. First, a memo from station manager John Fisher who was "forming an exploratory committee to better assess audience needs." Blah, blah, blah. John was the Christopher Columbus of cable TV, always exploring. She tossed the note aside. Next the usual administrative chaff from her secretary. "I really, really need your expense reports by Friday."

And then the *piece de resistance* from Cynthia Stallworth, outlining the following day's show: Daria was to interview Mary Catherine Sullivan, a nun—no, a former nun—who ran a place in Hanniford called Healing House. Daria lifted the book Mary Catherine had recently written, called *Healing*

House, Healing Light. According to the book jacket, women who visit Healing House "are invited to share their stories in order to explore, deepen, or refresh their connection to the Holy Spirit, to one another, and to themselves. Though Healing House was founded—and is administered—by women of the Christian tradition, individuals of all faiths, or of no faith at all, often find relief from physical, spiritual, and emotional wounds."

"Here," Cynthia had written, "are suggested questions, followed by supporting research and a media kit for Mary Catherine's new book." Cynthia had signed the note in her oversized, loopy script in the insipid aqua ink she always used.

A nun? Healing light? Daria refluffed the pillows on her bed, cursing both herself for not staying on top of things at the station and John Fisher for hiring "that stiletto-stomping upstart," as Daria had more than once described Cynthia to Frankie. It was too late to arrange for a different guest, so Daria read through Cynthia's notes, scribbling comments on the supporting materials. Then she turned out the light.

Chapter Six
March 1992

"Our guest today," Daria said to the camera, "is Mary Catherine Sullivan, a nun—a former nun, I should say—who has written this book called *Healing House, Healing Light.*" She held up the copy Cynthia had placed on the set's coffee table. "It's about her work at Healing House, in Hanniford, where women get help with all types of physical, emotional, and spiritual wounds. Let's welcome her."

As the audience applauded, Daria rose from her chair with practiced graciousness. When Mary Catherine Sullivan walked onstage, Daria tilted her head slightly. She had anticipated that Mary Catherine would remind her of the Holy Redeemer nuns, the Witches in Wimples, as she used to call them. The ones who wore long black habits and threw their often-considerable weight around while prowling for punishable offenses.

But when Mary Catherine, in her trim black pants and multi-colored jacket, walked toward her, Daria decided her guest's media kit photo hadn't captured her at all. Slim and petite, Mary Catherine might be ten years older than Daria, given the resume that had been included in the kit. But with her clear, bright skin, and confident posture, she could easily pass for Daria's age, maybe younger. She had apparently eschewed the services of the show's makeup artist and hair stylist. Her dark hair, only beginning to thread with grey, was done in a simple pixie cut. All she wore on her heart-shaped face was lip gloss.

Daria hesitated before extending her hand. If she had seen Mary Catherine walking down the street, she might have pegged her as a librarian—one who would know just when and why to prescribe Austen or Angelou, Woolf or Wolfe. Or maybe a frame shop owner, one who, after studying a landscape with half-closed eyes, would be certain whether a gold or silver frame, one inch or two, would best suit the painting. Someone who spoke with authority, but probably biked to work or ran half marathons. Daria took the woman's hand in both hers. "So glad you could join us."

"It's an honor to be here," Mary Catherine said, a touch of Boston in her voice. Her eyes locked on Daria's. Blue eyes. But not merry-making blue like Frankie's. Deep grey-blue. Intelligent. Probing. Too probing.

Daria was used to guests who held her gaze too long. Most of them, it seemed, wanted to show they *knew something,* that their practice—whether yoga or acupuncture or medical intuition—had delivered them to an ethereal plane that ordinary people couldn't access without their expert help. Many of them struck Daria as trying too hard.

Mary Catherine, though? Nothing seemed suspect or disingenuous about her. Daria released her guest's hands and motioned for her to take a seat. Then, between one heartbeat and another, Daria's camera-ready smile faded. Her throat went dry. Mary Catherine had seen something in her. Or she had seen through her. Daria was certain of it. She paused, then reached for the water glass on the coffee table and took a sip. *You've interviewed mayors, senators, best-selling authors,* she reminded herself. *Why is this woman, this* nun, *rattling you?* She sat forward in her chair, pulled back her shoulders, crossed her right leg over her left. She rediscovered her smile, then retreated into protective competence.

"So," she began, "by way of background, you founded Healing House seven years ago."

"Yes." Mary Catherine sat back, her elbows resting on the chair's arms. "That's true."

"And your new book tells of your work there? What exactly is that? I mean, the work you do?"

Mary Catherine explained how she and others at Healing House helped women. "Some might be facing a crisis in physical health. Cancer maybe or a chronic condition like MS. Others may be divorcing. Still others might find themselves pregnant and alone. And some might just need a safe place to rest and renew."

Daria's stomach clenched when she heard the words "pregnant and alone."

"But a woman doesn't need to be in crisis to visit. Any woman, any woman at all, is welcome," Mary Catherine continued.

"And what kind of healing can a woman expect to find at Healing House?" The words came out faster—rat tat tat—than Daria intended.

"Well, we can't know in advance. That's where the Holy Spirit comes in. What we believe at Healing House is that we all have choices. Maybe not about whether we get cancer or chronic illness, but how we respond to it. Or any other life experience. We simply ask women to tell their stories, to look back over their lives, and sometimes their families' lives, to find patterns that can be exposed, then changed."

"Patterns? What kind of patterns?"

Mary Catherine leaned forward. "Research shows that many conditions, whether physical, emotional, or behavioral, repeat through generations. Until women do a little research, they're often unaware of those patterns. Take alcoholism. A woman may be having trouble with substance abuse. But with a little digging, she might find that a grandparent, a cousin, even a parent faced the same challenge. The same may be true of women who have children outside of marriage or who face cancer."

Daria had expected Mary Catherine to talk about prayer or some other spiritual magic-making, but not about storytelling or family patterns or children of unwed parents. "I can see how addiction or cancer might run in families, but having children outside of marriage?" Her voice had gone screechy, like pieces of Styrofoam rubbing together. "And even when—or if—these patterns are discovered, what can be done to break them?"

"Everyone's situation is different, of course," Mary Catherine said, relaxing into her chair. "There's no exact formula. But it's generally community, prayer, forgiveness, if necessary, that bring clarity, and clarity opens the door for healing."

What wispy, diaphanous remedies. Where was the *science*, the *data* that substantiated this, this *healing?* "That sounds simplistic."

"Simple, perhaps. But not simplistic," Mary Catherine said. "We're not doctors. We don't perform surgery or prescribe medication. And we're not therapists. All we do is help women do the work to facilitate spiritual healing. Then we step back and see whether other healing takes place."

"Work? What kind of work?"

"Well, for one thing we invite the Holy Spirit into our conversations or our silence. And we bring in the teachings and experience of other women. Maybe you've heard of Saint Clare, for example?"

Daria remembered that Saint Francis prayer Frankie and her AA friends often went on about. Something about channeling peace and how it was better to understand than to be understood. "She worked with Saint Francis, I think?"

"That's right. And—as with anyone on a spiritual journey —there's a story behind her calling to do that." Mary Catherine explained how, when Clare's mother was pregnant —back in the thirteenth century—her inner voice, which she identified as the Holy Spirit, told her she would have a daughter who would bring light to the world. She shared that message with her sisters so that, even before she was born, Clare was blessed with loving women around her—her mother, her aunts—who mirrored that light, that gift to her.

"So, by the time Clare—her name means light, by the way —was a teenager and heard Francis speak, she was prepared to hear—again, the Holy Spirit—that she was called to reflect that same light into the world. She wasn't certain where she would be led, but she chose to follow."

Daria knew she should be furrowing her brow, acting amazed, captivated, leading the discussion where she wanted it to go. But no words came to her.

Mary Catherine, however, continued without prompting. "Maybe it was a little like the way you were called to do this show." She waved toward the set and audience. "The idea came to you. And, like the show's name implies, you awakened to it. Then someone allowed you to pursue that idea, and money to produce it was made available. Events came together in a way you wouldn't have been able to predict, and you made choices that put your talents to work to benefit all the people you help every day."

Daria silently ran through the circumstances that led her to create *Awakenings*. Yes, things came together in ways she couldn't have anticipated, but only because she worked her tail off, with the help of that ice water in her veins. She was guided by the need to make money and resuscitate her career, not by any spirit, holy or otherwise. As for the women she supposedly helped? They were as interested as Daria was in looking and feeling as good as they could, not in any healing. Weren't they?

Daria's lips parted slightly. She would defend herself, set her guest straight. But the audience started to fade in front of her. She saw only Mary Catherine, and those deep blue eyes looking through her.

"That's how Clare found her way," Mary Catherine said, "by making inspired choices."

You have a choice. That's what Frankie had hammered into her when Daria found out Lizzy was pregnant, but Mary Catherine was getting at something different.

"Yet," Daria said, finding her voice and the point she wanted to make, "we all make choices every day."

"True. Everything from what to make for dinner, to how we treat strangers on the street, to how we behave when someone close to us betrays us or dies. But we also choose how we make those decisions." She paused. "Have you ever made a decision you thought in your head was right but felt in your heart was wrong?"

Daria tilted her head as if she were weighing that possibility. "I'm sure I have at some point," she said, knowing damned well she'd made consciously bad choices. Getting involved with Stefan. Giving away her daughter. Slapping T.J. away as if he had been an annoying insect. Even marrying Ted.

"We all have. But this is where women have such power," Mary Catherine said, her eyes narrowing. "In their stories, and the wisdom that's revealed or reflected to them. Then they have the clarity to choose differently and encourage others to do the same."

Daria tightened her grip on her chair's arms. She nodded but said nothing. Relieved to see the technical director's cue to break for commercial, she turned to the camera. "We'll be right back to follow up with Mary Catherine on that intriguing point."

"I'm afraid I'm a little lightheaded," Daria said. "The flu maybe."

"Maybe." Mary Catherine's eyes lingered on Daria's.

Daria knew, and was sure Mary Catherine did too, that she didn't have the flu. She had simply looked into Mary Catherine's eyes and couldn't find purchase. If that's what mirroring light felt like—slipping and sliding with no rail to steady herself—she wanted no part of it. "More water?" Without waiting for Mary Catherine to respond, Daria called to the production assistant off-stage. "Todd? We could use more water here."

When Todd hustled onstage with another pitcher of water to replace the one that was still three-quarters full, Daria looked back to her guest. There was nothing overtly threatening about the woman. Yet that . . . what was it? Resolve? Confidence? Daria gripped her chair again so no one would see her fidgeting.

"Welcome back," Daria said on cue. "We're talking today with Mary Catherine Sullivan about her work at Healing House." She turned toward her guest, determined to steer the conversation in a different direction. "Your book tells how you had been a cloistered contemplative. And now you're out in the world. I'm curious about why you left your order."

"It wasn't so much that I left," Mary Catherine said, slowly shaking her head. "I was called to bring what I had learned through my previous experience to this new work."

"Called? How were you called?"

"Cancer," she said calmly. "I got thyroid cancer."

"I'm sorry to hear that." Daria found her footing in Mary Catherine's revelation. Cancer was physical, tangible. She could talk about that. "But now you're cured? Through this mirroring, this storytelling?"

"If by cured you're wondering if my physical symptoms were taken away, then, yes, I was cured. But, more importantly, I was healed."

Daria tilted her head, prompting further explanation.

"By looking back through my family history, all the way back to my great-grandparents, I learned there were patterns of both cancer and abuse. Things I didn't know about until I started looking.

"I was sexually abused—no, let's call it what it was. I was raped. By a family friend. Which I didn't know until cancer pushed my back up against the wall and said 'remember me,' 'take a look over here if you want to save your life.' And when I remembered, I felt rage I didn't know I was capable of—at the man, at my parents for not seeing what was going on, and, yes, even at God for allowing it. It took a while, but by telling my story to other women in the presence of the Holy Spirit, and with their help and experience, I was able to forgive and, yes, heal."

Rape? Forgiveness? Rage? Daria glanced to the studio clock. She hadn't prepared for the direction the interview had taken. Over twelve minutes to go. "Those are powerful revelations." She motioned to the audience. "It must have been difficult for you to share them. To a roomful of strangers. And to our viewers at home."

"Difficult?" Mary Catherine shook her head. "No. Keeping secrets is difficult. Hiding is difficult. But telling the truth? Most people—Christian or not—know that verse from the Bible about how the truth shall set you free. People toss it around all the time, thinking that if they don't tell little white lies or they don't cheat on their taxes, they'll be free. But until women dig deep enough to ferret out the truth inside themselves and learn to live in the light of that truth, they have no idea what freedom is.

"That's what we do at Healing House. We help women learn to mirror truth, one to another. And not for totally unselfish reasons. If we receive the gift of knowing our truth, our power, and we don't use that knowledge to benefit others, well, that's more about narcissism than it is about healing."

As if cued, the audience applauded. Daria used the pause to plan how to pivot away from Mary Catherine's admissions, her truth-telling, and from the pinprick Daria felt when Mary

Catherine brought up narcissism. "So," she said when the clapping stopped, "if someone in the audience wants help from Healing House, what do they have to do?"

"It's not so much what they have to do when they come to us. Sure, they might be asked to fill out a family tree that traces back any illness or patterns, hopefully as far back as four generations. But then they just need to talk. And allow us to sit with them, to invite them to invite the Holy Spirit into our conversation, confident that healing—on some level —has begun and will continue."

Daria thought again about other practitioners on *Awakenings* who claimed they could cure whatever ailed her audience. But the Church? No, she couldn't let that claim go without challenging it. "I went to Catholic school. This goes back a few years, of course. But healing? That's something I never heard about."

"First," Mary Catherine said, "a woman doesn't have to practice Catholicism or even Christianity to come to Healing House. Like I said before, all are welcome. As for your childhood experience, back in the fifties, when they had fewer workplace opportunities, women flocked to religious orders. And they did amazing things. Like founding hospitals and schools. Sometimes more energy was devoted to administration than spirituality. Yes, mistakes were made. As mistakes are made by all people in all walks of life.

"But now," she said as she leaned forward, "those institutions are thriving, so there can be more focus on spirituality. And there are also more opportunities for women to become their best selves without taking formal vows." She paused, smiled, and said again. "Like when you were called to do this show."

I was called, Daria insisted to herself, *to put food on the table.* Had she prayed to find a way to do that? Was she guided by the Holy Spirit? No. If she hadn't clawed her way back after getting fired, then getting divorced, if someone or *something* had pulled her through, she would have nothing to point to that said *I'm important. I matter.* She needed to make sure both her audience and her guest knew and remembered that.

"I'm curious why you think I was called to do *Awakenings.* It's not a religious show. And a lot of the programming we do is, I imagine, contrary to Church teaching."

"True." Mary Catherine sat back in her chair. "But *Awakenings* is a show for women who, at least on some level, want to become their best. And you were the channel called to create this venue for them.

"Every day, you,"—she gestured to the audience—"hold up a new garment and say, 'Try this on. If it fits, wear it. If it doesn't, come back tomorrow and try something else.' That's another way," she concluded, turning back to Daria, "of reflecting light, one woman to another. Not necessarily the light of the Holy Spirit. But we don't yet know what role *Awakenings*—and you—might play in a future plan, do we?"

That smile on her face. And that look in her eye. If I could, I'd start this interview over. On my terms. Better yet, I would never let it happen.

While the studio audience applauded, Daria turned to avoid Mary Catherine's eyes. *A future plan? No. You don't understand.* Daria looked back into the audience. *You're a means to an end. I'm not who you think I am.*

"Thank you," she said to the audience. "And thank you, Mary Catherine." Her words didn't sound as hollow as she expected, but Daria hurried on. She had had enough light reflected her way for one day. "How about if we take a few questions?"

At the end of most shows, women asked questions to clarify which yoga posture they could practice to get rid of back pain or which acupressure meridian they could tap to relieve migraines. Simple questions with simple answers. But the woman Daria called on first wanted to know how prayer and forgiving her husband—"He's the one who cheated, not me."—could help her heal from lupus. Another wanted to know how mirroring light from other women could help her deal with her daughter, a heroin addict. "One week she promises to get clean. The next she steals another thousand dollars from me." A third woman, trembling as she stood to speak, said that ever since she had an abortion in her twenties, she felt banished from the Church and from the God she loved so much when she was a child. "I was so alone. And scared." Her tremulous voice found its footing, got stronger, louder. "And when I hear homilies on the right to life, the ones that come across like draconian judgments, I still feel that way. Maybe worse. Where's forgiveness and mercy, where's Christ, in that?"

As this last woman spoke, Daria's heart began to race. Her head began to pound. Judgment. Anger. *I know how you feel.* She could say that. Instead, she shook her head slightly. "How difficult this must be for you," she said. It was okay for her to show sympathy for the woman. But empathy? Out of the question.

In the meantime, Mary Catherine responded to each woman with a variation of a theme. This is how healing begins. By telling your stories, by exposing your thoughts and feelings and questions to each other. And when that's done in the light of the Holy Spirit, we mirror that light to one another, then make choices—new choices in line with the guidance we receive.

"What we're really talking about is conversion," she concluded, "which is simply exploring undiscovered parts of ourselves. Coming home to ourselves. The paradox is that we come home to a place within us that's been there all along."

Relieved when the technical director cued her, Daria cut in. "I'm afraid we're out of time. Thank you, Mary Catherine, for a stimulating show. You obviously shared a message our audience was hungry to hear. Am I right?" Daria asked as she turned to those in the studio. When the audience applauded, some of them standing, she turned back to her guest. "I can tell they want to hear more about Healing House and your work there. Come back, will you?"

"I'd love to."

When the lights dimmed, Daria silently upbraided herself. Storytelling. Mirroring. Conversion. Those weren't the topics she intended to cover in the show. It was as if the hour had been a big, fat cumulus cloud, ambling through the sky, changing shapes as it drifted. Instead of wrapping her arms around it, steering it where she wanted it to go, she had been carried away, flailing. Mary Catherine, however, seemed to just sail along on it, delighting in the view, wherever it went.

Even worse was the way she felt transparent to Mary Catherine, as if her thoughts, her fears, her past were unwrapped and on display under harsh fluorescent lights. At least it was over. She fumbled to remove her mic.

"That was a different kind of discussion than we're used to on *Awakenings*," she said. A simple, hopefully unrevealing, declarative sentence.

Mary Catherine smiled. "You see what a service you offered those women? They had so many thoughts that they had kept hidden, so much to say. And you provided the forum to bring them out of isolation into community."

Cynthia Stallworth came click-click-clicking onstage in her waist-nipping tangerine-colored suit, smiling her Miss Ohio smile. She wedged herself between Daria and Mary Catherine. Then, clutching her clipboard in one arm, she hugged Mary Catherine with the other. "That was wonderful."

"Well, thank you. But we haven't seen you enough at our healing circle."

"You're right. And you heard it here first. I'll be there this Saturday."

"Good." Mary Catherine turned to Daria. "You're welcome too, Daria. Ten o'clock."

"Oh. No. I can't make it." A healing circle? Whatever that was, Daria wanted no part of it.

"Well, you're welcome any time. We have a lovely garden. People who visit say all kinds of revelations come just from sitting on the benches, looking out over the grounds."

Daria crossed her arms. "That's very kind of you." She nodded and smiled as if she understood how sitting on a garden bench could be at all revealing.

"I need to wrap up with the director," Cynthia said as she sashayed off. "Back in a sec."

"You have a beautiful face," Mary Catherine said to Daria when she turned back to her. Daria breathed deeper. She knew how to deal with someone who complimented her hair, her skin, her posture, her teeth. Before she could thank her, Mary Catherine continued. "But your soul . . . it's been scraped from you. The light inside. It's gone dark, hasn't it?"

Scraped from me? Yes, that's how I feel. As if my insides —call them my soul if you want—have been carved out like the insides of a jack-o'-lantern. Daria opened her mouth to speak, but any thoughts or words froze in her throat.

"And the wound has never healed, has it?"

Daria swallowed hard. She wanted to shout *No. No, it hasn't.* But she avoided the question. "Can we take you to lunch? Or make arrangements for a ride home?"

"Oh, no, thanks. I'm not hungry. And I drove. Can you tell Cynthia I'll see her Saturday?"

"Sure."

Mary Catherine started toward the door, then turned back to Daria. "Remember, you're welcome too."

******

"Did Frankie call?" When Daria arrived home, she found Lizzy rummaging through the freezer.

"Uh-huh. We're out of chocolate chip."

Why, even now, especially now, Daria wondered, did conversation with Lizzy seem as enjoyable as a root canal without Novocain? "And?"

"She said she'd get back tomorrow with the best place." Lizzy pulled out a pint of mocha almond fudge, opened the utensil drawer, and reached for a spoon.

Daria started counting to ten before speaking, but only made it to seven. "An agency you mean?"

"Yeah."

"And how are you feeling about that?"

Lizzy shrugged as she dug into the ice cream.

"Lizzy, help me out here. And put that back until after dinner."

"Chill, Mom. This *is* dinner."

"No, it's not." Sweeping by Lizzy, Daria extricated the ice cream from her daughter's hands and tossed it, spoon and all, into the trash. "For the next seven months, you're going to at least try to think about someone other than yourself and your cheerleading squad. No sugar, no smoking, no caffeine. And no alcohol. Not even beer. Now turn the oven on to three fifty and reheat that chicken in the fridge."

Lizzy sulked but did as she was told.

After a mostly silent dinner, without letting the chicken cool, without covering the salad, Daria put them in the refrigerator and made a cup of tea. In the living room, she lit a fire and sank into the sectional sofa, trying to lose herself in the flames.

She closed her eyes to slow the migraine brewing between her temples. As if that day's show hadn't sucked enough life out of her, she had called Ted to deliver the news about Lizzy. She didn't need his support. Of course not. She could manage the situation on her own. But when he ranted that Daria had "the mothering skills of a mollusk," she had slammed down the phone. On that point, he was probably right.

Daria leaned back and massaged her temples. She ached all over. She thought of Mary Catherine and that business of women mirroring light to one another. Nana had done that with Daria. Hell, it was because Nana encouraged her that Daria became a dancer. How would life have been different if her mother had? Would Daria have made better choices? Would the stage feel like a place where Daria could, in Mary Catherine's words, become her true self, rather than a place to hide?

Then, remembering her behavior with Frankie the previous night at the diner, she cringed. Wasn't Frankie trying to mirror too? Maybe not in the light of the Holy Spirit, but still. Instead of taking in Frankie's kindness, Daria had slapped it away like a hockey stick against a puck that was threatening to score. Admitting her own faults didn't come easily; but no matter how awkward it felt, she needed to apologize. She reached for the phone and dialed.

"It's Daria," she said when Frankie picked up. "Did I get you at a bad time?"

"Not at all. I'm just out of the tub. Slatherin' my thighs with some greenish seaweed slime that's supposed to get rid of this cottage cheese I've got goin' here." Frankie laughed. "I can always hope, right?"

"Right." Daria felt a little lighter. If Frankie had been upset last night, she wasn't now. How was it she could let go of the grudges they both used to nurse for weeks?

"First," Daria started, "I'm sorry I jumped down your throat at Silverman's."

When Frankie said nothing, Daria continued. "When I'm on the air, I know how to control myself. Most of the time anyway. But outside the studio? I still haven't learned to put the brakes on my thoughts before they spill out of my mouth. Even if I know I'll regret them later."

Frankie was silent for a moment. "It wasn't till I got sober," she said, "and realized I could possibly *ever* be wrong, that I learned how tough it was to admit a mistake. I appreciate the courage it took for you to call."

Daria felt as if a cloud had broken overhead, allowing warm sun to shine on her. "Thanks. For hearing me out, I mean."

"I'm not sayin' I wasn't annoyed. I just know better than most what it's like to open my big mouth when I shouldn't. Remember the time I went down to Town Hall and raised hell with Tom Hardy when he tried to open the beach to non-residents?"

Daria laughed. "I don't remember the event so much as the photo in the paper of you shaking your fist in Tom's face. You had him pinned against the mayor's office door like a trapped rabbit, while you looked like a wild-eyed Celtic warrior priestess."

"Lordy, I must have had too many Bloody Marys that mornin'. You know he still crosses the street when he sees me? Even after I went down there with a homemade pecan pie. I never before met a man who didn't melt under the spell of my pecan pie."

"But you don't do that anymore, Frank."

"Oh, I still slip up now and again. Like I did with you at Silverman's. I had no right to say what you should do when you didn't ask. But when I stopped drinkin', people sober longer than me said if I didn't change, I'd drink again. And I don't want to go back, Dar. I *can't* go back."

Daria slumped into the couch. "You talk about stopping drinking as if it split your life in two parts—before and after."

"I know it's tough to understand if you haven't been there. But when an addict puts down the booze or pills or needle, she starts over. From the day she started usin'. For me that was high school. Too bad," Frankie mused, "you don't get new sixteen-year-old thighs in the bargain."

"You're right. I can't understand." Daria disregarded Frankie's levity. "You asked," she said in a softer voice, "what I wasn't telling you. At the diner, I mean."

"I just had the feelin' you had more than Lizzy on your mind."

Daria tucked the phone on her neck. She grabbed a pillow and held it close, to insulate her chest, her stomach, her heart. "You remember that I was raised in Mount Laurel and that I went to MacMillan University, about an hour away from home?"

"Yes, honey, I remember. Can you talk louder? I can barely hear you."

"Sorry. I'm so . . . I don't know." Daria hesitated.

"Scared?" Frankie volunteered. "Is that what you are?"

"Scared's a little tame. Terrified feels more like it."

"Well, just remember it's me you're talkin' to. Good ole flawed Frankie." When Daria sniffled, Frankie softened her voice. "Do you trust me, Dar?"

Trust? Daria knew that wasn't her strong suit. But, she reasoned, if she couldn't trust Frankie, who could she trust? "Yes," she answered tentatively. Then louder, "Yes, I do."

"Then just start talkin'."

Chapter Seven
March 1968

"Great job, everyone. Let's wrap for tonight. Same time tomorrow."

When T.J. Townsend, student director of the theatre department's revival of *Carousel,* dismissed the cast, Daria clasped her hands behind her neck, rolled her head side to side, and groaned. "Finally," she muttered. T.J. might look like a well-bred teddy bear—tall, a little thick in the middle, a reddish cast to his face, and curly blonde-ish hair—but his easy smile and way-too-happy brown eyes belied the obsessive taskmaster lurking within.

"Daria? A word, please?"

A word? Daria wasn't used to twenty-year-olds talking that way. Then again, she wasn't used to anyone like T.J. No one back in Mount Laurel wore perfectly creased khakis, white button-down shirts, cuffs rolled, and Top-Siders, no socks, even in winter. Most other creative types on campus slouched around wearing shapeless black turtlenecks, faded jeans, and tortured demeanors, and were prone to loquacious—and to Daria, unfathomable—ramblings on Sartre and Baudelaire. But T.J., even though he was pre-med, didn't need to try too hard to navigate his way around MacMillan's fine arts department. He had started racking up theatre credits as soon as his mother—Ginia Vaughn, best known for roles as Ladies Macbeth and Guinevere—and his father—documentary filmmaker Spencer Townsend—started carting him to rehearsals and film sets when he was still in diapers.

Daria, on the other hand, felt she was shouldering a hundred-pound knapsack monogrammed I've Got to Prove Myself. She had grown up among the sinkholes and strip mines on the other side of the Allegheny Front from MacMillan, where oil and coal had been scraped from the Appalachian Plateau's underbelly beginning a hundred years earlier. Those sinkholes and strip mines left behind a stench she was convinced had penetrated her skin in some irreversible way. So, whenever an easterly breeze pushed a whiff of sulfur stink across the Plateau, up over the Front, and onto the idyllic MacMillan campus, Daria took extra pains to look pretty, to carry herself more gracefully. If I look okay, she believed, I am okay.

It had been one of those days. Late winter, but especially warm. The air laconic, a storm threatening. The scent of pink and purple hyacinths, blooming too early in the arts quad planters, bordered on invasive as Daria, already ten minutes late, hurried to Professor Richardson's twentieth-century poetry class. But in between one footstep and another, she stopped, turned around. The sulfur smell. Had anyone else noticed? Apparently not. Other students were still tossing Frisbees to German shepherds wearing blue bandanas around their necks. Or walking hand in hand or passing joints. Daria reached into her macramé bag, pulled out a mirror, checked her makeup. She went on to class. But when she came out an hour later, there was the smell again. She felt sickish. One more year to go, she reminded herself. Then she could leave this part of the world without so much as a wave in Mount Laurel's acrid direction.

Daria brought her thoughts back to the stage. It was evening. The rain had passed and taken the smell with it. But T.J. seemed about to deliver what would no doubt be another annoyingly accurate assessment of her performance. To brace herself, she walked stage center, bit the corner of her mouth, and looked deep into the theatre's seats, avoiding T.J.'s eyes.

"So," T.J. laughed, as the blue velvet curtain whooshed closed behind Daria and the footlights dimmed, "you want the mountain to come to Mohammed?" He smiled, took the steps and bounded onstage. "I can do that."

Daria knew that, having grown up in the wake of his mother's vacillating moods, T.J. was unswayed by tantrums and tears. She had tested him several times, and he never ruffled, nor did he back down. Still, she stood erect, right foot perfectly turned out, chin raised, just so, and tugged at her long-sleeved black leotard. She flashed her eyes at him before looking away again.

"I know," she said, holding up her hand to fend off the sting, real or imagined, of impending criticism. "I screwed up that final sequence."

"You didn't mess up," he said. "Granted, you missed the final *jeté*. It was late. You were tired. Otherwise, you were technical perfection. Can you look at me please?"

She raised her face warily. "But?"

"I can't help wondering what you're holding back and how absolutely,"—he leaned toward her and raised his hands —"compelling your Louise would be if you could let her be a little more, dare I say, angry." He clenched his raised hands for emphasis. "Not remote and cool, the way you're playing her now. But fiery.

"When Louise dances with the carnival worker, she's not just flirting. Which you do expertly, by the way. She's also giving form to her amorphous anger toward her father. For committing that stupid crime. For going off and dying and leaving her mother penniless. And for leaving her, Louise, without a father."

His voice lost some of its punch as he continued. "Dar, didn't you say the other night that your father had an affair and left? And your mother fell into a black hole that she never really crawled out of?"

So much for Rathskeller confidences. In a moment of weakness, over one too many Budweisers, she had told T.J. a bit about her life in Mount Laurel. She should have kept her mouth shut.

"Look," she said, defenses shutting around her like steel gates, "I'll do better."

"Not better, Daria." T.J. placed his hands on her arms. "Just go deeper."

"Better, deeper, what's the difference?" She shrugged off the thought that she wanted his arms to wrap around her so she could bury herself in his chest. She wanted his steadiness, not this criticism, though she could never, would never tell him that.

T.J. shrugged before he spoke, which Daria had figured out was his way of hinting he knew he was right, but that it would take her a while to figure that out. "You'll know it when you see it," he said. Then just before she could tell him how annoying he could be, he changed the topic. "I'm going over to Bailey. Stefan Janaczek is receiving the MacMillan Award. Come with me."

"Stefan who?" Now that T.J.'s critique was over, and it hadn't been so bad, Daria allowed herself to relax.

"Janaczek. The Catholic chaplain."

Daria rolled her eyes. "I gave up the Catholic thing years ago."

T.J. laughed. "It couldn't have been *that* many years ago. You're only nineteen."

She shot him a challenging look.

"Maybe when you hear the guy you'll see the tent's a little bigger than you think."

"Tent? What tent?"

T.J. smiled and shook his head. "Trust me, Stefan's not your typical priest."

"Stefan? You're on a first name basis?"

"That's what he likes to be called. He's not exactly a Father Janaczek kind of guy."

T.J. explained how, two summers earlier, his father had gotten him an internship on a documentary filmed in El Salvador. Stefan, a recognized photographer and civil rights activist, had taken photos of Salvadoran communities to raise awareness of how farm workers were mistreated. He was a consultant on the film.

"Not just one renaissance man, but two," Daria teased.

"I don't know about me, but yeah, Stefan qualifies. It's really his photos that he's receiving the MacMillan Award for. Not just of El Salvador. But the civil rights movement. Plus, there's his class in liberation theology. There's always a waitlist." He checked his watch. "It's seven fifteen, so we better go. I'll tell you more on the way."

"Maybe." Daria released her hair from its clip and shook out her curls. "But I need a shower more."

T.J.'s eyes softened. "Didn't you hear me before? You're perfect just the way you are."

Daria looked away. T.J.'s post-rehearsal chats had become more frequent the last two weeks. She knew he was smitten, which might have been okay had he cut her some slack on stage. But whenever she felt he could see through her, like she did now, she recoiled. After all, even if she wanted to get involved with him—and she was sure she didn't—he was bound to leave. Wasn't that the way it worked in her life? With Nana? Her father? Even her mother? Still, T.J. had all those theatre connections. She needed to keep him close, just not too close.

"Okay," she said. Without looking back to him, she scurried backstage to change her shoes, pull an oversized sweater and skirt over her leotard, and get her book bag.

******

"An educational institution of open doors and ideas." That's the promise the MacU catalogues held out to Daria when she was a starry-eyed junior at Mount Laurel High School. All those glossy photos of students—"from all 50 states and 113 countries"—yukking it up over brewskis at the Rathskeller, cheering their teams on to conference titles, leaning forward in their seats, rapt, in classes taught by Nobel winners and poets laureate.

But once on campus—whether at the Rathskeller, the stadium, or the classroom—Daria found only hard-cast and exclusionary cliques, so difficult to break into that she intentionally stayed outside them. Sure, she sometimes hung out at post-rehearsal happy hours. And she occasionally worked on team projects with other theatre and communications majors. But most often, she kept company with her dreams of dancing her way to New York after graduation. Or, of course, with T.J.

So, when Daria walked into Bailey Hall that night, she scanned the crowd to figure out where she and T.J. could sit. Somewhere she would feel the least excluded, the least different, from those who sat near.

On the right, sorority girls—coy or vivacious, depending on which house they had pledged— in cardigans and shoulder-length bobs. They chatted among themselves. Or they sent much-practiced smiles toward the nearby packs of thick-muscled Psi U's in blue-and-white varsity jackets, or leaner Signa Chi's in Shetland crew necks.

On the left sat several dozen members of the Black Student Association, their hair grown out into insistent Afros. Some were aspiring photographers from fine arts, others were studying poly sci, intent on eviscerating "the system." The slogans on their tee shirts—"Out of Vietnam, White Man," "Black Men Should Fight White Racism, not Vietnamese"—made clear their feelings, not just on the war in Southeast Asia, but on race relations—or lack thereof.

Near them was a group of older graduate students and teaching assistants—black and white. Daria recognized them from a feature she read in the *MacMillan Mirror* about how they had participated a few years back, before she arrived at MacU, in voter registration drives down South during what was called Freedom Summer.

In the last few rows, a couple dozen veterans, home from Vietnam, slouched with their feet up on the seatbacks in front of them. Intentionally separate from other students—the ones who "don't know shit" about life or the war. It wasn't just that they were a couple years older now; it was that they had seen hell, they had lived there, felt its burn. And though they had wanted more than anything to get out, to return, they learned that return wasn't possible. Not to life on an idyllic campus, not in a country that, more and more, blamed rather than supported them. So, separate and apart, they wore the fatigue jackets they had brought back to the States and absent glares, brought on by whatever reefer they had smoked or memories they couldn't shake.

The rest of the audience wasn't as easily categorized, since most were dressed in the new campus anti-establishment uniform—bell-bottom jeans and tie-dyed tee shirts, some printed with peace signs or anti-war slogans, MAKE LOVE NOT WAR, and an abundance of oversized turquoise and silver rings, pedants, or belt buckles.

******

The war. Even Daria, who didn't pay national news or politics much attention, had felt a chilly shift on campus beginning in late January. After Tet, the lunar new year, the First Morning of the First Day of spring in Vietnam. When, as every year, North and South had called a two-day truce. A time to celebrate, to visit grandparents and cousins, and to pay tribute to ancestors at temples. A time for sticky rice and young bamboo soup. A time for elders to toss coins and kisses to giddy boys and girls.

But this year, bells hadn't rung and drums hadn't rolled in Saigon's streets. Masked celebrants hadn't paraded through villages outside the capital. Not like they had in previous years. Instead, eighty thousand North Vietnamese and Vietcong overran the South in a surprise attack, patiently planned for six months, brutally executed. They blasted through the U.S. embassy's perimeter in Saigon—Sovereign Territory Violated—catching the Great American Power unawares. They savaged Hue, the Imperial City, razing sacred temples and royal palaces. What recourse for U.S. and South Vietnamese forces but to respond with even greater force? And when they did, thousands died and thousands more were maimed, burned, dismembered.

Victory, General Westmoreland later proclaimed. And what do we need to prevent further ravaging, further death, Mr. President? More troops. We need more troops.

But while the general might still have had the president's ear, other voices were heard in living rooms across the country. Huntley and Brinkley, for example. Every night at six on NBC. Ten, then twenty, thirty, finally forty thousand dead, they reported, in the war that wouldn't quit. Walter Cronkite, war hawk, patriot, admitting to his trusting CBS viewers that we couldn't win. And images, in the *Times,* the *Post,* the *MacMillan Mirror,* shocking, even more mobilizing than words. A South Vietnamese police chief shooting a Vietcong prisoner point blank. Eighteen-year-old marines cradling orphaned infants or fallen friends. Napalm victims —grandmothers, toddlers, and soldiers alike—bearing scars that rendered them unrecognizable.

Accelerants these words and pictures were, poured onto smoldering anti-war sentiments on campuses from Berkeley to Ithaca to Cambridge. Even remote, *polite* MacMillan University was finding its protest voice, largely because

Father Stefan Janaczek had arrived and started to *stir things up*.

Students and faculty held all-night vigils outside the Henrietta Hopkins administration building and the George William Hurd engineering school, where chemical companies subsidized research to develop even more potent alternatives to napalm and Agent Orange, which U.S. forces used to scorch both the North Vietnamese countryside and its citizens. A small but purposeful branch of Students for a Democratic Society—SDS—organized a sit-in at the campus ROTC office. Of the hundred or so veterans who'd returned to campus after being drafted and serving, almost half signed on as members of Vietnam Veterans Against the War.

******

"How about there?" Daria tugged on T.J.'s jacket as she started toward a couple center aisle seats, about halfway to the stage.

"Unless you really want to sit this far back," T.J. said, "I think we can squeeze in up there." He pointed to a few rows of seats near the front that had been roped off for the press.

"You're so damned privileged." She playfully tapped his arm.

"Believe me. I've paid my dues. Someday, if you're nice," he whispered, "I'll tell you the seamy side of growing up on Central Park West."

"Nuh-uh, my friend." Daria shook her head as they walked to the second row. "Seamy is my side of the street. In Mount Laurel. Privileged is yours."

Once settled in their seats, Daria leaned toward T.J. "Okay, I want the dirt on Janaczek. Excuse me. Stefan."

87

"Only because you asked nicely." He edged closer. "He's wired pretty tight. You'll see that for yourself. But with a little sugarcane vodka or weed—both of which were in plentiful supply in El Salvador—even he loosens up.

"He's Czech. His parents were intellectuals in the resistance against the communist regime. When he was a kid and things heated up over there, they sent him to the States to live with his aunt in Brooklyn.

"He went to Fordham—was as good a track star as he was a student. Even had a shot at the Olympics in the hundred meter. But by then he had his sights on the priesthood. After he was ordained, though, he became a little too hot to handle for the Church hierarchy. So, they shipped him to El Salvador—*adios*—where he helped out in the slums and on the farms.

"It was his photos of the poor there that started getting him noticed by the liberation theology crowd. You know, the ones who believe the Church should actually do something about poverty. From there he got connected with the international arts scene too."

The auditorium lights flickered. "There the details get a little fuzzy." T.J. lowered his voice as Dean Livingston walked onstage and took the podium. "I'm not sure why he came back to the States or exactly how he landed at MacMillan. But I know he's been hanging with the Berrigan brothers and Dr. King. The Who's Who of anti-war and civil rights activists. He'll probably tell us more tonight."

Daria shifted her eyes to the stage. The only activism she was interested in was increasing her chances of getting to New York. Stefan probably couldn't help with that. But he couldn't be all bad if he had the guts to buck the Church hierarchy.

"We're here tonight," the dean began, "to recognize the work of Stefan Janaczek, Catholic chaplain here at MacMillan." He held up the wooden plaque he planned to award to Stefan. "Many of you have taken his stimulating liberation theology classes and may know he won a Pulitzer for his photos of the civil rights movement here in the States and farm workers in El Salvador. We're delighted that, after his comments, we'll be able to see some of his work in the gallery at the back of the auditorium. Please welcome Professor Stefan Janaczek."

Stefan bounded on stage, looking to Daria more like the undergrad track star he had been than the paunchy priests she had known back in Mount Laurel. Instead of track shoes, though, he was wearing brown, tooled cowboy boots, so shiny new she doubted they had ever kicked up so much as a speck of dirt. From the corner of her eye, Daria saw that a few sorority girls to her right were checking him out too. The way Stefan's sandy hair swept back from his high forehead and prominent cheekbones. The way his jeans, cinched at his waist with a silver-studded belt, hugged his lean legs. The way his collarless red shirt opened at the neck to reveal a silver cross on a leather cord.

"His trademark vestments," T.J. whispered. When Daria looked puzzled, T.J. explained that, just as black turtlenecks, tennis shoes, and berets had become Daniel Berrigan's signature uniform, so had red shirts and cowboy boots become Stefan's.

Stefan accepted the plaque, but quickly stowed it on the lectern shelf. He turned from the dean, gripped the podium, and looked into the audience. "I suppose most of you," he said, dispensing with hollow pleasantries, "or at least many of you, expected to hear me talk about the photos I took in Latin America. Or maybe the ones I shot during the Freedom Rides in Alabama and Mississippi." He leaned forward, looking around the audience.

A few students on the left clapped or whistled. A few more shot raised fists in the air.

"Those were certainly glorious, groundbreaking days, my friends. Not five hundred miles from here, not that many years after blacks in our own country—*their* own country—had the courage to take seats on buses reserved for whites and to drink from water fountains labeled Whites Only. And, yes, finally, as a result of the blood, sweat, and tears shed by the Student Nonviolent Coordinating Committee—and so many others—they wore them down. President Lyndon Johnson and his equally full-of-fear cronies, I mean. Until he finally pushed through the Civil Rights Act of 1964."

When some in the audience stood and clapped or whistled, Stefan addressed a few directly. "That's right, Lucien. You were there. You know. And because you marched and sang and taught in the Mississippi Freedom Schools, you know that power—*our* power—can push a stake through the heart of *their* power and claim what for too long has been denied. Equality under the law.

"And don't think I don't know the sacrifices you made on that trip. Sherilyn, tell everybody what your mother said when you told her you were going down South."

Sherilyn stood and turned toward the auditorium's center. She spoke loudly and clearly. "She said, 'If you go, don't come back home.'"

"Don't come back," Stefan repeated. "That's the price Sherilyn paid. She lost her home. But I'm here to tell you, each of you has a new home. Right here. With those of us who are willing to do what a great teacher told us.

"'I have come to bring fire on the earth.' That's what the greatest of all activists said. 'Do you think I came to bring peace on earth? No, I tell you, but division. They will be divided, father against son, and son against father, mother against daughter and daughter against mother.'

"So, yeah, Sherilyn paid the price. But she also answered to that voice of truth inside her that told her not only 'you can do this,' but 'you must.'"

Daria sat forward. She knew what it was like to pay the price for leaving home, for not feeling welcome.

"I repeat," Stefan said. "You have a home here. With those of us who hear the call and make the sacrifice.

"And just because you're Jewish or a Buddhist, or you follow Mohammed, not Christ, or you don't follow anyone or anything, don't think you can weasel out of your responsibility. It's one thing to not know the truth. It's another to hear it and not respond."

Stefan chuckled. "And you, over there." He pointed to the students on the auditorium's right side. "You took my class because I'm an easy grader. Well, that's true. But when you signed up you probably didn't know how challenging, uncompromising even, I would be in pushing you to seek and know truth. And now that you've heard the truth tonight, you, yes each and every one of you, you are different than you were when you walked into this auditorium tonight. You cannot know the truth and not be changed by it. Unless you come to terms with it, some day it will rear up in front of you, and you will either say yes to it or it will beat you down. With regret, big bad regret, that will balloon up inside you and lay you low.

"Now friends, I know if that truth has not yet awakened within you, if you ask that it be revealed to you, it will be. And as you have heard many times, the truth shall set you free. But not if you don't continue to seek it by actions that fertilize its growth."

The longer Stefan spoke, the quicker his words spilled out, his Czechoslovakian accent becoming more pronounced. Anyone who wanted to hear him needed to focus. Daria leaned further forward.

"Who here knows how three SNCC workers—James Chaney, Andrew Goodman, Gavin Schwerner—disappeared in a Mississippi swamp the summer of 1964? Freedom Summer it was called."

A few dozen hands went up, mostly grad students old enough to remember, though a few younger, informed students, like T.J., also raised their hands.

"Look around you, brothers and sisters. That's how many of you? Ten percent? Fifteen?" He paused. "And how many of you—male or female—are eighteen or older?

"Almost all of you, right? You know how we hear that if you're old enough to fight, you're old enough to vote? Well I'm here to tell you that if you're old enough to study engineering or genetics or art history, you're old enough to know your own history and to take responsibility for the truth. Not the thin gruel the government doles out. I'm talking about the truth of who you are, what you're meant to do in the world. Look around you. If you want to live in this world, really live in it, you need to know the forces that have shaped it, continue to shape it, and you need to accept your role and your mandate for changing it. And that's whether you want to become a teacher, an architect, a parent, or even a priest.

"So, yes, look around. You in your varsity jackets and cashmere too. In case you're thinking, 'oh I have nothing in common with Lucien or Sherilyn.' Or—who's that in the back? Sam Wisniewski? Danny Costa? Yeah, there they are. Not long ago they were over there in the Delta or in Saigon, sweating their asses off, pasting their bloody brothers back together, trying to save kids or grandmothers whose faces or limbs got burned away by napalm. And what were you doing? Shooters? Serving up chocolate chip at ice cream socials?

"Are you squirming yet?" He looked around, a self-satisfied smile on his face. "I hope so. Because discomfort is the precursor to action. Look, I'm not saying anybody here's bad. I'm just saying that if you're not engaged, you're either not informed or you're misinformed. But now that you know the truth, you're responsible.

"So, whether you're from Watts or Greenwich, the Bronx or Orange County, I'm afraid you no longer have an excuse. Not after tonight. You need to get on board or quit dragging the rest of us down. Because we've got a world to change."

"He might be cute." Daria overheard one Tri Delt tell another. "But this is getting a little too intense for me."

Daria nudged T.J. "Did you hear that?"

T.J. nodded and leaned toward her. "If she thinks this is intense, she'd better buckle up. Trust me, he's just warming up."

Daria smiled. If her classmates were intimidated by Stefan Janaczek, if he could make them feel excluded the way she felt excluded around them, that only increased her interest.

"So, no," Stefan continued. "I'm not just here to show you photographs of those three men, now gone from us, taken from us. Or the workers in El Salvador, or Mario Savio, who with others from Berkeley, knocked on sharecroppers' doors in Mississippi. With one single question—Do you want your children to be able to vote?—those men and women persuaded thousands of blacks to march for the right that had long been denied them. And guess what? Many of those marchers lost their jobs or homes. But they kept on marching.

"I repeat, I'm not here to make you feel good. I'm here to tell you that in the four years since Chaney, Schwerner, and Goodman were dug up from the swamp where their murderers burned then buried them, the government of this land of the supposedly free and brave continues to subvert our rights. Yes, the rights of each and every one of us.

"Oh, Lyndon Johnson may have signed the Freedom of Information Act into law on the Fourth of July almost two years ago. But, come on. Listen up now. Did you know that draft language argued that 'democracy works best when the people know what their government is doing,' but the final product was changed in his very own hand? And what did it say? 'Democracy works best when the people have all the information that the security of the nation will permit.'

"Now, ladies and gentlemen, let me ask you, all of you, whether you're in cashmere and khaki or denim and tie dye." He banged the lectern. "Who, my friends, gets to decide your right, our right, to know? Are you as willing to speak up for your rights as you are to advertise with your sorority and fraternity logos and your varsity letters and your Brooks Brothers logos what sets you apart from your brothers and sisters on campus? Are you as willing to include as you are to exclude?"

A small smile eased across Daria's face when she saw the fidgeting, the side glances, the wary faces on the students who sported the logos and letters Stefan had derided. *Schadenfreude.* That's what Professor Melton had called it in comp lit class. Pleasure in others' pain. Maybe they now knew how she felt. Excluded, superfluous.

But her smile prompted possibilities too. Maybe she could belong in Stefan's world. Put roots down there.

"Tonight," Stefan shouted as he banged the lectern, ending Daria's dalliance, "I want to talk about Vietnam and the reasons we—all of us—must fight to end the war NOW."

T.J. leaned toward Daria. "I told you he isn't exactly the Father Janaczek type. Look around." He nodded to the auditorium's right side. "The faint of heart are restless."

The squirming Daria had seen a few minutes earlier had ended. Now, the students who had looked so playful, so innocent before Stefan's speech, were gathering their gear and eyeing the exits.

Stefan continued, undeterred. "In case you're as hopelessly unaware of events in Southeast Asia as you are about the civil rights movement, know this. Four years ago, in 1964, Lyndon Johnson used the allegation that North Vietnamese gun boats fired on U.S. destroyers in the Gulf of Tonkin to beat Congress into passing the Tonkin Gulf Resolution. And what did he get out of that? The right to take any steps necessary to protect South Vietnam. But let's say you already knew that. And you bought into that claim. Maybe because your Daddy, who worked for the Pentagon, told you that. Or because you watched the news and believed what you heard before the truth started coming out. What you probably don't know is that there's evidence, including a cable from one of the U.S. destroyers in the Gulf, that the attack never occurred. Did you hear me? I said IT NEVER EVEN OCCURRED.

"I ask you this, my friends. If our president and his well-oiled machine are willing to lie about Tonkin, why should we trust him not to interfere with the Kerner Commission that is, right now, studying and recommending solutions to what they insipidly refer to as *civil disorder?* Can those two tidy little words adequately convey the sound made when heads are cracking in our streets under the weight of policemen's nightsticks?

A photographer from the *MacMillan Mirror* made her way to the foot of the stage to get closeups of Stefan. Another turned his camera toward the crowd. "That's Alex Eames from the AP," T.J. whispered to Daria. "Watch what happens now."

When the camera pointed their way, fifty or so students on the auditorium's right side stood up, covered their heads with their jackets or sweaters, and headed toward the rear exit. It would be one thing for their photos to appear in the *Mirror* at what had been billed as an award ceremony. Not many parents read the student paper. It would be quite another if their photos showed up in the *Times* or the *Post,* where a firm partner might see another partner's daughter participating in a political protest, or where a senator might see the photo of a constituent's son—for whom he had wrangled a draft deferment—at an anti-war rally.

"You can run," Stefan called after them, "but you cannot hide." Then, with the walkout fueling his delivery, he turned back to the remaining students. How many, he asked, had heard how Father Philip Berrigan, Daniel's brother, had entered the Baltimore Customs House last October and poured human and animal blood on draft records to protest the war. "Blood," he said, "as red as that being shed by our brothers and sisters, American and Vietnamese, half a world away, their bodies, minds, and souls having been bought with our eighty-billion-dollar military budget. You heard me. Eighty billion.

"Think, ladies and gentlemen, how many lives could be improved rather than destroyed, if even half, even a quarter of that money were used to improve public education in this country. Or feed hungry people around the world.

"If you care at all," he challenged, "I want to hear you say so now." When most of what was left of the audience stood and cheered, the dean came back on the stage. "And," Stefan shouted as Livingston urged him aside, "I want you to join me in Taylor Chapel this Thursday at seven. Together, we'll figure out how we can support Father Berrigan and the other spirit-guided men and women awaiting trial, simply because they had the courage to act in accordance with their God-given consciences."

"Thank you, thank you, Professor Janaczek," the dean said as he leaned in front of Stefan to reach the mic. "A stimulating discussion, to be sure. Unfortunately, there won't be time for questions. Those who want to see Professor Janaczek's photos can proceed . . ."

But most of the crowd, what was left of it, was already out of their seats, heading toward the gallery at the rear of the auditorium.

Daria remained seated. Stefan's objections to the war were convincing, to be sure. But the fact that he had sent some of her classmates scurrying away as if they didn't matter—well, that's what made him compelling. That and the fact he promised a home in his circle. And then, of course, there were his passion and his good looks.

The more she thought about it, wasn't Father Janaczek, *Stefan,* doing what T.J. had counseled her to do on stage: to tap her anger, to transform it. If that's what T.J.'s after, she thought, if that's how it looks and feels and sounds, I want to do it too. I *can* do it. I *will* do it.

"So, what did you think?"

Daria, smiling, turned to T.J. "He's amazing."

"That," T.J. said, "he is. And so is his message."

Daria shot T.J. a questioning look when he shook his head and took her hand. He had seen the spark she felt while watching Stefan, she was sure of it. She tried to take her hand from his.

"Come on," he said, keeping her close. "I'll introduce you."

While they walked to the exhibit, Daria wished she had had that shower she wanted. Or that she had at least put on some makeup and changed clothes. Then again, mascara and lipstick probably weren't compatible with the protestor look she would want to create. Not one who wanted to be taken seriously anyway. Her clothes, though? She looked down at the prim little skirt she was wearing, one she had brought with her from Mount Laurel. She needed some jeans. And peasant tops and tee shirts and dangling earrings. If she wanted to fit in Stefan's world, she would need to look the part. She would go without lunch the next few weeks if she had to.

She started rehearsing in her head what she would say when T.J. introduced her to Stefan.

"Stefan," T.J. called when they entered the gallery.

Stefan turned and smiled when he heard the familiar voice. "T.J." He opened his arms and hugged his friend.

Then T.J. introduced Daria. With her eyes focused on Stefan's, and her brow furrowed to communicate the gravity she felt was appropriate, she delivered the line she had prepared. "You're so right about responsibility. If we don't take charge, who will?"

Stefan held Daria's gaze long enough for her to take in the way his jaw muscles worked beneath the surface of his face. He took both her hands, pulled her slightly toward him. Didn't he?

"So, that means you'll join us next Thursday?"

Up close, without his rhetoric filling him out, Stefan seemed smaller to Daria than he had onstage. She rounded her shoulders, stooping a bit before she answered.

"Absolutely." She nudged T.J. "Providing this tyrant of a director lets us out of rehearsal in time."

T.J. grimaced. "I'm not that bad." Daria narrowed her eyes to suggest otherwise. "I'm directing this semester's theatre department student project," he explained to Stefan. "And it seems I've developed a reputation as a bit of a brute.

"Tell you what." He turned back to Daria. "Think you can give Louise a little more of what I'm looking for by next Thursday?"

"You know I can."

"Then we'll wrap by seven, just in time for the committee meeting."

"Deal." Daria tilted her head, a coy little smile lighting her face. But she was looking at Stefan, not T.J.

Chapter Eight
March 1968

She knew it wasn't clicking. Not by the way she felt, but by the way T.J. looked. Still supportive, still almost, but not totally, satisfied. Daria knew if she wanted to get to Stefan's committee meeting on Thursday, she had to figure out a way to learn something new about Louise, then translate that into her *pas de deux* in the second act. So, after two nights of no improvement, she pulled out the journal she had bought after she met Stefan. She sat down with the script and her choreography notes.

She wrote down what she knew about Louise. How her father had mistreated her mother. How, when he died, he left Louise and her mother alone and not provided for. How her friends shamed her. Check. Check. Check. When she wrote the similarities on paper, she saw them, felt them differently than she had, even when T.J. mentioned them to her.

Okay, she thought. Now I'm making progress.

But that was what went on before Louise met the barker. The sexy, ne'er-do-well who literally and figuratively swept her off her feet. Him, she couldn't relate to. At least not until she started writing her reactions to Stefan. The way he exhorted his audience without fear of consequences. The energy that came, not from the right words, but from the passion behind them.

The next two nights, she planted images of Stefan in her mind while she rehearsed. The way he worked the stage and his audience. Even before T.J. said "You're getting there. Keep going," she knew she had brought something new to Louise.

More? He wanted even more? Could he never be pleased? The next night Daria brought out her journal again. How could she take it further? She started doodling, lazy scribbles, until, almost on its own, her pen took off. If she wanted to reach out to that rascal of a barker, she needed to fly to him, to land in his arms. How to do that? Images of Stefan again, exhorting the audience without fear of consequences, no governor on his words, no matter how they might hurt or shock. The feeling of flying on truth. That's what would enervate her arms, her legs, her shoulders. Whether that was the energy T.J. was looking for, she wasn't sure. But when she felt it, she wanted more of it.

******

"Bravo." T.J. clapped as he climbed onstage after Thursday's rehearsal. "You were beyond wonderful tonight. All of you." He scanned the cast, though his eyes settled on Daria. "See you tomorrow. Same time, same place."

Daria began to rush off as the others drifted offstage, but T.J. called for her to wait up.

Damn. She wanted to shower and fix her hair before going to Taylor Hall.

"You've been working hard," T.J. said.

"And I've got the throbbing calves and feet to prove it."

"Well, you're definitely tapping into new energy."

When he didn't say more, Daria tilted her head. "But?"

"I'm still not sure you're down to the anger part. But if you put this much sizzle into it, no one's going to object."

"I've been working my ass off." Her face flushed as T.J. stood, head nodding empathetically.

"I know."

He remained placid as a summer lake, which maddened Daria further. If he would just react, she could let loose on him. But faced with tenderness, the only thing she knew to do was flee. Besides, she wanted to see Stefan. "I'm doing the best I can."

"That's just it, Dar. I don't think you have any idea what your best is."

"Look," she said. "I've got to run."

"Okay. Do you want to head over to Taylor?"

"After you ran us ragged?" Relieved that T.J. had backed off, Daria managed a coy smile. She couldn't afford to push him too far away. He was her connection to Stefan, after all. And he had all those New York contacts. "All this sex appeal takes its toll, you know. I really, really need to grab some juice, a couple aspirin, not to mention a shower. How about I meet you there?"

"We could pick up juice at the deli. And I've got aspirin in my backpack."

Why was he always so damned helpful? Daria bit the inside of her mouth to keep from saying anything rash.

"And I'll sound like a broken record if I tell you you're perfect just as you are," T.J. continued, "or that sweat only activates those pheromones that are supposed to be inhaled by the opposite sex. But you know best."

"Okay, then," she said. "See you there." She started offstage at an energetic clip.

"Daria?"

She didn't stop. "Yeah."

"Be careful."

She turned to face him. "Careful?"

"You wouldn't be the first is all."

Daria twisted her face as if she didn't know T.J. was referring to Stefan. "What's that supposed to mean?"

"Daria, please. We're rehearsing *Carousel,* not *Taming of the Shrew*. The virago in you isn't all that attractive. And it's not as good a cover as you think."

Daria wasn't exactly sure what a virago was, but T.J.'s tone gave her a pretty good idea.

"When we shot that film in El Salvador," he said as he walked toward her, "there was another intern. Lynette. She had the same *'he walks on water'* look you get when you talk about Stefan. And he flattered Lynette the same way he did you the other night. But once we got back to the States? Stefan rode off into the sunset of his next cause. And Lynette? She was left in the dust.

"He's like that, Dar." His voice softened. "He talks a good game about responsibility. He's just not that great at living it."

Daria's chest tightened as T.J.'s constancy, his protectiveness, began to press in on her. If she didn't need him and his contacts, she would shoot him a withering stare and dismiss him. Instead, she smirked and shook her head. "Don't be silly."

"You're a good actress, Daria." T.J. descended the stage steps. "But I'm a better director." He picked up his jacket from the front row seat. "See you there."

"Screw him," she muttered. She might not be a very good virago, whatever the hell that was. But T.J. needed to back off.

******

Daria dashed to her apartment, showered, and changed into her new hip-hugging jeans, a bright pink peasant blouse, and her turquoise-and-silver dangle earrings. She set her hair loose from its braid so it splayed around her shoulders. Then, looking at her watch—she was twenty minutes late—she put on her denim jacket and took a quick look in her bureau mirror. The jacket covered too much. She slipped out of it, grabbed a fringed shawl instead, and hurried off.

When Daria reached the basement meeting room at Taylor, she stopped to catch her breath at the door. Being late might be rude, but it would make her entrance more noticeable. On the other hand, she didn't want to look asthmatic.

Stefan sat at the front on a tall stool, wearing his usual red shirt, jeans, and boots. T.J. was right about Stefan's uniform. Then again, T.J. had a disturbing habit of being right about most things. She shrugged off his warning about Stefan, though. If anything, it fueled her interest.

"So, at the risk of repeating myself," Stefan said, looking up from his notes, "all contributions—cash or otherwise—for the MacU Activist Defense Committee are welcome. We'll be sending out a mailing next Thursday, so get yourselves back

105

here to help. And if you can donate a few extra hours to man the phones, even better."

Daria spotted T.J. in the fifth row on the right. She had hoped he would be nearer the front so she could sit behind him, out of his view, but still close enough to Stefan.

"Daria," Stefan called as she made her way up the aisle. "Glad you could make it."

His smile seemed welcoming enough, but his voice? Maybe it was the little bit of an accent that made him sound sarcastic, even critical. Daria couldn't be sure. She smiled and squeezed into the second row while Stefan picked up where he left off.

"The next item on the agenda is the antiwar march in New York in April. This, ladies and gentlemen, is going to be the big daddy of all protests. Everyone who's anyone in the movement will be there. You don't want to miss it. But the City's going to be packed so we'll need to carpool. In the meantime, we need to form committees and assign tasks. We've only got, what, four, five weeks to go?"

Stefan's voice dulled as he enumerated opportunities to get involved. When he wasn't talking about ideology, he lost his fire.

"We'll need," he concluded, "promotion and recruiting, both on campus and in the community." Daria leaned forward. Here was a chance to use what she had learned in all those insipid communications electives. And impress Stefan.

"That's it from me. Before you leave, pick up some flyers to post around campus. They're back there." He pointed to the tables near the exit. "And don't think you can sneak out without signing up for a committee." He pounded his fists on the lectern. "We all need to contribute."

Daria fumbled for a notebook and pen in her purse. She jotted notes, hoping everyone, including T.J., would head to the sign-up tables so she could talk to Stefan alone. But another student had already reached him at the lectern. At least T.J. had been cornered too, by one of the *Carousel* understudies.

Daria walked to the tables and stuffed a few flyers into her purse. Then she picked up one of the signup clipboards and headed back to the lectern.

"So, there's a ton to do," she said when Stefan finished with the other student. "And maybe detail work isn't exactly your strong point?"

He chuckled. "That's the understatement of the evening."

"Well, lucky for you, it's my forte." She wrote her name and phone number on the sheet marked *Committee Preference,* checking the box next to *Publicity.* Under the heading *Are you willing to chair your committee?* she checked *yes.* Then she smiled and handed him the clipboard. "Let me know when you want to talk."

Without waiting for a response, she turned and left, letting those new jeans speak for themselves.

"People . . ." Daria heard Stefan call out to the remaining volunteers. "Don't forget the Peace Mass this Sunday in the chapel. Five o'clock. Bring your guitar, your harmonica, drums. And if you don't play an instrument, just bring your voice and your passion."

She turned back to look at Stefan. Peace Mass? Sure, she could bring her voice. And her passion. But, no. Not even Stefan could persuade her to show up at Mass.

At the End of the Storm

******

The next day Daria scribbled in her notebook, feigning interest in Professor Richardson's rapture over Wallace Stevens's red wheelbarrows and green cockatoos. Then the idea came to her, energizing as a cold shower: Stefan needed a video to recruit for his cause. Or causes. Granted, the technology was new. Equipment was bulky and expensive. But T.J. could help with that. Or his father could. And Stefan would be a natural on camera.

While Richardson read *Sunday Morning* aloud, Daria made a list of questions she would ask Stefan on camera. For sure, she would do the interview. After all, she wouldn't look bad on camera either.

When class ended, she raced to her apartment, sat at her typewriter. *Recruiting Video,* she typed, mapping out her ideas and a production timeline.

******

"A video?' T.J. set down his beer, crossed his arms, and rested them on the rough-hewn Rathskeller table. But then he leaned forward, and Daria knew she had his attention. T.J. didn't want to follow in his filmmaker father's footsteps. Not for a career anyway. But he had a social conscience. It was when his father arranged for him to work on a documentary called *Mississippi Freedom,* when he saw firsthand civil rights workers beaten and bloody, that he knew he needed to do more than make others aware of injustice. That's when he decided to become a doctor. In the years before he could practice medicine, though, he wanted to do what he could to right social wrongs. So, even if he

108

didn't approve of Daria's getting involved with Stefan, Daria knew he believed in Stefan's mission: the Vietnam War had to end. Besides, if T.J. didn't like the idea of Daria getting close to Stefan, he would want to be nearby to protect her.

"Yeah." She reached into her bag to pull out a pack of Parliaments. "A video. What do you think?"

T.J. tilted back his beer and finished what was left. "If you won't stop smoking for health reasons, will you at least stop because it'll add those awful little lines women get around their mouths?"

Daria lit up anyway. "I'll worry about that t'mahrah, Rhett," she said in a pretty decent Scarlett O'Hara.

"You really want to know what I think? About the video?"

"Sure. I wouldn't have asked if—"

"I don't trust Stefan," he cut in. "Not only because I think you're hanging around him for the wrong reasons. But because I'm not sure he's as committed as he wants us to believe."

She drew on her cigarette, leaned back against the oak-paneled booth, and exhaled a long and lazy stream of smoke. "Ridiculous."

"That you're attracted to him or that his motives might be suspect?"

"Both."

"Look, Dar, you're smart and talented and beautiful . . ."

Daria waved to dismiss his flattery.

"You don't need me telling you what to do."

"Finally, you're making sense."

He held his mug with both hands, rotated the base on the table. "Maybe," he said looking away, "maybe I'm just jealous."

"Jealous? Of a priest?" She laughed. "Absurd. Or ab-ZURD, as Professor Richardson would say." She shrugged, then leaned closer. "Know what I think?"

T.J. raised his eyebrows. "What?"

"I think if you're worried about me getting involved with Stefan, other than for the cause, you're wasting time you could spend on those fruit fly experiments or whatever else you do in that genetics lab at two in the morning." She set her cigarette in the ashtray on the table. "Seriously, T.J. Maybe my interest in the movement isn't as strong as it could be. But the video would make a great addition to my resume. I mean, I want to go to New York and dance after I get done at MacMillan. But I can't dance forever. Eventually I'll have to get a real job. On-camera experience could help."

"I guess you're right. About that anyway."

Daria grinned and bounced in her seat. "You mean you'll do it?"

"Did you think I wouldn't?"

She leaned across the table, stroked T.J.'s face. "You had me wondering there for a minute." She reached into her bag and pulled out the production notes she had typed. "I promise you won't regret this."

"There's a condition, though," T.J. said, reaching for her hand. "Promise me you won't get hurt."

"Me?" Daria laughed. "Hurt?" She laid her notes on the table as she pulled his hand from hers.

"Good song," he said, referring to the background music.

She looked puzzled.

"'Fakin' It.' Simon and Garfunkel's latest."

******

"Since we're doing a Q and A format," T.J. counseled when he and Daria met to outline the video script, "you'll need to keep a tight rein on Stefan. If you don't, he'll run like the bulls at Pamplona, and you'll never catch up."

"Pamplona?"

"Hemingway," he said.

Daria shook her head. "What's he got to do with this?"

"Never mind. Just keep the questions tight. And don't be afraid to interrupt him. We can do a lot in the editing room to get a good product. But it'll help if you keep him focused on the war. Period."

******

"Tuesday night? Maybe around seven, at the Rathskeller?"

When Daria finished the video production outline, she stopped by Stefan's office to set a time to review it with him. Tuesday night would be best since T.J. would be hatching fruit flies in genetics lab.

"Tuesday's good. But not the Rathskeller." He tore a piece of paper from a notebook and scribbled his address. "It'll be quiet and private."

Daria read the address, then tossed her hair over her shoulders. "Cool."

******

"I like it." Stefan set the outline on the coffee table as he stood from the orange bean bag chair in his studio apartment. He had stepped out of uniform, exchanging his red shirt for a black turtleneck, his jeans for olive drabs, and his boots for sneakers. He had also taken off the cross he usually wore. "Wine?"

"Sure." Daria sat forward on the futon, setting aside her copy of the outline.

"What about production arrangements?" Stefan made his way to the portable bar, uncorked a bottle of Chianti, and poured two glasses.

Daria explained how T.J. had arranged for the cameras—it would be a two-camera job—and for two of his father's cameramen and a lighting guy to come to MacMillan from the City.

"And Spencer Townsend's going to produce it?" He sat next to Daria, hesitating before handing her a glass.

"Well, no." Daria tucked a strand of hair behind her ear. His voice had taken on an insistent edge. "Mr. Townsend's loaning us equipment, but T.J.'s taking care of everything."

Stefan set down his glass forcefully enough that a little wine sloshed onto the coffee table. "If we do it, we need to do it right."

Now there was no mistaking the shift in Stefan's voice. He reached for a pack of matches and lit a yellowish candle on the table, sending a saccharine honeysuckle smell into the small room. Daria coughed. When Stefan's tone changed, she had already felt the oxygen draining from the room. The candle sucked up even more.

"T.J.'s got lots of experience with this kind of—"

"If Spencer Townsend's name's not on this thing," Stefan interrupted, "we don't go forward. Period." He finished his wine, took his glass and hers, still half-full, to the sink, and washed them. She was dismissed.

"I don't know what to say," Daria said, standing to leave. "I mean, we'll do everything we can."

He turned to face her. "You understand, of course."

"Of course," she said. "It's just that we've already got the people and equipment lined up." She felt deflated. Was it that sickening, smelly candle? She walked toward the door, then turned back to try to rescue the chance to work with Stefan.

"But what if . . . What I'm trying to ask is, do you really want to miss this opportunity? Shouldn't we at least start the project?"

"I need to meet Townsend."

Daria paused. She needed a solution that would salvage the project.

"What if T.J. takes you to meet his father when we're in New York?" She wasn't sure how she could arrange that, but she would find a way.

"All I need is to get in front of him."

"Okay, then. We'll find a way."

Smiling again, Stefan took Daria's hands. "Go in peace." He kissed her lightly on the cheek, his lips lingering. At least she thought they lingered. She knew she was mercurial, but this guy? He had her beat. Hands down.

After the door closed behind her, Daria began plotting. T.J. had mentioned that his father was in between projects, that he would stop in to see "Spence"—as he said his father's friends called him—when they were in New York for the march. Getting T.J. to take Stefan along was only a matter of inviting T.J. to dinner, opening a box of pasta, a bottle of wine, and lighting a few candles.

Trickier was how to prepare so that the next time Stefan challenged her, she wouldn't respond like a flustered schoolgirl.

******

"You're still going to visit your father when we're in New York?" Daria called from the kitchen as she poured hot fudge sauce over a bowl of mint chip ice cream. If T.J. was the least little bit tempted to refuse her request, her tight jeans and sweater, not to mention his favorite dessert, would clinch the deal.

"Yup." He sat on the floor at the coffee table where they had eaten. "All set. Want to meet him?"

She walked into the living room, carrying the ice cream like a sacred offering.

"That's not mint chip hiding under there, is it?"

She smiled and set down the dish. When T.J. dug in, she gingerly continued. "I'm not quite up to meeting the great Spencer Townsend," she said. "But I know who would like to."

T.J. finished a taste of ice cream, then put down his spoon. "Well, I guess I walked right into that one." He raised his eyes to hers. "Let me guess who that might be."

"It wouldn't be an imposition, would it? I mean, you've already made plans to see your father, right? Stefan just wants some reassurance that we're on the right track."

"This isn't an academy award contender we're putting together." T.J. wadded up the paper towel Daria had set out to serve as a napkin, tossed it onto the table, and pushed away his half-full bowl.

"You're finished?"

"I'm finished," he said as he stood. "Thank you for dinner."

After the door closed, Daria went to the window overlooking State Street, where T.J. had parked his Beetle. When she heard its familiar puttering engine, and T.J. drove off, she turned back to the room.

Don't leave me. For a moment, the thought that T.J., reliable and constant, might be angry, that she might have pushed him too far, left Daria feeling hollow and scared. But not for long.

"He'll come around," she said softly. "He always does."

Chapter Nine
April 1968

On the last Friday in April, Daria, T.J., and three other students piled with Stefan into his rusty van and headed east out of Pennsylvania to Manhattan for the big demonstration.

In the weeks since T.J. had been at her apartment, Daria had shown up for rehearsal and worked hard. She never mentioned Stefan, the video, or the march. And ten days earlier, when T.J. stopped her for another post-rehearsal debriefing, she kept her cool. As she had suspected, he relented.

"Sorry I walked out on you the other night," he said. "Thanks again for dinner."

"You're welcome." Confident she was in his graces again, Daria brought up the subject that had pushed him away. "I just don't see that it's that big a deal . . ."

T.J. held up his hands. "You're right. It's not. Besides, no one appointed me your personal knight in shining armor."

Daria bit her lower lip. She couldn't rush him into saying what she wanted to hear.

"What I'm trying to say is, yes, I'll introduce Stefan to my father in New York."

"You," she said, throwing her arms around him, "are the best." She planted a big kiss on his cheek and squeezed him close.

T.J. stroked her hair, then shook his head, disentangled himself, and walked away.

Daria smiled. She had gotten what she wanted. Which meant Stefan would get what he wanted. Which meant he would be thrilled with her—she hoped.

******

Not long after her first lessons at Miss Marie's Dance Studio in downtown Mount Laurel, Daria dreamed of going to New York. It had taken twelve more years, but she had finally made it.

She had never imagined politics and a priest with a cause, not dance, would get her there. But when Stefan's van crossed the George Washington Bridge, Daria felt as wide-eyed as she had at her first recital, tapping and bowing to what she remembered as thunderous and adoring applause. Not that she could let her childish exuberance show, of course.

She pretended to rock to the Dylan that was playing on the radio. But even from inside the van, she could feel how life danced to a different rhythm on this island, thirteen miles long, two-point-three miles wide. The Hudson River gleamed to her right; the cacophony of taxis and delivery trucks blared from the left. And the billboards advertising *Hair, Promises, Promises,* and other Broadway shows? Well, they just screamed: *Daria. Someday, your name, your picture will be up here.*

That's when excitement wore down her reserve. She rolled down her window and, wind blowing her hair, yelled, "Hello, New York. I'm here!"

Stefan made his way south to Seventy-Second Street and entered the park at the transverse. "That's the Sheep Meadow," he said as he drove along West Road. "Tomorrow, we'll be there, over a hundred thousand strong." Daria found it hard to imagine since there was no activity now except for a few men constructing a platform at one end of the wide green lawn. Stefan, hunkered over the steering wheel, already seemed to be feeding on the anticipated crowd's energy.

He navigated the van out of the park, past Fifth to the East Side. Then he drove north, to Morningside Heights, to the apartment they would all squeeze into for the next two nights. A few blocks away—he couldn't find parking any closer—the six of them grabbed their gear and worked their way to the brick walkup where Stefan's friend from seminary rented a third-floor studio.

With the others, Daria climbed the stairs, trying to ignore the water-stained plaster walls and the oniony smell. But when a mouse darted up a hole in one floorboard and down through another, she jumped and grabbed T.J.'s arm. She needed to get back outside, where the energy made her feel like she had never felt.

The apartment wasn't much bigger than Daria's freshman dorm room, and a lot less cozy than MacMillan's Hunt Hall, with its leaded windows and charming dormers. The kitchen consisted of a grimy three-burner stove, miniature sink, and refrigerator wedged into a closet. What precious little light filtered through two small windows was dulled by the ominous-looking purple batik fabric lengths that served as curtains.

They moved aside the orange-crate coffee table and each claimed space for their sleeping bags among the piles of books, magazines, and copies of the *Times*. The sole bed went unclaimed. Much too bourgeois.

"Listen up, everybody," Stefan said. "We've got to be ready to roll tomorrow by seven. So, if you decide to take in the City tonight, try to restrain yourselves and get back in time to get some rest. You're in for a long, exhilarating day."

Stefan's promise reignited Daria's enthusiasm. She felt she could go for days without sleep. Where would they go exploring? But as she spread out her sleeping bag and blanket, Stefan pulled a white sweater from his knapsack. "I'm going out now," he said after changing from his red shirt. "You're on your own."

Daria felt her insides lose shape, like the beanbag chairs on the room's perimeter. She wakened with a thud from her daydream of walking arm-in-arm with Stefan, inhaling the City's sights and smells and frenzy.

"Don't wait up," he said, closing the door behind him.

Rummaging through her bag, hoping to hide her disappointment, she pulled out a brush and took it vigorously to her hair.

"You want to catch a nap?" T.J. asked after he organized his things. "Or get a taste of the City?"

Was he gloating because Stefan left without her? Did his smile signal *I told you so?* She wasn't sure. But who cared? The City called. "Are you kidding?" Daria tossed aside her brush, grabbed her denim jacket, and looped her arm through T.J.'s. "Let's go."

At the End of the Storm

******

"Go away." When T.J. gently shook Daria awake the next morning, she turned over and groaned. The tour he had given her had run almost the length of Manhattan, which they explored by subway, by cab, and on foot, and culminated with a little too much red wine at a jazz club in the Village.

"I'm happy to oblige," he said. "But don't complain later when you miss the march and your opportunity to star in your first feature film."

Daria propped herself up on one arm. "What?" She squinted. "What time is it?"

"Six fifteen." T.J. held out a cup of coffee. "I thought you'd want a little time in the bathroom before the others get up."

Daria eased herself back down into her sleeping bag. "I need sleep more than a shampoo."

"Your choice. But a couple guys from my father's production company are showing up around seven thirty to shoot b-roll. I thought you'd want to be in it."

"B-roll?"

"Background footage. Q and A format can get a little deadly, even with a luscious interviewer like you. So, we'll want to edit in some atmosphere."

"Really?" Daria sprang to her feet. "Why didn't you tell me?"

"Really. I wanted to be sure my father didn't pull the plug on this whole thing at the last minute. He has a way of doing that."

"Is Stefan awake?"

T.J. shrugged. "Don't know. Looks like he didn't make it back last night."

Daria glanced toward Stefan's sleeping bag, still untouched. Where the hell was he? She grabbed her knapsack and headed to the shower. Fifteen minutes later, she reappeared in her gauzy blouse and jeans, hair pushed back with a multi-colored headband.

"Perfect." T.J. beamed.

The group was functional by seven, thanks to the coffee and bagels T.J. had picked up. They all made do with the tiny bathroom and dressed in appropriate protest attire. Even T.J. traded his khakis for jeans, though he couldn't give up his Top-Siders.

Then they waited for Stefan.

"If we don't leave," T.J. said at seven fifteen, "we'll miss some of the speeches."

"He said he'd be here," Daria said, too quickly, too sharply.

T.J. raised an eyebrow. "Suit yourself. I'm going."

Daria followed, as did the others.

******

Daria stopped suddenly when they arrived at the Sheep Meadow. As Stefan promised, the space that had looked bucolic the day before was filling with fifty thousand people? A hundred? She couldn't tell. All she knew was that the crowd spilled out of the park onto Fifth Avenue, and she couldn't see the end of the stream of people wending its way uptown.

Daria had expected the protestors would all look like their little band from MacMillan: students, accompanied by a few stoic or shaggy professors. Most fit that profile, some carrying bouquets of daisies and daffodils to hand out or posters bearing hand-painted peace signs. But gray-haired women in conservative dresses congregated next to businessmen wearing Brooks Brothers button-downs and flannel slacks. Young mothers pushing infants in strollers or shepherding toddlers gathered next to clergy. And then there were the burly Magnificent Riders from Newark, revving their Harleys in front of the crowd.

T.J. guided the group to the corner of the meadow where he had arranged to meet his crew. "Blows your mind, huh?"

Daria, with wide eyes and childish grin, grabbed his hand and squeezed it. She was part of this. But when T.J. drew closer to her, she released his hand and looked away. Where was Stefan?

"They're going to lead the way down Fifth," T.J. said, pointing to the Magnificent Riders. "For Dellinger and Sloane." He turned Daria toward two men at the front of the crowd where a cordon of bodyguards formed a hand-locked square around them. David Dellinger, T.J. explained, had been a World War II draft resister and now headed the National Mobilization Committee to End the War—the Mobe —while William Sloane Coffin Jr., chaplain at Yale, had been indicted for counseling young men to violate draft laws.

The names meant nothing to her, nor did their stature as anti-war icons. But she, Daria Petrauskas, from Mount Laurel, Pennsylvania, was there with them. She looked beyond the Sheep Meadow to the rest of Central Park. Just outside its perimeter, she knew, were Fifth Avenue's museums and shops, the Plaza Hotel, exclusive apartments overlooking the park. All waiting for her.

"Let's head down." T.J. led Daria and called for the crew to follow. As they moved closer to the stage where Arlo Guthrie and Pete Seeger were singing, T.J. instructed the crew on shots he wanted of the performers, the upcoming speakers, the crowd. And, of course, Daria.

Only Stefan, wherever he was, could make the moment better.

When Coretta Scott King stepped to the mic, the crowd quieted, and all attention turned toward her. She read from the "Ten Commandments on Vietnam," notes found in her husband's pockets after his murder weeks earlier.

"Thou shalt," she began, "not believe that the world supported the American mission in Vietnam, that military leaders knew best." By the time she read "Thou shalt not kill," some wept unashamedly. Others linked arms and sang "Blowin' in the Wind."

When the whole crowd joined in, their voices reverberating for blocks, police, wearing riot gear and brandishing nightsticks, charged.

Daria reached for T.J., but they separated in the crowd's current. When she turned and saw a policeman's nightstick aiming her way, she covered her head and ducked. Then she felt a hand around her waist.

"This way," he said.

"Stefan!"

Chapter Ten
April 1968

They ran from the park to Sixty-Eighth Street, caught their breath at Lexington Avenue, and slipped into a diner. How was it, Daria wondered when they sat in a booth at the window, that just a few blocks away New York's finest were cracking heads? But in this little neighborhood haunt, with its Formica counters and stainless-steel stools, New Yorkers were eating oatmeal and drinking orange juice, checking box scores, and scoffing at newspaper headlines, like they might any ordinary Saturday morning?

"We were worried about you," Daria said when they sat down. Stefan tilted his head, as if he didn't understand. "When you didn't show up this morning."

"These things don't just happen by themselves," Stefan said, dismissing her concern. "There's work to be done behind the scenes." He leaned back against the leatherette booth and draped his arm along it.

What work? Where had he been? With whom?

The greater the gap Stefan set between them, the more Daria wanted to close it. "You act like all this, like what we just went through, is just part of another day." She kept her voice cool. At least she hoped she did.

He shrugged. "You get used to it after a while."

When he looked away, she sipped the coffee the waiter had poured, then tried again to get something from Stefan other than distancing nonchalance. "T.J. had a camera crew there. I bet he got some great footage. B-roll. For the video."

"He did that?" His Czech accent intensified, his consonants became more clipped, which, Daria knew, meant he was annoyed. About what, she wasn't sure.

"Why do you sound so . . ."

"He should have run it by me." He leaned forward, tapping the tabletop. "I want to know everything on this project. Every detail."

Then why weren't you there?

When the waiter arrived with their eggs and toast, Daria attacked hers. Stefan just picked at his breakfast, then set down his fork. He reached for the *Times* someone had left on the next table.

Moments later, with no apparent reason for breaking his silence, Stefan put down the paper. He reached across the table and took her hand.

"I bet if we left now," he said, "we could beat them all back to the apartment."

She looked tentatively at him, not wanting to misread him. But from his little smile, the way his eyebrows arched, the way his hand lingered on hers, the signals were clear. "I bet," she said as she pushed away her plate, "we could."

Without waiting for their bill, they each tossed a few dollars on the table and left the diner, arms wrapped around each other's waists. Outside, Stefan took a joint from his jacket pocket, lit it, and took a hit. He passed it to Daria while they walked to the subway, lingering at every intersection. Each time they stopped, they pressed closer, tighter to each other. When he kissed her neck, her head lolled back like a rag doll's as the thrill of the City faded. Where were they? On Sixty-Eighth Street? Amsterdam? She didn't know. She didn't care. All that mattered was this moment, this anonymity, this freedom, with Stefan.

Stefan took Daria's hand as they ran up the apartment building steps. After fumbling with the locks, they stumbled through the door into the previously unused bed, leaving behind a trail of denim. *Just don't get hurt.* When she heard T.J.'s warning in her head, Daria tried to silence it by reaching for Stefan. But as she held him, she tensed. Was it because, lying next to her, he was so small? So ordinary, so seemingly inconsequential? Or because she couldn't muffle T.J.'s meddling voice?

"What's wrong?"

"I'm a little scared is all. I just . . . what about a rubber? Do you have one?"

He shook his head. "Look, if you want," he said, his voice edgy again, like it had been at the diner, "I'll pull out before I come."

Was that possible? Daria had a few high school flings in Mount Laurel, ones that involved sweaty, furtive sucking and hand jobs in pickup trucks or old Chevys. And then there were those freshman-year encounters with MacMillan upperclassmen. Didn't she know, they grumbled when they pulled on their jeans and stalked out, that she shouldn't get them jazzed if she wasn't going to follow through? That they couldn't stop?

If we don't take responsibility, who will? That's what she had asked Stefan the night she met him. It wasn't T.J.'s voice she heard in her head any longer, it was her own. But this was Stefan. She couldn't back down. "Okay," she said.

He moved on top of her. Then—how long was that? That's it? All that buildup over the last weeks, and that's it? And what happened to pulling out?

"You had me going there," he said, his breath still racing as he closed his eyes, leaning his head back into the pillow. "Next time," he said as he grazed her cheek with his hand.

Anger borne of disappointment burned in her chest. But no matter what T.J. had told her about tapping into those feelings, that was for the stage, not real life. If she showed her anger, if she needed too much, Stefan might leave, right? Besides, there would be a next time. He said so.

The easiest way to take cover was to get Stefan talking about himself. "So, tell me," she said, forcing a smile, "who are you, Stefan Janaczek? How did you end up doing the work you do?"

He tilted his head as if to ask if she really wanted to know.

"It's complicated," he said when she nodded. "But if you want to know about me, you have to know something about my country and my family."

She edged closer. "Well, I'm not going anywhere."

He was born in 1934, sixteen years after the Czech lands and Slovakia united under a shaky new constitution, doomed from the beginning because it didn't account for centuries of the Czechs' and Slovaks' different histories, religions, and cultures. "My father was an engineer, my mother a professor."

After that, a montage of historical upheaval. From when he was a toddler and Hitler's forces rolled in to the end of World War II, when the Soviets, a Czech-coalition government, and American troops took over, to the communist takeover three years later. The details were confusing to Daria, but not the fact that he—and his country —were shaped by instability and uncertainty.

"Political and cultural freedoms?" He slammed his hand on the bed. "They were squashed like bugs. And by the fifties —I had already come to the States by then—dozens, maybe hundreds, of intellectuals and artists were put on trial and executed. The rest were forced underground."

He turned to Daria. "That's probably right around the time you were born. The fifties?"

Daria hesitated. "About then." Stefan's energy, his body, made him seem so young. But he was almost fifteen years older than her. Almost old enough to be her father. He had traveled the world and lived in it in a way she couldn't imagine. *No wonder I feel like a kid around him.*

He chuckled and shook his head. "I was even younger than you are now when my parents sent me to Brooklyn to live with my Aunt Bernice. I didn't want to go, but it was the only way they could keep me safe while they protested the rape—yes, I said, rape—of intellectual and creative freedom over there.

"My father, like many of the intelligentsia, drifted away from the Church. Or any other religion. My mother found a way for her faith and her intellect to coexist, though, so I went to Catholic schools. And when I landed here, my aunt enrolled me in St. John's Prep. A couple years later, when she told me my parents died in a car accident, I convinced myself and everyone else I had a calling for the priesthood. But that's another story."

Daria tried to decipher Stefan's enigmatic smile. What it was saying about his choice, his commitment. Or maybe he was simply remembering his mother. Whatever the reason for its ambiguity, it faded once he spoke again. He went on to say how restrictions on the press, education, and the arts began to loosen under the 1960 constitution.

"And now," he said, as proudly as if he had engineered the country's evolution, "Czechoslovakia's creativity—its literature, theatre, filmmaking—they're finally getting their due. And not just in Eastern Europe.

"*Closely Watched Trains*? You know it?"

Of course, she knew it. She had seen it with T.J. at MacMillan's international film festival. Then she had written a paper on it for her film class.

"Even the *Times* and the *Globe* named it one of the year's best," he said.

In large part, Daria recollected, for its earthy story line and bawdy sex scenes. Not exactly priestly material. Where was T.J. anyway? She pulled the covers over her breasts.

"When my aunt died late last year," Stefan continued, "I found a box of unopened letters from my mother." He wasn't smiling anymore.

"It turned out my parents weren't killed in an accident. I don't know why my aunt lied. But the letters told, in cryptic ways—remember the mail was heavily censored, still is to some degree—how they were involved in protests that sparked reform.

"So now," he said, propping himself up on his elbow, "I have my chance to find them."

Daria tried to catch his gaze, but he was looking beyond her, as if he had already left the States and was flying across the Atlantic.

She stayed silent for a moment, trying to figure out how to reel him back. "So maybe it's your parents you've been looking for in your work, all your travels?" She stroked his arm. "Maybe if you find them, I don't know, you might settle down a little?"

Stefan pulled away. "Settle down?" He laughed. "I'm as unsettled as my country's history. Always will be. Besides, things are really opening up over there."

In January a Slovak named Alexander Dubcek had become party leader. Press censorship was loosening, and creative communities were thriving.

"Prague Spring they're calling it," he said. "I'm heading over there in a couple weeks."

Daria inched away from him. Hadn't he just promised there would be a next time?

"You look surprised."

"Surprised?" She flushed. "I guess . . . I just didn't know you'd be leaving. I mean, what about the video?"

"An activist's work," he said, a seductive smile turning up his lips as he took her chin in his hand, "is never done." He kissed her lightly as he avoided talking about the video. "At least not a serious activist's."

She wanted to brush off his insinuation that her commitment to the anti-war movement wasn't solid. But his tone? His hypocrisy? He was the one who was abandoning their plans. Had he always been this condescending?

He reached for her, but Daria backed away when she heard footsteps on the stairs. She leapt up and struggled to get into her jeans, though Stefan tried again to ease her back to the bed. "You're embarrassed to be with me?"

"Shouldn't you be embarrassed?" Shrill. I sound so shrill. But he was leaving anyway. She didn't care how she sounded. She jerked her arm from his hand. "You're the priest."

The door opened, and the others spilled in, still energized, still going over their adventures on the march.

Daria turned from them to light a cigarette and to avoid T.J.'s eyes. But she saw how he looked from the mussed-up bed linens to her to Stefan and back to her.

He tossed on a table the couple six-packs he had bought. Without offering any, he grabbed a can for himself.

"So," he said with a sourness Daria had never heard in him, "tough day at the demonstration, Dar?" He popped the tab and slugged down the beer.

"No rougher than it was for anyone else, I guess." She crossed her arms. She held his gaze.

T.J. motioned to the rumpled bed. "Looks like you needed a nap."

"You could use one too. Might loosen you up a little."

******

Reliving the march through a smoky reefer haze, the group brainstormed how they would stoke their activism back on campus. Stefan encouraged them but said nothing about his plans for Prague. Daria stayed silent.

Around seven, T.J. took a paper and pen from his knapsack.

"My father's expecting you." He handed Stefan the address he had scribbled down.

"You're not coming?"

T.J. glared and said nothing.

"In that case," Stefan said, heading to the door, "I'll catch you guys later."

Daria slipped into her sleeping bag, hoping to warm the chill T.J. had sent her way.

******

Tired and hungover the next morning, no one spoke as they packed up to drive back to MacMillan.

Once inside the van, the mood was somber. Daria had disappointed T.J., and Stefan had disappointed her. But the City? When they crossed the George Washington Bridge, she turned in her seat to catch another glimpse. There it was. Her new friend, extending an invitation. *You belong here. Come back. Soon.*

Chapter Eleven
May 1968

T.J. had been slated to present the production schedule for the recruiting video at Stefan's planning meeting two weeks after they returned from New York. When he didn't show, Daria wanted to know why. "Where were you last night?" she asked when she ran into him between classes the next day.

"Let me get this straight," he said, shaking his head. "You still expect me to do this? To sit back while he takes advantage of you? And, by the way, me too? Sorry, Dar. I've got my hands full with more worthy endeavors, like this show. And if you want to keep your place in the cast, I suggest you give it a little more time and energy than you've doled out these last couple weeks."

Daria turned and left. If T.J. wouldn't finish the video, she would figure out how to put it together on her own. But when she called Stefan the next day—and two days after that—to get production back on track, she got no answer.

******

"You heard about Stefan?"

Daria braced herself when she ran into another student who had driven in their van to New York. What about Stefan? Whatever it was, she hadn't heard.

"He tacked a note on our meeting room at Taylor. Said he'd be gone a couple weeks. Everything's on hold. The administration building sit-in. The video. Everything."

Stefan was gone? Where? For how long?

"Oh, yeah." Daria shrugged. "I meant to get the word out."

******

Daria carried her tray to a cafeteria table and set down her tuna salad sandwich and iced tea. She picked up the *MacMillan Mirror*. The headline stared back: *MacMillan University Chaplain Trashes Pittsburgh Draft Board.*

According to the article, Stefan and six others had walked into Local Draft Board 27 in Pittsburgh and staged a protest like one the Berrigan brothers had organized months earlier in Catonsville, Maryland. They had barreled past workers, stuffed handfuls of files into wire trash baskets, and set them on fire with homemade napalm. Then they held hands and recited the Lord's Prayer. Stefan ran off afterward, but the others stayed until they were escorted to jail.

Daria lit a cigarette. Stefan had told her how he met the Berrigans at the civil rights march in Selma, Alabama, and how much he admired them, even before Catonsville. Daniel, a Jesuit priest and poet, had already rankled the Catholic Church with his unconventional Masses and his civil rights activism. His brother, Philip, also a priest, was known for his work with the poor in New Orleans and Newburgh, New York.

"They'll do anything to try to stop them," Stefan had said, referring to how the Church had transferred the Berrigans from city to city to try to cool their activism. "What the powers that be don't see is how that interference only strengthens their will to crack open the system and watch it bleed."

Daria remembered how Stefan's words had thrilled her then. Now T.J.'s warnings, and her own experience, tainted her impression of Stefan and his motives. Yes, he was impassioned, charismatic. He was also erratic and unreliable. She glanced again at his picture in the *Mirror*. How much of his activism, his inability to stay put, was shaped by the fact that his parents sent him off when he was so young, rather than by his pursuit of justice, his calling? And as for the Pittsburgh break-in, how much did he do it to win favor with other activist heavyweights, or to compete with them, rather than to support the anti-war cause? She didn't know. But he had run off again, and where he was, no one knew.

Daria pushed away her sandwich. Either the tuna had gone bad or she had just gotten a taste of tough-to-swallow truth.

******

"I'm sorry." T.J. approached Daria after Wednesday's dress rehearsal.

Daria's eyes hardened as she caught the towel T.J. tossed her. She'd felt inexplicably tired the last few days, which forced her to work harder to make her dancing look easy. Though it was only mid-May, it felt as if spring had passed MacMillan by. The temperature was in the eighties, and the air—heavy and humid—was tinged with the sulfur smell that made its way to MacMillan from the other side of the Front. At least Daria thought it was.

"You're sorry?" Daria suited up in her armor of arrogance. Was he taking her out of the show? He wouldn't. Couldn't.

"Yeah, I'm sorry for whatever forced you to dig deep enough to dance like this. But . . ."

He looked so damned serious. "But what?"

"But . . . you're magnificent, Dar," he said, smiling now.

Daria slapped T.J.'s arm, but she smiled too. "You're very mean." She might feel like she was falling apart, but at least she was holding it together on stage.

******

"Listen to this."

When Daria opened her apartment door, she found T. J. waving two flutes in one hand and a bottle of champagne in the other. A copy of the *MacMillan Mirror* was tucked under his arm. After he set the champagne and glasses on the coffee table, he read from the review in the *Mirror's* Arts section. "Daria Petrauskas, a Broadway star in the making, set the stage on fire."

"To the leading lady," he said, toasting Daria after he uncorked the champagne.

Daria beamed. T.J. could be such a pain in the ass. But thanks to him, all the work she put into *Carousel* had paid off. She lifted her glass to his, savored the bubbly, glad to be one step closer to New York.

Chapter Twelve
June 1968

"Miss Petrauskas?"

Daria sank into her lumpy couch when she heard the nurse's tinkling voice over the phone. "Yes?"

"The test was positive. I hope that's good news."

Daria's breath stopped short. She reached down to the sofa cushion, clenched the edge of it. She was sinking, falling, spinning. *No, that's not good news. Not at all.*

"You'll need to see Doctor Zimmerman this week. How's Tuesday at three?"

"Tuesday? Three o'clock? Sure."

When Daria hung up, she went weak-kneed to her bedroom, peeled back the bed's blankets. Even though it was almost summer, she crawled under the covers and pulled them over her head. Maybe, just maybe, her secret would wither and die if she deprived it long enough of air and light.

She slept through the afternoon and night but woke the next morning with a jolt. Was it the thunder from the storm that had wakened her? Then she remembered. *Pregnant. By a priest. A man she had slept with once and barely gotten the time of day from since.*

Daria wasn't sure whether it was shame, disgust, or dismay that rose up in her belly. Whatever it was, she wanted to spit it out, be done with it; but it was lodged too securely in her throat. She struggled from bed and changed out of the jeans and shirt she had slept in, leaving a trail of clothes behind her. A shower would help. But afterwards, when she put on a long, tiered skirt and white blouse, that dirty feeling still clung to her, as penetrating as the Mount Laurel stench she so wanted to escape.

In the living room, she lit a cigarette and tried to weigh her options. But she was nauseous. From what? The pregnancy, the cigarette, or the truth?

She put out the cigarette and reached for the phone.

"What's up?" T.J. sounded happy to hear from her.

"I . . . I . . ."

"Daria? What's the matter?"

"Nothing. Nothing's wrong at all. I just wanted to see how you're doing and—"

"And I'm Mick Jagger." She could hear T.J. opening and closing a dresser drawer while he juggled the phone. "I'll be right there."

******

When she heard him bounding up the stairs to her apartment, Daria met T.J. at the door. "What's wrong?" He reached to her, but she backed into the apartment, turned, and sank into the couch.

"Whatever you do," she said, reaching for a cigarette, "don't say you told me so." She lit up, inhaled, and blew a long, urgent curl of smoke into the air as she slouched back into the cushions.

"You know I wouldn't do that." He sat next to her, took the cigarette from her hand, and rubbed it out in the ashtray on the coffee table. "But whatever's wrong, a cigarette's not going to help."

"I'm pregnant."

T.J. nodded slightly, as though he'd just solved a riddle.

"What?" she demanded. "Say something."

"It makes sense, is all," he said.

Her jaw clamped shut, eyes narrowed. Why had she called this self-satisfied know-it-all? She said nothing.

"How did I know, you want to know? For one thing, I'm going to medical school, remember? I'm trained to observe. I could see that you're a little puffy. Right here," he said, gently pressing his hand along her waist. "And at rehearsals, you were starting to look tired. A little sickish."

She turned away. A flaw, even something natural like fatigue, even to T.J., felt like imperfection, and imperfection felt like failure.

"When did you know? Why didn't you say something?" She stopped assaulting him with questions when he reached for her.

She allowed him to hold her. Then, feeling safe enough to come out from behind her self-protective shell, she broke down.

He rocked her until her tears stopped. Then she pulled away. "Now what?"

"I guess that's your decision. But whatever you decide, I want to help."

"No." She shook her head. "I got myself into this mess. I'll get myself out."

"You know that Stefan's not going to help, right?"

"Of course, I know." When Daria snapped, tears came to her eyes again. She wasn't sure if she was angrier that T.J.

had said what she didn't want to face or that he had detected the slim possibility she still held on to. Her face felt rubbery, like it was wobbling out of shape from trying again to hold back her hurt, her fear.

"You've seen a doctor?"

"Not yet. I just found out yesterday."

"Have you had time," he asked, "to think through your options?"

"Options? I don't have any."

"Yes, you do. There are three."

"An abortion." He held up a finger, ticking off the first possibility.

"An abortion," she snapped. "I'm Catholic, remember? I was, anyway. I mean, I don't think I could live with myself."

"Okay," he said, "we're just exploring options."

When T.J. raised his hands as if to defend himself from her sharp response, Daria shook her head and managed a laugh.

"What's so funny?" he asked.

"If I really was Catholic," she said, "I wouldn't be in this mess. Especially with a *priest*."

"Maybe, maybe not." T.J. shrugged his shoulders. "Last time I checked, even my worn-out old copy of the Baltimore Catechism doesn't say we're perfect. Any of us. And anyway, we're looking ahead, not back, right?"

She hesitated, then acquiesced. "Right."

"Another option," he continued, methodically, "is to put the baby up for adoption. And the third," he said, taking her chin in his hand, gently urging her to look straight at him, "you could marry me, have the baby, and we could all live happily ever after."

Daria wasn't as surprised by T.J.'s back-door proposal as she was by her response. For a moment, she thought about it, turning it this way and that in her mind, admiring its angles. T.J. would be protective and affectionate toward both the baby and Daria. He would be faithful. And money wouldn't be a problem. *I could just leap over the edge of this cliff, freefall, and land in a soft, safe place.*

But Daria's suspicion of soft landings got the better of her. "I've already made one mistake," she said, fear yanking her back from possibility.

"I didn't think I was that bad an option." T.J.'s voice remained calm.

"You're not," she said. "It's me. You deserve someone who adores you. Someone who knows how to treat you the way you treat me."

He shook his head, looking at her the way he had when he told her, after rehearsal, that she didn't know how good a dancer she was. When Daria turned away, he changed course. "So, you're thinking adoption is the way to go?"

Daria was grateful he didn't push, even though she suspected he hadn't given up. She nodded.

"Okay, how about this? You can go to my father's place in the Berkshires for fall semester. There's a good hospital up in Stanton. My father's given them tons of money, including enough for the Townsend Memorial Cancer Center after my mother died. With a couple phone calls, an ob-gyn and family friend—his name's Dan Holcomb—can handle everything. Discreetly." He paused. "He'll even place the baby. If you're sure that's what you want."

Daria felt as if an escape hatch had opened. She could breathe again. When she looked back at T.J., her eyes softened. She nodded.

"Okay then. All your records can be mistakenly misplaced," he continued. "So there won't be any trace you were ever at the hospital. I'll be in New Haven, taking courses at Yale. I'll visit when you want. And after you recover and the baby's placed, you can come back to MacMillan, finish school, then head to New York like you planned."

Daria bit down so hard on her lower lip to keep from crying again that it began to bleed. Why didn't she just accept T.J.'s proposal? But as soon as she asked herself the question, the answer sprang to mind. T.J. couldn't see the layer of coal dust that she imagined clung to her. He couldn't smell the sulfur stink she was sure had drifted over the Allegheny Front, following her to MacMillan from Mount Laurel. Eventually he would, though. And then he would leave. So, the best thing was to hold him at a safe distance so he could continue to admire her, but never, never let him close enough to learn the truth.

She reached out and grazed his cheek with a sisterly kiss. "Thank you." But when she tried to lean back, he held her.

"Just remember," he said, "my other offer still stands."

This time when she pulled away, he let her go. "If there are strings," she said, searching his eyes, "any strings at all, I can't let you do this. I could never—"

"Shhhhh." He held his finger to her mouth. "You're not who you think you are, Dar," he said. "You just need a little more time to see that." He stood. "Will you be all right when I leave? I can stay if you want."

"I'll be fine." The small door she had opened to reveal herself slammed shut, the bolt secured across it by the artificial smile she put on. She stood, then tried to dust off the makeup that had rubbed onto T.J.'s white shirt when he had held her.

"Don't worry about that," he said, gently pulling away. He walked to the door.

With his hand on the doorknob, he turned back, wearing the boyish grin that, to Daria, always gave him the look of an oversized Cub Scout. "Do you need any saltines? Dill pickles maybe? Mint chip ice cream?"

"I'll tell you one thing, Mr. Fix-It-All." She picked up a throw pillow from the couch and tossed it toward him. "I may be pregnant. But I'm not going to get fat."

Arms up, he pretended to protect himself by ducking behind the door. Then he peeked back. "You're not going to starve yourself, are you?"

"You're smothering me."

"Okay, Okay. I just . . ." He thought better of finishing the sentence. "I'll call you tomorrow," he said over his shoulder.

I need him, Daria thought as she closed the door. *I just wish I could want him.*

She picked up the month-old paper again and stared at Stefan's picture. Just a few weeks earlier, two other anti-war activists, Father Tom McCarthy and Sister Mary Clark, married shortly after they destroyed draft records in Syracuse. It wasn't impossible that a priest would leave the priesthood and marry. *Maybe.*

٭٭٭٭٭٭

When the phone woke her, Daria looked toward her bedside clock. One ten. Since becoming pregnant, her sleep, despite her anxiety and fear, had become deliciously deep. It took a minute to decide whether the ringing was real or the remnant of a dream. Then she leapt from bed, stumbled on the pile of clothes on the floor, and ran to the living room. It had to be Stefan. No one else would call at this hour.

"Hello."

"Daria?" The connection was staticky, but when Stefan said her name, she sat on the edge of the couch.

"Stefan? Where are you? I read about—"

"We're winning," he interrupted, his voice jubilant. "I swear, before this thing is through, freedom's going to spread across Czechoslovakia. No, all Eastern Europe. That's how big this is." He described students spilling into Prague's streets without fear of being rounded up, writers and filmmakers publishing and producing work that had simmered for years, cafés filled from dawn to dusk, theatres packed every night.

Fueled by an adrenaline rush, Stefan's words tumbled out too quickly for Daria to understand. Plus, in the time he had been in Prague, his accent had become more pronounced.

"Too bad you're not here to see it."

Daria's heart sped up. *Maybe.*

He didn't wait for a response. "I need to send you some photos and interview tapes. Get them to T.J. and ask him to deliver them to his father, okay? There's a story here, and it's got to be told."

She fell back, resting against the couch cushions.

"Daria?"

"I'm here." Her voice chilled. "Why can't *you* send them to him?"

"The mail's still censored. Some of it anyway. We can't risk that anything we ship to someone as visible as Spence won't be confiscated."

Spence. He met the man once and now he's nickname-chummy?

"If the package goes to you, it's less likely to be stopped by customs."

When she paused, the jigsaw puzzle pieces tumbled into place, and the picture T.J. had seen all along came clear. Stefan had courted her because he knew T.J. would do whatever she asked, including arranging for Stefan to connect with Spencer Townsend. As for his trip to Prague, to find his family? He hadn't even mentioned them.

"Daria? This damned connection. Daria?"

"I'm pregnant."

"What? Pregnant?"

"And you're the father."

"You're sure?"

"That I'm pregnant or that you're the father?" Her world was shifting beneath her, but clearly hearing Stefan grounded her. She rose from the couch and stood tall.

"I'm sorry," he said.

"Sorry?" Had he mastered that technique in seminary? The ability to speak hollowed-out empathy, void of sincerity? "I'm pregnant with your child, and the best you can say is you're sorry?"

"I just assumed you took precautions," he said. "No, you were the one who . . . oh, what does it matter now?"

She wanted to vomit. Not because she was pregnant, but because she had been manipulated, then tossed aside. *Nothing. You get nothing more from me.*

"Do you want to have the child?" he asked.

She grabbed a vase from her nearby desk and threw it against the wall. It shattered, the water staining the painted plaster, the shards and daisies falling to the floor. When she heard banging on the wall from the apartment next door, she lowered her voice. "It's not a matter of what I *want* to do," she spit into the phone. "You're the priest, remember?"

"That's true," he said hurriedly. "But it was a mistake. We got carried away in the moment." He paused and his tone went cold. "You need to know that, if you decide to go ahead, either to keep it or give it away, I won't be involved."

"It? Give it away? Like a pair of shoes that hurt because they don't fit right?"

"No, no. Of course not." He batted away her bothersome gnat of a question. "Now, how can you get T.J. to deliver to Spencer the things I'm sending you?"

Daria held the phone at a distance. Stefan rattled on while her body numbed and her thoughts cleared. All those warnings T.J. had given her about Stefan. *You wouldn't be the first.* Now she saw the truth for herself. People earned a spot in Stefan's chaotic game-of-life as long as they helped him flit from one cause to another. As for his calls for justice and responsibility? Those lofty aspirations apparently mattered only while weaving spells over people—his groupies —who believed they needed and wanted what he said he stood for. But individuals? People close to him—as close as they could get to him anyway? They were on their own.

Daria hung up and curled on the couch.

She hadn't taken Stefan's class in liberation theology. But she had learned from him all right. Lying there, she admitted she needed T.J.'s help with the baby. After that? She would get what she wanted, and no one would dismiss or obstruct her. Not ever again.

Chapter Thirteen
September 1968

"T.J." Dan Holcomb walked into his reception room and extended a hand to his friend's son. "Good to see you." Trim, well-groomed and tanned, he seemed to Daria nothing like the doughy, white-haired doctors she was used to in Central Pennsylvania.

While the men shook hands, Daria took in the cream-colored walls, glossy white crown molding, and bookcases lined with leather-bound volumes. Signed photos of Martha Graham, Erich Leinsdorf, who would bring the Boston Symphony to nearby Tanglewood for the summer, and Ted Shawn, director of the nearby Jacob's Pillow dance center, hung on the walls. This was no smelly university clinic like the place her pregnancy had been confirmed. No, this was the setting for another glimpse into T.J.'s world. All polished and concealing, all Ivy League-tidy. She ran her hand through her long, rambunctious hair, as if to tame it, as if to make it look acceptable in a world she knew nothing about.

"You're in terrific shape for ski season," T.J. said.

"Only ten, twelve weeks to go. In the meantime, I've got a couple pounds to work off on the squash courts before I hit the slopes." The doctor patted his sweater where anyone who really needed to lose weight would have a belly. "But we're not here to talk about me." Smiling, all bright-white teeth, he held out his hand to Daria. "I'm Dan Holcomb."

"My apologies," T.J. said. "This is Daria. Daria Petrauskas."

Daria took his hand but had no idea what to say. It's a pleasure to meet you? Thank you for your help? She managed only a weak smile.

"Step into my office and we'll chat." It was Saturday afternoon, and the receptionist's desk was unattended. As T.J. had promised, Holcomb would be discreet. At least Daria could be thankful for that.

"And you?" the doctor asked as he looked to T.J. on their way into the office. "All set for Yale?" He motioned for T.J. and Daria to sit on leather chairs facing his desk.

"All set. Thanks again for the recommendation. I'm sure it tipped the scale my way."

"My pleasure," Holcomb said. Then he turned to Daria. "Now, young lady, you brought the forms I sent T.J.?"

Daria nodded, handing over a manila envelope.

"Good." He took the envelope and undid the clasp. As he started to review the papers, he motioned toward a raised-panel door to his left. "Why don't you get changed in the next room," he said, without looking up, "while T.J. and I wrap up a few details. You two can meet up somewhere in, oh, about an hour."

"I think I'd rather stay," Daria said, shooting a look at T.J. She was the one having the baby, not T.J. Shouldn't she be able to discuss whatever *details* needed *wrapping up*?

When Dan Holcomb raised his eyes, clasping his hands atop the papers, he looked at Daria squarely. "We do everything possible to insure you get the best care and to preserve your privacy. Which is why I'll refer to you as Miss Smith from now on. Now, if you don't mind, Miss Smith." He motioned again toward the exam room door.

She held the doctor's gaze long enough to show she did mind. She wanted to be called by her name. Daria Petrauskas. And she wanted a voice in how her *situation* was handled. But feeling she had no choice, she agreed.

"How about we meet at Toby's?" Daria ignored T.J.'s hand as he reached to squeeze hers. "The coffee shop with the blue awning. Down a block at Elm and Main."

"Sure." Daria said. Why did Dr. Dan have to be so damned clean and chilly, like his pristine white clapboard office building? The one that blended seamlessly with Stanton's consistently quaint architecture. When she stood, her eyes lingered on three pictures on his desk. Two of girls. Around ten and seven, blonde curls tumbling around their cherubic faces as—one gleefully, the other sheepishly—they tossed rose petals from baskets while walking down a white-carpeted aisle at a wedding. Another of a boy, about sixteen, square-jawed as a Kennedy, hiking out over his sleek little Sunfish in a yacht club race. No, there was nothing unseemly in the office except Daria and her *situation*.

In the exam room, Daria wished she could disappear into the velvety center of one of the oversized Georgia O'Keefe poppies that hung on the wall. Remaining inconspicuous might not prove too difficult through September. T.J. had arranged for her to dance at Jacob's Pillow so she would keep in shape. After that, she thought as she took off her skirt and sweater and slipped into the pink robe set out for her, she and her *situation* would be visible, no matter what she did.

When she heard T.J. leave, she braced for Dr. Holcomb.

"So," he said, walking briskly into the exam room, his manner purposeful and sterile as the instruments set out next to the exam table. "You believe conception took place on April twenty-seventh?" He set down the folder of papers Daria brought with her. It was labeled "Miss Smith 37." Thirty-six Miss Smiths had preceded her. No doubt more would follow.

"Yes."

"Okay." He turned to the sink and washed his hands. "Why don't you hop up here, and we'll have a look."

Hop? I'm not a rabbit. She shuddered at the thought of Dan Holcomb's hands on her. Still, she did as she was told.

After the mercifully short exam, Daria rewrapped the pink robe around her while Holcomb confirmed that she was approximately eighteen weeks pregnant, that she was in excellent physical condition, and that the pregnancy should proceed smoothly toward delivery in mid-January.

"I'll want to see you three weeks from today," he said. He stood from the stool-on-wheels where he had been seated, turned his back to her, and washed his hands again. She had been dismissed. Daria moved to the edge of the table but didn't stand.

"I'm wondering," she said, her voice sounding too small for the question she was asking, "about the family."

"The adoptive parents, you mean?"

"Yes." She tried willing him to look at her, but he opened her file on the counter, scribbled in it. "Who are they?"

"Well, that needs to remain confidential." Dan Holcomb opened a locked cabinet drawer, placed the folder in the drawer, closed the drawer, and locked it. He turned to her and crossed his arms on his chest.

"I know you can't tell me their names," Daria persisted. "But something about them. Where they live, what they do, how you know them."

"I'm afraid," he said, "I can't." He started for the door, opened it, then turned back toward her. "T.J. tells me you're a fine dancer, with a future. You're fortunate. You can pour yourself into your work and, literally, move on." He smiled his chilly smile. "Now, if you'll forgive me, I have another patient coming, and I need to ensure her privacy just like I insured yours."

Daria reached for her skirt and sweater on the hook next to the door. "Miss Smith number 38?"

Dan Holcomb didn't respond. "Use that back door." He pointed to the opposite side of the exam room.

When the door closed, Daria clasped her belly. "Maybe," she whispered, "I'm a temporary intruder in Dan Holcomb's world. But you, little girl—and I know you're a girl—can be a full-time resident."

Once dressed, Daria walked to the back door to leave the exam room. But when her hand touched the doorknob, she turned to face the center of the room.

"Even before you see daylight," Daria said softly, hand on her belly, "I'm going to teach you how to belong here. Or anywhere else."

She walked to the door leading to the reception area and opened it. The newest Miss Smith, a slight woman a little older than Daria, was handing an envelope to the doctor, just as Daria had a short time earlier.

With Dan Holcomb's eyes fixed on her, Daria entered the room and smiled.

"I'm Daria," she said, extending her hand to the young woman. "Daria Petrauskas. What's your name?"

Chapter Fourteen
October 1968

Every morning, no later than seven, Daria packed the Townsends' Jeep with her lunch, her leotard, and her ballet shoes, then drove to the dance center. The Berkshires' hilly landscape wasn't all that different from the Appalachian Plateau, which wasn't as flat as its name implied. But even on the foggiest mornings or most humid afternoons, when she drove between the roadside columns of white pines, she felt as if they protected her like fragrant, faithful soldiers. Never changing, never judging. She felt safe in their shadows, safe enough to get to know her baby. A girl. She just knew.

With the child inside her, changing shape day by day, Daria didn't even try to dismiss the questions that rose up. Will she look like me? Will her parents take good care of her? Will she dance? Become a doctor or a waitress? Live in New York? Or California? Then occasionally, the most unsettling question—am I doing the right thing? Which Daria chased away by insisting she had no choice but to give up her daughter.

At least everything was going according to plan. She would deliver around January eighteenth. She would spend three days in the hospital, recovering. She would be back in

MacMillan for spring semester, her last. Then on to New York.

Her future was all tidily laid out, just like the town of Stanton.

No one had to know that in bed at night, she sang to the tiny person inside her that, somehow, someday, just like the song from *Carousel* promised, a golden sky would appear at the end of this storm.

******

By mid-October, belly swelling, Daria lightened her dance schedule. She took a beginner's ballet class at a local studio to keep up her form, and a seminar at the local U Mass campus in history of musical theatre.

At night, she made a fire in the fieldstone hearth, then remembered Nana's tale of Gabija, the Lithuanian goddess of fire. "To please Gabija," Nana had said, "care for fire like dog or cat. Like pet." As Nana taught, Daria placed a bowl of water on the hearth, so the goddess would visit, bringing protection from thieves and safety in childbirth.

But sometimes, as she fell into murky sleep, Nana's story of the Laumės and the Babe, the fairies and the child, insinuated itself into her thoughts.

A long time ago, the story went, a woman set her daughter down by the flower bed while she harvested her zinnias and dahlias. When her basket was full of red and yellow and purple blossoms, she went home, forgetting her child, who had been small and weak since birth. The woman milked the cows. She twisted a chicken's neck, and plucked its feathers before simmering it for dinner with carrots and potatoes and dill.

"Where's my child?" her husband asked when she set out the meal.

"Oi," the woman gasped. "I left her in the fields."

The field fairies, the Laumės, taunted the woman as she ran. "*Čiūčia liūlia.*" Forgotten child.

"Please," the woman begged the Laumės, who hid behind rocks and trees, in bushes and clumps of grass. "Help me find my child."

"Come, woman," they said, directing her to a large linden tree. "Take your child. We know you work hard and that you didn't intend to leave your dear daughter."

The woman scooped up the infant and ran home, thanking the fairies. From that day on, the Laumės showered the woman with good fortune. Her husband's fields yielded bountiful corn and rye. The woman's gardens flourished. The red-and-yellow blankets she wove from her sheep's plentiful wool sold for good prices. And the baby grew strong, her eyes blue as a late spring sky, her hair the color of summer wheat.

When a neighbor heard of the woman's good fortune, her skin turned the green of envy. "I shall take my son to the linden tree where that good-for-nothing mother left her sickly child. 'My child, my dear child,' I'll call out for the Laumės to hear. 'I was toiling so hard I left my poor boy in the fields.' Ahh, how much spun wool I will sell at the village market. The fat prices my barley will fetch."

But when she reached the linden tree, the fairies were pinching the screaming boy. "Child of a mother who left you for her good, not yours." "Take him, cursed woman," they called as they tossed the child to his mother. She reached out her arms and caught the boy. But when she huddled him to her chest, the child was dead.

Daria often woke from these nightmares of field fairies and wrong intentions with her heart racing and her nightgown clinging to her body from fearful sweat. Would she be punished, she wondered, for her bad judgments in the same way the jealous mother had? Worse yet, would her child suffer?

******

As they strolled downtown that weekend, Daria took T.J.'s arm. "Tourists," she said, shaking her head as she steered him past a couple with Boston accents who, like most of Stanton's visitors that weekend, had come to the Berkshires to "leaf peep."

"You sound like a native." T.J. smiled as he finished his ice cream cone, melting in the Indian summer sun. "If you don't watch it, you might even admit you like it here."

"Well, I'm not sure if I like it here so much." She turned toward the gallery they were passing to avoid T.J.'s thinly veiled invitation to settle with him in Stanton, or anywhere else. "But I like that." She pointed to the landscape in the window. "The way the clouds are hanging there on the horizon, waiting."

"That sounds ominous." T.J. studied the painting. "I guess I see it differently, that the clouds aren't threatening, but parting. See how the sun's peeking through there?"

"Maybe." She released T.J.'s arm and walked closer to the window. "But I like big weather. Like the twisters that used to skitter across the Pennsylvania hills."

"Well, there's plenty of big weather here, come January, February." He paused. "You don't talk much about home, you know."

"Home?"

"Mount Laurel."

"I'm not sure I'd call it home anymore."

"Well, whatever you call it, someday I want to hear more about it."

Daria focused on the painting, but from the corner of her eye caught a whoosh of yellow, vibrant as the maple and elm leaves on Stanton's trees. When she turned toward it, a heavily made up woman, dressed in a flamboyant, loose-fitting, mustard-colored dress, rushed open-armed and beaming toward T.J.

"Why, Thayer!"

"Lorna." T.J. hugged the woman and kissed her lightly. When he tried to back away, she hung on to his upper arms.

"Look at you, all grown up and ready to conquer the world." Her voice drifted into a nostalgic tone. "I haven't seen you since your mother's service. How are you, darling?"

"I'm well, Lorna. Very well."

Daria had moved to the next gallery's window to escape an introduction but turned when T.J. called her. "Daria, come meet Lorna Bennett."

Daria looked straight ahead as Lorna's eyes dropped to Daria's belly, then moved to her barren ring finger, and back to her face. "Daria, is it?" To try to mask her surprise, the woman forced a bigger smile.

"Yes."

"What an interesting name." Daria tensed as Lorna looked from T.J. to Daria and back to T.J., waiting to hear a wedding date, or at least a due date. Getting none, she continued.

"I've known T.J. since, well, since he was a glimmer in Spencer's eye. And Ginia and I used to do off Broadway together. You'd never know it by looking at me now. I got fat. Tell this stunning young lady I wasn't always this fat."

"Lorna," T.J. assured, "you're as lovely as ever."

"Well," she said, "I'm going to pretend that's true and get on with my day. Call me, darling. I'm in Stanton through Christmas. Pleasure to meet you, Darlene."

"Daria," T.J. corrected.

Lorna tapped her head. "I'm such a ninny when it comes to names. Forgive me, Daria, won't you?"

Daria waved, then turned back to the gallery window.

"She's always been a little spacey," T.J. said, walking behind Daria, putting his hands around her thickening waist. "It's none of her business, Dar. You're the only one who matters. You and your little girl."

She caught his reflection in the window and managed a smile. "Well," she said, "at least I now know your name is Thayer. What's the J stand for? And how come you don't call yourself Thayer?

"You know, I'm not the only one who's a little stingy on the personal history."

"True," he said.

Instead of responding further, he took her hand and started down the street. "There's a little gallery around the corner with some outstanding Ansel Adams," he said. "Did you know Adams actually wanted to become a concert pianist but decided . . ."

******

Dan Holcomb sat at his desk and scribbled in Daria's file. "Everything," he said, "is still on track for January eighteenth."

Daria, seated across from him, wondered if he could be anymore aloof. Then again, she hadn't exactly endeared herself to him.

"That's good news," Dr. Holcomb said, looking up, smiling his thin smile, "isn't it?"

Daria nodded.

"I'm going up to Stratton for a couple weeks of skiing around the holidays," he said, closing her file and clasping his hands atop it. "But I'll be back in plenty of time."

With any luck, Daria thought, his chairlift would keep on going right off Stratton Mountain and propel him into Iceland.

"All I want to know," Daria said, "is what arrangements have been made."

"For the adoption, you mean?" He checked his watch.

Daria glared. Maybe he had a squash court reservation. She might not fit in Dan Holcomb's world, but she would be damned if she allowed its trappings to intimidate her, to take away her voice the way he had taken away her name. "Yes, for the adoption."

"Well, yes, of course." He stood. "They're all finalized. Now, if you don't mind . . ."

"Actually, I do mind." She leaned forward, refusing to be rushed. "You haven't told me anything. Not about the parents, where they live. Nothing." She paused, swallowed. "What if I change my mind?"

"Miss Smith."

By now she wanted to strangle him so no other Miss Smith would ever have to suffer his demeaning money grubbing. She had no idea how much the doctor's services cost. T.J. had taken care of that. But there must be a hefty price for discretion. One significant enough to fund his trips to Stratton, to the Amalfi Coast, for this pristine office?

After Daria had left Mount Laurel, she had always been squeamish about her name. It was so ethnic compared to all those Merediths and Sarahs and Janes who lived in MacMillan's Pi Phi and Tri Delt sororities. But here, with Dan Holcomb's Yale degrees on the walls, with the void she felt when her name had been taken away to protect her privacy, she wanted it back. "My name is Daria."

"Very well, Daria. I'm afraid the time for changing your mind has passed. And even if there were time, I assume you have limited financial means? On your own, I mean."

Daria's heart raced. Money. Now she felt the anger T.J. wanted her to tap when she danced with the barker in *Carousel*. Why did her father go off and leave her? Why did he piss away what little money they had, leaving her feeling adrift? She clung to the chair arms to hide her trembling. Her left eye twitched.

"Miss—Daria." Dr. Holcomb's voice softened as he walked to the front of the desk, then leaned against it. "A lot of girls get squeamish toward the end." He placed his hand on hers. "But I assure you, the ones who avoid contact with the baby—which you agreed to do—the ones who have goals —which you have—they do the best."

For a moment, Daria wondered if Dan Holcomb kept his chilly distance because, if he came close, like he was now, he might not be able to stomach what he did for all his Miss

Smiths. Maybe he wasn't so much of a beast. Maybe she was angrier at herself than at him.

She blinked three times, trying to keep her tears from falling. Yes, when she agreed to the arrangement, she had planned to give up her child, go back to school, then to New York. But that was when she was reeling from Stefan's rejection, when she was vomiting and so tired, and, despite T.J., feeling so alone. That was before she spent time with her little girl.

Now, she wanted to exchange two little words, *give up*, for one, *keep*. She would worry about the details later. Somehow, she could manage. And there was always T.J. He would find a way.

"In case you're thinking T.J. can rescue you," the doctor said, anticipating Daria's solution to her situation, "you need to know that Spencer—that's T.J.'s father—when Spencer hired me, he stipulated that if you attempt to keep T.J.'s child—"

"It's not T.J.'s child."

"Of course, it's not." He smiled, as if he knew the truth but chose to placate her. "But if you attempt to keep the child, by marrying T.J. or otherwise implicating him, Spencer will cut off support like that." He sliced the air with his hand. "No money for you, the child, T.J.'s medical school. None."

Daria held his gaze, then looked away. She might have made some bad decisions, but she couldn't force T.J. to make one too. Before she could digest that realization, the office door opened. Two girls—the same two whose pictures were on Dan Holcomb's desk—ran into the office, followed by a thin, blonde woman in a luscious sable coat.

"I'm sorry," the woman said. "I didn't know you were with a patient." She attempted to corral the girls back to the waiting room, but the younger girl ran to her father.

"Daddy," she called while she twirled in front of him, modeling her new pink parka. "Look what Mommy bought me for our trip."

Daria felt dizzy looking at them. A perfectly cast family. Without speaking, she rose from her chair, steadied herself, then walked out the front door into the chilly air. "That damned coat," she muttered, thinking of the full-length sable Mrs. Holcomb wore. "I need one of those."

Chapter Fifteen
December 1968

"I'll be back on Thursday." T.J. slipped his sheepskin jacket over the cabled crewneck Daria had knit him for Christmas.

For the last few days, Daria had felt she was playing a role in a documentary called *How the Holidays Should Look, Feel, Sound, and Taste.* She and T.J. had cut down, put up, and decorated a crooked, but endearing little tree. They baked and assembled a gingerbread house, sang carols at Stanton's white church on the green on Christmas Eve. On their walk through town, they made snow angels—no easy feat for Daria, with her ballooning belly—near the green's bandshell, then sipped hot chocolate at home in front of a fire.

They ate Christmas dinner at the Stanton Inn, where the hearth fire warmed the room, and Scotch pine garlands with big red bows decorated the mantle and banisters. No one looked anything like anyone from Mount Laurel. Hair trimmed just so. Teeth all straight and impossibly white. Men wearing tasteful ties, starched white or blue shirts under navy blazers. Women in cashmere and pearls. Boys looking like miniatures of their fathers. Girls in lace-trimmed taffeta. All entertained by strolling carolers, the men in cutaway jackets and top hats, the women in rabbit-trimmed velvet.

When she and T.J. sat at their table, Daria looked down at her long black gabardine skirt and now shapeless wool cardigan, her only clothes that still fit. She fingered her cheap silver and fake turquoise necklace.

She refocused on their meal of goose and candied sweet potato soufflé and Christmas pudding. It wouldn't be long, she vowed, before she would be wearing cashmere and pearls and dining at the Stanton Inn or wherever else she chose. Maybe she shouldn't be so hasty about turning down T.J.'s offer to take care of her and the baby. Even if Spencer cut him off, T.J. would make it on his own. She was sure of that.

So, when they returned to the Townsends', she reached for T.J., took off his tie, unbuttoned his white shirt, and urged him to make a fire so they could cuddle in front of it. They dozed off and on, and when they woke around three, T.J. led her to his room. Under his down comforter, his arms wrapped around Daria's belly, he nestled against the curve of her back.

"Everything's going to be just fine," he said.

And when Daria drifted off, no taunting field fairies interrupted her sweet, peaceful sleep.

When they woke the day after Christmas, though, the spell she was under the night before dispersed. At breakfast, she avoided T.J.'s eyes, retreated from him when he tried to kiss her.

"I can stay if you want," he said as he wrapped his scarf around his neck. If he was disappointed that Daria had once again danced away, he didn't show it. "I'll just call Professor Kleinberg and get someone to cover the lab. Smitty owes me for all the times I filled in for him when his daughter was born.”

Daria shook her head. “T.J., it’s not the same. It’s not your baby.”

“Details, details.” He smiled. “I know it’s not my baby. And for, what, the ten thousandth time? I know you don’t want to marry me. I’m just saying I don’t like your being alone, especially with the baby coming in a couple weeks.”

“You’ll only be gone five days. And you’re only four hours away.” She had never mentioned to T.J. that she knew about the strings Spencer Townsend had attached to the deal he had brokered with Holcomb. The temptation she felt the night before had dissipated in the light of day.

“Okay,” he said, hopping on one foot then the other as he tugged on his L.L. Bean boots, “I’ll leave under one condition.”

“Be careful,” she laughed as T.J. bumped into the door jamb in the entryway. She reached to steady him. When T.J. righted himself, his eyes softened.

“No conditions,” she said, trying to ward off any impending advance. “Remember?”

“Just this once, can you please cut me a break?” He reached for her arms and held them, forcing her to look at him. “If you change your mind, about anything, promise you’ll call.”

“Cross my heart, hope to die,” she said, making an X on her heart.

“Don’t,” he said, his grip tightening, “even joke about that.”

"It's just a figure of speech." She reached for his face. "Thank you. For everything." Then she stepped away, crossing her arms.

When the door shut, Daria lingered at the front window as he backed his Beetle from the turnaround and proceeded out the driveway. She may have teased T.J. about being superstitious, but she was the one who, since she had become pregnant, constantly worried. *What if? What if? What if?* She imagined everything from a bear clawing its way into the house, to the electricity going out, to the baby being born with some indelible, contemporary scarlet letter that would brand her as illegitimate. Then again, Daria reasoned, if she remembered from nineteenth century American Lit, Hester Prynne, not her child, bore the big red A for adultery. Daria, not her little girl, would bear the scar.

Daria made a fire and a cup of tea. She went to her room and pulled out her journal. Wrapped in a quilt on the couch, she sipped her tea, flipping through the journal, reading what felt like someone else's recordings.

March 31. *Happy,* she had written. *I'm happy. I feel alive, like I could fly!* She ran her finger over her flowing script, underlined and heavily peppered with exclamation points. She wished she could recapture the exuberance she had felt that day, less than a year earlier.

She flipped to the entry for April 27, the day of the peace march. Then to May, when *Carousel* had opened on campus. More ebullient exclamation points. Then June 18, the day she found out she was pregnant. That writing was in bold block letters. To June 23, when she drove to Mount Laurel to tell her mother. Just a few short sentences. *I couldn't do it.*

At the End of the Storm

I'm never going back. I don't want to be the kind of mother she was to me.

Some days all she wrote was a phrase or two from *Carousel*'s lyrics. *At the end of the storm is a golden sky. . . .* Those lyrics had seemed so corny when she sang them at first in rehearsals. But now she hung onto them, even dared to believe them.

Interspersed with her daily entries, she had written the stories Nana told her. Like how, when a woman gave birth, the grandmother was supposed to lay out gifts of towels and lace-trimmed pillowcases. She had written, too, about Ausrine, the dawn goddess, and the Asvieniai twin horses. Today, she planned to write about Laima, the goddess of childbirth, domesticity, and pregnant women.

Laima and her two sisters, Karta and Dekla, controlled a woman's destiny. It was Laima, Nana had said, who determined a newborn's fate. What, Daria wondered, did Laima have in store for her little girl?

When Daria looked up from her journal, it was five-thirty. The days had started inching longer as of the equinox a few days back; but it would be weeks—right around the time her baby girl was to arrive—until the sky stayed light past five or so. Especially since the Townsends' place was at least a mile from town, far enough that ambient light from the street lamps and shops didn't reach.

Goddess Laima, Daria continued writing, most often called at night, outside a window, waiting and watching.

She tossed aside the quilt and set her journal on the coffee table. She clumsily eased herself to standing. Then she went to the windows and peered out, pressing her hand to the pane, feeling its chill on her palm. *Laima, determiner of destiny for newborns, are you there?*

But all she saw was a deep, dark grove of pines. And all that was certain was that she would never know who her little girl would grow up to be. She only hoped that Laima or Nana or someone was keeping watch.

******

The morning after T.J. left, flurries swirled in the wind along the driveway among the pines. By noon, the snow fell straight and steady until four, then eight, then twelve inches accumulated. When T.J. called at six as usual, Daria insisted she was fine, even though the pains had started. False labor. It must be. It had to be. The baby wasn't due for almost three weeks, and her water hadn't broken. There was no reason to ask T.J. to drive back up from New Haven. But she did ask Gabija for protection. Laima too, for the baby.

She turned on the local radio station and heard that "the roads have been closed to all but emergency vehicles" and that many residents had lost phone and electrical service. At eight, she picked up the phone to call T.J.; but when she heard the dial tone, she put it back down.

She was uncomfortable, but she could wait until morning. She went out to clear the path to the Jeep—just in case she needed to get out—when a single, sharp pain sent her to the ground. She stumbled to the house. It was time to get to the hospital.

She picked up the phone again, but this time there was no dial tone. Slowly, carefully she loaded the bag she had packed into the Jeep, then drove along the road she'd traveled every day to dance class. "It's not that far, little girl," she said. "You can be a little bit patient. Just a few more miles. Just a couple more minutes. Ahhh, aahhh, ahhh, aahhh, ba-a-by," she sang, just like Nana used to sing to her. She drove carefully, slowly, sitting tight, ice water in her veins. Just like her father taught her.

******

"Miss Smith?" The young woman in blue scrubs and a white lab coat walked into the room and shut the door behind her. A private room was part of the deal Dan Holcomb struck for each of his Miss Smiths.

"My name's Daria. Daria Petrauskas." She wanted her words to sound insistent but . . . had she been drugged? She didn't know, but her voice sounded lazy.

"I see," the woman said. "Well, I'm Dr. Krevina. Alexandra Krevina. And I'm going to do an exam to see how long it'll be before we get you into the delivery room."

"The baby's not due for—" Another contraction, this one longer and more intense than the last, forced Daria to truncate her sentence.

"Your paperwork's a little thin," Dr. Krevina said as she checked Daria's chart. "You weren't scheduled to deliver for another three weeks?" She set down the file. "Feet up here." She placed Daria's feet into the exam table's stirrups.

"The eighteenth," Daria said as she looked more closely at Alexandra Krevina. Her voice. A Russian accent. Familiar. Not just because Daria had grown up around a lot of Russians in Mount Laurel. Who was she?

"Your contractions are running fifteen minutes apart, and you're dilated four centimeters." The doctor moved and spoke with efficiency bordering on brusqueness. "I'm guessing you'll be a mother before midnight. A nurse will be in in a minute to get you prepped for the delivery room."

"Dr. Holcomb?" Daria tried to raise herself up. "He'll be here?"

A storm, it turned out, had stranded Dan Holcomb in Vermont. "So, who's going to deliver my baby?" As much as Daria disliked him personally, she trusted him professionally. She tried to prop herself up, but a contraction forced her on her back again.

"I'll deliver your baby," Dr. Krevina said as she finished the exam. She patted Daria's arm. "And, yes," she said, anticipating Daria's question. "I've done this before. Many times."

I should know more about this girl-doctor, Daria thought. But with the next contraction, Daria's curiosity skulked away. *Laima, you goddess bitch of pregnant women, where are you? And T.J.? Why didn't I call T.J.?*

******

"A girl?"

"Ten fingers, ten toes," Dr. Krevina said as she reached to take Daria's pulse. "She's a tiny little thing. Only five and a half pounds. We'll need to watch her a few days, but there's no need to worry. Now, up, up, up." She snapped her fingers. "I want you to sit up."

When Daria heard the doctor's fingers snapping, she realized where she had heard her voice. At the dance center. In the room where the high school girls practiced, across the hall from the studio where Daria danced. "Up, up, up. *Relevé. Plié.*" Daria had heard Dr. Krevina order her students many times. "Again, again."

"You teach at the dance center," Daria said, trying to find a way to sit that didn't hurt.

Dr. Krevina looked at Daria differently, less clinically. "You dance there?"

"Only since summer. I came up here to have the baby." Daria turned her face to the wall so the hot tears rolled down her face, onto the starchy white linens beneath her. "I want to see her."

"The baby's fine." Alexandra Krevina placed her hand on Daria's arm, then hesitated. "I wasn't in on your arrangements, but when Dr. Holcomb phoned, he said you asked not to see her."

"No." Daria shook off the fuzziness from her fatigue. "*He* decided I shouldn't see her. And even if I agreed, I changed my mind."

"You're sure?"

Daria nodded.

"Miss Jacobson," Dr. Krevina called out to the nurses' station. "Please bring Baby Girl Smith to her mother," she said when the nurse arrived.

Miss Jacobson cast a sideways glance to Daria. "Dr. Holcomb usually doesn't permit that. Under the circumstances."

Dr. Krevina moved toward the door. "If you won't get her," she said, motioning for the nurse to leave, "I will. And Miss Jacobson? No matter how short-staffed we are tonight, don't come back in this room as long as Daria is in it, do you understand?"

Maybe, Daria thought, Laima had been watching out for her after all.

******

Daria took her little girl in her arms, afraid she might break her, yet knowing she would do anything, *anything* to make sure no harm came to her. She stroked the baby's cheek, her plentiful hair, the same color as Daria's. Her tiny fingernails and toes, her little red face, all wondrous. She snuggled the little girl, inhaled her baby smell, and wept into its sweetness.

She had spent the last days, weeks even, thinking about this moment, steeling herself against the possibility of attachment to her daughter. But here she was, wondering how she had ever thought she could just hand her over to someone else to feed and dress, send off to kindergarten, then college.

"Daria?"

T.J. stood at the door, carrying a dozen yellow roses, smiling like the proud father.

******

The morning after leaving the hospital, Daria picked at the eggs and toast T.J. set in front of her.

"Juice?"

She shook her head as he held out a pitcher.

"Okay." He smiled, trying to lighten her mood. "But I'm as tough a taskmaster behind the wheel as I am on stage. I only stop when the gas gauge is hovering around empty."

She looked up, face expressionless, eyes vacant. "I'm taking the bus back." Her voice carried the same bite as the January wind whistling through the barren birch branches along the driveway. "I want to be alone."

T. J. hesitated. "The bus will take forever," he said, setting the pitcher on the table.

"It's leaving at eight-thirty." She pushed back from the table. "And I'm going to be on it whether you drive me to the station or I have to walk." She stood, then turned and headed down the hall to get her bags.

Chapter Sixteen
March 1992

"After college," Daria said, continuing the story she was telling Frankie, "I was off to New York. And that's when I became a Rockette."

Frankie laughed. "I'm sure you had the body for it, *chère*. But I just can't imagine you dancin' to anybody else's tune."

"Well, it's true. For two years, I dressed up in fur-trimmed velvet at Christmas, floppy ears at Easter. I shivered my way through Thanksgiving Day parades and shimmied my way through USO shows.

"The Rockettes were all about precision and perfection. And I figured if I looked perfect enough no one would see who I really was, where I was from, and how flawed I was for getting pregnant, then giving up my little girl."

"It's a wonder you could dance at all, given all that baggage you were carryin'," Frankie said. "What about Ted? When did he come into the picture?"

"I first met him at a USO show he organized in Saigon. Even in his fatigues, Lieutenant Demarest looked pretty darn good. But can you imagine? Only a couple years earlier I'd been toting Bring Home the Baby Killers posters at anti-war protests. And there I was tapping and kicking for an audience of cat-calling enlisted men.

"When Ted returned to the States, I had just started doing special segments for *Wake Up*. We met up again at a holiday party. Then and there, I decided he was the one, that his Princeton degree and country club pedigree would legitimize me and obliterate—or at least sufficiently disguise—my past."

Within three months after they eloped, she explained, they were sniping at each other. "He wanted kids right away. I didn't. So, the sensible thing to do, I thought, was to take birth control pills on the sly. In the meantime, I got the job as Gavin's co-host on *Wake Up*. On the surface, life was going just how I wanted. Until Ted insisted I see a fertility specialist.

"When we were told there was no apparent reason we couldn't have children, I knew the jig was up. I stopped the pills and 'miraculously,' within weeks, I was pregnant. I took time off work—being pregnant on camera was unthinkable back then—and that was a low point. Whenever I took Jack to Central Park, I couldn't stop staring at the little girls who were around seven, the age my daughter would have been. Could that be her swinging on the swings? Teetering on the teeter totter? I was having nightmares about her by then, and this unshakeable feeling that one day she would run up to me, arms flailing, crying, '*Mommy, why did you leave me?*'"

By the time they moved to Connecticut, Daria continued, Jack was three and she was pregnant with Lizzy. They renovated an old farmhouse on White Oak Shade in Greenvale, enrolled Jack in Greenvale Country Day pre-school, hired a live-in nanny, joined the club, and eventually bought a second place on Nantucket. "And," she said, "I smiled through it all, hoping no one would see who or what I really was."

She paused. "You know the rest, Frank. The way you and I met at the club when we were out sailing with the Donaldsons. Remember that afternoon? The way you looked from me to Ted to Bitsy Donaldson? That's what tipped me off to their little dalliance."

When Frankie remained uncharacteristically silent, Daria prompted her. "What are you thinking, Frank?"

"Amazing, isn't it," Frankie said, "the pains we take to build those big old fortresses around us, brick by brick, so no one can see who we really are?"

"I'm not really sure what to say."

"You've said a whole lifetime in the last hour or so, sugar."

When Daria said nothing more, Frankie continued. "You know, life has a way of keepin' after us till we learn the lessons we need to learn. This situation with Lizzy is gonna be a roller coaster for you *and* her. But maybe it's an opportunity too?"

"Opportunity?" Daria let out a cynical little laugh. "You're kidding, I hope?"

"A chance to do things different. What I mean is, maybe if you let others help you be there for Lizzy, you'll learn to be there for yourself. All that shame you felt—or feel—all that need to pretend to be somebody you're not, maybe that'll all melt away."

Daria tossed aside the pillows she had clutched while she told Frankie her story. "You've been reading too many self-help books, Frank."

"Could be. But I'm not gonna let up on this one, Dar."

Daria glanced at her bedside clock. "It's almost midnight. I've got to get at least a couple hours' sleep or I'll look like hell on camera tomorrow."

"You, darlin', could never look like hell. But will you do me one tiny little favor?"

"What's that?"

"With Lizzy, just remember, you have a choice."

"About what?"

"Look, I know Lizzy's a handful. She and I get along because I don't live with her. If I did, we'd hit our rough patches too. And this situation's not gonna sweeten her up. Not right away. But when she tries to get under your skin, to get you all riled up?"

"Just thinking about it makes my head hurt."

"I bet it does, sugar. But you don't have to get into an adolescent, tantrum-throwin', shootin' match."

Daria balked at Frankie's implication that she and Lizzy operated on the same emotional level. But Frankie was right when she said Daria needed to do things differently if she was going to get through Lizzy's pregnancy. The only problem? She didn't know how. "And what do I do instead?"

"Easier said than done. But when things get tough, walk away for a few minutes if you have to. Call me. But just remember you don't have to do to her what your mother did to you. Or, what was that rascal's name, Stefan?"

"Yes."

"All you have to do is be there."

"I hear you," Daria said, "but I'm not sure I've got it."

"You know how those gurus on *Awakenings* are always talkin' about how yoga's a practice?"

"Yeah."

"Well, if we try new things, we're bound to make mistakes. And, that old saying that practice makes perfect? It's probably still true for the Rockettes. But for us normal folks, we just keep doin' our best, and hopefully get better, bit by bit by bit."

Hearing Frankie's permission to fumble, Daria's shoulders relaxed. "Thanks, Frank."

"No problem. I'll call tomorrow with the name of an agency, okay?"

"Okay."

"Sweet dreams, sugar."

******

Daria hung up and slid under her linen duvet. She closed her eyes, ready to escape into merciful sleep until her alarm went off at five fifteen.

But less than a minute later, she rolled back the covers and sat up. What was the date? She checked the program notes she had set on her bedside chair. The twenty-seventh. Her mother's birthday. The last thing she wanted to do was call this late. Not that her mother wouldn't be awake. Helena had always been a night owl, yet still able to get up before dawn.

Daria reached for her phone and dialed. As it rang, she braced herself for the inevitable challenge ahead—a civil, communicative conversation with her mother.

"Hello?"

"Happy birthday." Daria's voice was as chipper as she could manage.

"It's almost over," Helena responded.

"I'm sorry it's so late. The day got away from me."

"We're all busy."

"You got the sweater?"

"It's too soft."

"Ma, it's cashmere. It's supposed to be soft."

"Don't waste your good money. I got all I need."

Daria refrained from telling Helena she could return the sweater. There was no way her mother would drive to the Saks in Pittsburgh or bother sending it back by mail. "Okay. Well, did you and Rosa go out to celebrate?"

"Same as we always do. Down to Wojtzak's for a fish fry."

"I hope you had a good time."

Like trying to deadlift a Volkswagen. That's how this conversation felt. But what could she talk about? Lizzy's pregnancy? No, not now. Maybe never. Something safer. Maybe her mother would like to hear about Mary Catherine.

"I had a guest on the show today. Mary Catherine Sullivan. She's a nun. A former nun, anyway."

"What, she broke her vows?"

"Well, she left her order, but she's doing great work now helping women—"

"I hope she doesn't burn in hell."

"Ma, she's a good person. She helps a lot of people. Why would she go to—"

"She broke her vows."

There it was again. The mile-high, concertina-wire-topped fence Helena put up to set apart right from wrong. Good from bad. Helena from Daria. No, Daria wouldn't talk about Mary Catherine. Or Lizzy. Or herself, for that matter.

"Well, I hope you had a happy birthday," she said.

After Helena said she was tired, Daria hung up.

The sleep she had hoped for eluded her.

Chapter Seventeen
March 1992

Daria parked on the street in front of her house. Seventeen-year-old Megan Conway's black Mercedes was in the driveway, blocking her from getting into the garage.

Daria had lived in the New York Metropolitan area for twenty years, over a dozen of those in Connecticut. She knew from the demographic data her staff collected for *Awakenings'* advertisers that the disposable income in Fairfield County was rising at twice the national average. Close to seven percent of Greenvale's households owned four or more cars. Four or more.

Annoyed, she gathered her purse and briefcase, remembering how she had learned to drive on a '63 Chevy C10 pickup. Just why had she denied Lizzy the lessons learned from working hard to earn what she got?

She made her way up the icy sidewalk and stepped into the house.

"Girls." No answer. Not surprising with the stereo blasting.

"Girls." No answer again. Daria set down her purse, kicked off her shoes, and padded to the family room. Though the windows were open, a diaphanous haze had settled in the room. "Girls!" When they finally heard her, Lizzy and Megan went silent. They sat up on the facing couches where they had draped themselves like Grecian goddesses, then hastily rubbed out their cigarettes in the saucers-turned-ashtrays on the end tables.

"You're early," Lizzy said.

Okay, Daria reminded herself, *like Frankie said, I have a choice.* She could stomp to the stereo and turn it off, bark at Lizzy, and send Megan packing. Or she could try a different approach.

"Actually, it looks like I'm right on time." She walked toward the windows. "How was school?"

"Hi, Mrs. Demarest." Megan smiled. "It was good."

"How'd the show go?" Lizzy asked.

The girls' stifled giggles and sideways glances didn't escape Daria.

"It's pretty chilly out," she said as she closed the windows. "About twenty-five degrees actually. We don't need the windows open. Not even to help get the smoke out."

More sideways glances.

"Did you hear from Frankie, Lizzy?" She rounded up the saucers without commenting on the girls' creative use of her china.

Lizzy tied her hair into a ponytail while looking past her mother. "She left a message."

Daria heard Frankie whispering in her ear. *Don't take the bait, sugar.* There was a remote chance that Lizzy hadn't told Megan she was pregnant, so Daria kept her questions vague. "And?"

"She left a number."

"Did you call?"

"Nuh-uh." Lizzy aimed the remote at the stereo and kicked up the volume again. When Daria left the room, the girls snickered. She wanted to give each of them a good slap but remembered drinking her share of Boone's Farm Apple Wine and smoking pot in the bedroom at their age. At least they weren't drinking or drugging. Not that she knew of. But the smoking would have to stop.

In the kitchen, Daria rinsed the saucers, then pressed the play button on the answering machine. She poured herself a glass of mineral water and reached into a drawer for a pad and pen.

"Hi Lizzy. It's Frankie, honey. The name of the agency is the Adoption Option. The number's 203-555-2324. Ask for Katrina Wilkinson. Good luck, sugar, and let me know how it goes."

Daria scribbled down Katrina's number, listened to the other messages on the tape, all annoying telemarketing calls. Then she went back to the family room.

"Megan," she asked, "could you excuse Lizzy and me a minute?"

"Sure."

Lizzy handed the stereo remote to Megan. "I'll be back in a sec." She followed Daria to the kitchen.

"It's time for Megan to leave. Then you need to call that agency and set up an appointment."

"Megan just got here. We're gonna—"

"Did you hear me?" *Stop*, Daria thought. *No badgering.* "We have work to do."

Without answering, Lizzy skittered off. A few moments later Daria heard more giggles—no doubt at her expense.

Then Lizzy, followed by Megan, waltzed through the kitchen to the front hallway.

"See you tomorrow," Lizzy said. Then she whispered, loudly enough for Daria to hear, "once the wicked bitch of the west flies out on her broom."

Megan covered her mouth to avoid laughing. "Goodbye, Mrs. Demarest."

"We'll see you soon, Megan. But when you come back, you need to park in the street instead of the driveway."

"Oh, sure. Sorry."

Lizzy rolled her eyes then closed the door as Megan sauntered down the steps.

******

"Before you call this woman," Daria said as she checked the name and number she'd written. "Katrina, her name is. There's something else to settle." Daria pulled a chair from the kitchen table, motioning for Lizzy to sit down. Lizzy dragged the chair out as if it weighed the same as the refrigerator behind it. "We talked about keeping the driveway clear so I can get in the garage."

No answer.

"Lizzy?"

"Since when did you start playing housemother?" Lizzy got up, went to the refrigerator, pulled out a Diet Coke, and popped the tab on the can. Then she plopped back in her chair.

Daria paused. "Lizzy, it's time for both of us to grow up." She took the can of soda from Lizzy and set it at the other end of the table. "That stuff's not good for the baby. And while we're at it, neither is the smoking."

"And while *I'm* at it, I just hope I don't grow up to be like you."

Daria leaned forward, ready to snap, then thought better of it. Restraint—the kind Frankie had learned to show, the kind she wanted Daria to practice—well, it took work, a lot more work than just spilling out whatever she wanted to say, however and whenever she wanted. Daria passed the paper with Katrina's number across the table, then sat back in her chair. "I can meet with Katrina any afternoon this week. Just let me know what works for her."

She stood, handed the phone to Lizzy, and went upstairs to change. "Dinner's at six," she called over her shoulder, leaving her daughter to sulk as long as she chose. For a moment, she regretted getting on Lizzy's case about the cigarettes. One would sure taste good right about now.

"And Lizzy?"

"What?"

"I'm your mother. Not the wicked bitch of the west."

******

When Daria pulled into the circular drive in front of Sound Shore High School that Thursday, Lizzy stood at the center of a group of perky girls, all blonde except Lizzy, all dressed in their shiny cheerleading jackets and flirty little skirts. The sky was spectacularly blue, the purple crocuses and pink hyacinths just beginning to color the lawn. A perfect made-for-TV movie set, though she would prefer that Lizzy's situation not provide the storyline.

Daria honked the horn and Lizzy reluctantly said goodbye to her friends. She noticed her daughter's bare legs. It was still March, still chilly. "Did you bring something to change into?"

Lizzy rolled down her window. "Tomorrow at five in the gym," she yelled. "Be there." As the girls shouted back, Daria drove off.

At the signal light near the I-95 entrance, Daria turned to Lizzy. "How are you feeling about this?"

"Fine." Without looking at her mother, Lizzy pulled a brush from her backpack, bent forward so her hair formed a curtain over her face, and started brushing. Apparently, Lizzy didn't want to talk.

Don't you see, Daria wanted to shout, how your life is going to change? Don't you know that whatever innocence you thought you had left, even if it was clothed in all your Fairfield County sophistication and disdain, has just been stripped from you? But she said nothing. Twenty minutes later, they arrived in Hanniford, on the New York-Connecticut state line.

"Can you read me those directions?" Daria nodded to a paper on the console as she exited the highway.

"Turn left at the first light," Lizzy rattled, "then go three blocks to Maple. Number thirty-seven, a white Victorian with green shutters." Then she turned her attention to the boutiques and chain stores along Hanniford's main street, the ones that catered to credit card-carrying girls her age. "Can we stop at Banana on our way home?" She tugged at her waistband. "My pants are getting tight."

Chapter Eighteen
March 1992

Not long after Daria and Lizzy took their seats in the Adoption Option reception area, a tall, trim woman entered the room.

"I'm Katrina," she said.

Daria hesitated before reaching to take Katrina's extended hand. She had expected an adoption counselor to wear a long, gauzy skirt and clogs, foraged for on Macy's clearance racks. But Daria had seen Katrina's taupe knit outfit at Saks a couple weeks earlier. She had tried it on herself but didn't like the way it draped on her. On Katrina, though, it looked perfect. Casual, yet tasteful and professional. The only thing that seemed out of place was the little gold cross Katrina wore around her neck. Something big and statement-making. That's what was needed to complete the outfit.

"Daria Demarest," she said. Why, she wondered, was this striking blonde woman, with her confident handshake and steady eye contact, working in social services in Hanniford, when she carried herself like an ad exec who had missed her train to the City?

"It's a pleasure to meet you." When Daria released her hand, Katrina turned to Lizzy. "And your name?"

"I'm Lizzy."

But instead of shaking the counselor's hand, Lizzy grabbed the book she'd been reading and stuffed it into her backpack.

"Lizzy," Daria prompted. "Manners." It was one thing for Lizzy to act out at home. But in public?

"It's okay." Katrina held up her hand, signaling for Daria to refrain from chastising Lizzy. "My office is upstairs, third door on the right. Have a seat and I'll be there in a minute. There's coffee and water in the kitchen out back," she said, motioning down the hallway, "if you want to grab something."

Daria declined the coffee, but she and Lizzy each took a bottle of water with them upstairs.

Katrina's office, a little more cramped than cozy, was pleasant enough, with its Bonnard prints and vase of pink tulips. But it did nothing to calm the uncertainty roiling in Daria's stomach. She sat on the couch, and Lizzy took the armchair to the left of the desk, both sipping their water without speaking.

Katrina entered the room, closed the door behind her, and sat in her desk chair. Without any pleasantries she said, "So, tell me why you're here today, Lizzy."

No wedding ring, Daria noticed, no polish on her nails. And her cuticles, shredded. Like the cross, incongruous with Katrina's outfit and persona. Still, her voice was clear and confident.

"I'm pregnant." Lizzy's words snapped like a rubber band, stretched taut, then sprung. She didn't have to voice the question her tone implied. *Why else would I be here?*

"What she means," Daria said, sitting forward in her seat, again rushing to gloss over Lizzy's insolence, "is that we're exploring ways to handle the pregnancy."

"Mrs. Demarest? May I call you Daria?"

"Please."

"Daria, here at the Adoption Option, we ask that, when a young woman comes to us because she's pregnant, she takes responsibility for her actions and decisions. I'd like Lizzy to answer the questions I direct to her."

Daria forced herself to sit back in her chair. This woman seemed competent enough. But expecting Lizzy to behave responsibly? If Katrina could manage that in a matter of minutes, she would be the first to applaud. "Of course." She reached for her water bottle to keep from fidgeting. "I guess I'm a little edgy."

"Perfectly understandable," Katrina said. "We're here to help Lizzy, and you, get through this as comfortably as possible."

Daria nodded, and Katrina reached for a pad and pen. She turned back to Lizzy and began asking basic questions: her age, what class she was in, how she was feeling.

"Sixteen." "I'm a junior." "I feel pretty good. A little tired. Especially in the morning. But mostly fine." To Daria's surprise, Lizzy began to warm to Katrina.

"And the baby's father," Katrina asked, "does he want to participate in your decision?"

Lizzy shook her head. "Nuh-uh. He's going to college this fall."

"He's not cooperating," Daria started. "And his parents . . ." When Katrina looked her way, Daria caught herself. "Sorry."

"I see." Katrina turned back to Lizzy. "And what about you? Are you planning on college?"

"Sure." Lizzy looked perplexed. Didn't everyone go to college? "I want to be a writer. Or a photographer. Maybe work in film. Or at a magazine. You know, like *Elle*."

Katrina nodded and made more notes. "And what are you thinking about the baby?"

Daria's stomach tightened when Lizzy squirmed. What we want, Daria refrained from saying, is to turn back the calendar a few months, to the time when Lizzy's biggest challenge was teaching her squad a new cheer or getting decent PSAT scores.

"I haven't really decided," Lizzy said. "I mean . . ." She waved toward Daria. "So far, we've only talked about how I was feeling."

"Feeling physically, you mean?"

Lizzy nodded.

"Okay." Katrina set her pen and pad on her desk, then leaned forward in her chair. "We have some time pressure, so we need to get down to business."

For the first time during the conversation, Lizzy looked to her mother. "It's okay, honey," Daria assured her. Lizzy looked back to Katrina, then nodded again.

"You know there are three choices. Abortion. Adoption. Or keeping the baby."

"I don't want an abortion." Lizzy jumped in. "I mean, at first I did. I know a lot of girls have them. But that would be wrong. For me, I mean."

Before this, Daria had found it so easy to judge those girls and their parents for taking what she thought was an easy way out. But when Lizzy dismissed the possibility, Daria closed her eyes for a moment, her mood sinking. In many ways, abortion seemed the expedient choice, the option Daria thought Lizzy would choose. Here today, gone tomorrow. No scars. No visible scars anyway. When Lizzy responded so quickly and definitively, Daria figured Jack had most likely convinced Lizzy to make a different choice.

"And I don't want to give the baby up," Lizzy continued.

Daria's eyes popped open. "You want to keep the baby?" Daria could no longer keep her thoughts to herself. She turned to Katrina, shaking her head. "This is the first I've heard of this."

"So, it must be surprising. But we need to focus on Lizzy right now."

Daria's skin felt too tight and close around her. *All this damned restraint.* She tapped her foot against her chair as Katrina continued with Lizzy.

"So, you've given this some thought," Katrina said to Lizzy.

"Uh-huh."

"You feel you could care for your baby and finish high school, then go to college? All on your own?"

"Well, not exactly. I mean, my mother would take care of the baby." Lizzy shrugged. "I figured she would, anyway."

Daria drank again from her water bottle. She suspected that Katrina would eventually lead Lizzy through the absurdity of keeping the baby, but why couldn't she speed things up?

"And how," Katrina continued, "do you know your mother would take on that responsibility if you haven't asked her?"

"Because, she takes care of everything."

Daria couldn't fault Lizzy for coming to that conclusion. What had she done all these years but ram her way through whatever life presented? Lost job? No problem, find another. Divorce? Get a lawyer, sign the papers. Need money? Make more. Life was that simple. Just move on.

"Daria," Katrina asked. "How do you feel about raising Lizzy's baby?"

Daria looked first to Lizzy, then Katrina, then back to Lizzy. She shook her head. "No, honey. I can't raise another child. For a lot of reasons. There's the money, the time."

"Dad could help. With the money, I mean. And what about the Fitzgeralds?"

After the divorce, Daria had never asked Ted to contribute to her or the kids' support. She wasn't about to ask him for help now. Besides, Ted had remarried and had a son with his new wife. For all Daria knew, he was still tossing his money away at blackjack tables. "It's a complex situation with your father, Lizzy. And even if the Fitzgeralds contributed financially, they made it clear they don't want to help take care of the baby."

"Then we'll get a nanny. Like the one we had in Greenvale."

Daria looked to Katrina for help. "I think what your mother is trying to say, Lizzy, is that raising a child takes commitment, time, and energy. Not just money. Even if there's a nanny."

Lizzy glared at Daria. "I'll do it then."

"Okay, let's try to envision what it would be like for you to do that," Katrina said. "You said you wanted to go to college, then maybe work for a magazine?"

"Sarah Lawrence would be good. I mean, it's nearby, so I could commute. And a lot of people who go there end up with good jobs in publishing. That's what I heard at the college fair, anyway."

"That's a great school and an exciting field. I know because I was in the magazine business myself."

"You were?" Lizzy's eyes brightened. But after conceding that the field had a certain glamour, what with photo shoots, fashion shows, and afterparties, Katrina helped Lizzy walk through the challenges of getting through high school, college, then working, all while raising a child. Passing up time with friends to get home before bedtime. Taking time off for doctors' appointments. Waking up for nighttime feedings. Making time to study or meet work deadlines. Falling asleep bone-tired, then waking up to do it all over again.

"I guess," Lizzy admitted while twirling a strand of hair around her index finger, "there's more to it than I thought."

So much more, Daria thought. For the first time since Lizzy announced she wanted to keep the baby, Daria felt she could breathe.

"Okay," Katrina continued. "Let's go over the other options. You said you didn't want an abortion?"

Lizzy shook her head. "What about adoption?" Lizzy asked. "Isn't that what you do here?"

"Yes," Katrina said, "we do help place babies. As long as it's the right decision for young women like you, and men too, when they want to be involved. Not just in the moment, but down the line.

"So," Katrina continued, "there are three types of adoption. We call them closed, open, and semi-open.

"Women who elect closed arrangements, when the birth mother doesn't meet the adoptive family and doesn't communicate with them later, often feel that the less they're involved, the less attachment they'll feel to the baby, and the less they'll hurt later."

"Is that true?" Daria interrupted, too quickly, she realized once the words were out. "I mean, does it hurt less if a woman chooses closed adoption?" She wanted to spare Lizzy the pain she had experienced when she gave up her child. But after her question, she shifted in her chair. Had she exposed her own history?

"Birth mothers experience a range of feelings," Katrina said. "Anger, grief, acceptance. Sometimes the feelings surface in waves, long after the birth mother thinks she's come to terms with her choice. That's why . . ."

Daria retreated into her own thoughts. Anger? Grief? She had felt both over the years. But acceptance? No, even all these years later, acceptance had eluded her.

"I see." Daria turned back to Katrina, who spoke about how the Adoption Option's goal was to help provide a safe place for birth mothers to experience whatever emotions came up, even after adoption.

"One reason closed adoptions aren't as popular as they were ten or twenty years ago," she said, "is women found there was no way to escape their feelings. And if they eventually wanted to know what had become of their children, they often had no way to do that."

Daria's thoughts drifted as Katrina spoke. When pregnant with her first daughter, she hadn't wanted to know who the child's parents might be, or what might become of her. Not in the beginning. All she wanted, needed to do was to move on. But then came the weeks and months of singing to the girl inside her, feeding her, imagining her prospects. She needed to know the child would be placed with parents who would love her and provide opportunities, even though Dr. Holcomb counseled, no insisted, it was better for her not to know. And once she saw her daughter? Once she felt her warm breath and stroked her soft skin? How, why did she acquiesce so easily? But here, now, all these years later, if she could somehow find her daughter, could she face the sorrow and regret that felt powerful enough to swallow her? Unable to answer her questions, and unable to reconcile her actions and feelings, Daria shifted her thoughts back to Lizzy.

"You still with me, Lizzy?" Katrina asked.

"Sure."

When Lizzy responded so casually, no big deal, Daria wanted to shake her daughter. It is a big deal, she wanted to say. You have no idea how very big a deal it is.

But Daria then caught Lizzy's eyes drifting toward the clock on Katrina's desk. If Katrina didn't pick up the pace, Lizzy would check out altogether. "What about open adoption?" she asked.

"That," Katrina said, "is when the birth mother and adoptive family share first and last names and decide how often they want to be in touch." Katrina turned to Lizzy, who was again twirling her hair.

"We're almost done for today," she said. "Can you hang in just a little longer?"

Lizzy squirmed in her chair. "Umm-hmm."

"Good." Katrina then described semi-open adoption, in which first names and maybe phone numbers, but not last names or addresses were shared. "Any correspondence goes through the agency." She paused. "Do you get the differences in the three choices?"

Lizzy nodded.

"Okay. So, at the Adoption Option you tell us which option you want to choose. Then, if you want to be involved, we give you profiles of families who meet your criteria. After that, you pick one and we make an adoption plan."

Daria's thoughts again retreated to her first pregnancy. If she had been able to rewind this scenario a couple decades, she would have been called a birth mother, not an unwed mother. No holing up in the Berkshires. She wouldn't have given up her baby, but would have placed her daughter, after making an adoption plan. And the possibility of keeping her daughter at least would have been raised. Not just by T.J. Where was he now, anyway? Why had she cast him off like a no-longer-needed skin? She forced her attention back to Katrina.

"If you want to meet the family," Katrina explained to Lizzy, "we schedule a time and place. Then we help you work out details like whether you want to receive letters or photos or if you want to set up a visitation schedule."

She reached for a green and blue binder on her desk. "This kit explains what we've talked about. Take it home, and after you and your mother look it over, we'll talk again." She checked her day timer. "Say, next Tuesday at four?"

"Tuesday at four is fine," Daria said when Lizzy didn't respond.

"Good." Katrina noted the appointment in her calendar. "Any questions before then?"

When Lizzy stood up without answering, stuffing the binder in her backpack, Daria handed her the car keys. "I'll be out in a minute, Liz," she said.

"Call me anytime," Katrina said. But Lizzy, after knocking over the opened water bottle next to her chair, was already on her way out the door.

"I'm sorry," Daria said, reaching into her purse for tissues to mop up the water. "For a while, I could see she wasn't listening at all."

Katrina dismissed Lizzy's early exit. "For what it's worth," she said, "it's not unusual for very young mothers to react the way Lizzy did. If they haven't already thought through their situation, this first meeting can be overwhelming. Sometimes they detach or act as if they're detaching. Usually they're feeling more than they let on.

"Is there anything you'd like to ask, Daria? Anything at all?"

Daria tossed the wet tissue and near-empty water bottle into the wastebasket. Then she hesitated. Katrina was a professional. A little young, maybe, but well-grounded. She had probably met dozens of women who had given up children and, years later, were plagued by warring feelings. Why not tell her? Why not trust her? "I . . ." Instead of continuing, Daria shook her head. Maybe because Katrina looked and dressed more like a fashion editor than an adoption case worker. Maybe because the chewed-off nails telegraphed something at odds with her calm, professional demeanor. Or, more likely, just because it was too scary to admit the truth. "No," Daria said. "Not now." She forced a smile. "I guess Lizzy's not the only one who's overwhelmed."

"That's natural too," Katrina said. "But feel free to call any time."

"Thank you." When Daria closed Katrina's office door, her legs felt leaden. She looked at her hand on the door knob. Her polish was chipped. Katrina wasn't the only one who needed a manicure. *Move*, she ordered her feet.

In the car, Lizzy was rummaging through her backpack.

"You okay?" Daria asked.

"Fine." Her face a little pale and tight, Lizzy continued clawing through her things. She didn't look fine.

Daria tossed her purse into the back seat, buckled her seatbelt, and put the key in the ignition. Before turning it on, she hesitated. Maybe not too long ago, she would have shouted for Lizzy to snap out of it. But not today. "It's okay to not be okay, you know," she said tentatively. "Having a baby, when you're young, still in school. It's a big deal."

"I said I'm okay. And even if I wasn't, it's not like you'd know how I feel anyway." Pulling out her Walkman, untangling the headphone wires, Lizzy slid in a tape.

Oh, yes, I do, Daria was tempted to say. But now wasn't the time to come clean. Or was it? She tapped Lizzy's shoulder to get her attention. Lizzy begrudgingly took off the headphones.

"You still want to go shopping?"

Lizzy shook her head.

Daria stroked Lizzy's arm. "How about dinner?"

"Okay."

"The Clam Bar, maybe?"

"Silverman's. I want more cheesecake."

******

Daria drove down Mason Street, then up the I-95 entrance ramp. Concentrating on the stop-and-go rush hour traffic provided a merciful reprieve from the memories that had reared up during the meeting with Katrina. By the time she pulled into Silverman's, she had plotted an agenda for dinnertime discussion. Top priority: making sure Lizzy understood that Daria wasn't going to raise her child.

Lizzy ran out of the car ahead of Daria and was eyeing the dessert carousel when her mother joined her. After the hostess showed them to a booth in the back, Carla came to the table. "Oh, hi," she said. "It's you."

"It's me." Daria rolled her eyes and grimaced. "I was such a beast the last time I was here, I'm surprised you ventured over here."

Carla laughed. "Believe me, I've seen worse."

"I tried the breathing, by the way."

"And?"

"Not bad."

"I'm hungry," Lizzy interrupted.

"Oh, sorry, Carla. This is my daughter, Lizzy. We're both famished."

"Then let's get to it." Carla handed them menus. "If I were you, ladies, I'd seriously consider the oriental chicken salad, then one of those monster brownies." She pointed her yellow pencil toward the dessert case. "Lots of walnuts, double chips, and topped with caramel sauce."

"The chicken salad sounds good to me," Daria said as she handed back the menu. "But I'll pass on dessert. Lizzy?"

"Cheesecake. Strawberry. And a Diet Coke. Large, lots of ice."

"Another excellent choice. Coffee for you, Mrs. Demarest?"

Daria thought better of lecturing Lizzy on prenatal nutrition when they were both tired and hungry. "Call me Daria," she said, smiling at Carla. "And yes on the coffee."

"Okay, I'll be back in a jiff."

When Carla walked away, Lizzy pointed her chin in Carla's direction. "She the Good Humor lady or what?"

"She's only trying to be nice."

"Well, she's too nice."

Daria clasped her hands on the table. She took a breath. This wasn't going to be easy, but there was no point in stalling. "I meant what I said before, Liz. I'm not up for caring for another baby. You need to know that."

Once Daria spoke, the edges of Lizzy's mouth turned down. "I thought," she said, "you'd want to help me."

"I do want to help you." Being direct and gentle at the same time still made her feel like a colt on shaky legs trying to secure her footing. "I just don't want to raise another child."

Lizzy leaned back against the booth, her lower lip trembling. She glared. "It's not just another kid," she spit out. "It's my baby. Your grandchild."

Carla returned, placing Lizzy's Diet Coke and a straw in front of her. She poured Daria's coffee and set down a breadbasket. "How's everything here?" she asked. But she picked up on the tension and didn't wait for an answer. "Your orders'll be up any minute." She headed for the kitchen, then turned back. "Breathe." She mouthed the word, and Daria managed to follow her suggestion.

"I know that, Lizzy. And I know this must be confusing for you," Daria said. "Probably scary too. All I can say is I'm trying. I want to help. But it's confusing and scary for me too."

Lizzy unwrapped the straw, stuck it in her soda, and stirred it around.

"Honey, can you please talk to me?"

"What do you want me to say?"

"Anything, whatever's on your mind. We need to work this out now so it doesn't reach up and grab you by the throat later, when you're off in school somewhere or working and don't have me or Katrina around to help you."

"You want me to talk? Fine." Lizzy shoved her soda away from her. "It's bad enough that the best you could manage when you showed up—if you showed up—at a cheerleading competition was to keep checking your watch and to tell me I went a little heavy on the eye shadow. Or, when something went wrong at school and you turned up late at Mr. O'Donnell's office when I got caught smoking to say something like, 'Damn it, Lizzy, don't you know I'm taping in half an hour?' But if you think I'm going to fall for this new best friend thing, you're wrong. Especially when you say you want to support me, but you don't do what I want."

Daria leaned back in her seat. She looked around the room, filled with other early diners. Her eyes settled on a dapper man in his seventies seated across from a petite white-haired woman whose pink lipstick and rouge looked electrified against her papery skin as she buttered a piece of bread for the man. When she handed it to him, he bit into it as she held it, her hand quivering. Then he leaned back and smiled.

That was the way people should end up, wasn't it? Tenderly feeding each other? Had they ever been on a roller coaster ride like Daria had been on for most of her life, like the one she was on now?

"Lizzy," she said, turning back to the table. "Do you remember how, when we were in the car, you said I couldn't know how you feel?"

Lizzy said nothing.

"Well, I'm afraid I do."

Lizzy sipped her soda. "Yeah, I'm sure."

"No, I mean it. When I was in college, a little older than you, but not much, I got pregnant too. I had a daughter and gave her up for adoption."

When Lizzy looked up from her Coke, wide-eyed, Daria kept going.

"In some ways, once I made my decision, it didn't seem all that important then. But it was. And now? It hurts just about every day, because I never let myself feel anything back then. I just barreled through it and moved on.

"At least I thought I got on with my life. But I had a big hole inside. And I couldn't fill it. Not by marrying your father or having a career. I was always running. Trying to cover things up. Thinking if I did enough or made enough money or looked good enough, everything would be okay. That's a big part of the reason I wasn't the best mother for you. I couldn't sit still because I was afraid that, if I did, I would crack into a hundred pieces that no one would be able to glue back together.

"I had one friend who tried to help me back then, but I pushed him away. And I never felt I could tell Grandma. So, I don't want you to go through this feeling like I'm not on your side."

"Mom?"

When Lizzy squinted at her, as if making sure the woman sitting across from her was really her mother, Daria looked back across the table, her eyes filling.

Lizzy reached and took Daria's hand. "Mom?" she said again.

"Yes, honey, you have a sister. I don't know anything more about her than you do now."

Chapter Nineteen
April 1992

"Can I get you anything before we get started?" Katrina offered before their next appointment. "Soda? Water?"

"I'll take a Diet Coke," Lizzy said as she stood from her reception area chair. Then she hesitated. "No, maybe water."

"Nothing for me, thanks," Daria said, pleased by Lizzy's choice. Since their dinner at Silverman's, she and Lizzy had been working together. Most days, at least.

Two days after their diner conversation, Lizzy called Katrina to tell her she wanted to place the child through an open adoption. She asked if Katrina could have profiles of potential adoptive parents for her and her mother to review when they came in the following week.

"Promise me you'll meet with Katrina too," Lizzy said to Daria that night at dinner.

"Sure. Like last time." She reached for her water glass, as if she didn't understand what Lizzy was after. "We said we'd see her on Tuesday, right?"

"No, Mom. Not like last time. I want you to make an appointment for just you. To talk about your other daughter."

Daria hesitated. "I don't know." She pushed back from the table, took her barely touched plate to the sink. "Let's take care of you first."

But Lizzy persisted. "How can you support me if my sister's on your mind?"

Her sister? In just a couple days Lizzy had made Daria's first daughter part of the family, something Daria had never allowed herself to do. It was a manipulative approach, but, Daria conceded, an effective one.

"Okay," Daria said. "Just give me some time."

"Some time, maybe. But not too much."

******

When Daria shook Katrina's hand on Tuesday afternoon, she clung to it a moment before letting go. She hadn't yet made an appointment with Katrina, but she had promised Lizzy. *Soon*, she told herself. *When I'm ready.*

Katrina reached for a pile of folders and held them in her lap as she swiveled her chair to face her clients. "You've taken a big step, Lizzy."

"A little scary." Lizzy inched toward the edge of her seat.

"Of course." Katrina nodded. "Before we look at profiles, do you have questions? About anything, no matter how small."

Daria's eyes fixed on Lizzy, looking to see if her lips quivered or her hands fidgeted, any sign of indecision or regret. Lizzy lightly gripped the edge of her seat cushion and remained still, except for her jaw muscles, which tensed the way her father's did when he made a firm decision. "No," Lizzy said. "The papers you gave me answered all my questions."

"Okay, good." Methodically, Katrina described the couples whose hopes to adopt were laid out on a few pages of paper in each folder. A farming couple from Indiana. Two physics professors from Stanford. An investment banker and attorney from Boston. "Any immediate reactions?"

"I like the couple from Boston."

There, Daria observed, was Ted again. Decisive, determined, and resolute. "They sound nice. Smart too. And they've been waiting a long time for a baby, so I think they'll appreciate her. Or him."

"Any comments, Daria?"

Daria was slow to answer. When she did, her voice was more tentative than Lizzy's. "I just wonder . . ."

"Yes?"

"Can she take some time to think about it?"

"Of course." Katrina set the folders on her desk, then looked back to Daria. "Once a decision's been made, we ask birth mothers to take forty-eight hours to reconsider."

"I won't change my mind," Lizzy said.

"Probably not," Katrina said. "But I still want you to take the two days. Maybe some questions will come up, maybe not. In fairness to the prospective parents, we want you to be sure before we notify them to come in. How about if you call me on Thursday?"

When Lizzy acquiesced, Daria warmed with pride. Frankie had been right when she told Daria that Lizzy was going to grow up "real quick." Things had gotten off to a slow start, but now there were small changes. Like the fact that Lizzy was making good on a promise to keep Megan from parking in the driveway. But making the considered decision that open adoption was the best choice for everyone? That was huge. And different from the way she had reacted and behaved when she was first pregnant.

"Good," Katrina said. "After I hear from you, if you still want to meet this couple, I'll contact them and arrange a meeting."

"Okay." Lizzy stood. "Thank you." She reached out and shook Katrina's hand.

Things, Daria thought, were going to work out just fine. For Lizzy anyway.

******

"I have good news."

When she heard Katrina's voice, Daria carried the phone from the kitchen to the living room.

"You heard from the Boston couple?" Daria sank into the couch. The farther along the placement process moved, the more relieved she felt about Lizzy and the more anxious she felt about herself. She was going to have to make good on her promise to Lizzy.

"I did. Their last names, by the way, will be kept private until there's an agreement to move forward. But June and Richard are thrilled. They'd like to meet you and Lizzy as soon as possible. Does some afternoon next week work?"

"I'll check with Lizzy, but should we tentatively say Tuesday? Unless you hear from us by this evening? No, let's try for Monday. The sooner the better."

"Three o'clock?"

"Fine." Daria hesitated. She felt paralyzed, as if she had stepped into a frigid mountain lake. "Katrina?"

"Yes?"

The water was too cold. She couldn't ask Katrina to meet about her first daughter. Not yet. "Is there anything we need to bring?"

"Just yourselves."

******

Daria and Lizzy arrived at the Adoption Option the following Monday. It was still chilly for early spring. Clumps of hopeful yellow daffodils dotted the Adoption Option's front lawn. Lilacs, anxious to bloom, hugged the trellis near the front steps.

Inside, Katrina escorted Daria and Lizzy to a room that, before the house was converted to an office, had likely been a parlor. Lizzy, in pull-on pants and an oversized knit top over her rounding belly, took one of the yellow-and-red-print chairs. Daria sat opposite her.

"June and Richard are here," Katrina said. "I'll get them in just a few minutes. I'll introduce everyone, and after that, you can ask whatever questions you want, except last names or phone numbers or addresses, anything that would identify them. All set?"

Lizzy nodded.

"Yes," Daria said, her voice soft. Why, in the last days, had Lizzy matured, while Daria seemed to regress into uneasy adolescence?

"Good." Katrina rose from her chair. "I'll be right back." She walked through the room's rear door, then closed it.

When Katrina returned with the young couple, Daria's breath deepened. Her one reservation about their profile was that they were overachievers. They might be too hard-edged, more dedicated to their careers than to raising a child. She knew from experience how that kind of drive could undermine a family's chances.

Richard, tall and lanky in his blue blazer and khakis, looked like any of the Wall Street men walking around Fairfield County on any weekend afternoon. His angular face might have seemed stern, except that it was softened by an easy smile, warm brown eyes, and slightly ruffled light brown hair. He carried a leather portfolio in one hand and held June's elbow in the other.

June, though, looked incongruous with the image Daria had anticipated. Almost a foot shorter than her husband, June was dressed in a longish print skirt and pullover sweater, a little loose-fitting on her petite frame. She came across the way Daria had expected Katrina to look before they met. No makeup. Long, wavy hair free-flowing past her shoulders. Her one concession to appearances was her engagement ring. Tiffany, Daria guessed, based on its luminous sparkle, no less than two carats.

When Richard reached out to her, she looked at him. "I don't need you to get me where I want to go," her glance seemed to signal. Not unlike the way Daria might have dismissed someone's act of kindness, even in a situation that would seemingly require her to be on her best behavior. June was a woman who wasn't afraid to be herself.

"Lizzy," Katrina said, "this is June and Richard."

"Hi."

"And this," Katrina continued, "is Lizzy's mother, Daria."

Richard and June smiled at Lizzy. Then they shook Daria's hand before sitting on the sofa.

"I'm sure," Katrina said, "you're all anxious to get started. So, let's just dive in. If any of you have questions as I go along, please ask them." Katrina summarized the situation, provided a profile of Lizzy and the child's father, the date the baby was due, and June and Richard's history. Richard, it turned out, was a partner at a private equity firm, while June practiced family and immigration law. "Any questions so far?"

"Honey?" Richard turned to his wife.

"Everything seems consistent with what you told us," June said in a lawyerly way.

"Daria? Lizzy?"

Daria smiled when Lizzy jumped into the conversation. "Katrina said you had a house in Boston and one in the Berkshires."

"We do," Richard said. Then he turned to Katrina. "Would now be a good time for pictures?"

"Lizzy?" Katrina asked.

Lizzy nodded and sat forward in her chair, ready to look through the portfolio. Richard rose from the couch. "Please," he said, motioning for Daria and Lizzy to sit on either side of June.

As Lizzy and Daria moved next to June, Richard walked behind the sofa and placed his hand on June's shoulder. June then led them through the album of pictures of their townhouse in Cambridge, their mountain house, their chocolate-colored retriever. "His name's Falstaff," June said. "Richard's into Shakespeare."

"Henry the Fourth," Daria recollected from her college days. "He's probably quite the trickster."

"I like that," Lizzy said, smiling.

"Do you mind," Daria asked, tilting her head toward the album, "if I take a closer look?"

"Not at all."

Daria flipped through the photos while June asked Lizzy how she was feeling and how she was managing in school. A beautiful home in town. A mountain retreat. Two accomplished parents. Richard seemed kind and protective. But June? She must have a heart, given the kind of work she did. Still, she seemed a little distant. What kind of mother would she make?

"I don't get sick anymore," Lizzy was telling June. "So that's good. But it's been tough keeping my grades up. Plus getting to all the doctor's appointments and trying to help with cheerleading practice. I'm still the squad captain, well, co-captain now that I can't work out as much. Don't worry, though. I won't do anything to hurt the baby."

When Lizzy smiled, June did too.

Daria looked to Richard when he asked if she had any questions. "No," she said, and when she looked up at him, eager to make his wife happy, she thought of T.J. and how he would have walked across continents just to see her smile when she was pregnant.

Katrina then said that after a few days she would follow up with each of them to see if they had questions. "Then I'll contact you for your final decisions. If you all agree to proceed, the child would typically leave the hospital three days after birth."

"And that's September?" June asked.

"Around the fifth, the doctor thinks," Lizzy said.

"Before that," Katrina continued, looking to Richard and June, "you'll all need to agree on the involvement Lizzy can expect. How often you'll send pictures. Visitation rights. That sort of thing. Is everyone clear on those points?"

After they worked out the details, everyone stood except Lizzy.

"Mom?"

"What is it, honey?"

"The baby." She placed her hand on her stomach. "I think it's kicking."

June sat back down next to Lizzy.

"I bet June would like to know what that feels like," Daria said. "Is it okay?"

Lizzy nodded. June inched closer on the sofa. Uncertain where to put her hand, she looked back to Katrina and Daria. "Here," Lizzy said, placing June's hand firmly on her belly. "Can you feel it?"

"I can't really . . ." she said, her face serious. But when she felt the tiny thump-flutter-thump, she turned to Richard, smiling.

Her grandchild, Daria decided, would be in good hands with June and Richard.

******

"Mom? You there?" Lizzy spoke into the phone in her bedroom to make sure Daria was on the kitchen extension.

"I'm here."

"Good."

"It's Lizzy. Lizzy Demarest," she said when Katrina picked up. "My Mom's here too."

"You've been doing some thinking?" Katrina asked.

"Uh-huh. We decided, my Mom and me, I mean, that we want June and Richard to have the baby."

"You sound confident about your decision."

"Um-hmm. They're the ones."

"Okay, then, what about arrangements? Visitation? Pictures?"

"I want to see pictures," Lizzy said. "But we don't think, what I mean is, I won't want to see the baby in person."

"And you're sure about that?"

"We're sure."

When Katrina suggested photos every three months for the first three years, every six months after that, Lizzy and Daria agreed.

"Okay then," Katrina said. "I'll phone June and Richard and get back to you as soon as I hear from them."

******

Lizzy was at practice when Katrina called back. June and Richard, she told Daria, had agreed to Lizzy's requests. "They're thrilled, of course."

"They'll make good parents," Daria said.

"I hear reservation in your voice. Is there something you want to say?"

"I need to see you," Daria said. "Alone."

Chapter Twenty
May 1992

Daria checked her office clock and drummed her fingernails on her desk. Forty-five minutes until her appointment with Katrina. Still time to cancel. Reaching for the phone, her stomach clenched. Again. Right now, Katrina seemed the best person to help loosen its grip.

Pulling her purse from her desk drawer, she stood without checking her makeup, without clearing her desk. She grabbed her coat from the hook behind her door, stuffed her arms into it, and stepped into the hall. In the main office area, she leaned into her secretary's cubicle.

Slouching in her desk chair, her back to Daria, Therese uncoiled the little red string that secured a light brown interoffice envelope while she cradled the phone between her shoulder and ear. "No way," she said in an exaggerated, disbelieving whisper. "He's *married?*" She tossed aside the envelope and slapped her desk. "Now listen, girl, if you're serious about finding a husband, you gotta drop this loser. And I mean pronto."

When Daria stepped into her line of sight, Therese bolted upright. "That's absolutely right," she said, her voice morphing from chatty to professional. "I need three new toner cartridges by end of business tomorrow. No excuses."

She hung up, grabbed a pencil and pad, and, with an enthusiastic smile, made ready to record any orders. "Hi, Daria. How'd the show go?"

"Fine." Working with Therese had its challenges. She arrived late at least once a week and wasn't as malleable as her previous assistants. But at least she didn't whine to Human Resources every time Daria barked an order. "I'm leaving for the day."

Therese's eyes sliced to the digital clock on her computer screen. It was barely past noon. Daria only left early after urgent calls came from the principal's office at Lizzy's school. "Lizzy okay?"

"She's fine." Daria felt an unfamiliar need to explain herself. "Just a few personal things to take care of." She turned to leave.

"Oh." Therese's eyes narrowed. Daria never left, even for a doctor's appointment, without detailed instructions about how to reach her, when she would be back, what to do if she couldn't be located. "Well," she said, "before you run out, Mr. Fisher called twice." She pulled a couple pink message slips from under the mail. "He said it's crucial you get back to him by one. At this number. It's about those focus groups."

Focus groups? Daria turned back to take the messages. She vaguely recalled that memo about *exploring* research to improve ratings. "Critical, crucial." Daria stuffed them in her pocket. "Everything's an emergency with Fisher," she said. "If he calls again, tell him I snuck out before you got to me. That you don't know where I went." Without waiting for a response, Daria hurried to the elevator. "Hold that," she called to the mail clerk wheeling his cart into the waiting car.

At the End of the Storm

******

Daria studied the second hand, ticking its way around Katrina's office clock. Still time to change the reason for her visit. She could make up something about Lizzy, that she was acting out. Or maybe she could concoct some office emergency to run back to.

But before Daria constructed a plausible scenario, Katrina arrived and shut the door. "So," she asked as she sat down, "how's Lizzy?"

Dressed in another striking outfit, Katrina looked as put-together as always, except for those fingernails. And those cuticles. And that cross. And, as Daria had come to observe during her meetings at the Adoption Option, a lingering sadness. Granted, she and Lizzy had come to Adoption Option to do serious business, but she had never heard Katrina laugh. Her smile was cordial, but always controlled.

"Lizzy's handling everything better than I expected," Daria said. "It's as if she's living a schizophrenic, girl-woman existence, shopping for an album for baby pictures one day, coaching cheerleading the next."

"That's terrific," Katrina said. "I hope you know you're responsible in large part for how well she's doing. Some parents aren't able to rally around their pregnant teen the way you have."

Daria's eyes drifted to the window, soft rain skittering down the pane. "It hasn't been easy."

"It never is." Katrina paused. "And you?"

"Me?" Daria turned back to Katrina.

"How are *you* doing?"

"Well, for starters, I agree that June and Richard look like ideal parents."

"But?"

"I'm . . . we . . . I'm not sure." She paused. "The reason I'm here," she said, "it's not about Lizzy."

Katrina picked up a pitcher of water on her desk, poured a glass, then extended it to Daria.

"Thanks." She reached for the glass, took a sip while Katrina poured water for herself.

"A long time ago," Daria started, "when I was in college. A little older than Lizzy. I had a child. Another daughter."

"I see."

"Things were different then," Daria continued. "We didn't have places like this." She waved her hand around Katrina's cozy office. "Or if we did, I didn't know about them. Anyway, back then, if you had a child and weren't married you had to hide. At least I thought I did." She drank again from her glass. "Sorry."

"Take your time."

"And now . . ." Daria looked up, lost.

"Now," Katrina suggested, "you're seeing how different things could have been if you had a place like this?"

Daria nodded. "But it's not just that I didn't have a place to go to. All these years I tried to convince myself I had no choice but to give up my daughter. Now I see I did have choices. That I might have found a way to keep her." Daria turned away before continuing. "I was ashamed. Because of what I thought my mother might say. That sounds infantile, but it's true. And I believed what the doctor told me. That it was best for me to have nothing to do with the child. So, I did to my little girl what all—or at least most—of the people in my life did to me. I abandoned her. Left her. Because she was inconvenient and because I was afraid."

Daria tried to hide her tears; but when she began to sob, she reached for the tissues Katrina held out to her. "I'm sorry. I keep trying to stuff it in a little box and keep it contained. But it won't stay put any more."

Katrina clasped her hands around her knees. "This may sound callous, but I don't mean it to be. I'm glad that your feelings are making themselves known. I know it's tough now. But I also know you'll feel better if you can make some peace with all this."

"Peace?" Daria shook her head and wrapped her arms around her belly.

"I know I'm a little younger than you are, that you lived through more of the sixties and seventies than I did." Katrina leaned closer as she spoke. "But maybe it would help if I gave you some historical context, some facts and observations about what was going on back then?"

Daria nodded, though historical context was of no interest to her. What she wanted was for the ache in her chest to go away. She wanted to be able to breathe deeply. Daria listened, but Katrina's words faded in and out in fragments. Roe v. Wade. Abortion legalized. Complicated transitions for men and women. Blurred workplace identities. Women's independence inching forward. The sexual revolution. Cryptic hygiene classes about how girls could get pregnant and how not to. Laws against selling contraceptives to single women. One and a half million babies surrendered.

As she listened to Katrina, a montage of images raced through her mind, fast-forwarding through the decades, the experiences that had formed and misinformed her. But when Katrina talked about the millions, yes millions, of women who were whisked away in secret to maternity homes, she focused again.

"Carol was vacationing in Switzerland," Katrina said. "Or Maryann was nursing a sick aunt in Iowa. Lies, lies, lies. All to cover what was considered the shame of pregnancy outside marriage. Which, by the way, only increased the shame for the young mothers." Daria took another sip of water. She was all too familiar with the secrecy and shame Katrina described.

"Most women who relinquished children were flanked by a Greek chorus of family, social service agencies, doctors and clergy, all singing the same tune: surrendering a child was the only way to salvage a reputation, to have a chance at a respectable future. Meaning a husband and what was considered an acceptable family. From what you've told me, you know firsthand that doing what their families wanted was sometimes young women's only safeguard against being ostracized."

Daria nodded slowly but paused before speaking. "So," she asked, "this need to hold onto family, to try to please, could be as powerful as any other motive for giving up a child?"

Katrina's voice softened. It sounded less clinical and more empathetic. "We all want to be loved, Daria. Especially by our families, good, bad, or indifferent. No matter how we try to distance ourselves from that need or pretend it doesn't exist. And if we don't get what we need, sometimes we try that much harder to be or do what they want. Or, in more extreme cases, to shut them out before they can shut us out."

"I see."

"Do you really? Because, if you made a decision because you wanted to please, or to avoid rejection, you really didn't have as much choice as you now think you had."

"Well, maybe . . . I guess I don't know. I mean, I can see that might be true for other women. But that, because I really am so selfish, or somehow so flawed, it's not true for me."

"That's something we could work on."

Work on. So that meant some relief, some resolution might be possible. "I hope so," Daria said.

"Do you want me to keep going?"

When Daria nodded, Katrina went on to say how some women tried to keep their secret under wraps by drinking. Or by eating too much chocolate. Or by becoming promiscuous. "Anything to keep the genie inside the lamp." She paused. "And, in more than a few cases, they took their own lives. So, in some ways, your ambition, your perfectionism were the lesser of many evils."

Daria wilted into her chair. She squinted as if looking through a thick haze, trying to make out a distant shore. Sometimes it came into view, only to disappear behind another wave of thick, soupy fog. "No one ever told me any of this. That I wasn't the only one who felt the way I did, I mean. And I never tried to find out. I felt like if I let out my secret I would self-destruct."

"When really the opposite was true, wasn't it? That keeping the secret was what was ripping you apart."

Daria remained still, looking straight ahead.

"Do you want to tell me about it?"

Tentatively at first, Daria told her story. From Mount Laurel to that day. When she finished, she closed her eyes.

She felt so tired. Spelling it all out at one time left her depleted.

"And you never stopped dancing, did you, Daria? Always onstage, always performing? Trying to please? To achieve? Hiding in plain sight?"

Daria opened her eyes but looked away.

"If you want," Katrina said, reaching into her desk, "I have information you can read." She pulled out a slender brochure. "This might help."

Daria grabbed another tissue, wiped away the remains of her eye makeup, and took the pamphlet. *Coming to Light—Destroying Adoption Myths from the Sixties.* As she flipped through, she stopped at page three.

Myth Number One: These women were having a lot of sex with a lot of different men.

Truth: A majority had sex with only one man, and some became pregnant through their first and only sexual experience.

Myth Number Two: These women were all eager to surrender their children.

Truth: Many women were forced to give up their children, sometimes by their families, their religions, or their fears of rejection and isolation.

Myth Number Three: These women got on with their lives easily after surrendering their children and suffered few after-effects.

There it was in black and white. She wasn't the only one who did what she did and felt like she felt. Daria refolded the brochure, tucked it in her bag. When she looked up at Katrina, her shoulders curved forward, her lips parted slightly, though she didn't speak.

"Is there something you want to say, Daria?"

Daria nodded, but no words came out. Then she sat forward, and her voice became clear and strong.

"It wasn't as if I didn't know how babies were made. And for years I deluded myself into believing that I wouldn't have done it if I hadn't been stoned." She hesitated. "But I wasn't stoned. A little high, but not so out of it I couldn't tell right from wrong. There was that moment, though. That one split second where I thought 'you can tell him to stop. You don't have to do this.' But I didn't say anything. I just let it happen. There was nothing in it for me. No pleasure, I mean. Just the desperate feeling that if I wanted to keep him—even though I never had him—I had to sacrifice my better judgment, I had to go through with it. And then the moment passed. There was no gun pointed at my head. *I just did it.*"

"Yes," Katrina said. "You did it. But I'd like to suggest that if you felt that desperate to win that man over, there *was* a gun to your head. The weapon of love denied. For whatever reason, whether because your father left when you needed him or because your mother was unable to accept you, you felt you needed that man. And if you can understand why, maybe you can forgive yourself. And then forgive them. All of them."

Daria shook her head. "Impossible."

"Maybe today," Katrina suggested. "But maybe not forever."

"I'm not sure. But now with Lizzy . . ." Daria tossed up her hands. "You'd think with what I went through I could have prevented her from getting into the same situation."

Katrina smiled. "It's a pretty tall order, don't you think, to expect you could control a teenaged boy's hormones? Or

Lizzy's choice. Would it surprise you to know that more than half of all teenagers who get pregnant outside marriage are the children of mothers who also gave birth out of marriage?"

"I'd be more than surprised. More like shocked. How does that happen? I mean, I never told Lizzy. Not until the other day anyway. Or her brother. I never even told my former husband or my mother."

"We're not sure why, but that's the case. When a young woman comes to us, and her family supports her, it's not uncommon for all kinds of secrets to come to light. Especially from the mother, if she had a child and, pressured or not, chose adoption. Or abortion. And in the rare case, from the man, if he knowingly fathered a child but removed himself from the situation."

Maybe this was one of those patterns Mary Catherine said could be broken with generational healing. But what good would that do now? She had already passed down the childbirth-out-of-marriage syndrome to Lizzy.

"Still with me, Daria?"

Daria nodded. "I was just thinking about someone who came on the show a while back. A former nun. Mary Catherine, her name is. From a place called Healing House. Have you heard of it?"

"I know Mary Catherine well." Katrina reached for the cross around her neck. "They do a lot of good work there."

If Katrina knew Mary Catherine, and if they did such good work at Healing House, why did Katrina's hand linger protectively on her chest at the mention of the place?

"Is it safe to assume," Katrina continued before Daria could speak, "that you had no say in selecting the adoptive parents? And that you never saw the child?"

"I didn't meet the parents or know anything about them. I wanted to—not at first, but eventually—but was told I couldn't. And even though I wasn't supposed to see the baby, I did." Daria's eyes filled again. "For a while I even wanted to change my mind. But I honestly don't know if I just say that to try to absolve some of the guilt. To try to blame the doctor, or my mother, or anybody."

"And now that you see Lizzy's options?"

"I feel so petty." Daria wadded up her used tissue and stuffed it in her purse. "But I'm jealous. There, I said it. The way you support her, with such understanding, such kindness—it's as if a flag is being raised, everyone honors her with respect and dignity. But me? My insides are burning, like I want to spit out some poison that's eating away at me, but I can't bring it up."

"Whatever your feelings, Daria, they're understandable. That includes anger or frustration over how you were dealt with years ago and even resentment over the way things are going for Lizzy. That doesn't mean it's healthy to hang on to those feelings." Katrina paused and leaned forward. "Have you thought about whether you'd like to try to find your first daughter?"

Daria shook her head slowly. "Not really." She felt exposed and frail, like a springtime dandelion whose flower had gone to seed, its froth so tentatively attached that it could fly off in the faintest breeze. "I mean, after all these years, I still think of her. Especially these last few months, with Lizzy and all. But try to find her? I'm not sure."

"Think about it. And, if you want, we can help. No promises, of course. Back when your daughter was born, the tracking mechanisms weren't very good. Often by design. The best chance we have of locating her is if she's registered with an agency to try to find you."

Daria paused. "Right now, I've got my hands full with Lizzy."

"That's fair." Katrina scanned Daria's face. "As long as you're not hiding behind Lizzy."

"Hiding?"

"What I mean is, Lizzy's situation is straightening itself out. And when things calm down, I wouldn't want to see you fall back into denial."

Daria sniggered. "I've been in an emotional hell, maybe. But denial?" As soon as the words came out, she started to cry again. "I'm sorry."

"It's okay." Katrina looked out her office window, then back to Daria. "Would it help you to know I was adopted as an infant and didn't find out until my late teens?"

Daria nodded. "I guess it would. On the other hand, I had the feeling you wouldn't work here unless you had some personal reason. I mean, you still dress and carry yourself like you work in Manhattan."

"Well, you're right." Katrina laughed as she reached for the pitcher and refilled Daria's water glass. "You can take the girl out of fashion, but you can't take the fashion out of the girl. Or something like that." She set the pitcher back down. "I think I told you and Lizzy I used to work in magazine publishing?"

"Umm-hmm."

"*Vogue*, actually. I was the accessories editor. But what's more important for you to know is that, even though I was raised in a five-bedroom house in back country Greenvale, went to Sacred Heart Convent School, then Columbia, I had a son when I was seventeen and surrendered him. And even though I had a lot more support than you did, I still feel it." Katrina worked her cuticles, drawing blood on her left thumb.

"Oh." Daria's eyes shifted away from Katrina. Her response felt paltry, insignificant. She looked back to her. "I don't know what to say."

"You don't need to say anything. But it might help to know that when I worked at *Vogue*, my career consumed my life. Or maybe I should say it consumed my ego. It gave me an identity that had nothing to do with the fact that I'd given up my son. Designers didn't dare not return my calls, for fear I'd pan them in print. My underlings wouldn't even consider crossing me, afraid they'd be fired and forced to find work on lesser publications.

"But even though I was the envy of many women who would have loved to see me fall off my pedestal, I felt as empty as this cup." She picked up her coffee mug, turned it over to show Daria it had nothing in it, then set it back on her desk. "And all the trips to Paris or Milan or London couldn't fill me up. All the Louis Vuitton luggage, the Italian shoes, beautiful as they were, couldn't give me what I needed most."

"And that was?"

Katrina's eyes softened. "Connection with women who had been through what I had. Or who had at least been through other things they were willing to talk about.

"Then one day I got called out for a spread I'd done on spring handbags. It was if a switch was flicked and my sparkly little life went dark. I just walked out. I went to Fordham, got my masters in social work, then came to Adoption Option.

"So, yeah, I still like to dress up. And maybe sometimes I'm still vain and shallow enough to think the right clothes help me feel better. But I also know I help someone now and then. And that helps fill the hole inside that Paris and Milan couldn't."

Daria nodded as she juxtaposed Katrina's revelations with her appearance. "That's why you always looked a little unexpected to me. Before I met you, I imagined you'd be a little more, I don't know . . ."

"Rumpled? That I'd wear long skirts and baggy sweaters and Danskos?"

Daria smiled. "I guess so."

"A lot of men and women who were adopted end up either working in the field or volunteering to help others locate their birth parents. I'm not suggesting," Katrina said, "that you're going to abandon your career and apply for a job here."

"Good." Daria laughed. "A new career isn't what I need right now." Serious again, she shook her head. "I'm not ready to find my daughter. Not yet. Maybe never. I don't know." She hesitated. "Have you . . . I mean, did you ever . . ."

"Find my son?"

"Yes."

"No." Katrina shook her head. She reached to her neck again and held the cross. "But I still hope."

Chapter Twenty-One
September 1992

"Mom?"

Daria heard the excited, fearful, happy, frantic sound of Lizzy's voice, opened her desk drawer and grabbed her purse. "Is it time?"

"How'd you know?"

"Lucky guess. Did your water break?"

"All over. Sorry. It's a mess."

"We'll worry about that later." Daria fumbled inside her purse for her car keys. "Is everything else okay? You called Frankie?"

"I'm fine, I guess. I don't know. Aunt Frank's on her way."

That was the pre-arranged plan Lizzy and Daria had agreed upon. Lizzy would call Frankie first, since she was only five minutes away. Then Lizzy would call Daria, then Jack. They had a plan. Everything would be fine.

"Give me fifteen minutes max." Daria grabbed her coat hanging on the back of her office door. "And get the bag we packed."

"We already put it by the door, remember?"

"Oh, yeah. Right." Daria wriggled into her coat while she balanced the phone between her neck and ear. "Okay, then. Call your brother."

"Yup. But Mom?" Lizzy's voice sounded at once plaintive and in charge.

"Uh-huh."

"Don't be late, okay?"

"Not a chance, honey."

Fifteen minutes later, Daria tore up to the house. Frankie and Lizzy waited on the front steps. If it were a typical day, Daria would have noticed that it was unseasonably mild for September, that she didn't need the coat she was wearing, that the sun was bright, and that the sky was a brilliant cobalt blue. But nothing could keep Daria from focusing on one consuming thought: Lizzy, her youngest child, was hours away from becoming a mother.

Frankie, with one arm wrapped around Lizzy's shoulder, carried a cluster of pink and blue and silver balloons in the other. How she got them so quickly, Daria had no idea. It wouldn't be unlike Frankie to buy a new batch every day, just to be prepared for this moment. And Lizzy, her stomach full, her face as round as it had been when she herself was a baby, had one hand on her belly, the other on her duffel bag. If she had time, Daria thought, she would fall into tears just looking at the two of them, their faces jumbled with apprehension, urgency, and joy. But time she didn't have.

The car still running, Lizzy, supported by Frankie, started to the car.

"Hello, darlin'," Frankie called. "We're gonna have a baby today."

"I'm so glad you're here, Frank." Daria cast an appreciative glance toward her as she wrapped her arms around Lizzy. "You ready, honey?"

Lizzy nodded, managing a smile. "Even if I wasn't," she said, "I don't think I have a choice."

Daria grabbed Lizzy's bag. As Daria stowed the bag in the trunk, Frankie stuffed the balloons on the back seat beside her, then reached into her purse and pulled out a bright yellow Baby on Board road sign, which she affixed by its suction cups to the back window. "Let her rip, Dar."

"I think," Daria announced as she hunched over the steering wheel, "this is a perfect time to try that visualization technique my guest talked about last week on the show. Everybody repeat after me: we will have a clear, safe, and construction-free drive on 95."

They did. Eleven minutes later, Daria pulled up to the circular drive to Greenvale Hospital. And almost six hours afterward, at 7:19 that night, Lizzy gave birth to a healthy girl.

******

"She is, without a doubt," Frankie pronounced as she and Daria hovered over Lizzy's hospital bed, "the most precious baby ever."

"Look at her little feet," Lizzy said. "And all that hair." Lizzy stroked the baby's face, held her tiny hand, and examined her fingers, counting them one by one. "Want to hold her, Mom?"

"Of course, I want to hold her."

"Careful," Lizzy said.

Struck by Lizzy's maternal concern, Daria smiled, then reached for the baby. "I promise." The red-faced yawning little girl, stretching then clenching her fingers as if grabbing onto her new life, nestled in Daria's arms. "She's perfect," Daria said, cradling her, kissing the top of the baby's head.

"You're right about that, sugar," Frankie said.

Daria looked from Lizzy to the baby, to Frankie, then back to the baby. This is how a child should come into the world. Surrounded by wonderment, by love. Maybe this is what Mary Catherine meant that day on *Awakenings* when she talked about mirroring, one woman to another.

"Jack!" Lizzy called, interrupting Daria's thoughts.

They all smiled more brightly when Jack walked in the room. That was the effect he had on people, from the time he was as tiny and red as Lizzy's baby. And was it possible that Daria saw a hint of Jack's smile in the baby's?

"Hey, LizBiz," Jack said, calling Lizzy by the childhood nickname he had given her. "Whatcha got there?" he asked.

"I had a baby girl." Lizzy beamed. "Mom, let me have her so I can show Jack."

When Daria passed the baby back to Lizzy, she remembered the awe she felt when she held her first daughter for those three short days before she gave her up. Then the overhanging despair that came from knowing she would never see her again.

She looked again from Lizzy to the baby to Frankie, then to Jack. Her family. Not a perfect family, to be sure. Not even a typical family. But a family all the same. So different from the way things were when Jack and Lizzy were born. Whatever else happened, Daria hoped Lizzy would always know she could count on them.

Her thoughts shifted to a family member who wasn't in the room. Her first daughter. If she'd kept her, she'd be here now. Should Daria have found a way to help Lizzy keep her daughter? *My granddaughter?* June and Richard would be good parents, Daria knew. But, in the end, would surrender prove to be the right decision for Lizzy? For the family?

Daria tried to make peace with the fact that she had no way of knowing, no way of controlling the future. She could only hope that the support Lizzy received would buoy her, whatever feelings or circumstances might surface in the near or long term.

Then, she knew. Whatever the consequences, it was time. She needed to try to find her first daughter.

******

After leaving Lizzy at the hospital for the night, Frankie, Jack, and Daria returned to Authors Street.

Outside her house, Daria looked on as Frankie hugged Jack goodbye, pronouncing her godson "the sweetest, handsomest man on earth."

Daria couldn't disagree. Now standing over six feet, his always-restless brown hair framing his square jaw and blue eyes, Jack looked every bit the charmer he had always been.

"And you, Grandmama." When Frankie reached to hug her, Daria felt none of the dismay she had anticipated about being a grandmother when Lizzy first announced her pregnancy. She was the little girl's Nana—at least for a few days—and proud of it.

Daria held Frankie close. "You, Frank, are Auntie Extraordinaire. We couldn't have done this without you."

"Nonsense," Frankie said. "You would have done just fine. But I'm glad you let me play an itty-bitty part in the whole thing."

After one more round of hugs, Frankie drove off, promising to visit Lizzy again the next day. Daria went into the house while Jack brought his duffel in from his car.

"Looks like LizBiz's been heavy into ice cream," he said when he headed straight to the kitchen, taking a pint of peanut butter fudge from the freezer.

"That's for sure." Daria looked closely at Jack as he scooped a generous serving into a bowl, hoping that, with a child of her own, Lizzy would still be Jack's little LizBiz. "I won't be surprised if she goes back to carrot sticks and celery when she starts cheerleading again. I just hope she doesn't pick up the cigarettes."

Jack grunted in affirmation.

"I'd tell you not to ruin your dinner," Daria said as she turned on the oven, "but there's not much to choose from. How about grabbing that leftover lasagna and I'll heat it up?"

Daria set the table, and Jack took the casserole dish from the refrigerator. While it was reheating, they retreated to the family room. As Jack brought her up to date on his studies and plans to become a surgeon, Daria sat back, waiting for the opportune moment to say what she wanted him to hear.

"Are you happy?" she asked when he finished speaking.

"Uh-huh. I was a little worried about Lizzy. But now that the baby's here and Lizzy's good, I'm okay too."

"I'm happy you're happy, honey. Lizzy really wanted you to see the baby." She paused. "But there's something else I want to say." Her voice caught. "This isn't easy for me."

"Don't tell me you're pregnant."

When Jack laughed, Daria did too. She wished she could roll back the clock so she could have enjoyed more time with him, laughed with him more, which seemed so easy for him.

"Fortunately," she said, "the answer to that question is a big fat no." Then she became serious again. "Lizzy already told you about your sister. Your other sister, I mean?"

"Uh-huh."

"I'm just so sorry."

Jack set down his ice cream. "For what?"

"That I kept that secret from you and Lizzy. And that I put other things—work mostly—ahead of you so often. I just thought that if I accomplished enough and made enough money to take care of you, I was doing enough. I wasn't.

"Mostly," she continued, "I'm sorry I didn't spend more time with you. That I didn't tell you how special you are. The way you have with people, the way your smile puts people at ease at the same time it makes them feel alive."

"Well," Jack said, slouching back into the couch, "you've got a pretty killer smile too, Mom. I see it every time I watch the show."

"I guess I do," she conceded. "Or at least I did. But mine keeps people away. Yours draws them in. It always has. Remember the first time I saw you on stage? In *Anything Goes*. When you came out in your navy blazer and white pants, that blazing smile, the whole auditorium wished you were their son or boyfriend or brother or grandson."

Jack shrugged, not used to this kind of talk from his mother. "That's nice to hear, Mom." He reached for the ice cream but set it down again without eating any.

Daria's heart quickened when she saw that he wasn't smiling, he wasn't joking.

"I know you didn't always have time for us," he said.

Daria reached for his hand, but he shook his head and leaned away. "Maybe this sounds a little weird, but you being the way you were probably helped me. I mean, sure, I wanted you to visit more. I wanted you to look at me the way you looked at Lizzy's baby today. But I didn't get those things, so I forced myself to get along with people. I learned how to do that because of how you accomplished whatever you wanted. The way you kept on going, even when things looked pretty grim around here. You know, the divorce and everything.

"You sent me to Saint Gregory's so I'd get into a good college. And, sure, I had great teachers who knew their stuff and who pushed us to do well. But some of them—especially Brother Francis and Brother Dominic—they helped me learn how to take what we learned in chapel into the world.

"You and Lizzy never had that. I mean, I know you went to Catholic school. And I know Grandma's religious. But she doesn't seem to practice what church is all about. To me anyway. You know, Christ, love, mercy."

That, Daria thought, was certainly true.

"How is Grandma, anyway?"

Daria diverted her eyes. She shrugged. "It's been a while."

"Mom?"

Daria looked back to him. Even if he had always been as gentle as Lizzy could be petulant, there was no mistaking a new look in his eyes now, a new persistence. Whether that had been her influence or his teachers', she couldn't be sure. But she knew as well as Jack that she should be in closer touch with her mother.

"It's just not easy with Grandma," she said, trying to rationalize her distance from Helena.

"She's tough," he said, nodding. "No doubt about it. But, she's, well, she's Grandma."

When Daria said nothing more, Jack circled back to his previous thought.

"Anyway, Brother Francis and Brother Dominic helped me see that, even when things hurt, they're part of a bigger plan. And that I never see the whole picture. Only bits and pieces. And only from my point of view. But if I'm patient, I can look back and see how the pieces fit together.

"I guess what I'm trying to say is, yeah, I missed out on some things, but I got other things too."

Daria reached across the couch and hugged him close. "I'm so sorry I wasn't around when you were learning those lessons," she said. "I'm so very proud of you."

Then she leaned away from him, still holding his arms. "I don't want you to have to substitute other things and people for what I didn't give you. Not anymore. I want things to be different. I want me to be different."

"That's just it, Mom," Jack said. "I mean, sure, I'd like to see you more often and talk to you more. And not just about school or sailing. About this kind of stuff. But even if we don't, even if you don't change a thing, you're still my mom. Like how I said Grandma's Grandma?"

Daria nodded.

"You're you."

Daria looked at her son, her eyes soft. There it was again. The feeling that Jack couldn't possibly be her and Ted's son. The feeling that someone must have exchanged her child at the hospital for the one that had become this incredibly wise and wonderful young man. And how was it that the more she tried to be a better mother —to both Lizzy and Jack— and the more she tried to grow up, the more childlike she felt?

Chapter Twenty-Two
September 1992

"Daria?"

When Katrina answered her call, Daria hesitated before responding. Her thoughts and feelings were still tumbling from the experiences of the last few days. "Daria, you there? How did everything go?"

"Yes, yes I'm here. Everything went beautifully. Lizzy's labor was mercifully short, and the doctors pronounced the baby healthy and ready to leave the hospital as soon as June and Richard come for her.

"Frankie was a huge help. Jack—he's my son—he visited too.

"The baby's got Lizzy's hair and eyes, but I saw a little bit of Jack in her too. With that combination, we won't have to worry about how she'll make her way in the world.

"As for Lizzy, the next day her friend Megan came, and they were already talking about cheerleading. I think she'll do fine."

"And that leaves you feeling how?"

"If there's such a thing as a mega-Cyclone roller coaster, I'm on it. Riding high one minute, plunging into the depths the next."

"Understandable."

Daria paused. "I want to try to find my daughter."

Silence.

"Are you there? Katrina?"

"Yes, yes. I'm here. You sound quite certain. Your voice is clear, strong. I just want to be sure you didn't decide based on a romanticized notion of how things might work out. Based on seeing your granddaughter, I mean, and your experience with June and Richard. There's never any guarantee of outcomes in these situations."

"Of course, I understand," Daria said, not caring that she sounded impatient. Katrina had done such a great job with Lizzy. Why was she being such a wet blanket now? For a moment, Daria recollected Jack's confidence, his certainty that, even in hurtful situations, a bigger plan was unfolding. Then she dismissed the thought. She had a plan. And she would make it work. "I want to find her," she said. "I need to."

"Okay, then," Katrina said. "We'll submit your profile to a couple registries of children trying to find their birth parents. Whether we get any responses depends on if your daughter knows she was adopted and if she wants to find you."

Daria's enthusiasm flagged. "What are the chances of that? I mean, if her adoptive parents were as secretive as I was back then, they probably didn't tell her."

"True. But it's also true that adoption secrets have a way of coming to light no matter how hard people try to keep them under wraps. Either way, once we send out word that you're looking for your daughter, all we can do is wait."

Wait? No, Daria didn't want to wait. Her next question hung in the air, unspoken. *How long will it take?*

"Unfortunately," Katrina said, sensing Daria's concern, "there's no way to gauge when, or if, we might hear something." She paused. "And, of course, there's the risk we may never find her."

Unacceptable. That's what Daria thought of the possibility that she might never find her daughter. She would find her. Somehow. And, by the way, everything would work out just fine.

******

As the days shortened, maple leaves flared red, then retreated to brown. Snow would fall. Then crocuses and daffodils would insinuate themselves again through cold, dark soil in spring. If nothing else were certain, Daria mused, at least the seasons could be counted on.

But the prospect of finding—or not finding—her first daughter seemed to thicken the air, making it more difficult for Daria to move through the world. For the first few weeks after June and Richard took Lizzy's baby to Boston, Daria woke each morning thinking—*will this be the day Katrina finds my daughter?*

******

A week later, Daria left the studio after taping her show. It was only four, plenty of time to make an early dinner for her and Lizzy. As she drove between the Sound Shore pillars, the heavy-bellied clouds and the Sound's raucous waves pulled her past the turnoff to Authors Street and led her to the stone wall at the end of Shore Road. She parked the car facing the water, rolled down the windows, and leaned her

239

head back to let the breeze, the damp air, the sound of the advancing and receding waves lull her.

When Daria spotted a flock of geese overhead, their V formation drew her out of her car, urging her to follow them south. She exchanged her heels for the running shoes in the trunk. Walking past the concession stand, closed for the season, she took one of the benches facing the water. Sunset was less than an hour away. The little light breaking through the clouds was fading fast.

She shut her eyes and took in the weather's impending intensity. She rolled her head back to loosen the tension that had settled in her neck. It wouldn't be long now, not long at all. Soon her fears and regrets, like the brown leaves falling from nearby trees, would be carried away by the waves, never to return.

******

Daria faced the hallway mirror. Turning her head left and right, she decided Jean-Paul should go a little lighter on her hair color to better disguise the gray that was growing more insistent. *Gone to the hairdresser,* she scribbled on a note for Lizzy. *Back by 8:30.* Then, grabbing the ringing phone, she picked up her purse and keys.

"Hello."

"Daria? It's Katrina." Daria checked her watch. It was after six, later than Katrina usually left her office. That meant one of two things. "Do you have a minute?"

Daria set her keys and purse on the hallway table. "I was just running out. But, yes, of course." Then, more tentatively, "You heard something?"

"Your daughter is in Manhattan," Katrina said. "She's been trying to find you for a year or so." She paused to let Daria absorb the news.

"Manhattan?" Daria tried to make sense of the fact that her daughter lived only a train ride away. "All this time she's been less than an hour from me?"

"Well, we don't know how long she's been in New York. But she's there now. With your permission, I'll contact her registry agency." Katrina gave Daria another moment, then continued. "If she still wants to meet you, do you still want to see her?"

"Of course." Daria tried to calm her voice. "I mean, yes." She hoped her words didn't sound as uncertain as she felt.

******

The following Monday, Daria reached for her ringing office phone, tucked it between her ear and shoulder, and kept scribbling comments on Tuesday's production notes. "Daria Demarest."

"I have good news." Recognizing Katrina's voice, Daria put down her pen, took off her reading glasses, and set them on the desk. She pushed back in her chair, feeling as if a sharp wind had blown through her and drained the breath from her lungs. "Daria?"

"Yes. I'm here. I was just . . . catching my breath, I guess." She hesitated. "Do I really want to know this?" She picked up the can of Diet Coke from her desk and took a healthy swig, wishing it were Scotch.

"Before you answer that—and I think you already know you're the only one who can, right?"

"Right."

"—would it help to know it's not unusual to get cold feet? A lot of people think they want contact. But when the possibility presents itself, well, they freeze."

"Yes. Yes, it would. I mean, it does. I . . . okay, go ahead." She picked up her pen and began tapping it against her desk.

"Your daughter's name is Angela Rush. She's an actress and a dancer. And she's performing on Broadway in a play called *River*. Her run ends the beginning of December. After that, she'll be touring." Katrina paused. "She'd like to meet you in a few weeks. In the meantime, she's leaving two tickets at the box office for this Sunday's matinee if you want to see her perform."

"Sunday," Daria said. Too soon. She needed more time. "Are you sure she's my daughter? I mean, how do you know? After all these years?"

"The details each of you provided on your forms match perfectly, down to the day, the time, the hospital in which Angela was born, and the doctor who brokered the adoption."

"Oh." She paused. "She's an actress? A dancer? What kind of cosmic coincidence is that?"

"Interesting." Katrina paused. "Coincidence can mean something different from happenstance."

"I don't get it." There was that impatience again. "Sorry. What are you trying to say?"

"Just that things seem to happen at the right time, even if we wish they happened sooner. Or even if we don't want them to happen. Like they're part of a bigger plan that we can't control."

Katrina sounded like Jack now. But that didn't matter. What was important was that, coincidence or not, Katrina had found her daughter. Angela.

Katrina shifted the conversation. "Does that time work for you?"

"I don't know. What I mean is I've wondered about this for twenty years, and now, I feel like it's opening night and I've got paralyzing stage fright."

"Understandable," Katrina empathized. "May I make a suggestion?"

"A suggestion?" Daria managed an anemic laugh. She had heard enough of Frankie's suggestions to know that they were really directives dressed up in sheep's clothing. "I guess that depends."

"All I'm hoping," Katrina said, "is that you take this step by step. And the first step is a decision about whether you want to see your daughter on stage this Sunday. That's all. It doesn't mean you need to meet her face to face. And you don't have to answer now. Sleep on it and get back to me tomorrow. Then, if you decide to go, take a friend. No matter how disarmed or sad or elated you feel after seeing Angela, you'll probably want to talk about it. And Daria?"

"Yes."

"How about we pencil in a time for you to come in next week to debrief? And if you decide not to go, we can talk about that too."

******

"She wants to get together." Daria's words rushed out as soon as Frankie picked up the phone.

"Who wants to get together?"

"My daughter. Angela. That's her name. Angela Rush. Katrina found her. She's an actress, playing in something called *River*." Daria didn't try to tame her voice. "She's leaving tickets at the box office for Sunday's matinee. Will you go with me?"

"Why, honey, I wouldn't miss it—"

"I'll pick you up around twelve?"

"Whoa, darlin', slow down a sec," Frankie said. "How about we take the train? What I mean is you might not feel up to drivin' afterwards. And I'm not all that fond of takin' the car into the City anymore. Too stressful."

"You're right. Hang on." Daria set down the phone, rummaged through her desk, and ferreted out a Metro North schedule. "I'm back. The eleven fifty gets in at twelve forty."

"Sure, sugar. But Dar, can you take a breath, for heaven's sake?"

Daria continued, measuring her words. "I guess I'm a little wound up."

"Now there's an understatement. Hang on a minute, will you? There's somethin' I want to read you from the *Times*. But I need to run downstairs to find it." Without waiting for Daria to comment, Frankie put down the phone. She returned a few minutes later, out of breath. "I'm way too old for this, you know."

"For what?"

"Nothin', sugar. Just give me a minute."

Daria heard Frankie flipping through the newspaper.

"Okay, you ready?"

"For what?"

"Stephen Pope reviewed *River* in last Sunday's *Times*. Here we go. 'This,' he says, 'is theatre for our generation. The choreography in this production is at once sexy and sublime, and the casting is sheer genius.'

"Then it goes on about the male lead, Robert Hayworth, blah, blah, blah." Frankie skimmed the rest of the review. "Okay, here, 'Angela Rush is as naughty as she is nice. Her *pas de deux* with Hayworth is one of Broadway's most enigmatic yet powerful performances in years.' Then he goes on. Here. 'She's even better in this production than she was last year when she won the Tony for her role as Louise in *Carousel*.'"

"Not bad, huh? Especially from Pope."

Daria was impervious to Frankie's banter. *Louise*. She drifted back, remembering the spring, over two decades earlier, when she played that same part at MacMillan University, the two *pas de deux* she danced in every show: one with a carnival worker, the second with her father. *Go deeper*, T.J. had encouraged. *You're breaking out of your drab little life by embracing a dangerous yet tasty relationship*, he had said about her dance with Billy Bigelow. *Now, when he leaves you, show the audience your anger. Use your arms, your feet, your heart to let them know how much you hurt.*

Then, Louise preparing for graduation, when her father returns from the heavens to visit his daughter. *This is your father, Daria. The man who left you even before you were born. When he offers you the star he's been sent from heaven to deliver for you, reject him, let him know how much he hurt you. And when he slaps you, let the audience see how his anger overpowers even yours.*

And the final scene. *At your graduation, show the audience you believe what Aunt Nettie is singing, that you'll never walk alone, that there really is a golden sky at the end of the storm. Let them feel your hope, your fragility. Let them see all of you, Daria.*

Finally, after the show, in her apartment. By herself. "When you walk through a storm," she used to sing, hands clasped around her belly, her child. "You'll never walk alone." How she wanted her baby to know that, despite the fact that, there, in the dark, Daria felt nothing but alone.

"Dar? You still with me?"

"I'm here," she said, her voice subdued and slow. "I used to sing that song to her, when she was inside me. 'You'll Never Walk Alone,' I mean. I wanted her to believe it. I wanted to believe it too. Because, except for T.J., I *was* alone."

"T.J.?"

"My college friend. Remember? The one who helped arrange for the adoption?"

"That's right," Frankie said. "Too bad you let that one get away, huh?" When Daria ignored her, Frankie changed the subject. "Listen to the rest of this. "Run, don't walk to see this glorious, feel-good production.'"

"I guess it doesn't get much better than that," Daria said. "A favorable review in the *Times*, I mean."

"It's not too shabby, no. At least you know that one part of her life is goin' well. Hell, better than going well. It's fantastic. Whoever her parents were, they must have done somethin' right."

Daria said nothing.

"Dar?"

"Did you have to say it that way?" She slammed her pen on the desk. "About her parents?"

"I only meant that at least she got opportunities."

"You're right. I'm just so . . . scared."

"I'd be worried if you weren't." Frankie paused. "You know you did the best you could back then, right? With the hand you were dealt?"

"No," she said quickly, her criticism aimed at herself. "I don't know that. I got myself into a mess, and I took the easy way out. Lizzy did a better job than I did."

"That's true in good measure because you've been walkin' her walk with her. Can't you see that?" When Daria didn't answer, Frankie kept going. "Nobody's heapin' a mountain of shame on Lizzy the way people did on you. That's not to blame anybody. It's just the facts."

"But I was the one who—"

"But, but, but. No more buts. Just consider the possibility of puttin' down that baseball bat of guilt you keep clubbin' yourself with and give yourself a break."

"I just don't know, Frank. I just don't know."

"Well not knowin's a step above 'I can't' or 'I won't.' Things with Angela are just gonna unfold the way they're meant to. No amount of plannin' or organizin' or controllin' is gonna make them go the way you imagine. Good or bad."

"You're probably right. As usual." But Daria had no idea how whoever or whatever was in charge could have the situation under control when she couldn't keep her own thoughts, and the situations around her, from spinning every which way. "I've got to run, Frank. See you Sunday, okay?"

When Daria hung up, she sat on the bench and faced the front window, drifting into the place Frankie called projection-land. She would see the show this weekend, then have dinner with Angela sometime soon. Sure, things might be rocky at first. But they would take it slow, get together a few times while they learned how they took their coffee, whether they preferred Asian Fusion or Indian cuisine. And once the post-reunion jitters settled, Angela would take the train up for holidays. They would shop for clothes or antiques on weekends. In time, Daria decided, everything would be just fine.

She grabbed her purse and keys again and ran out the door so she wouldn't be late for her appointment.

Chapter Twenty-Three
September 1992

Daria checked her watch as she hurried to the train platform. Eleven forty-six. Less than five minutes until the train arrived.

Not that she hadn't allowed herself enough prep time. She had gotten out of bed at six, hoping a three-mile sunrise run and its foot-to-pavement rhythm would calm her. When that didn't work, she soaked in a tub of lavender bubbles. Still no luck. The Carla-approved breathing method worked for a bit, but once she sat at her dressing table, any benefits were lost on her. She tied up her hair in a chignon, then let it fall loose around her shoulders, wondering whether to aim for sophisticated or hip. She changed three times, finally settling on a tailored taupe suit with navy blouse, shoes, and bag.

By the time she reached the platform steps, her insides felt like they were trapped inside a Cuisinart work bowl while someone intermittently pressed the pulse button. What, she wondered, would it be like when, no *if,* she actually met her daughter, talked to her? No, not *my daughter.* She had a name. Angela. Angela Rush.

Frankie, already seated on a bench beneath the ironwork clock, looked up when she heard Daria's strident click-click-

clicking along the concrete. Gathering her oversized tote, she waved and stood, opening her arms to greet Daria. In her bright red, loose-fitting cape, flapping in the noontime breeze, Frankie looked like an extremely large and happy bat, ready to envelop Daria in her protective wing span. "I was startin' to worry. The train'll be here any sec."

When Frankie reached to hug her, Daria pulled back. "How do I look?" She smoothed her jacket and stood for inspection.

"Gorgeous, of course," Frankie said, stifling a smile. "Why would today be any different? But it doesn't really matter, does it? You're not the one performin', are you? Besides, I think you're gonna be a little too far away for Angela to notice if you're mascara's smeared."

"My mascara? What? It's running? Clumping?" She reached to her purse for a mirror, but Frankie put a steadying hand on hers.

"Your mascara's fine. I was just tryin' to provide some perspective."

Daria extricated her hand from Frankie's and reached to remove a stray hair from her jacket. "I guess I'm a little jumpy."

"Well, precious girl, who the hell wouldn't be?"

As the approaching train's whistle blew, Daria took Frankie's arm. "Come on." She tugged her friend behind her. "Let's move up so we can get the first car."

******

Outside the theatre, Daria stopped Frankie as she opened the door.

"Am I sure I want to do this?"

"Well, honey, I suspect only you can answer that. All I know is you look like Lot's wife standing there, all pale and frozen, like you looked back and turned to a pillar of salt." Frankie put her hands lightly but squarely on Daria's shoulders. "Like I said before, you did the best you could back then, Dar. And now all you can do is the very same thing—the best you can, one step at a time. Just because we're gonna see Angela onstage today doesn't mean you're gonna meet her next week or next month or ever."

"Right," Daria repeated. "You sound like Katrina. One step at a time." She turned back to the heavy brass and glass door, opened it, and walked in.

Daria picked up the tickets at the lobby window. Then she grabbed Frankie's arm and steered her through the crowd to their seats, third row, orchestra, center. A few minutes later, as the theatre's crystal chandelier dimmed, Frankie took Daria's hand. "I'm right here, sugar," she whispered.

"You're the best, Frank." Daria withdrew her hand, fixed her eyes straight ahead, and waited.

******

When the blue velvet curtain went up, Daria clasped her hands over her mouth. Angela, like Daria, stood about five eight. Her hair—though dyed yellow-blonde—was as thick as Daria's, enveloping a similarly shaped face. And she had Daria's graceful, muscular legs. But the way she danced. Committed to every *jeté*, every *pirouette*, yet knowing when to step back from her edge, when to withhold, when to let go. Whatever else Angela might be, she was definitely in control.

"She's somethin', isn't she?" Frankie said.

Daria nodded, though she continued leaning forward during the six-minute *pas de deux*. When Angela left the stage, Daria melted back into her seat, breathless, as if *she,* not her daughter, had just performed.

Stephen Pope, she decided, had been right. The choreography for this show was definitely sexy and sublime. And Angela was coy and seductive, and then shattered and vulnerable when her hard-shelled lover left.

That's how she could have danced, *should* have danced, if she'd been able to do what T.J. had wanted of her. To reach inside, beyond technical precision, and feel.

******

"I knew she was my daughter the minute I saw her. If her hair hadn't been bleached, maybe someone else would have seen that too." Daria sat in Katrina's office, not bothering to take off her coat. "I felt as if I was seeing a twenty-four-year-old film of myself. Except that she's a better dancer than I was. Less afraid of herself, I think. More willing to put herself on the line."

"That must have been quite an experience." Katrina wheeled her desk chair closer to Daria. "But when you get into comparing yourself with her, let's not forget, Angela probably had advantages you didn't. Given the family she was placed with, I mean. Only child of a comfortable middle-class family, her profile said. Besides,"—Katrina removed her cabled cardigan and draped it over the back of her chair —"it's possible your vision of yourself is a little distorted now. Don't you think?"

Daria shrugged. "Maybe, maybe not."

"Perhaps that's the subject for another conversation. What about next steps with Angela? Do you want to meet her?"

"Yes. Yes, I do."

"Okay," Katrina said. "Many birth parents and their children write to each other before they decide on a visit. Just to break the ice."

"Maybe," Daria said thoughtfully, "writing first makes sense. So neither of us is risking everything all at once."

"Exactly."

Katrina said she would contact Angela through her agency to confirm that she wanted to meet. "No matter what she decides, it will be cathartic for you to put your thoughts on paper."

******

Dear Angela,

I'm not much of a writer, though I suppose this would be difficult even if I were.

It's hard to know where to start.

First, thank you for the tickets to your show. Stephen Pope was right in his review. You dance like an angel, even if the choreography was deliciously seductive.

Though I saw you for the first time in over twenty years yesterday, you've never been far from my thoughts. Almost every day I've tried to imagine what you look like, what your voice sounds like, whether you were happy and in good hands.

I can tell from your singing and dancing that you received excellent training. That makes me happy. I know you're doing what you were meant to. You're gifted and tenacious. I also want to tell you that, in seeing you, I received a part of myself that has been missing ever since I allowed you to be taken from me.

Of course, I want to know all about how you were raised, what your parents are like, where you studied. If you want to meet—and I hope you do—I would like to hear whatever you want to say.

I know my thoughts aren't all in logical order here. Please bear with me.

When I read the review of River, it mentioned how you played Louise in Carousel last year. That threw me back to when I played the same part in a college production. Maybe that sounds too coincidental, but it's true. I wasn't half as good as you were, not nearly as expressive or free-spirited, but the music always stayed with me. And when I was pregnant with you, I sang that one song to you over and over, hoping we would both know we would never need to walk alone. Sad to say, the message didn't stick with me, and for many years, I've felt I needed to keep a deep, dark secret, and that secret was you. Feeble as this may sound, I never told my family or friends about you. I was too afraid.

I hope you can understand, even a little, that I don't know if I'll ever find the right words to express to you the depth of the confusion and hurt and disappointment that have spun in my head, my chest, my heart all these years.

I can try to tell you the reasons why I did what I did. That I was young, irresponsible. That I didn't feel I had the makings to be a mother back then. And, while this is no excuse, things were different in the sixties.

Living with the shame of being an unwed mother —that's what we were called back then—along with the self-loathing for doing something I knew deep down was wrong, kept me for a long time from wanting to be a mother again. But after I was married a couple years, I had two more children, a boy and a girl, and I can't say I was the best mother to them either. Not when they were young, anyway. But I'm trying now with them, and I'd like to try with you.

I know I can never make up for the past, and the best I can offer you now is this flimsy explanation. I hope it helps you understand, at least a little bit, what I did and why.

In the meantime, if you want to see me—and I very much hope you do—please call or write Katrina Wilkinson at the Adoption Option.

Daria read and re-read the note, crossing out words, sentences, paragraphs, trying to get it right. Finally, she decided she could never craft anything even close to perfect. How would she sign it? *The formerly irresponsible, frightened young girl who gave you away to strangers, but who's trying to make things right?* Or, how about the sanitized, 1990s, politically correct moniker? *Your birth mother.*

In the end, she signed the letter *Daria.* Before she gave herself the chance to second guess, further edit, or rewrite, she folded the letter, put it in an envelope, and addressed it to Katrina. Then, she pulled on her coat, grabbed her car keys and ran out the door, headed for the Adoption Option.

******

"Hello." Daria balanced her phone as she opened a file drawer to retrieve a folder of background material for the next day's show.

"Daria?"

It had been two weeks since Daria had delivered her letter to Katrina. She tried taking things one day, one step, at a time, as Frankie and Katrina had suggested. But as each day passed, Daria slept less and wondered more. Maybe it was better to just know Angela was alive and well and leave it at that. Twice Daria called Katrina to tell her that, since Angela hadn't responded, she had decided against meeting her.

"I'll do whatever you want me to do," Katrina had told her. "But I want you to think it over and get back to me tomorrow."

Both times, Daria decided again to move forward. Last week, she bought a calendar and propped it up on her desk, though. Each day, she crossed off the date as it passed. If Angela didn't respond by December 1, that would be that.

Daria set the file on her desk. "Katrina? Is that you?"

"Yes, it's me. Is this a good time?"

"I guess that depends." She hesitated, reluctant to ask the question that stuck in her throat.

"A letter came in today's mail," Katrina said without prompting. "From Angela."

Daria sank into her chair.

"Should I forward it to you? Or do you want to come in and read it?" Katrina continued when Daria didn't respond. "It's hard to predict what emotions might come up, so how about if you read it here?"

"No," Daria said. "I'd rather be alone." But as she leaned back in her chair, she picked up the marker she had been using to count down the days. "No," she said again, this time making a big black X through the whole month of October, "that's not right. I want you there when I open it." At that point, she wasn't sure what felt worse, the fear of what Angela had written or the fear of exposing herself even more to Katrina.

"Good. Unfortunately, I'm tied up tomorrow morning. But my afternoon's open. Say, two?"

"I tape in the morning anyway," Daria said. "So, two's fine."

Daria stood quickly after hanging up. Getting back to work would help quash the fears, the hopes that were jostling for position inside her. But as she went back to her filing cabinet, she felt dizzy and sat back down.

******

The next day, Katrina entered the Adoption Option waiting room, her hands empty. "I'll take you back to the conference room," Katrina said. "The letter's there."

How could Katrina have left the letter out of her sight? Didn't she know how precious it was? Daria managed a weak smile as she nodded. Then she followed Katrina to the conference room.

As Daria took a seat at the shiny mahogany table, Katrina sat next to her and handed her the small, pale blue envelope.

Daria held it tentatively. *Daria* was written in narrow, controlled script on the front. "I guess it's now or never."

"Do you want me to stay? Or leave and stop back in a few minutes?"

"I'd like privacy, thanks." Daria paused. "But come back. Please."

As the door closed, Daria slid her finger under the envelope flap to unseal the letter. She took it out gently but deliberately, unfolded it, read it, put it back in its envelope, then took it out and read it again.

When Katrina reentered the conference room, Daria was staring out the window. She turned toward Katrina and slid the letter across the table. It took Katrina, as it had taken Daria, only seconds to read.

> *Let's meet at Tableau, in the City at Twenty-Fourth and Fifth, at 1:30 on October 24.*
>
> *There's no need to contact me before then, unless you can't make it.*
>
> *Angela*

"It couldn't be much chillier, could it?"

Katrina folded the letter. "This is never easy." She handed it back to Daria. "Even when both parties want to get together, there's always some bobbing and weaving that goes on.

"The only advice I can offer, if you still want to see Angela, is to try not to overreact to whatever she says. Or does. No matter what her circumstances, it's unlikely she could understand you before she meets you. Maybe not even after she meets you. But no matter what she says, or how she acts, you'll be helping both of you piece together parts of your lives' puzzles."

Daria considered Katrina's counsel. "She didn't know she was adopted until just last year? That's what you said, right?"

Katrina nodded. "In some ways," she said, resting back in her chair, "that may make things more difficult. If she thought for over twenty years she was the Rushes' natural child, then found out otherwise, it would be normal for her to be conflicted. About them *and* you."

"I couldn't control what her adoptive parents did or didn't say."

"True." Katrina paused. "Just like you can't control Angela's feelings or reactions when you meet. The best thing is to try to accept her without expecting too much of her. Or yourself."

Chapter Twenty-Four
October 1992

A taxi rolled to a stop outside Grand Central. Daria grabbed the door handle and got in. "Tableau," she called as she scuttled into the back seat. Along with glasses thick enough to raise suspicions about his driving abilities, the cabbie wore a faded blue Yankees cap pulled tight over his head, forcing his cantankerous gray hair to spew around his ears. The remains of an unlit cigar dangled precariously from his mouth. "What's 'at?" He leaned into the corner between the seat and door, waiting, meter running.

"Tableau. Twenty-Fourth and Fifth," Daria clarified. "A block up from the Flatiron."

"Oh." The driver jolted the car from the curb. "Tahh-bloooww."

She wasn't sure whether his affected pronunciation was meant to swipe the restaurant's upscale clientele or her.

"Where the rich kids go."

Daria closed the plexiglass screen between her and the cabbie-comic. Muttering something about tight-assed rich broads, the driver lurched right from Vanderbilt onto Forty-Second Street, then left onto Fifth past the public library. Daria opened her purse and took out a twenty, folded it in quarters, unfolded it, folded it again. She picked a piece of lint from her navy pants, then brushed her matching coat's shoulders in case any dandruff had settled there. Why hadn't she worn the camel coat, the one that didn't show anything? She re-crossed her legs, tapping her foot against the front seat.

As the cab pulled up to Twenty-Fifth Street, a block before the restaurant, Daria handed the driver the twenty. Before he could reluctantly begin making change, she was already dodging traffic across Fifth. She paused when she reached what, before the area's redevelopment, had been the United Bank and Trust building. *Tableau* a little brass plaque read in modern type, right above a larger one telling how the landmark site had been converted into "a mixed-use residential, commercial, and lifestyle complex, complete with restaurant, shops, and gym, while maintaining the building's architectural integrity." Architectural integrity it may have, Daria thought. But the building—sleek and stark against the steely sky—struck her as cold. Too angular and sharp. What if her meeting with Angela proved the same?

After making her way through Tableau's glass double doors, she arrived at the severe, wedge-shaped pedestal that served as the reception desk. Waiting for the *maître d'*, she surveyed the dining room, its terra-cotta walls, the sleek banquettes, flanked by mirrors, covered in mustard- and moss-colored velvet. Dozens of skeletal women and well-chiseled men—most in their twenties and thirties, most dressed in black, hair glossy as cellophane—sat at the tables, either smiling too obviously, tossing back their heads to blow orchestrated smoke streams into the air, or leaning forward in their seats, utterly engaged in what they were saying and how they were saying it. "That's why," Sinatra sang in the background, "the lady is a tramp."

The boomerang-shaped bar, with calla lily deco light fixtures and smoky haze hanging over it, could have served as backdrop for Bogart and Bacall banter. Twenty years earlier, a place like this would have provided Daria the opportunity to meet people without getting to know them, a place to look good and feel nothing.

She spotted Angela, seated at the bar, exhaling a long, seahorse-shaped curl of cigarette smoke. She was lavishing the Kevin Costner-lookalike bartender with an exaggerated laugh in response to the apparent joke he had leaned close to tell. Her short black skirt was hiked up by her bar stool pose, showing off black fishnet stockings over her long, toned legs.

My legs, Daria thought. *Twenty years ago, those were my legs.*

Angela's black turtleneck fit snugly across her small, high breasts. Her purse, a squishy leather shoulder bag with a leopard print scarf tied around the strap, hung, along with her leather jacket, over the back of her chair. For no apparent reason, she turned from the bartender toward Daria.

Thinking Angela might have felt her gaze, Daria smiled tentatively and waved. But a waitress carrying a tray of salads passed in front of her, eclipsing her view of the bar and Angela. By the time Daria could see her daughter again, Angela's attention had shifted back to the bartender. Feeling invisible, passed over, Daria held her hand to her stomach. She wanted to wretch.

The *maître d'*, a slender young man in tight black pants, tailored black shirt, and tie matching the color of the restaurant's walls, swept into the reception area. "May I help you?"

She turned from him, looking around aimlessly. "The ladies' room?"

"Past the coat check to the left."

Daria hurried down the hallway where the young man pointed. When the bathroom door swung closed behind her, she fished through her purse for her lipstick, applying it with a heavy hand. She pulled out her mascara and twisted it open, pumping it a few times. When she leaned into the mirror to flutter the wand through her lashes, all she saw was fear. Doe-eyed fear. She swallowed hard, stuffed her makeup back into her purse, and headed for the door.

But when she reached it, she stopped. Should she just leave the restaurant? There was still time. Help. She needed help. She turned back to the mirror. No help there. What would Frankie tell her to do? Mary Catherine? Only one word came to her. Pray. But pray for what? *To what?* Frankie's Higher Power? Nana's Gabija? Mary Catherine's Holy Spirit? She closed her eyes. "Whoever you are," she whispered, "help me. Give me the right words. Please."

When her heartbeat slowed, she opened her eyes. She hoped for results but dared not expect them. She stood still, not wanting to move, even the slightest bit, so she didn't shake loose the calm she felt. But after a few moments, her breathing shallow, her heart pounded again. She'd asked for help, and she got it, no matter how fleeting. The memory of the momentary quiet stayed with her though. She could do this.

She opened the door and went back to the reception area. "All set?"

At the End of the Storm

As Daria nodded toward the *maître d'*, she saw Angela, now seated near the windows facing Fifth, and nodded toward the young man. "The reservation's in the name of Rush, I think," Daria said. "I see her over there." She motioned toward the banquette where Angela sat, hands wrapped around the base of the glass before her, eyes on the shoppers, the traffic, the Saturday pace of downtown New York.

"Right this way."

Daria followed until the young man stopped at Angela's table, motioning for Daria to sit opposite her daughter.

"Angela?"

The young woman looked up, expressionless. "Daria."

"Yes." Daria's legs wobbled. Should she reach down and hug her daughter? Extend her hand? She tried to reincarnate the confidence she'd felt minutes earlier. She could do this. She leaned slightly forward but checked herself when Angela remained stiff in her seat.

"Sorry I'm a little late." She slid into the banquette, taking in Angela's mouth, her jaw, her hands, all familiar to Daria. They resembled her own. She expected the young woman—her daughter—to seem softer up close than she had on stage. Instead, her eyes done in dark shadow and thick liner, her all-black clothes, barricaded her in an edgy, brittle shell. "It was tough getting a cab. A lot of people in town for matinees, I guess." Daria caught herself. It was barely past one and getting a taxi hadn't been difficult at all. There was no need to lie. "You don't perform on Saturdays?"

"Sundays," Angela said, "but not Saturdays." Her face remained unreadable as she reached for the glass in front of her and finished her Scotch.

"Something to drink?" the *maître d'* asked as he handed them menus.

"Another Dewar's," Angela said. "Rocks. With a twist."

"Pellegrino for me." Daria clutched the menu. "Nice place," she said as the *maître d'* walked away. When she realized her hands were shaking, she set the menu on the table. "It wasn't long ago this part of the City was a mess."

"You know the City pretty well?"

"I used to live here. In Manhattan, I mean. Upper East Side, though. When I was married. Before we moved to Connecticut."

"You're divorced?"

"Yes."

Angela rubbed out her cigarette in the ash tray. "Two kids? That's what you said in the letter."

"Yes. Two. Besides you, I mean. Jack and Lizzy."

A waitress, dressed like the *maître d'* in black pants and shirt, approached the table, carrying their drinks. "Dewar's?"

"That," Angela said, with considerably more ease than she was showing Daria, "would be mine."

"And the Pellegrino?" The waitress held it out toward Daria.

"Yes." Daria waited for the waitress to set down the glass. There was no way she would attempt to hold it. "Thanks."

"Would you like to hear today's specials?"

"I don't need to," said Angela with a New Yorker's insistent nonchalance. "I'll have the wasabi-crusted tuna."

"Sounds good." Daria handed over the menu without reading it. "I'll have the same."

"Salad with that?"

Angela nodded. "Balsamic vinaigrette."

"Why not," Daria said. "But no dressing for me. Just lemon on the side?"

"Sure."

When the waitress left the table, Daria unfolded the linen napkin at her place, smoothing it across her lap. She should take control. Just jump in. "You know from my note that I used to be an actress? Like you?"

Angela didn't respond.

"This might be easier," Daria said, attempting levity, "if we had a script?"

"Maybe." Angela lit another cigarette, then blew a stream of smoke sideways into the air. "Maybe not. Depends on what roles we'd be cast in, I guess."

"Good point." Daria wanted to reach across the table and take the cigarette from Angela's mouth. Didn't she know smoking would ruin her voice? Give her lines around her mouth?

But when she looked at this young stranger, the daughter she had held when she was hours old, she saw in Angela the same bitter crust she herself had served up to the world for many years. Damn it, where was that calm she felt in the ladies' room?

"I guess," she said, trying again, "I hoped the right words would just come out, but it doesn't seem to be working that way. For me anyway."

Angela drank from her glass of Scotch, saying nothing.

"Maybe you have questions. About me? About you?"

"All I have is questions." But she asked none.

"I'll do my best," Daria said, "to tell you anything you want to know."

The waitress returned, carrying two salads. "Vinaigrette?" Angela nodded and the waitress placed one plate in front of her. "Lemon on the side for you."

"Thank you," Daria said, lifting her fork. "You got my letter?" she asked, though she knew Angela had received her note.

Angela leaned back in her seat, ignoring her salad. "We wouldn't be here if I hadn't, would we?"

"You're right, we wouldn't." Daria placed her fork back on the table. "So, you know that I've wondered all these years where you were, how you were?"

"I know that's what you said."

"Well, it's true." Angela's armor was impenetrable. Of that, Daria was certain. Seeing she had nothing to lose, her confidence began to build again. "And you know I wish I could do things over, that there would be some way to take away whatever hurt I might have caused you?"

"What," Angela asked, cracking the door to possibility, "would you do differently?"

"Well, if I knew then what I know now, that there's no shame in being an unmarried mother, I might have been brave enough to find a way to keep you."

"You *might* have?" Angela tossed back her hair. "That doesn't sound very convincing. Not convincing at all." She turned her eyes from Daria to the bar. She waved to the bartender, who served up his leading-man smile in return.

"Maybe this would be easier," Daria said, finally hitting her stride, "if I told you things you wanted to hear, rather than the truth. But I can't say with total certainty what I would have done. Only that I might have done things differently. Based on what I know now."

Angela turned back to her. "What you know now? You keep saying that."

"What I mean is that my other daughter, Lizzy, she's sixteen, and she had a baby just a few weeks ago. When she went through her pregnancy, I saw how different things could be. Katrina—she's the woman from the Adoption Option where Lizzy went, the woman who found you for me —helped us all see that Lizzy's pregnancy might have been unplanned, but it didn't need to be the prison sentence it seemed to be back when I had you.

"I felt I needed to keep you a secret. I never even told my husband or other children about you because I thought I might upset our family's ballast, though it was already listing to port. And my mother—that would be your grandmother— never knew about you because she was—is—a devout Catholic. We weren't close to begin with, and I guess I thought if she knew she would be even more ashamed of me. All that means I lied to myself, always trying to cover up who I was. Always performing."

She reached for her Pellegrino, took a healthy sip, then continued. "When I was your age, I was a dancer too. A Rockette, if you can believe that. After I got married, though, I started working at WNYY, then got a job as co-host of a show. Maybe you heard of it? It was called *Wake Up Manhattan*."

"Oh, I heard of it all right," Angela said. "My mother," she hesitated, "is that what I'm still supposed to call her? Her name is Sally, or it was anyway. Thanks to cable, we started getting the New York channels up in Albany when I was a kid. Sally used to set up the ironing board in front of the television and watch, imagining what it would be like to get to dress up every day like a glamorous talk show host—like you."

"That would have been when? The early eighties?"

Angela shrugged. "Whenever it was, Sally would have settled for a seat in the audience. When you used to do audience interviews, she would set down her can of spray starch and answer questions as if you were talking to her. 'Someday, Angela,' she used to say, 'I bet I'll be watching you on TV.' Ironic, huh? That the woman I thought was my mother was fantasizing about my real mother?"

Daria averted her eyes, resisting the temptation to reach into her purse for a tissue to wipe down her daughter, to clean her up, soften her so she could break through to her. But Lizzy had used similar guerilla tactics. Hell, she herself had waged the same kind of warfare with the world. She knew what it was like to feel the amorphous anger Angela was spitting out. And, yes, now she understood what it was like to be its target.

"Angela," she started when she looked back, "it's a complicated situation. Of course, you're confused. And if you're angry, that's probably natural."

But Daria's attempt at empathy failed, and Angela's words took on a sharper edge. "Then she'd walk me to the school bus, remind me I had dance or piano lessons that afternoon. And with a smile on her face, go back into the house, starching and ironing her linen tablecloths and napkins. 'Someday Sally,' I used to call her. But we were talking about you." She lifted her glass to Daria, as if toasting her. "And here you are in the flesh."

When Angela said nothing more, Daria took a deep breath. Tired. She felt so tired. She began again. "Once we moved to Connecticut, I moved up the ranks of *Wake Up*. Ted and I—that's my husband, my former husband, I should say—we looked pretty good from a distance. He was a partner in his firm, and I was doing well at *Wake Up*. We had a picture-perfect house, belonged to the right clubs, had the requisite two children and three cars. Then Ted started getting sloppy about his affairs with other women. And his gambling debts. I got fired, ostensibly because the show needed what management called a fresh face. And the house that Daria and Ted built came tumbling down."

"And now?"

"Now I do a show out of Connecticut called *Awakenings*. I got the idea after Ted left. It's targeted to mature women who want to fill a spiritual void in their lives."

"A spiritual void?"

"A need that can't be met with club memberships or cars. We introduce women to everything from yoga to acupuncture to meditation."

Angela's left eyebrow raised suspiciously. "Astrology, numerology, snake oil?"

"Admittedly, it started that way. I mean with a little bit of snake oil. I had no alimony. I had two children to support."

Daria caught herself, imagining that by mentioning her other children Angela might feel dismissed. "This is all very awkward. Talking to you as if we've never met. And none of my work history feels important now. Except that, in honesty, by pouring myself into it, I tried to erase all the guilt and shame and remorse I didn't even know I felt for letting you go."

Angela's left eye twitched, but other than that, her body, her silence, betrayed nothing of her feelings.

Daria pushed away her plate, clasped her hands in her lap, and leaned forward. "I'd very much like to know more about you. Anything, anything at all." She tried to meet her daughter's eyes, but couldn't.

Angela was fixed on the mirror behind Daria, the one that reflected multiple images from all the other mirrors at various angles around the room. "I look like you, don't I?"

Daria nodded. "You do. Except for your eyes. They're your father's. Deep and brown and intense." For a moment, Daria remembered how she felt with Stefan, falling into those eyes, magnetized by his passion. For so long she wanted to paint a monochromatic, all-evil picture of him, just as she had wanted to with Ted. But she was learning, as much through the experience with Angela as with Lizzy, that the truth of any situation changed shape and color and texture, depending on a person's point of view. Just like the restaurant's mirrors reflected different light from different perspectives.

"Who was he?" There was no denying that now Angela's voice had softened. "My father, I mean."

Daria sipped her Pellegrino, set down her glass, clasped her hands atop the table. "I met him when I was in college. Back in the sixties. He was an anti-war activist, and I skirted around the movement, as we called it then. He was involved in other causes too. In Latin America, Czechoslovakia. That's where he was from. Czechoslovakia, I mean.

"He was also a photojournalist, and for a long time after he left me, I used to see his pictures in the *Times*. I haven't for a while, though. He seems to have vanished." She paused. "He's a priest too. At least he was when I knew him."

"A priest?" Angela's eyes narrowed. When Daria nodded, Angela tossed her head back and laughed. "A priest," she said again. "Can it get any more bizarre than that?"

"Not much," Daria admitted. Her hope for lasting detente had passed.

The waitress arrived, setting down their lunches. "You can take that." Daria pointed toward her salad plate, grateful for the interruption.

"Fresh ground pepper?" the waitress asked.

"I'm fine," Daria said.

"No." Angela leaned back in the banquette, oblivious to her meal, still eyeing her mother as if she were a museum piece, one that needed to be looked at from all angles to make sense of it.

Daria tried again to focus the conversation, as Katrina had advised, on Angela. "Did they treat you well?" When Daria heard the crack in her voice, the little fissure that seemed to her to loosen twenty-four years of regret, she turned away. She looked out the window, struggling to keep herself from feeling as if she were falling into a heap of rubble, like the pile of stones and dirt across the street, where a building was being demolished. "Your parents, I mean."

Angela hesitated.

I'm your mother, Daria wanted to plead when Angela didn't respond. *You can tell me anything. And if you can't tell me everything, just tell me something.*

"They treated me well," Angela began. "So well I could barely breathe. Anything I wanted, I got. Dance lessons, voice lessons, Barbie dolls, a swimming pool. Always poking a camera in my face, making videos and taking snapshots they forced on visitors, bank tellers, anyone polite or bored enough to give their attention. Quick to see I was the first of my friends to get a car, to go to Paris. And someday to land on Broadway. But someday never came for Sally. She died of breast cancer a year and a half ago, six months before I got my break."

"I'm sorry."

"You know." Angela breezed past Daria's condolences. "I always suspected I didn't belong. I know lots of kids fantasize about being adopted. But I knew.

"It wasn't just that I didn't look like them. Don, my father, was tall like me but wide in the waist and hips, with a big red Irish face. A golden retriever of a guy, always eager to make everyone happy. And Sally, well she was a little slip of a thing. Petite, blonde. Not this kind of blonde," she said, running a hand through her bleached hair, "but the real thing. If Don was a retriever, Sally was a hummingbird, always, and I mean always, hovering but in motion at the same time.

"They were so, I don't know, even, solid. Which I knew I would never be. Don was a CPA. Everything—the tools in his shed, the shaving gear in his medicine cabinet—always organized into neat compartments. And if there was a decision to make, he'd pull out one of those yellow legal pads, draw a line down the center. 'Let's put it down on paper, hon,' he'd say to Sally. 'Pluses and minuses.' If they were choosing between a vacation in the Outer Banks or California, there he'd be, comparing cost, travel time, climate. And the option with the most pluses won.

"Sally was the perfect little wife, hosting dinner parties of beef Wellington and cheesecake. Volunteering at the hospital. Baking cupcakes for school birthday parties and bake sales. You never would have guessed she graduated from Vassar.

"We lived in a four-bedroom colonial with a flawless lawn and symmetrical arborvitae guarding the front door. Everything trimmed and tidy in their little world. Except me, that is. First it was an occasional comment on my report card. *Bad attitude.* Then it was drinking too much at a party, which for them meant drinking at all. And while they thought acting and dancing were good outlets, they wanted me to branch out. Get a summer internship at a newspaper. Study French at least. Learn something *practical,* Don would say, to help me get into a good school. Fat chance. I had as much interest in college as I had in driving a bus.

"When Sally got cancer, all hell broke loose in their little world, but it wasn't more than four months after she died that old Don was engaged to his secretary, Lorelei. I never found the list he made of her positives and negatives, but I'd bet *River*'s box office net there was one. Anyway, Lorelei's impending move-in date gave me the perfect reason to come to the City and seek my fifteen minutes of fame."

"Well you've done that and then some," Daria said. "And I suspect you have a lot more success ahead of you."

Though Daria made her comment in all sincerity, Angela's eyes challenged her. When Daria didn't react, Angela continued. "After Sally died, I was going through her things, looking for the scrapbook she kept for me, thinking I should take it to New York. Clippings of my grade school dance recitals, high school shows, summer stock. Tucked in the same box as the scrapbook I found a notebook. One of those with the black-and-white-speckled cover. And on the line where *Subject* was printed, she had written in *Baby*. She started it after a couple miscarriages, when she and Don decided to adopt.

"There were notes about a couple adoptions that didn't work out. Under the heading *Chicago*, there were a plus column and a minus column, *a la* Don's Decision-Making Method. Plusses. Mother's health excellent. Minuses. Mother smoked marijuana during pregnancy. Then there was the page labeled *Local.* Sally's neat little cursive script got all raggedy when she got word from a doctor named Holcomb that you—she referred to you as "the girl"—were pregnant, in good health, smart, and pretty.

"So," she said, arching her eyebrows, tilting her head, "I found out why I always felt I didn't belong. Because I didn't. I was the product of one of Don's inventories, a couple of columns labeled pluses and minuses. He must've missed a couple of the minuses, huh?"

"Oh, I don't think that could be—"

Angela continued. "There were lists and more lists. What Sally needed to do to change one of the bedrooms into a nursery. Names for boys, names for girls. I was supposed to be called Margaret, by the way, after Sally's mother. But when Don first saw me and said I looked like an angel, they decided on Angela." She reached into her purse, still talking. "If they could have seen into the future," she posited with a laugh, pulling out her pack of cigarettes. "I guess they would have changed their minds."

You don't have to do this, Daria wanted to say. *You don't have to torture yourself with impossible standards and brutal, unwarranted criticism. I know how much you must hurt to need to do that to yourself.* "That must have been hard," she said instead. "Losing Sally, then finding out that way."

"Hard? That's one way to look at it. Another is to say it gave me an opportunity. Isn't that what we're told now? That we can start over whenever we want? Turn lemons into lemonade? Shapeshift just like that?" She snapped her fingers.

"Don was right, you know," Daria said.

"About what?"

"Angela's the perfect name for you. You really do dance like an angel."

"Angelic wasn't the effect I was going for." She shook a cigarette from her pack, then put it back. Her eyes fixed on Daria's, as if she dared not take them away, for fear the woman, the stranger, the mother before her might disappear.

"I guess that's not what I meant. You were seductive and sexy, and the choreography was torrid and the chemistry between you and . . . what was his name?"

"Robert."

"Robert. You and Robert could have lit up the Empire State Building with all the electricity you generated. But underneath you showed such grace and vulnerability. I could never do that the way you did."

"Well," Angela said, ignoring Daria's admission, "the show needed some sizzle, as Julian, the director, was fond of saying."

Daria kept going. "Remember from my note that I played Louise too?"

Angela nodded tentatively.

"I sang that song over and over when you were inside me. 'You'll Never Walk Alone,' I mean. I wanted both of us to believe that."

"Even though you knew you were going to toss me away? To strangers?" Angela took her napkin from her lap and lobbed it to the table, covering her untouched tuna.

"I wouldn't put it that way, but, yes, even though I knew I couldn't keep you."

"That's some way to tell a kid she'll never be alone. By giving her away."

"You're right." Daria paused, sitting with her admission. "And sadly, there's nothing I can do to change that."

"Did you ever see me? After I was born?"

Daria looked away, then back to Angela. "I wasn't supposed to. But I did." She leaned forward. "Angela, truthfully, once I knew I was pregnant and decided to surrender you, I thought the matter was taken care of. I made a decision and shut out the possibility of emotions. Any feelings whatsoever. Then I held you and something poured out of me I didn't think I'd be capable of. But I was told there was nothing I could do to change my decision. That turned out to be a lie, but I didn't know that." Her voice faltered. "I just hope you can forgive me."

"Forgive you?" Angela plucked the lemon twist from her Scotch, ran it around the rim of her glass, then dropped it back in. "What's to forgive?" She shrugged as if Daria had told her the sky was blue or daffodils were yellow. *No big deal.*

"What's to forgive?" Daria repeated the question. She searched her thoughts, trying to recall Katrina's counsel. No matter how Angela reacted when they met, her daughter would at least get a piece of her life that had been missing. Daria could only hope, beneath Angela's rancor and bulletproof shell, that was the case. She motioned to Angela's plate. "You're not hungry?"

Angela shook her head.

"Ready to leave?"

"I think so."

Daria caught the waitress's attention.

"Is something wrong with the tuna?"

"We're just not as hungry as we thought."

"Coffee then?"

Angela shook her head when Daria looked at her.

"No, thanks."

"Okay, I'll be right back with your check."

Daria reached into her purse and pulled out her wallet. She laid three twenties on the table. "Where," she asked, snapping her wallet shut, then putting it back in her purse, "do you live?"

"Upper West Side. I share a one-bedroom with another girl."

"How about we get a cab and you drop me off at Grand Central on your way home?"

Her daughter's eyes steadied on her, whether mining for guilt or searching for some word she wished her mother had spoken, Daria didn't know.

"I want to do some shopping in SoHo," Angela said. "I'll take the subway."

"Okay, then," Daria said, suspecting Angela's shopping would be done right there at Tableau, picking up that charmer behind the bar. "How do you want to leave things? Do you want to set up a time to get together again?"

"I don't know."

"I'd really like that," Daria said, "if you want."

"Well," Angela repeated, "I don't know if I would."

"Okay." Arms and legs and head aching from trying to construct a bridge that didn't want to get built, Daria acquiesced. "If you want to see me again," she said, fishing in her purse for a business card and pen, "here's how you can reach me." She turned over the card and wrote her home number and address, then handed it across the table. "I'll leave things up to you." She gathered her coat and purse.

"Isn't that what you've done for twenty-four years now?"

Daria paused, looked across the table. "Yes," she said. "I suppose that's true." She toyed with the possibility of trying one more time to find the right words to say but lacked the strength. "Well, I'm going to head out now. I wish you the best, no matter what you decide."

Angela's lips trembled slightly. But when Daria reached across the table to take her daughter's hand, Angela just looked down and bit her lower lip.

Daria left the table. She hugged her coat around her, hoping that if she wrapped herself tightly enough in it, she wouldn't shake.

By the time she reached the curb to hail a cab, a cold rain had begun to fall. She pulled up her collar, reached into her tote for her umbrella. But when she opened it, it folded in on itself. "Worthless piece of crap." After trying unsuccessfully to wrangle it back into its little nylon sleeve, Daria stuffed it in a curbside trash can. Her meeting with Angela had been as useless, and as badly mangled, as the flimsy umbrella.

******

"Damn," Frankie said when she heard Daria's voice. "I've been on pins and needles waitin' for you to call. How'd it go?"

"Not bad." Daria shook off her coat and walked to the couch. "If you compare it to sparring with Mike Tyson. That girl's got a mean left hook."

"Well," Frankie said, "at least she didn't KO your sense of humor. And don't shoot me when I say this, sugar. But did you really expect anything different?"

Daria sank into the down-filled sofa. She kicked off her shoes and propped her leaden legs on the coffee table. "I guess I hoped that because I wanted to work things out, maybe she would too."

"It's those expectations, hon. If they don't kill you, they're at least sure to disappoint. What's important, though, is that you showed up for her, you showed up for you. That took guts."

"Well," Daria said, "if courage is this exhausting, I can see why I've been a coward all these years. I need sleep."

"Night-night, darlin'."

"Good night, Frank. And thanks."

"What in the hell for? You did all the work."

Daria hung up, curled into the couch, and closed her eyes. What else should she have said to Angela? What if she never called? Worst of all, she felt—what was that word Frankie used when she talked about alcohol? Powerless. That's how she felt. She grabbed a pillow, held it close, and fell asleep, still wearing her navy pantsuit.

When she wakened, she glanced at the hallway clock, saw that it was going on ten, and stumbled up the stairs to bed.

Tossing her clothes onto her bedside chair, she crawled naked under the covers.

******

The following day, Daria woke groggy and achy. Sunlight was already intruding through the slanted blinds, which she hadn't had the energy to close the night before. She glanced at her bedside clock. A little after eight. She was late for work. Forcing herself out of bed, Daria ran to the bathroom and turned on the shower. When she saw herself in the vanity mirror, her face looked pummeled, her eyes swollen. "Angela," she said softly. "I'm so sorry."

Trying to ease out of her fatigue, she remembered it was Sunday, not Monday. She shuffled back to bed, pulled the covers close, and stayed there until noon.

Chapter Twenty-Five
December 1992

When Daria breezed into the Channel 77 conference room, John Fisher and Cynthia Stallworth were already seated at the table.

"I guess I'm a little late," she said, her pace slowing, her eyes shifting from John to Cynthia and back again. As far as she knew, she was supposed to meet only with John. So, when they both looked up from the binders they were reading through, wide-eyed as high school juniors caught cheating on their SATs, Daria's tone stiffened. "John," she said. "Cynthia."

"Come in, come in. Have a seat." John motioned to the chairs across the table.

Daria sat down, noticing the Christmas wreath that hung on the opposite wall. If she focused on its piney scent, maybe she could keep from reacting to whatever John and Cynthia were up to. And up to something they certainly appeared to be, given their solicitous smiles. But the wreath only reminded her how, in past years, by this time in December, her house would have been decorated as meticulously as Saks Fifth Avenue windows. All the presents—too many— would have been wrapped and under a full and fragrant blue spruce. This year, though, distracted by Lizzy, then Angela,

Daria hadn't bought even a single stocking stuffer, hadn't put up a tree, hadn't hung a single mistletoe sprig.

Frankie, no doubt, would call that spiritual progress, that Daria had been doing the right things rather than making sure things looked the right way. To Daria, her lack of preparation only meant that yet another aspect of her life was spinning out of control. Even before John started talking, Daria drifted back to that day in Gavin McGee's office when she realized her days at *Wake Up Manhattan* were numbered. She crossed, then uncrossed, then re-crossed her legs under the table.

"So," she asked, a plastic smile on her face, "why are we here?"

John cleared his throat. "I think you know, Daria, that a while back we conducted some focus groups. Not only here in Fairfield County, but all around the Tri-State, just to put our finger on the pulse of what's happening out there." He waved his hand toward the station conference room window as if "out there" were a nebulous place awaiting exploration by the next space shuttle. His thinning brown hair swept back in a brave but unsuccessful attempt at diminishing the glare from his shiny pate, John sat forward, swiveling his chair with abrupt, jerky movements. Daria wasn't the only one at the station to notice that since Cynthia Stallworth's arrival, he had traded his Dockers for low-slung designer jeans. Then came the open-necked shirts, and now the audacious gold bracelets that peeked out from his cuffs.

Daria reeled herself in. She heard Frankie in her head. *Now be nice, sugar.* It was just, she thought as she opened her leather portfolio, that John was such an easy mark. She dated the pad, December 15. Then she settled back into her chair, prepared to spend most of the meeting making lists: groceries to be bought, errands to be run, Christmas presents for the kids and Frankie. And Angela?

Daria was used to John's tedious analyses, his intermittent suggestions about the show. During the years they had worked together, she had learned to implement his recommendations for a week or two, then proceed on her merry way until three or so months passed and he called her back in his office for "just a few more suggestions."

Then again, John had taken a chance on Daria. If he hadn't, *Awakenings* might never have been launched, she might never have hosted a show again, or garnered the Emmys that led to *Awakenings'* syndication.

But Cynthia? With her bottle of diet iced tea in front of her, perched at the edge of her conference room chair, her hanky-sized skirt hiked up more than mid-thigh? Careful, Daria was tempted to caution. If you move too fast on that scratchy upholstery, you might get a brush burn and John might have to kiss it and make it all better.

"Focus groups?" Daria leaned back, her head tilted to feign sincerity. "Interesting," she said. "And just when were these focus groups conducted?"

"When was it, Cynthia? September?"

"That's right, John."

"September?" Daria said.

"Yes, yes. I sent a memo way back in, I think it was March," John said, casually shrugging his shoulders. "And when I didn't hear back from you, we proceeded as planned." He picked up his glasses from the table, then put one of the stems in his mouth and sucked on it like a socially acceptable midlife pacifier.

Focus groups. Daria vaguely recalled the memo she tossed aside the night after Lizzy announced her pregnancy and the supposedly urgent phone message disregarded the day she rushed off to see Katrina about Angela. She straightened her posture. "So," she said, her voice clipped, "when you say *we* conducted them, who might that be?"

John removed the tortoise shell pacifier from his mouth, set his glasses back on, and leaned forward, hands clasped on the table in front of him. "Actually, it wasn't *we* so much as Cynthia." He gave Cynthia a big smile. "In addition to her production experience, Cynthia has a marketing background, you know."

"Marketing?"

"Yes. In her previous life, so to speak."

Previous life? Before coming to *Awakenings* Cynthia had some sort of job with Lancôme. At Lord & Taylor. No, even worse, it was Macy's. Daria suspected the extent of her focus group work had been polling customers on whether they preferred Défincils or Amplicils mascara. "How fortunate."

"Indeed. Anyway," John continued, "Cynthia conducted the focus groups, and we wanted to share the results and see how we can parlay them into some ratings mojo."

He's screwing her, Daria decided. Now it all makes sense. The red Mustang he bought last month. And that Tumi duffel bag he swings over his shoulder when he steps out of his office at lunchtime, announcing louder than necessary to his secretary that he's off to the gym to "pump some iron, ha ha." Daria would bet any amount of money that the duffel sat on the Mustang's back seat while he downed a personal size pie, extra cheese, at Milo's, his favorite neighborhood haunt. And now this ratings mojo nonsense.

"We've got solid data now. With a little tweaking," he continued, "we think we can increase viewership by three, maybe as many as five points."

"Tweaking?" Daria bit the inside of her mouth. If she lunged across the table, which one would she strangle first? Cynthia, she decided. All it would take would be a little perfectly applied pressure, then one deft little snap, one tiny little *tweak*.

"That's right," John said. "But Cynthia's the expert. How about I turn things over to her?" He swiveled his chair and smiled again at Cynthia—whose intentionally furrowed brow reflected the situation's gravity—then motioned toward the binders on the table. But weren't his eyes lingering on that Barbie-doll-sized skirt?

"Thanks, John." Cynthia smiled. "That would be my pleasure."

Daria picked up the binder Cynthia eased across the table. *Suggested Enhancements to Increase Awakenings' Ratings.* Then, when Cynthia rose from her chair and sashayed to a flip chart at the front of the room, she shook her head. How could this stiletto-stomper be a friend of Mary Catherine's?

"If you'll turn," Cynthia said, tossing her blonde curls over her shoulders and picking up the fat red marker from the easel's lip, "to the executive summary, you'll see the highlights of the recommendations I gleaned from the focus groups." She paused. "That would be page three, Daria."

"Yes, thank you," Daria said, fumbling inside her bag for her glasses.

Cynthia turned over the top blank flip chart page to the next, which was neatly printed with the heading *Focus Group Results*. "I've copied the results here."

Cynthia waited while Daria found her way to page three, then, with a staccato wrist flick, put a check next to the first finding: seventy-seven percent of focus group participants thought the show needed a new logo.

Fine. A new look wouldn't be so bad.

"Seventy-nine percent," Cynthia went on, checking the next item, "think the set looks tired, that it could use a little updating."

If she ever gets sick of television work, Daria thought, Cynthia would make a fine realtor. She already had the lingo down: tired, updating. As for a new set, that wasn't such a bad idea either. *Awakenings'* moody mauve chairs and dais were a little tepid.

"Finding number three," Cynthia said, "is that instead of the show opening with the host—"

"That would be me?" Daria balked at Cynthia's impersonal reference to "the host," as if she were a commodity as easily replaced as those old chairs on the set. She leaned forward, her antennae up. Was she as interchangeable as *Awakenings'* logo? In as much need of updating? Daria's foot tapped fast and hard enough that her silk-covered mule flew off and landed halfway under the conference table. Too far to reach without looking obvious. She would need to wait.

"Why, of course," Cynthia paused, blinking and smiling. "Instead of the host being seated onstage when the show opens, eighty-seven percent think she should enter the studio from offstage, making contact with members of the studio audience as she does so. You know, shaking hands, waving."

"Sort of a Miss America thing," Daria offered. "Minus the crown." No doubt Cynthia, in her interview as a Miss Ohio finalist, had cited world peace as her *cause célèbre*. Next, Daria supposed, she'll suggest I wear a sash and tiara.

"An excellent comparison," Cynthia said, not skipping a beat. "But we—John and I, that is—think of it more as the Oprah Meets Jane Pauley Effect." She smiled, pointing the fat red marker in Daria's direction.

"And," Daria asked, "the Miss America routine's designed to do exactly what?"

"Well," John said, taking his glasses off again, this time folding them and unfolding them as he leaned across the table. "That's on page six of the report. But since you raised the issue." He looked to Cynthia. "I'll take it from here," he said. "What the study shows, Daria, is that the audience finds you just a tad . . ."—he scrunched his face and shrugged his shoulders—"well, remote."

"Remote?"

"Yes."

"Just a tad?"

"That's right. As much as your audience wants to walk and talk and dress like you, they don't necessarily want to behave like you. They want you to be more approachable. Somebody they can sit down with over coffee, even if their nails aren't manicured and they didn't just walk out of the salon."

What felt like a quick kick to the belly left Daria feeling undressed. She'd been found out. Not just by Frankie. Or Mary Catherine. Or Katrina. But now by John and Cynthia.

Even by her audience. If she couldn't hide on stage, was anywhere safe?

"Interesting."

"It is interesting," John said.

Daria sat back, watching the scene in front of her unfold like a foreign film without subtitles. She could see what was going on, but she couldn't quite grasp it.

"And it gives us just the opportunity we've needed," John continued. "Cynthia, why don't you move on again so Daria can see what we're after."

"If you want to follow along," Cynthia said, "you can turn to page eight now."

"Oh, I'm following just fine, thanks." When Daria looked up, there was the smile again, those perfectly aligned teeth that Cynthia's parents probably paid ten grand for.

"What the audience really warmed to was the idea of theme programming." Cynthia leaned forward as if leaking national security intelligence. "You know, not just a single show on a single topic, but a series of shows, maybe some guests with opposing, contradictory opinions. Something to turn up the heat."

"Theme shows?" There was the parrot again. Daria want a cracker?

John smiled and nodded, smiled and nodded.

"Like theme parks?" Daria asked. "Disney on Parade, maybe?"

"Good one, Daria." John chuckled, but his smile quickly faded. "Cynthia," he said, "let's move on."

"Of course." Cynthia turned the page over and made another big red check on her chart. "The most telling finding is that over ninety percent—ninety-one point five, to be exact —favored introduction of a regular guest host."

"Not a co-host, you understand," John interjected. He splayed his fingers on the table. "A fresh face. More of an assistant, really."

Fresh face. Hadn't Daria heard that term right before she was shuffled off *Wake Up*? "I'm going out on a limb here— but maybe this fresh face would sort of nudge me off camera now and again? Just a tad, I mean," Daria said, borrowing one of John's favorite expressions. Where on earth had that little word come from anyway?

"That's a legitimate point, Daria," Cynthia said. "What we're thinking is—"

But John jumped in. "If you turn to page eleven, appendix C, Daria, you'll see that, while a guest host would decrease your on-camera time by approximately three percent, we'll have the potential to boost ratings by almost five percent. And, Daria," he said, as gravely as a surgeon recommending a liver transplant, "we need those points. When *Awakenings* started, you were the only game in town. But the competition's caught up and that means . . ."

"I get it, John." She pursed her lips. "Just curious, any suggestions for who that guest host might be?"

"We are so fortunate," John said, smiling in Cynthia's direction, "that Cynthia, in addition to her marketing and production background, also has on-camera experience. When she was at XXI in Cleveland, she hosted a show on people and their pets that developed a very respectable viewership of . . ."

Daria sat back, grabbing the table edge to offset the feeling that she was sliding down an icy slope. She had been so involved in Lizzy and Angela the last months that she had committed a cardinal career sin: she had rested on her laurels. She would figure a way out of this, but for now she would just have to play along. "And when will we decide on these recommendations?"

"Actually, Daria—"

"They've already been agreed on?"

John reached into the briefcase that rested at the base of his chair. "Cynthia did a pilot interview a couple weeks ago. With a guy called . . . who was he again, Cynthia?"

As John stood and got ready to pop Cynthia's pilot tape into the nearby VCR, Daria considered excusing herself. But, damn it, she would have to crawl under the table and rescue her shoe. She just needed to sit and listen.

******

Daria grabbed the front hallway phone and dialed. She turned her face left and right in the hallway mirror while she waited for Frankie to pick up. Her eyes weren't bad, not bad at all, but her neck? Clearly the firming treatments with her dermatologist weren't working any more. And her breasts? When had they migrated so far south?

"Who's that surgeon who did your breasts?"

"Rheingold," Frankie answered. "And hello to you too. That was years ago. Before I knew better. Why you askin'?"

"Because I've apparently got a shelf life, and I just passed the expiration date." Daria turned and checked her full-length reflection. "Don't you hate a flat ass?"

"Oh, I don't know," Frankie said laconically. "I guess I used to worry about that sort of thing, but—"

"Not another word," Daria interrupted. "You're only saying that because you had your breasts done before you got religion. If you're going to offer me some platitude about age being a state of mind, I'm going to vomit. Besides, I'm already hitting ten out of ten on the resent-o-meter, and I don't want you pushing me into the red zone."

"Okay," Frankie said. "I'm having a little trouble piecin' this quilt together here, Dar. You're resentful because . . ."

"Because that sniveling little Cynthia's after my job, that's why."

"I see. Now do me a favor and catch your breath, then take it from the top."

After Daria briefed Frankie on that day's meeting, embellishing her recollection of what she called *The John and Cynthia Show*, Frankie laughed until Daria suspected tears were rolling down her friend's face.

"Okay," Daria said, "now I'm really pissed. What's so funny?"

"It's just that you're still livin' under the illusion of control, darlin'. As if you can keep things from happenin' the way they're supposed to happen.

"You've come so far, Daria. You're so beyond this. Besides, remember the days when *you* were a kiss-ass? It wasn't so long ago you were toleratin' John's interest so you could get *Awakenings* up and runnin'. Granted you never slept with him, but you're not sure Cynthia's doin' him either.

"And what about that station manager at WNYY. What was his name?"

"Vince."

"Remember that dreadful birthday party you threw for him? Strippers and all?"

In spite of herself, Daria laughed too. "That was a god-awful night, wasn't it?"

"Yes, it was. And, Dar?"

"What?"

"Let me remind you how, just a few months ago, your world seemed so dark you couldn't laugh about anything."

"Things were looking a little grim, weren't they?"

"That's an understatement, darlin'. If somethin' like this happened six, nine months ago, you'd have been callin' me from a cell—either one in jail because you got arrested for murder or from a padded one in Connecticut State Hospital.

"Now, honey, let's look at the facts. "You've had a helluva run in that job, haven't you? I mean, you built that show from nothin'. You won awards, you supported your kids all on your own, did a terrific job with Lizzy. You're workin' your way through the situation with Angela. Besides, if I'm not mistaken, your contract runs well into next year. Am I right or wrong?"

"You're right. On all counts."

"So, the worst that can happen, if you decide you want out or if the station doesn't want to renew, is that you've got over six months for your next opportunity to come along."

"But . . ." Daria hesitated.

"But what?

"I'm older now."

"Yes, you are, sugar. And wiser. Nobody, but nobody, knows how to survive—no, thrive—like you do, Dar.

"Can I ask you a question? And it's not somethin' you need to answer now. Nor, I might add, is it somethin' I'm grantin' you permission to bite my head off for askin'."

"And if I say no?"

"I'm gonna ask anyway."

"You've got thirty seconds. But if you give me some cock and bull about silver linings . . ."

"Okay, I know you're gonna cut me off, so I'm gonna cut you off first and spit out what I have to say. Have you ever thought it might be time for you to move on? That maybe it's time to actually live the spiritual life you've been talkin' about on *Awakenings* these past five years?"

"Damn it, Frank."

Chapter Twenty-Six
March 1993

While Daria waited for Mary Catherine to come to the phone, she opened the cupboard beneath the sink. She took out a bottle of Windex and a roll of paper towels. With a vigorous hand, she wiped down the kitchen window her cleaning lady had done a decent job on the day before. But Daria was feeling uncomfortable, as Frankie would say, and when Daria felt uncomfortable, decent wasn't good enough. Her first instinct still was to do something, show results. There. Now she had a better view of the six or so inches of snow—a lot for March—that had blanketed the yard the night before.

She wished for a second she could run out and throw herself down in it, making snow angels, abandoning adulthood for a retreat into childhood bliss. She was happy there for a while, wasn't she? Before the fighting started? When Nana was still alive?

"I don't know if you remember me." Daria snapped back to the present when Mary Catherine picked up. "You were a guest on *Awakenings* a few months back."

"Of course, I remember, Daria. How are you?"

There was that calm, steady voice. "I'm well, thank you." She hesitated. "I'm wondering if I could come see you?"

"You're working on another show?"

"No. Well, maybe."

"Afternoons are good. Before evening prayer. Say around four next Tuesday?"

******

Daria noted the mailbox numbers along the road's edge. Eighteen ninety-seven. Nineteen thirty-three. Healing House would be coming up on her left. She hit the brakes, slowing so quickly that the BMW behind her, horn blaring, loomed suddenly on her bumper. In her rearview mirror, she saw the driver, face twisted with road rage, spitting invectives.

She prepared to return his verbal assault. But when she saw the simple sign marking the Healing House entrance, she swallowed the temptation. Without signaling, she steered sharp left and entered the dirt road just past the sign.

The narrow, hard-packed drive forced Daria to a crawl. Up ahead, a two-story, yellow clapboard farmhouse sat on a snow-covered hill. Cozy looking enough, but a bit ramshackle, more like a down-on-its-luck bed and breakfast than a place called Healing House.

On the right, a stand of pines. To the left, a frozen pond. Because the drive curved behind her, the main road was no longer visible in her rearview mirror. Not another car or person in sight. She lowered her car window. Quiet. It was so quiet. No traffic sounds. Nothing.

At the driveway's end, the land leveled where the house sat above the pond. She pulled her car into the parking area, which was little more than a patch of matted earth shoveled free of snow. It was a few minutes before four. She looked at the garden, barren except for the arborvitae that formed a semi-circle behind the sculpture at its center. Three figures, arms reaching toward heaven. Were they asking? Or receiving? No time to speculate. She needed to organize her thoughts.

******

The previous week Cynthia had started her Prayer Power series. Daria had to hand it to Cynthia. She was a fox terrier of an interviewer. She sank her teeth in and hung on, keeping her guest from wandering off topic. And, damn it, the camera loved her.

A few days later, *Awakenings'* next six-month preview crossed Daria's desk. The series' second segment would feature a physician who, in researching alternative treatment modalities, found that heart patients recovered faster when they were prayed for. Even by strangers. Even at a distance. And even if they didn't know about those efforts on their behalf.

Daria had to roll her eyes. She was willing to concede to a psychological boost if a loving mother or devoted spouse said a few Our Fathers or clicked rosary beads bedside. But strangers? Praying in a chapel or at home? Nuh-uh.

Then Daria opened the attached media kit. "Thayer Townsend," the bio stated, "received his BS from MacMillan University and his medical degree from Yale. After practicing psychiatry in New York for over twenty years, he recently founded the Department of Integrative Medicine at MacMillan University. His latest book is published by . . ."

It couldn't be. But when Daria turned over the enclosed book, there was Thayer's—T.J.'s—photo. She traced with her finger the lines that had formed around his eyes, the silver gray that threaded through his still-wavy hair, swept back from his brow, curling slightly at his collar.

When she had been living in Manhattan—a few years after he had dropped her off at the Stanton bus station on her way back to MacMillan—she had read his marriage announcement in the Sunday *Times*. He had married well, to the daughter of a Goldman director. Daria had tossed aside the newspaper, glad that New York was an anonymous place where she could live for years without running into him, even if he lived a few blocks away. A place where she could forget.

She took off her glasses and set them on her desk. The trouble was, she hadn't forgotten. She had just been consumed by other things, other people. *Wake Up. Awakenings*. Lizzy. Angela. Frankie and then Katrina had helped navigate Daria through those landmines. And they could probably help her prepare to meet T.J.—Thayer. But Mary Catherine came to mind instead.

******

Mary Catherine greeted Daria with a smile. "Did you have time to see the garden?"

"I did."

"It doesn't look like much now. Not like it will in April or May. But sometimes we can learn as much from barrenness as from abundance, can't we?"

Daria gave an agreeable little smile, though she wasn't convinced. Abundance—too many things and too much to do —that's what kept her sane. Barrenness, on the other hand, sounded way too ill-defined a place to venture.

Mary Catherine led Daria through the entryway, bordered by built-in bookcases stocked with as many books on art, music, and literature—Botticelli and Velazquez, Mozart and Bach, Hopkins and O'Connor—as on religion and spirituality.

"Careful," Mary Catherine said as they worked their way around stacked cartons and a bin full of mailing tape, bubble wrap, and black markers. "We're doing some packing."

They passed through the room that served, Mary Catherine explained, as the chapel. The space was only large enough to hold the simple altar—with its two candles and a crucifix—and a dozen or so folding chairs, each as carefully arranged as the china settings Frankie and Daria used to place on dinner party tables. But here there were no party favors, no meticulously constructed centerpieces. And the unadorned, cream-colored walls? They struck her as a little stark. Disarming, even.

"Have a seat." When they reached an alcove off the chapel, Mary Catherine motioned to a pair of armchairs in fading tweed, positioned in front of French doors overlooking the pond.

"You know," Daria said tentatively as she took off her coat, "when I drove into the driveway, it was so quiet. As if I were a hundred miles instead of a hundred yards from Hanniford."

Mary Catherine nodded as she sat down. "We're always happy when visitors connect to this place—the spirit in and around it—the way we do."

She reached to the table next to her chair and lit the candle that was there. "That's why we light a candle," she said, "when we come together to tell our stories. And sit for a few minutes in silence. To remind us we're in the presence of that spirit."

Daria nodded as if she understood. When Mary Catherine closed her eyes, Daria did the same. She waited. She felt nothing. Her eyes fluttered open. She tapped her foot, then closed her eyes again. Still nothing.

"So, what brings you here today?"

When Mary Catherine spoke—finally—Daria considered asking her to do another show. Or saying she wanted input for a book she wasn't really writing. Anything except the truth. That she just wanted to talk. And that she wanted answers, even if she wasn't exactly sure of the questions.

But unlike during Mary Catherine's *Awakenings* appearance—when words first escaped her, then hobbled out cautiously—this time they tumbled out freely. Like preschoolers on exercise mats. Not at all self-conscious. Unable to be restrained.

She told her story from its beginning to that day. The places. The experiences. The voices of those who had shaped, wounded, encouraged her.

Mount Laurel.

Her mother. *"More shame we don't need." "Hail Mary, full of grace."*

Her father. *"You got ice water in those veins a yours, and by God Almighty, that's all you need in life, Dairee Darlin'."*

Nana. *"The Laumės, Čiūčia liūlia. Forgotten child."* *"Dance for Nana. Sing stars and moon song of Ausrine, morning star."*

Sister Agatha Rose. *"Witchcraft is a sin. There is only one God." "Let's pray that God will forgive Daria for telling her story."*

MacMillan.

T.J. *"The tent's bigger than you think." "You're perfect just the way you are."*

Stefan. *"I came to bring division, mother against daughter and daughter against mother." "Don't think you can weasel out of your responsibility. It's one thing to not know the truth. It's another to hear it and not respond to it."*

Sound Shore.

Lizzy. *"I'm pregnant."*

Frankie. *"My higher power? It's not really somethin' I can put into words, sugar. It's like someone's always lookin' out for me. Knowin' what's better for me than I know for myself." "You have a choice."*

Jack. *"Even when things hurt, they're part of a bigger plan. If I'm patient, I can look back and see how the pieces fit together."*

Hanniford.

Katrina. The cross around her neck. *"I haven't given up hope."*

New York.

Angela. *"My father's a priest?" "That's some way to tell a kid she'll never be alone. By giving her away."*

"I'm sorry." Daria sat back. "I didn't expect to unload all that." A child again. That's how she felt. Ready for whatever punishment she would receive for telling too much.

Mary Catherine was slow to speak. "You've lived such a richly textured life."

No punishment. No judgment.

"And now you're here. At Healing House. With all these experiences and voices and apparent contradictions. A priest —someone who helped so many and preached responsibility, but who abandoned you. A mother whose religion maybe got in the way of her spirituality. A loving grandmother whose teachings contradicted those of the church in which you were raised. A friend who made a life-altering turnaround with the help of a power she can't quite define for you. A woman who helped you find your daughter, a woman of faith, who keeps hope alive through her connection to the cross. And your son, who's found a home in the church you left behind.

"And maybe you're wondering, at this point, out of all those people, who's right, who's got *the* answer?"

"I guess so. Yes."

Mary Catherine looked from Daria to the lit candle. "That's something I can't answer for you. Not without assuming I know best for you. I don't."

Then why did I bother? Why did I expose myself the way I just did if you can't help? Daria fought the urge to grab her coat and run out the door, back into the world that clamored for action, for results. Not like this place, where the pace and process crawled. Talk. Listen. Wait. Talk. Listen. Wait.

"But I do know," Mary Catherine said, "that each of those people, places, and experiences you described?"

Daria nodded.

"They all informed and shaped you, then led you here, to Healing House." She tucked her legs under her on her chair. "I'm curious. What specifically brought you here today? Why now?"

"It turns out T.J.—Thayer he goes by—now heads the Integrative Medicine Department at the college we went to. He's been researching how prayer helps people heal. Physically, I mean. And not knowing that he and I have history, Cynthia booked him for a show."

Daria sat back. "In a way, seeing him seems more challenging than all the other things I told you about. Not just because I treated him badly. But . . . well, I guess I'm not sure."

"So, you want support for when you see him again?"

"Umm-hmm."

"But you could have gotten that from Frankie, right? Or even Katrina."

"I guess."

"So, I ask again, why here? What are you looking for here that's different from what you might get from your friends?"

"When you were on the show," Daria said, feeling pressed, "you talked about mirroring light, one woman to another. I wasn't sure exactly how that's different from talking to Frankie, with her higher power, or Katrina, with her cross around her neck.

"But I wanted to know because—this sounds so shallow—I wanted to experience the way your eyes looked when you talked about it, the way your skin, your face . . . You just looked certain, peaceful even, when you talked about the abuse. I wanted to know how you got that look, so I could have it too."

"I'm not sure I see it as shallow," Mary Catherine said, "but rather, the next step. Even if you came here for what seemed like a superficial reason—maybe because you wanted a certain look in your eye, a certain clarity on your face or in your thinking—you were seeking, searching.

"The difference is that we come together here, in the presence of the Holy Spirit." She motioned toward the candle. "So, while Frankie has her higher power, it's hers, not yours. And Katrina, she relies on her experience of the Holy

Spirit in her life. But she works in a secular organization, where she can't openly discuss that relationship.

"Here we tell our stories—openly, unabashedly. We ask for information, for guidance from the Holy Spirit. We wait. And when, we receive it, we mirror it back so others can do the same. Eventually the waiting becomes easier and the light becomes brighter. And that's maybe what you see in me —the benefits of having had that light reflected to me for a long, long time. It's important to remember, though, that even during the abuse I experienced, even in the subsequent rage, I had faith. I knew I was protected. And, as a result, I have that certainty, as you call it, to offer other women."

Mary Catherine looked at the candle, then turned her eyes back to Daria. "Remember how, on your show, we talked about how *Awakenings* came to be? All those circumstances that came together, just at the right time?"

"I remember," Daria said. "But when I look back, all I see is chaos."

"Maybe your experiences seemed chaotic, possibly unfair. But, from a worldly perspective, you not only survived, you thrived. So, maybe there was a protector, a provider at work, even though you didn't feel like there was? And now that all those other challenges are out of the way, maybe now is the right time for Thayer to appear—reappear? We don't know what might happen when you see him. But maybe the time is right, whatever the result.

"What do you hear in your prayer life about T.J.? Or do you pray?"

Daria shook her head. "Not since I was a kid really. I mean the only time I recall praying—if you can call it that—is right before I met Angela. In the ladies' room at the restaurant of all places. All I said was 'Help me.' But I didn't know who or what I was speaking to."

"What happened then? Did you get help?"

"I did. For a little while, anyway. I felt calmer, stronger. Then Angela came at me with both barrels, and all I could do was sit there, let her attack, and try to keep the door open if she wanted to get together in the future."

"Well, you could have just gotten angry yourself, or you could have gotten frustrated and stormed out, right?"

"Yes."

"But you stayed. And did you come away thinking it was ice water in your veins that kept you there?"

Daria sat back. "It didn't really feel like that, no."

Mary Catherine reached for the Bible on the table next to her. "Another woman's story comes to mind." She flipped through, close to the end of the book. "It's from the Gospel of John. You know about the Magdalene?"

"The prostitute?"

"Well, the way I—and some others—read scripture, it's not clear she was a prostitute. But that's a topic for another discussion. What we know for sure is that demons were cast from her, that she was a devoted follower of Christ, and that she gave of her resources to support His ministry. "So, after He died and was taken to His tomb—can you imagine how bereft she felt?"

From the time she was a child, Bible stories had seemed impenetrable and distant. Daria had never considered, was never taught, that she might place herself in the middle of them, that she might see and feel, or at least imagine, what the people—yes, they were people—in them saw and felt. "She must have been heartbroken."

"That's what I imagine too. So, she went to find Him. But He wasn't there."

"And now she's desperate, maybe?"

"Desperate," Mary Catherine said. "Disconsolate. So, she asks the gardener. A stranger, she thinks. Where have they taken Him? Only instead of answering the question, the gardener calls her name, Mary, as if he knows her. And when she turns, she sees it isn't the gardener after all, but Jesus. He had been there all along, walking with her in her suffering. She just didn't see Him until she heard His voice and turned to Him."

Daria looked from Mary Catherine out to the pond. She felt safe in this place called Healing House, safe enough to tell her story to someone she barely knew. But no one had called her name. No one had whispered, "this is the right thing to do." So how the Magdalene's story, or the Holy Spirit, was supposed to help her face T.J., she wasn't at all clear. Still, tears came to her eyes when she turned back to Mary Catherine.

"It must have been awful for her to lose Him," she said. She didn't need Mary Catherine to point out the lesson she had just learned. She had listened to another woman's story, placed herself in it, felt what another woman might have felt. And during that time her own needs and concerns didn't press so hard on her.

"It's called compassion," Mary Catherine said. "It's how we all learn and grow. Together."

******

On the way out, Mary Catherine introduced Daria to three younger women who were packing books from the reception area shelves.

"We're moving." Mary Catherine lifted one of the packed cartons and stacked it near the door.

"Here, let me help," Daria said as she added a carton to the pile. "Where to?"

"We don't exactly know."

"You don't know?"

"The diocese used to help us when we first opened," Mary Catherine said. "But what we do here—like you pointed out on your show—doesn't quite mesh with some Church teachings. Our patrons are generous, and our workshops and retreats raise a good bit, but not enough to afford the property on our own."

Daria looked back to the women, organizing, labeling, packing, while leafing through any book that caught their attention. Even if they seemed at peace with their uncertain future, she wasn't. "There's nothing you can do to stay here? I mean it seems so . . ."

Mary Catherine tilted her head. "Unfair?"

"Yes, I guess so."

"We did what we could to save Healing House. But we came up short. Now it's time to let go." Mary Catherine smiled. "We're not giving up. We're just choosing to see what unfolds."

"And in the meantime?"

"In the meantime, we pack up and we wait."

Chapter Twenty-Seven
March 1993

Daria paused at the green room door. She dusted off the jacket to her favorite black pantsuit, tidied the collar on her silk blouse, then reached for the doorknob. Whatever was going to happen would happen. Whether that was Frankie's influence, Katrina's, or Mary Catherine's, Daria wasn't sure.

When she walked in, T.J. was seated with his back to her. Cynthia, brows knitted to convey rapt attention, waited an extra beat before shifting her focus from their guest to Daria. "Why Daria," she said. "What a pleasure. Come meet Thayer. Dr. Townsend, I should say."

T.J. swiveled his leather chair around to Daria. He rose and smiled, folding his hands in front of him. She started toward him. How long had it been since they had trekked the MacMillan campus hills, downed a few too many Budweisers at the Rathskeller, rehearsed and rehearsed and rehearsed that scene from *Carousel*? And, finally, awaited Angela's birth? More than twenty years. But it took her only a few seconds, a few steps, to travel back to him.

He reached for both her hands. "Daria."

"T.J. Or should I say Thayer?"

"We're all grown up now," he said. "But I'm still T.J. to my friends."

Cynthia rose from her chair, smoothed the wrinkles from her knit dress. "Well, my word. It looks as if no introduction is necessary."

Daria took a step back from T.J., but he held onto her hands. "As a matter of fact," he said. "We met years ago. It's been a long time."

"Why, how fortuitous."

"Indeed." When his smile widened, Daria's eyes drifted to his left hand. No ring.

"And," Cynthia said, "how unexpected. I wasn't aware—"

Daria pulled her hands from T.J.'s, checked her watch, and interrupted. "We're due on set in a couple minutes. If you're free," she said to T.J., "we can catch up afterwards."

"Terrific idea," Cynthia said. "I took the liberty of making a reservation at Nona's. I'm sure they can find a table for three instead of two."

"My pleasure." T.J.'s eyes finally left Daria's. He turned to Cynthia. "Daria and I have a few years to catch up on. We wouldn't want to bore you."

Still the gentleman, Daria thought, and still quite capable of directing a scene to his liking.

"So," T.J. continued, "how about she and I keep that table for two and the three of us get together next time?"

"Why, of course." Cynthia's smile weakened. "Well, one show at a time, as they say." She checked her watch. "You're on in five, okey doke?" She winked and left the room.

Where to start? This wasn't the time to apologize or to reminisce, though she wanted to do both. "You look well."

"As do you."

Cocktail niceties. Cardboard and unrevealing. She crossed her arms, when what she wanted to do was nestle close to him, listen to his heartbeat while he stroked her hair and assured her—like he used to—that everything would be just fine. But everything wasn't fine. She didn't need him to tell her that.

"This was a surprise." More cocktail party patter. "Seeing that you were booked for the show."

"I'm on a book tour. When my agent asked if I wanted to do this on my way to New Haven, it seemed, oh, a little too coincidental to be a coincidence. After all these years, I mean."

Todd, the production assistant, knocked on the door and ducked his head in. "You're on, Daria."

"You ready?"

"I've been ready," T.J. whispered, "for almost twenty-five years."

******

As she did every day now that the show had been reformatted, Daria stood at the studio's rear doors, waiting for her cue. "Daria," the technical director alerted her, "you're live in three, two, one." She entered the studio, clasping or shaking hands with a few audience members on the aisle, waving to others.

She usually abhorred this part of the show. But today she energetically made her way to Cynthia's newly designed stage. Done in lively Caribbean blues and greens, flattering to both Daria and Cynthia.

"Welcome," she said as she took her seat and the camera zoomed in. "Our guest today is Dr. Thayer Townsend, noted psychiatrist and head of the new department of integrative medicine at MacMillan University. He's also written this new book." She reached to the coffee table. "In it, Dr. Townsend shares some remarkable findings from his research on how a patient's spiritual life can affect recovery from illness. Please help me welcome Dr. Thayer Townsend."

When T.J. reached the dais, they shook hands. Then they relaxed into their chairs and casual conversation.

"Your research has yielded some rather astounding results," Daria said. "What would you say is the most important—or surprising—finding?"

As T.J. answered, Daria asked herself different questions. What would life have been like if I'd married you instead of Ted? What might have happened with Angela? Do you know I was more afraid of someone good, someone like you who wouldn't let me down, than of someone who treated me badly?

The interview was scheduled to take twenty minutes, followed by audience questions. But after only fifteen minutes, Daria turned to the audience. "I'm sure a lot of you have questions to ask or experiences to share," she said. "Cynthia, let's get the mic over to the woman in the third row."

As Cynthia worked her way through the audience, Daria turned toward T.J., content to sit back and listen to her friend answer whatever questions he might be asked.

******

"I admit I was skeptical." Daria removed her mic. "I mean, I could imagine how there might be some sort of psychological boost if someone knew he was being prayed for, but . . ."

"You were wonderful."

This was how it used to be. T.J. always seeing the best in her. Maybe this time she wouldn't push him away. "Thank you."

"Terrific job!" As Daria and T.J. rose from their chairs, Cynthia rushed over and wedged herself between them. "You were awesome, Dr. Townsend. Just awesome. Not one single dry eye in the studio—backstage, too—when you told how that six-year-old got cured of cancer."

"Your prep helped a good deal." T.J. shook Cynthia's offered hand but turned again to Daria. "I've done enough of these things, though, to know it's the interviewer who makes or breaks a show."

"That's one of the reasons the audience found you so very engaging," Cynthia said, overlooking his focus on Daria. "You're so modest. Willing to share the credit for all the remarkable work you've done."

"Well, I guess that's part of the message, isn't it? That a force greater than ourselves is at work. And," he said, still looking at Daria, "if we get out of its way, remarkable things can happen."

"How very true. Now I know you two have lots to catch up on, but I hope, after lunch, you and I can spend a few secs figuring out when you can come back. I just know we'll get deluged with requests."

"I would love to, Cynthia. Really, I would. But I'm a scatterbrain with dates, times. Give my PR guy a call. Mike Lombardo. His number's in my advance package."

"Why, I'll be sure to do that. Now, you two go on ahead and have a real nice reunion. After all, a lot can happen in ten, fifteen years." She winked over her shoulder at Daria.

"Good, good." T.J. smiled but turned back to Daria. "I've got to check in with my secretary. Can I use your phone?"

******

Daria closed her office door behind them. "Pretty presumptuous to assume I'd be available for lunch. Even for an awesome, engaging guest like you."

"If I had to, I would have told that woman I had an appointment with the president. She's one tenacious assistant."

"Tenacious is a very kind descriptor. Just don't make the mistake of calling her an assistant to her face. She's now a guest host." Daria stood on her tiptoes to imitate Cynthia on stilettos.

"You're evil, you know that?" T.J. took the chair opposite Daria's desk.

"Old habits die hard." She picked up her phone, pressed the button for an outside line, and held it in his direction. "You wanted to call your secretary?"

He shook his head. "Another ruse. But if you're really free for lunch, I'd like that. Miss Broadcast News said she made a reservation?"

"Well, Doctor Townsend, you're a lucky man." Daria hung up the phone. "I just happen to be available. But where we're going, we won't need a reservation."

******

When Daria and T.J. walked into Mai Lan's at the Sound Shore marina, a diminutive woman of around sixty ran to meet them, batting the menus she carried in greeting.

"Miss Daria, too long! Miss Frankie we see, yes. But you? No. Mad at Mai Lan?"

"Mad at Mai Lan? Impossible. I've just been—"

"Who's this?"

"Oh, sorry." Daria turned to T.J. "This is Thayer, Thayer Townsend. But his friends call him T.J."

When T.J. held out his hand, Mai Lan took it in hers. "Mr. T.J." Then she leaned toward Daria as if imparting a secret she hoped would be overheard. "Very handsome."

Daria looked T.J. up and down. "Not bad."

Mai Lan bowed as she laughed. "Mr. T.J., how lucky you know Miss Daria long time."

"Yes, I am."

"You see, I watch Miss Daria every day. On kitchen television. But I tell you," she said, her tone again conspiratorial, "that yellow-haired girl?"

"Cynthia?"

"Yes, yes. Cynthia. I smell trouble."

"She does like the spotlight."

"No one fool Mai Lan." She tapped her temple before leading them to a table near the back window. "Now, sit, sit." She called to a young server who was hustling from the kitchen with an order for a table near the front door. "Make extra special nice lunch for Miss Daria," she ordered, before turning back to Daria, smiling. "Crab," she said. "Very nice today." Then she scurried off, waving her menus toward the front door. "Mr. David," she called to her next patron. "Long time! Mad at Mai Lan?"

Daria looked after their hostess as she dashed away. "She's something, isn't she?"

"Yes, she is."

But when Daria turned back to the table, T.J.'s eyes were on her, not Mai Lan. For a moment, she held his gaze—its familiar comfort and constancy. Then she picked up her menu without speaking, glanced at it, and set it aside as the waiter approached.

"The food's great here," she said after the waiter took their drink orders. "But whenever I come, I remember all that protesting back in college. Blaming the soldiers. They were victims as much as the South Vietnamese. And a lot of them still suffer. Addiction, Agent Orange, post-traumatic stress. We did a show a few months back on how meditation was helping."

"You're right." T.J. leaned back in his chair. "They were victims. And we were kids, finding our way without all the facts. Full of passion, hope, and anger. Some of it properly channeled, some of it not."

"Still," she said. "I always feel a little guilty."

"A donation to a veteran's organization might do more good than a sackful of guilt."

"Always the pragmatist." Daria smiled and leaned back.

"Guilt's made me a pretty wealthy man, so I can't knock it completely."

"You were wealthy anyway."

"Growing up, yeah. But after med school, I never took a dime from my father. And once I started working, I paid him back for my education."

"That always confounded me," she said. "The way you never let all that money and position affect you."

"Oh," he laughed, "it affected me plenty. Just not in ways that show."

The waiter arrived with their drinks. When the young man left, Daria started in.

"None of that worked out the way we hoped, did it? I mean, how the war dragged on," she said. "And how many died. Then again, who would have thought that a lot of people like Mai Lan would end up here, building new lives?

"Mai Lan and a friend started cooking in their kitchens and selling hot pot beef and cellophane noodles and coconut ice cream to local groceries. Once they got established, they started a takeout business, then this place." Daria waved to her surroundings. "You can't get in here on weekends, it's so crowded. She sent her daughter to Yale, by the way, and now she's an oncologist at Yale New Haven."

"That's pretty remarkable," he agreed. "And Mai Lan apparently likes you."

"She likes everybody. Except her landlord. Oh, and if you're one of her suppliers? Don't think you can slap on a surcharge or hide some bad bok choy under the good stuff. Not without living to regret it."

The waiter approached again and readied his pen and pad. "Ready to order?"

T.J. looked across the table to Daria. "Just a spring roll for me, thanks," she said.

"And I'll have the Pho Bo."

When the young man gathered their menus and left, T.J. reached across the table. He loosened the grip Daria had on the stem of her empty water glass and took her hands.

"Amazing," he said, returning her smile, "as your associate would say, how ten, fifteen years can fly."

Daria rolled her eyes at his reference to Cynthia. "That woman's the thorn of all thorns in my side."

"She's after your job, is she?"

"It's that apparent?"

"Well, if I were a betting man, I'd say the chances were pretty good."

"That she's after my job, or that she's going to get it?"

T.J. shrugged. "Depends how much you want to hang on. If I recall, you've got a pretty mean left hook when your back's in a corner."

"Like I said back at the office. Old habits die hard." Daria took her hands from his, reached for the lemon perched atop the water carafe. She cut it in half, squeezed it into the water, filled her glass, then tipped the carafe in T.J.'s direction.

"Please."

"Getting back to guilt. Just humor me a minute, okay?"

As she set down the carafe, T.J. checked his watch. "You've got ten. After that, the guilt-o-meter shuts down."

"I behaved badly," she said. "In MacMillan. Stanton."

"Yes." He took a drink of water then set the glass down. "You did."

"You were the one friend I had, and I tossed you away like a pair of old jeans."

"Those are the best kind, you know. The ones that are already broken in. The ones that don't have enough starch left in them to hurt."

"It's taken me a while to learn that. But you knew that, even when you were a smartass college know-it-all. All these years later, and I'm just starting."

"Some people never get off the dime," he said. "So, take a bow for doing what you're doing now. As to my being a smartass know-it-all, I owe all my wisdom to the succession of shrinks and coaches and tutors my parents paid to teach me. One of the fringe benefits of being raised in New York by parents of means who were simultaneously aware and too busy to be directly involved. If it looked like I knew what I was doing, it was because I got a lot of help."

He paused. "You didn't have that. I mean your father left. And your mother, she wasn't exactly the nurturing type."

"True on both counts. So, I ran roughshod over anyone who got in my way. Especially you. Anyway, I'm sorry."

"I appreciate the words. I really do. And I can't say it didn't hurt. You were so damned defensive." He shook his head. "All I wanted to do was to take a pickaxe to that fortress you barricaded yourself behind and tear it down. Folly, of course, to think that one person can do another's work. Especially with you swiping at me every time—well, almost every time—I got close."

"I really was a beast."

T.J. checked his watch. "The guilt-o-meter has officially shut down. No more looking back, no more regrets. Tell me about today."

This was T.J. There was no need to hide or to veneer the truth. "I met her."

She spoke so softly T.J. leaned closer. "I couldn't hear you."

"I met her."

"Your daughter?"

She nodded.

"Tell me."

"She's an actress. A dancer. What a coincidence." She laughed.

T.J. looked past Daria. "I'm not sure I believe in coincidence anymore." Then he faced her again. "I've come to see—in my own life and in my patients'— that once we're open, situations unfold just like they're supposed to. And coincidences, if you want to call them that, are just part of the plan."

"You sound like my friend Frankie. And Mary Catherine. She was a guest on the show. And Katrina, the woman who helped me find Angela after my other daughter . . . This all sounds impossible, unbelievable as I'm telling you, like an overwritten, made-for-TV movie."

"Not as unbelievable as you think. How do you think they come up with those scripts?"

Instead of responding, Daria finished her story. "My other daughter. Lizzy. She got pregnant at sixteen."

"Also not that unusual, you know. For children to repeat that pattern."

"You mean pregnancy? Outside of marriage?"

T.J. nodded.

"I know that now," Daria said.

"How's Lizzy doing?"

"Lizzy is like a cliff diver, always jumping off the edge, always surfacing from the depths."

"We're all survivors. Mai Lan, you, me. We all do what we have to do."

"I guess I ended up on top of things. But it's getting harder. Staying on top, I mean. Old age, I guess." She regretted that comment as soon as it passed her lips.

"Either that or enlightenment." He smiled. "Personally, I find they go hand in hand."

The waiter arrived, set down their orders. "Anything else?"

"I think we're fine," T.J. said, and the young man left.

"Tell me more about Angela. What was it like seeing her?" T.J. picked up his fork and took his first bite, but Daria's spring roll went untouched.

"It was the strangest thing," she said. "I thought that after all those years of feeling ashamed and afraid, then finally sucking up the courage to try to find her . . . I don't know, I guess I thought meeting her I could mend fences, maybe become friends with her."

"And that didn't happen?"

"She got angry. I got frustrated."

"Sounds about right. Both of you taking each other's measure. The whole story's not been told, though. This," he said, motioning toward the Pho Bo, "is delicious. Want a taste?"

"No thanks." She hesitated. "You make it sound okay. Just like you always did."

He set down his fork, picked up his beer. "Because it is okay. You can't deny Angela her anger, though. And you can't deny your own frustration. Not if you have any chance for an honest relationship with her or with yourself."

Daria poked her fork around her plate, picked up a piece of spring roll, but set it back down when T.J. spoke again.

"What are you holding back?" he asked.

"Just that . . . I don't know how to say this. Well, I didn't really like her." When he didn't react, she continued. "And I had the feeling that all those years of shame and secrecy—by the way, did I mention that I never told anyone about Angela, not even my husband or kids or my friend Frankie? Not until Lizzy got pregnant anyway."

"Things were different back then."

"Anyway, even though things didn't work out with Angela, it was like a five-hundred-pound gorilla let go of my neck when I met her and told her the truth. And when the beast went galumphing off? I felt so tired. From all the energy it took to keep everything around me looking just right. All so no one could see what was really going on inside me."

She picked up her napkin, wadded it up, then set it back down. "Now, though? Sometimes I feel like I'm free for the first time. Like I can breathe."

T.J. finished his meal, pushed away his plate. "You, my friend, have covered a helluva lot of ground."

Daria felt her face flush. "Just like old times. Me usurping the conversation while you pay rapt attention."

"You always did a little better front and center than I did. I'm still a behind-the-scenes kind of guy."

She sipped her tea, now gone cold. "Well, sorry," she said, "but you've just been cast as the handsome leading man. So, come out stage center and take a bow for all *you've* accomplished."

He laughed, then waved off his successes as if anyone with a pulse could have achieved them. How, after med school, he did his residency at New York Hospital, then treated homeless schizophrenics in a Harlem clinic. "That's," he said, "when I still thought I could save the world. And when I met Jennie. At a fundraiser for Vietnam vets with post-traumatic stress."

So, he was still married—he just didn't wear a ring. Her stomach tightened. Not the least bit hungry, she picked up her fork and ate the spring roll.

"When we had two boys and I realized I actually had to feed, clothe, and shelter them, I went into private practice. On Park Avenue. Talk about culture shock. One day working with vets who lived out of cardboard cartons on Lexington Avenue grates, the next prescribing Seroquel for manic bond traders, Neurontin for neurotic publishers, and beta blockers for stage-frightened actresses. No offense intended."

"None taken. Stage fright may be one neurosis that passed me by. But this kind of performance, one-on-one? That's what scrambles me. Is there a pill for that?"

He leaned toward her. "It's called," he whispered, "TLC."

She smiled, but then lowered her eyes. He was married.

"Jennie died last year. Lung cancer." He hesitated. "She was a lovely woman. Accomplished—she was a curator at the Cloisters—a devoted mother, and she certainly gave the marriage a fair shot." He downed what little remained of his beer. "But I was unfaithful."

Steady, honorable T.J. had an affair? "That doesn't sound like you."

"Not an affair in the traditional sense. No lying about working late. No sneaking off to supposed AMA conventions. It was what my priest called spiritual adultery. I never really committed to Jen—not emotionally anyway—because a tiny part of me was wrapped up in the possibility that one day I could be with the woman I wanted to be with." He looked away for a moment, then back to her. "You, Daria. I never stopped loving you."

There was a chance. So why, after thinking that's what she wanted, did she want to run again? Cautious. She needed to be cautious. And where was that guidance Mary Catherine talked about? The Holy Spirit. *Help me.* "Tell me more."

"When Jennie got sick, we were still in New York and had access to the best doctors in the world—or so we thought. But no one came up with anything other than a grim prognosis. But one guy in New Haven—Stanley Garfinkel—had been using meditation and visualization and reconciliation to ameliorate the agony of chemo and radiation and to help heal what couldn't be cured.

"We went to see him. And even though Jennie didn't make it," he continued, "we made peace with each other."

"How?"

"By admitting the truth. That she married me because she thought I was different enough from her controlling father that she could be happy with me.

"And," he continued, "that I married her because I thought you and I could never be together."

"You told her? About me, I mean?"

"I did," he said. "For her, it confirmed what she suspected for almost twenty years. For me, it exposed the guilt. You don't have the market cornered on that commodity, by the way."

"And that healed the two of you? I would have had a contract out on you. Your knees broken. Something like that, anyway."

"You're not giving yourself enough credit. We've changed, and you're on a new path now."

Daria still wasn't sure she wanted to be on a new path, even if the old one was beginning to feel too well-traveled. "Maybe, maybe not."

"The truth shall set you free, Daria. No matter how painful at first. Isn't that what happened with you and Angela? Maybe things didn't work out the way you hoped.

But you got rid of that shame and guilt that weighed you down all those years. Yes?"

She nodded and glanced away. How many times had she heard that about truth-telling? First from Stefan. Then Mary Catherine. Now T.J. But it had meant something different for each of them. She thought back to the time she visited Healing House and how, with Mary Catherine's help, she imagined herself in the Magdalene's story, a witness to it, but one who walked away with her own awareness, the messages sent to her and her alone by the Holy Spirit. Maybe the same could be true in this situation. How would the truth set her free?

"It still sneaks in now and again, but it's better than it used to be." Then she forced herself to look back at him. "Anyway, I'm still sorry for all the times I manipulated you, used you."

"That's where you're underestimating me, Dar. I may play the softie, but even back in MacMillan, I knew you were trying to stage-manage me. I made the decision to let you. If I could only get part of you, I tried to be content with that. Most of the time, anyway."

"So much for what I thought were my feminine wiles." She picked up her water glass, held it toward him as if toasting. When she took a sip, then set down the glass, her hand lingered.

"We can change all that, you know." He leaned forward. He took her hand from the glass, held it. "Starting today."

This was the moment. She imagined herself like Lizzy, on a cliff's edge. But unlike her daughter, she hesitated. Jump or turn back? Try or preclude possibility? She slipped her hand from T.J.'s and motioned to the waiter. "Check, please."

At the register, Mai Lan pulled Daria aside. "He's a good man, Daria," she said in perfect English. No sign of the accent, the jumbled tenses and pronouns she used to charm her customers. She tapped her menus against Daria's arm. "Don't screw this up."

******

Daria rested her head on T.J.'s chest, listening to his heart, its steady rhythm reassuring her.

He adjusted his head on the pillow. "Now that wasn't so bad, was it?"

"Not bad at all." She grinned as she traced his mouth with her finger. "What an idiot I was for waiting so long."

"Point well taken. On the other hand, we both learned a lot from our marriages, we've each got a couple great kids, successful careers. All we have to do now is make every minute count."

"So where does that leave us?" She pulled her comforter up over them, then snuggled closer.

"Meaning?"

"Well, you're in MacMillan. I'm here. You're off to London for your book tour. And our kids may be wonderful, but they've still got to get launched."

"Details." He stroked her face. "That's all they are. We'll just have to sort our priorities and make the best decisions we can. As soon as we can."

She smiled, then worked her way on top of him, pressed her mouth to his, and let out a soft moan as he pulled her close.

"Mom?"

When Daria heard the front door slam, she rolled away from T.J., wrapped her comforter around her, and looked at her bedside clock. It was only two thirty. Lizzy didn't usually get home until four.

"I'm up here, honey," she said as she fumbled for her robe. "Give me a minute."

"Coach Williams's mother died," Lizzy called out as she started up the stairs. "Practice got cancelled."

Daria shot T.J. a furtive look.

He shrugged, jumped from the bed, and scrambled for his clothes.

"Megan's here. We're going to the funeral home."

"Okay. Good, honey."

"Are you sick?" When Lizzy opened Daria's bedroom door, Daria stood, still tying her robe, fluffing her hair. T.J., meanwhile, tucked his shirt in his pants and cinched his belt.

"Oh." Lizzy looked from her mother to T.J. "Hi."

"Hello," T.J. said.

"This is my friend, T.J.," Daria said.

"I'm Lizzy," she said with an impish grin.

"Nice to meet you," T.J. said.

"You, too. Well, sorry, but I've gotta run."

"Tell Miss Williams I'm sorry for her loss," Daria called as Lizzy went to change her clothes. Daria did her best to sound concerned, though she struggled to muffle the giddy laughter that wanted to rush out of her. "And be careful."

"You too, Mom."

"You too, Mom?" Daria looked to T.J. and mouthed the words Lizzy had spoken. "What's that supposed to mean?"

When Lizzy ran downstairs, Daria heard indecipherable whispers, then copious giggles.

"Well," T.J. said when the door closed behind the girls, "one thing we don't have to worry about is how you'll introduce me to Lizzy."

Chapter Twenty-Eight
May 1993

It was the first, deliciously warm Sunday in May. Daria had wakened early, as she still did, even on weekends. She made coffee and toast, brought them upstairs with the *Times*, and placed them on a bedside tray. When she settled back in bed, she reached for T.J. next to her, moved close to him, kissed his chest. Life, at least outside the studio, had become fluid. Easy. T.J.'s eyes blinked open, then shut again, but he turned toward Daria and nuzzled her neck. Why for so long had she denied them both the pleasure of waking to the certainty that the other would be waiting, warm-bodied and inviting?

"You're so wonderful," she said as she curled against him, looking up to meet his eyes.

He kissed her again, then took her chin in his hand. "Hadn't I been trying to tell you that twenty-five years ago?"

"True," she said. "Hearing impairment, I guess. Coffee?"

T.J. sat up against the headboard and smiled. "Sure."

After she poured coffee for both of them, she offered him toast and handed him the paper, minus the Week in Review section. He scanned the front page, then reached for the magazine and a pen.

Meanwhile, an article caught Daria's eye: "Russian Sex Slaves Enter U.S. Through Mexico." Halfway through the article, she glanced at the accompanying photos and captions. "Stefan Janaczek," one read, "political activist priest, meets with Mexican officials to urge controls on importation of sex slaves to U.S. buyers."

She studied the photo, Stefan's hair gray now, a goatee making a valiant attempt to cover his chin, his body still lean, countenance still fiery. At home again in the center of chaos.

Daria sipped her coffee, then looked across the bed to T.J., working the crossword, horizontally first, then vertically in a decidedly disciplined manner. She smiled when she thought of Mary Catherine, who would, no doubt, point out that Daria had chosen order over tumult.

"When are you heading back to MacMillan?"

He set down the magazine, stretched back. "Summer session starts mid-June. I should get back a week or so before that to get things in order. I guess that means I leave this week." He picked up his coffee mug, drank from it, though his eyes remained on Daria. "You're coming with me?"

Daria hesitated. "Why do I not feel ready for that?"

"Because," he said after he leaned forward and kissed her cheek, "we never feel ready."

The phone on the nightstand beside her rang, interrupting Daria's thoughts. Lizzy, no doubt. She and Megan were at her father's apartment in the City. Would she be asking permission to charge a pair of overpriced jeans at Bloomingdale's or to catch a matinee?

"Hi, hon."

But instead of an ebullient, ingratiating Lizzy, a stranger's voice responded.

"Mrs. Demarest?"

"Yes."

"My name," the man said, "is Paul Haslun. I'm a physician at Laurel Hospital in Mount Laurel, Pennsylvania."

Daria sat up, pulling the sheets around her. "Yes?"

"You're the daughter of Helena Petrauskas?"

"That's right."

"Mrs. Demarest, your mother was admitted during the night exhibiting stroke symptoms. She listed you as next of kin."

In the last months, Daria had done what she felt was her best to tidy her relationships. She and Lizzy were no longer at each other's throats. She talked to Jack a couple times a week and had gone to visit him twice. She had become a better friend to Frankie, being there for her as much as Frankie had been for her. After putting Carla off for months, she had returned to Silverman's diner and given her an hour-long interview. Daria was even warming to Cynthia and could manage civil, almost cordial conversations with Ted. But her mother? For years their only communication had been halting holiday and birthday calls that most often devolved into impersonal weather reports—"Cold, very cold. And windy." "Rain? Uh-huh, we've had rain too."—which Daria endured while filing her nails or doing yoga.

It wasn't as if she hadn't known this call—or one like it—might come someday. She just didn't think she would feel anything. But as she waited for whatever news this doctor was about to deliver, her heart pounded.

"Is she . . . is it serious?"

"She's still undergoing tests. So far, we're not seeing anything life-threatening. It may be a matter of what's called transient ischemic attack, or TIA, which mimics a stroke's symptoms. But even if that's the case, the first twenty-four hours are key in determining a patient's prospects. About forty percent of TIA patients are likely to have an actual stroke during that time."

"I see." Daria tightened her robe around her. "Thank you. I'll . . ." She couldn't finish the sentence, because she wasn't sure what to do or say next. "Thank you," she repeated. "Your name again?" She took a paper and pad from the nightstand drawer.

"Haslun. H-A-S-L-U-N."

Daria scribbled the name and, after it, the phone number he gave her.

She paused. "And you'll call me back when you know more?"

"I will."

When Daria hung up, T.J. had put down the crossword and propped himself up on his elbow. "What's up?"

"My mother. She's had a stroke. Or maybe not a stroke but something like it. A TIA, I think the doctor called it."

Before Daria said another word, T.J. sprang from bed as he must have hundreds of times as an on-call resident. "I'll gas up the car," he said as he made for the bathroom to turn on the shower, "and get us some coffee for the road."

"No," she insisted. "I can't . . . I . . ."

"Can't what?"

When T.J. returned to the bedroom, Daria looked up as if she hadn't understood his question. She was still sitting on the edge of the bed, absorbing the doctor's news.

"You were saying," he prompted, "you can't do something."

"I can't see her. I won't know what . . ."

"Yes, you can." He grabbed a towel and headed back to the bathroom. "And I'll be with you when you do," he called over his shoulder.

Daria was still on her bed when T.J. finished his shower. "Look, I know this is hard. Just take it a step at a time. And the first steps," he said, helping her to her feet, "are getting up, taking a shower, and getting dressed."

As Daria reluctantly went into the bathroom, T.J. stuffed his suitcase with the few things he had unpacked since his return from London.

"I'll be back in fifteen minutes." When Daria didn't respond, he stepped into the bathroom where she was staring blankly into the mirror. He reached for her arm and gently squeezed. "Honey, after you shower, pack a couple things and call the kids and let them know."

He bent over to tighten his Top-Sider laces, then stood back up. "I can't promise what you'll see will be pretty. But I know that if you don't go, you'll regret it. Okay? Dar?"

"Okay."

"Where are your keys?" he asked on his way from the room.

"On the hallway console."

He ducked his head back in and smiled. "Looks like you'll see my place in MacMillan sooner than you expected."

******

Daria made her way to her dresser, opened her lingerie drawer, pulled out a handful of panties, yellow, nude, and black, then reached to the back of the drawer to find the matching bras. She found a couple nude ones, one that was white, another one black-and-purple-flowered. She reached back into the drawer, this time scrounging furtively. *Where's the yellow one?*

When she caught sight of herself in the mirror, scratching in her drawer like a squirrel in search of winter stash, she stepped back and closed her eyes. Matching underwear didn't matter. She knew that. But she was going home. Going back. She needed to look better than where she came from. To suit up in her pretty, coordinating armor, to protect herself from that damned coal dust and that wretched sulfur smell. If things matched, if she looked okay, everything would be under control.

But hadn't she learned, *shouldn't she have learned*, in the past months that matching Natori lingerie didn't make life a damned bit more manageable, more predictable, easier to navigate? That what mattered was going wherever life took her—whether situations went well, as they had during Lizzy's pregnancy, or whether they stirred up more than they resolved, like meeting Angela?

She grabbed whatever underwear she could, matching or not, tossed it into her bag, and turned on the shower hot and full blast. "Mommy." A plaintive little cry. It just came out of her. A prayer. She should say a prayer. Maybe T.J.'s research applied to stroke victims as much as people who had heart attacks. Maybe prayer would help, would *heal,* even if her mother didn't know she was being prayed for. But what to say? And to whom? She still wasn't sure. "Help my mother," she said out loud. "Help me. Please."

At the End of the Storm

******

"Room three twelve." The woman at the nurse's station pointed down the hallway. "Last door on the left."

A few steps from Helena's room, T.J. reached for Daria's elbow. "Your mother might feel more comfortable if I'm not with you when you first see her. My being a stranger."

"Sure. Yes. You're right."

He squeezed her arm. "I'll wait in the reception area. If you need me, either come and get me or ask a nurse to find me."

"Okay."

"I love you." He kissed Daria's cheek.

"I love you too."

Daria watched as T.J. made his way down the hall. Then she turned and walked toward her mother's room.

Reaching the door, she stepped inside and froze. Of the two beds in the room, only the one nearer the window was occupied. But not by Helena. This was not her mother. Granted, even from the back, Daria could see that the woman's hair, though matted, was thick and full, like Helena's. But Helena was only sixty-seven. And she had never looked diminished, not the way this woman did, curled under a blue blanket, wearing a shapeless blue hospital gown.

"Ma?" Daria spoke softly, wishing, hoping the woman would turn and that this patient wouldn't be her mother. That Daria would be able to apologize, to say "Someone told me my mother was here, but . . ." Still no response. Daria walked closer to the bed. "Ma?" she said, louder as she went to the bed's opposite side.

When Daria faced her, Helena's eyes looked hazy at first, as if she couldn't tell if the woman at her bedside really was her daughter. Then she said simply, "You came."

Yes, this was her mother. "How are you feeling?" Daria put her hands on the cool metal bedrail, to steady herself, to hang on.

Helena cast a sideways glance. "My right side's all locked up."

Daria reached out and stroked her mother's immobile right arm.

"What happened, Ma?"

"It just came on sudden," Helena said. "When I was hanging out the wash. I reached up to pin a sheet to the line, and I went numb. Not all over, just here." Helena tried lifting her right arm. When she couldn't, her voice went frail. "I fell and couldn't get up until the neighbor kids called their mother to help. That was yesterday, I think. I don't know, I lost track of time."

"It was yesterday, Ma. On Saturday." Daria slid a nearby chair close to her mother and sat down. "Remember how Saturday's wash day?"

Helena nodded. "Saturday's wash day. Sunday's church. Monday, I bake bread for the rectory. Tuesday . . . Tuesday, I can't remember."

"It must have been terrible. To be alone, I mean. When it happened." Daria knew her words sounded choppy and stilted. *Help me.*

"Oh, I'm not alone," Helena said. "Mrs. Ludwig and Rosa Santoro and me, we keep tabs on each other. Besides," she said, turning from Daria, "I'm used to it."

There's the Helena I know, Daria thought. Or was Helena's complaint, backhanded as it was, appropriate? *I was the one, after all, who left*. Feeling she was accomplishing one of those feats of strength possible only under extreme duress, like when a mother lifts a station wagon off her child trapped beneath its wheel, Daria took her mother's hand in her own. "Well, Ma, you're not alone now."

Helena looked at Daria again, this time her eyes tentative as a baby rabbit's, unsure whether the person reaching to stroke its ears would feed it or skin it.

"He was a bastard."

"Who?" Daria hesitated.

"Your father," Helena said. "Who else?"

Here she was again, feeling as if she had regressed thirty years. Stuck between the two of them, knowing the result as well as she knew her multiplication tables. Picking one means losing the other.

"He spent all the damn money on horses and the Steelers and the Pirates. And that girlfriend of his. All I wanted was a damned Oriental rug."

"A rug?" Daria looked at her mother. Was this the drugs talking? Or was her mother finally worn down to the truth of her anger? Finally ready to spit it out and be done with it?

"I never knew you wanted an Oriental rug," Daria said. "But when you're up and around, we'll go down to Kleinman's and pick one out."

"Kleinman's?"

Had anyone else been in the room, they might have suspected, from Helena's tone, that Daria had suggested her mother shop for a rug on Mars.

"They still have nice rugs, don't they?"

"They moved out years ago."

Yes, Daria, thought in response to the way her mother turned her head away, *yes, I would have known that if I had come back now and again.*

"Somewhere else then. The MacMillan Store. Or we could drive to Pittsburgh."

"What's the use now? Just one more thing to vacuum. And what with this hand of mine now . . . I don't know."

Was there nothing she could do to please this woman? "Well," Daria said, taking the chair next to her mother's bed, "whatever you want."

******

"I'm Paul Haslun." The doctor checked the chart he held as he strode into the conference room. "You're, let's see, Daria? Daria Demarest?"

"Yes."

After shaking Daria's hand, he turned to T.J. "And you?"

"Thayer. Thayer Townsend." He shook Dr. Haslun's hand.

"From the university?"

"That's right."

"You're doing great work up there."

"We've got a long way to go. But, yes, we're making strides."

"Please," the doctor said, "have a seat."

"We've confirmed," the doctor said across the table to Daria as he clasped his hands atop Helena's chart, "that your mother had a minor transient ischemic attack. As these types of situations go, she's quite fortunate. She may have some lingering weakness. And temporary speech and memory

337

impairment. But with a little time and therapy, her prognosis is good. Like I mentioned on the phone, we still need to monitor her for a few days because of the possibility of an actual stroke."

"You sound hesitant."

"Not as far as the TIA goes, no. But we also want to adjust her meds if need be."

"Her meds? What meds?" As far as Daria knew, the only drug her mother ever took was aspirin, and she only took that when she was flat out from the flu.

"Her Depakote."

When T.J. looked at her, she sensed Depakote wasn't something someone took for an occasional headache.
"And that's for what?"

"Your mother's records indicate she suffers from a mild form of bipolar disorder."

"Bipolar disorder? Isn't that manic depression?"

"That's what it used to be called, yes."

Daria looked skeptical. "I thought manic depressives went on crazy shopping sprees and took extravagant vacations, then ended up in institutions. My mother clips coupons and hasn't been in a hospital since she had me."

"At one end of the spectrum, yes, behavior is extreme and hospitalization may be necessary. But your mother appears to have a milder form, which causes her to be volatile, out of sorts, but still largely functional. Does that sound like your mother?"

"Volatile? Yes. Out of sorts, on the other hand, sounds a little too innocuous. She was always prone to pretty bleak moods. Well, I take that back. Not until she was in her thirties. That's when she really started to go dark."

"That's not uncommon. For the symptoms to manifest at that age, I mean."

"Do you have a treatment plan?"

Daria leaned back, relieved, when T.J. stepped in. Manic depression—bipolar disorder, whatever it was called—sounded amorphous. Too big to absorb or understand. But Helena's darkness, as Nana used to call it, had a name. And giving it a name began to dispel some things Daria had supposed for a long, long time. That *she* had caused her mother's volatility, that if only she had been a better little girl, her mother would have been happy. That Helena wasn't at fault, either.

******

"After you."

As T.J. juggled their luggage, Daria stepped inside his house, shifting from one hip to the other the bag of dinner fixings they bought on their way from the hospital.

He had already briefed her on the history of what he called his retreat, telling her how, when town founder Martin MacMillan established the university a century and a half earlier, his wife, Mairead, arranged for a hundred faculty residences to be built on the fifty acres south of MacMillan Mansion on MacMillan Ridge. All with views of the Ridge, the Allegheny Front, or the university clock tower. And all resembling the stone cottages on Ireland's west coast, where Mairead was raised. Places, she insisted in her writings, that would "liberate thought and foster creativity. Places where imaginations would soar."

Daria took in the masculine, brown-leather-and-beige-tweed feel of the place. The Navajo rug. The oversized watercolor of the Berkshires that hung above the stonework fireplace. And the abstract oil painting of John the Baptist that hung near the staircase.

"How about we start dinner," T.J. said as he led Daria to the kitchen, "and I'll give you the tour."

After they turned on the oven and set the chicken and potatoes in a pan to roast, T.J. took Daria upstairs. No Fairfield County-like updating had been given to this place. It still had original moldings, crystal doorknobs, creaky floorboards in both bedrooms. Maybe that was why it felt comfortable, like those worn jeans she and T.J. had talked about the day he appeared on her show.

"The bathroom's to the left, if you want a shower before dinner.

"And here," he said, leading Daria to his office when they were back downstairs, "is where I work, think, read. I usually end up eating here too. There's a stellar view of the sunset from my desk," he said as he motioned to the west. "So, I draw the line on television. No TV allowed in the peace room, as I call it."

Daria stepped inside the space, which she guessed was only about sixteen-foot square. It felt more spacious, though, because its windows on three sides provided a clear view of MacMillan Ridge, even in the rapidly fading light.

It would be even more dramatic in a week or two, she figured, when the mountain laurels on the Ridge, all fluffy and pink, like so many bridesmaids, came in bloom. That's what she remembered about spring in MacMillan when she was there, when they were there. She went to the windows, looked up at the sky, the pale moon and stars as they eased into view.

T.J. walked up behind her and wrapped his arms around her waist. "Remember how we used to climb up there to get high," he said, pointing to the university clock tower to the right, "then run back down before the bells rang so we wouldn't lose our hearing?"

"My ears hurt just thinking about it." She squeezed her arms around his. "It feels like yesterday."

She turned to him, kissed him, then nestled her face against his chest. "Thank you for bringing me here. Not just to your house. To see my mother."

"There's nothing to thank me for. Besides, you saved me plane fare. You know how I hate that commuter flight from Pittsburgh. After all these years, I still have to fly west from LaGuardia to Pittsburgh, which takes an hour. Then get on one of those rickety little planes, which takes almost that long, to get to MacMillan."

"Well," she teased, "you'd better get used to those rickety little planes if we're going to have a long-distance relationship."

"Actually," he said, "I was hoping for something a little more traditional. Like marriage."

"Oh." Daria tried to back away, but his hands on her hips grounded her, kept her close. "I don't know. The kids. My mother. Not to mention my job."

"The kids—all of them—aren't as big an obstacle as you're making them. Jack's on his way to becoming a top-notch doctor. As for my guys, Spence has a year left in law school and Henry's working in the Madagascar Embassy."

"There's still Lizzy."

"I concede that point. But I still have a few contacts left in film. She can intern this summer to make sure she really wants to get into that business or anything communications related. Then she can study. Whatever, wherever she wants.

"And your mother, Daria? She may not admit it, but she'd probably like having you near. Once Haslun regulates her meds, it might be easier going with her."

She shrugged. "How could it have been that all these years she just had some neurons misfiring, making her say and do all those mean things? And why did it take so long for someone to diagnose it?"

"Time, Dar. All in good time. Just like there was shame in being a single mother back in the sixties, there's been shame in mental illness. I assume that's why she never told you."

Daria shook her head. "I guess if I had been more involved, I would have been able to help her."

He took her hands in his and held them up, signaling for her to stop talking. "I hear the guilt-o-meter ticking again."

"You're right." She looked beyond him, released his hands, then walked to the painting that hung above his desk. "That painting," she said. "We saw it in Stanton. The day we met your mother's friend."

He smiled, then followed her to the picture. "When you left town, I went back to that gallery and bought it. I liked it, too, mostly at the time because you liked it. But the more I lived with it, the more it grew on me. Even though you saw storm clouds gathering, I saw that tiny little clearing over in the far right there. I kept it to remind me never to give up hope that one day you'd see it hanging in my house. Our house."

Chapter Twenty-Nine
May 1993

"Ma?"

Helena, eyes roaming, seemed to size up Daria as she perched on the chair beside her hospital bed. "What?"

"What was it like for you growing up?"

Helena batted her left hand at Daria's question, as if it were an annoying gnat. "What's the sense in bringing that up?"

Daria edged closer. "You never told me about your father. Or how he and Nana came from Lithuania. Ma, will you please look at me?"

"What's to tell? Things were bad over there," Helena said. "First the Poles took over, then the Germans. Then the Russians. Everything got all mixed up. Everyone lying to the police about neighbors, friends. Anything to save their own skins. But who could blame them? It was either risk your life getting on a boat full of people poor as yourself or get shipped to Siberia. Those filthy coal mines over here," she said, "looked pretty good compared to freezing to death."

"That must have been awful."

When Helena spoke next, her voice was too soft for Daria to hear. "I can't hear you, Ma." She leaned closer.

"You were twelve when your Nana died." Helena turned back toward Daria, her eyes wet.

Daria took her mother's hand. "I remember," she said, "how she used to sit at the kitchen table, stirring cake batter with a wooden spoon or kneading dough. How she used to brush my hair. And ask me to dance for her."

Helena nodded. She wiped away her tears with her good hand. "She told me I was good. No matter what. And when she died, and your father left, that's when I started scrubbing the rectory floors and washing Father Kowalski's dirty underwear. So I could still be good."

"Why did you have to try so hard?"

"Because," she said, looking directly at Daria, "of you."

"Me?" Daria let go of Helena's hand. More truth. She hesitated. "Me," she said again. "Why me?"

"Because I got pregnant, and he didn't want us. You or me."

There it was. The secret. Katrina's statistics started rattling through Daria's head. The ones about how children of mothers who have children out of wedlock are more likely to repeat the pattern. But Daria had assumed she had been the first. The one who started the trend. The curse. Whatever it was. That it was her fault. "But," Daria said, "he married you."

"My father made him. Said he'd make sure Zack never worked the mines if he didn't. And your father never let me forget it.

"I don't know," she continued, her voice mellowing. "He was just a kid. I was a kid too." But then her voice toughened again. "We had to, back then. Get married. Not like today with everybody doing whatever the hell they want."

Daria brushed aside Helena's last words. Whatever their intent, she didn't care. She needed more. More information. More truth. "But Dad always treated me good." Daria sat up taller on the bed and corrected herself when she lapsed into Central Pennsylvania vernacular. "Well, I mean." she said. "He treated me well. Even after he moved in with Janette, he still took me places, taught me to drive."

"Daria, Daria." Helena shook her head. "He used you like a stick to beat me. If he paid attention to you and ignored me like I was some old rag he could wipe the floors with, he knew it would turn me against you. And I let him. That's when I decided all I could do was go to church and pray and hope I'd be good again. Like I was before I had you."

No, Daria insisted to herself, *I was his special girl. But if he loved me so much, why did he make such a mess of our lives with the drinking and gambling? And why did he leave?*

"Why didn't you tell me?"

Helena waved off Daria's question.

"No, Ma. I want to know."

Helena looked back to Daria. "I knew I wasn't doing enough for you. But no matter how much I tried to love you like Nana did, it just wouldn't come out. Like it was stuck right here." Helena made a fist with her left hand and tapped it against her chest. "Even if he paid attention to you to hurt me, I wanted you to know you didn't have to prove you were good. And if he could do it and I couldn't, so be it." She hesitated. "It wasn't enough, was it?"

Daria shook her head. "No, Ma, it wasn't."

Helena lowered her eyes. "I'm sorry."

An apology? Was that an apology? Daria wanted to ask Helena to repeat herself, to make sure she had heard correctly, but other questions intruded. *Why didn't you tell me this sooner? Why didn't you try harder?*

Still, she had a little bit of her mother back. A piece of her that had drifted off when Zack left. That was what was important. Truth and connection.

"It must have been so hard for you, Ma."

Daria sat still as Helena scrutinized her daughter's face. She felt no disdain, no judgment. When Helena reached out her hand, Daria took it. Her heart raced. If she really wanted connection, she needed to be as honest as Helena had been.

"You know, Ma," she started. "I had a little girl too. Before Lizzy. Before I got married." She hesitated when Helena's eyes narrowed, trying to assimilate what Daria was saying. "It was the year I went to Stanton. That's where I had her."

"A little girl?"

"I gave her up."

"You gave her up?" Helena's eyes widened, as if she couldn't imagine why Daria would even consider giving her child away. "Why?"

"Why what?"

"Why didn't you bring her home?"

Home? Because home wasn't safe. Because I thought you wouldn't want her.

"I . . ." Daria fumbled for words, tamping down the anger she thought had dissipated. "I was ashamed. I thought you wouldn't want us."

"But Darinnina," Helen answered, "it's the grandmother's job to set out the linens. The grandmother needs to call to Laima to bless the house, to bless the baby."

Regret was making Daria lightheaded, weak. She leaned forward in the bedside chair. "You mean you would have wanted us? What about the church? What about Mrs. Como next door?" Daria stopped herself. What for years had seemed certain and unyielding had, in minutes, changed shape. Her perceptions, her beliefs were separating and shifting, like glass pieces inside a kaleidoscope, forming new colors and patterns. If she had made a different choice about Angela, how differently would the fragments of her life have fallen into place?

She sat back in her chair. Now she had a different choice. She could continue to allow her anger to separate her from Helena, she could continue to blame Helena, in large part, for the choice she had made. Or she could try a different way.

Help me.

She reached for her purse on the stand beside Helena's bed, took out her wallet, and removed the copy of the *Times'* review of *River* she kept there. "Would you like to see a picture of your granddaughter?" She stood again and handed Helena the article.

"No," Helena said. "I'm all shaky. You read it."

"Angela Rush," Daria read, "one of Broadway's most enigmatic yet powerful performances in years." When she finished reading, Daria held the article to Helena so she could see Angela's picture.

"She's got your legs," Helena said. "But I don't like her hair."

Helena's critique was cut short when a man, a stranger, came to the door.

"Helena?" He walked into the room in his rubber-soled shoes, wearing a brown plaid shirt, brown pants, a black cord holding an oversized crucifix around his neck. He carried what looked like a saucer-sized gold compact.

Suspicious, Helena narrowed her eyes. "Who are you?"

"I'm with the hospital ministry," he said. "I've brought you the Eucharist."

When Helena looked from the man to Daria, but said nothing, Daria prompted her. "Ma, do you want communion?"

"I haven't been to confession," Helena snapped.

After the man assured Helena she could receive the sacrament, he walked toward her, lifted a thin, white wafer from the compact. Helena opened her mouth, and the man placed the host on her tongue.

"And you?" When he turned to her, Daria held up her hand.

"She hasn't been to confession, either," Helena said. "And I don't mean just for a week like me." She turned to Daria. "Tell him."

But the man looked at Daria and held up his hand. "I'm not a priest."

"What?" Helena tried to sit up. "Now Bishop Krolik says it's okay to break the rules?"

"Not exactly." The man paused, silent, as if listening to a voice neither Helena nor Daria could hear.

Meanwhile, Daria considered the situation. There was nothing in her past, or present, she hadn't already owned up to, either to Frankie or Mary Catherine or Katrina. No, she hadn't reconciled with the Church. Yet she had begun to reconcile with her mother. Was it so wrong to share more of this moment with Helena, even if doing so meant breaking the rules?

Daria closed her eyes, as she had as a child, waiting at the altar rail for the moment she would receive the host, flat and stiff, but nourishing. She wanted to hold her hands in prayer, waiting for that precious gift that promised forgiveness, redemption, renewal. Why exactly had she denied herself those assurances because of the way she was punished by nuns who were doing their jobs, by another girl, as young and unaware as she had been, and, yes, by a mother who was only trying to find order in a world that seemed so heartless and random?

When she opened her eyes, she shook her head. "Not now," she said to the man. "Not yet."

When the man nodded, Daria caught the look on Helena's face, relieved that the rules had been adhered to. At the same time, sad. *She wants it as much as I do. Connection. Peace.*

"Now," the man said after tucking the vessel into his pocket, "shall we say the Lord's Prayer?"

This I can do. Daria nodded, gently lifting her mother's weakened right hand. The stranger took Helena's left hand.

"Our Father,"—the prayer Daria had said how many times as a child?—"forgive us our trespasses as we forgive those who trespass against us. . . ." But now the words took shape and form. Breath and connection had rounded them out. Forgiveness was possible. She had received it. She had given it.

When they finished the prayer, the stranger left as quietly as he had arrived. But Daria still held her mother's hand.

There was much more for them to resolve. They hadn't even gotten around to talking about Lizzy. That would have to wait for another conversation, another day.

******

"Your mother's got a remarkably strong will," Dr. Haslun said as he reached for the coffee pot and offered a cup for both Daria and T.J.

"No, thank you." Daria said. But T.J. rose from his chair in the hospital conference room, took a paper cup from the dispenser, and held it out so Dr. Haslun could pour.

"Thanks," he said.

Dr. Haslun gave his prognosis. "I think she'll be fine. She'll need to continue the physical therapy on her right arm. We'll adjust the Heparin dosage over time and start her on half an aspirin a day. She'll need to watch her sodium intake. And she'll stay on the Depakote to keep her mood stable. She should be ready to go home soon, but I'd like to watch her for a day or two more before we decide exactly when. She lives alone?"

Daria nodded.

"Are there other relatives in the area?"

"No. She has friends at church. And she and a neighbor help each other."

"Okay. I'll recommend twenty-four-hour home care for a few days, then have a nurse come in a couple times a week to monitor her blood pressure and make sure she's eating properly. I think she'll be able to keep up the therapy with home visits."

"That's fine," Daria said. "But I want to bring my mother to Connecticut. When she's ready to leave the hospital. I'm sure there's someone at Greenvale Hospital or even Yale New Haven who could take over her care?" She addressed her question to T.J.

"I'm sure there is."

Before she could detect the detachment in T.J.'s response, she turned to Dr. Haslun. "When's the best time to tell her about the arrangements?"

****

"Ma," Daria said after wheeling Helena into the conference room where T.J. and Dr. Haslun were already waiting. "This is T.J.—Thayer his real name is. We're friends from college, and we just met up again a few months back. He's a doctor. We and Dr. Haslun want to talk to you about what happens when you're released from the hospital."

After Dr. Haslun reiterated what he had told Daria and T.J., Helena shook her head. "No, no one in the house. No nurse. No therapy. My friends and me, we'll manage."

Daria had anticipated Helena's reaction, so she cut in with her own proposal. "If you don't want people in the house, Ma, I want you to come home with me. To Connecticut."

Helena shot Daria a damning look. "Why would I do that?"

"So I can take care of you. Until you get better. Or longer. Whatever you want."

"I want," Helena said, pounding her healthy hand on the table, "to go home."

"But—"

"Don't think you can pull up here one day like the Red Cross and cart me off somewhere I don't know anybody."

"But you know me." Daria caught her voice rising, straining. She pursed her lips, regrouped, then spoke more evenly. "And you and Jack and Lizzy could all get to know each other better."

Helena looked away from Daria and locked her eyes on Dr. Haslun's. "I'm going home," she said. "I'll have the nurse come even though I won't need her. But I'm going home."

******

Daria and T.J. sat in the sunroom, each in armchairs facing the Ridge. Dinner plates propped on their laps, they ate the stir-fry they had picked up on the way home from the hospital.

Until T.J. spoke, the only sounds were light rain on the roof, Debussy on the stereo. "Nice," he said, "isn't it?"

"Mmmm." A single, lazy syllable was all Daria could manage in response. Getting to know her mother had left Daria drowsy, as if she had been drugged.

"So." T.J. set his plate on the end table. "I'm here. Your mother's nearby. Your kids are going to be off living their lives."

Not now. Daria reached for her cup of tea. Something warm to hang onto while she braced herself. She felt like she had in college—a dancer on T.J.'s stage—when he wanted more from her performance than she felt she had to give.

"Tell me one more time," he said, his words clipped, "why you insist on holding on to life in Connecticut?"

"My work," she said, as if her answer should be obvious. "*Awakenings* is my kid too. Besides, it's paying for Jack's schooling. And it'll pay for Lizzy's."

"Money doesn't have to be a consideration, Daria." T.J. said. "In the end, when my father died, he left his estate to me, minus a hefty donation to the Film Institute. There's plenty to go around."

"That's very generous, but . . ."

"But what? Why would it be so difficult for you to accept money? It's a necessary evil. No more. No less."

"It's more complicated than that for me. Money, I mean. I guess I'm still shell-shocked from my experience with Ted. My father, too, for that matter."

"Understandable." T.J. stood and started to pace. "But no longer necessary. In fact, it's no longer even valid. It's like you're clinging to that excuse as if it's the last brick in the fortress wall you built around yourself years ago."

She ignored his frustration. "I know I complain about John Fisher and Cynthia . . ."

"That," he agreed, "you do. And before you do again, let me ask just one more question. Is there anything Cynthia's doing that you didn't do at her age?"

Daria looked affronted. "I didn't sleep with my boss, for one thing."

"And you're sure about John and her? Do you have incriminating tapes or photos?"

"No, but—"

"Men, especially middle-aged men, are capable of the most idiotic behavior with even the slightest encouragement. A smile, a flash of the thigh, a peek down the blouse. Even the best of us become fools, utter fools, under the illusion that maybe, just maybe, we're the testosterone-laden heroes our flatterers think—or pretend to think—we are."

"Oh, come on." Daria waved to dismiss his admission. "You're so much above that."

He shook his head. "I'm afraid not. There was a receptionist once at my New York practice. A hostess at a restaurant. Most recently a teaching assistant here in MacMillan. And I was every bit as dizzied by them as John is by Cynthia.

"But," he said, "we were talking about you. You may never have slept with a boss to get ahead, but I'd be surprised if you didn't flatter one or two along the way."

Daria brushed away the memory of how she encouraged John Fisher the day she presented him with her *Awakenings* proposal. "Okay," she admitted. "Maybe I did. But I can't just let go. Not without knowing where I'm heading next."

"What's to know? You'd be here. With me. Your mother. The problem isn't that you don't know where you'd be headed. You know exactly where you'd be going, and you're scared to death. It's not that you can't let go. You won't."

"Can't. Won't." She shrugged as if she didn't comprehend the difference.

"Oh no, you don't," he said firmly. "You're not going to dismiss me like that. Not again."

"I'm not—"

"Don't even start." He held up his hands. "We're not nineteen anymore, and I'm not going to let you do the avoidance dance again. As much as I want a life with you, I'm not waiting another twenty-five years. Or twenty-five months. Not even twenty-five weeks."

Daria felt the room shrinking, the walls, the windows pressing in on her chest, her back, her sides. She squirmed in her chair. The Debussy on the stereo had ended, and Mahler had taken its place. She looked straight out to the Ridge, which was now hidden by heavy fog.

Chapter Thirty
May 1993

Driving over the Exit 4 bridge on I-95, Daria glanced at the inlet to the south. Even in the few days she had been gone, progress—if it could be called that—had been made on the townhouses being jammed onto the shoreline. The framing was complete, the siding, a non-offensive gray, had gone up. What did it matter if future occupants, just to claim a glimpse of the Sound, would need to look beyond the shuttered power station, sitting like an oversized, used-up battery on the shore's edge?

The energy of the traffic, the shiny German cars—the rush. She was back where she belonged. She ejected the CD she had been listening to, turned on the news, and drove straight to the studio. It was Sunday. No one else would be in. She could clear any desk clutter that had accumulated since she left and prepare for Monday's show.

Inside the building, Daria stopped at the office kitchenette to grab a bottle of Evian but found none. Someone had raided her supply. There was plenty of diet iced tea, though. Cynthia's. She grabbed one, unscrewed the cap, and headed for her office.

In her absence, Fisher had agreed to reruns, but the following week's lineup and advance materials had been sent to her in MacMillan. Monday she would interview a reflexologist, who would demonstrate on Daria. Cynthia would do a segment with a podiatrist on how to avoid foot fungus, ingrown toenails, and bunions. Lovely.

Daria kicked off her shoes and looked at her feet. Dancing might have kept her taut and trim, but all that *en pointe* work had mangled her toes. She needed a pedicure. If she waited until Monday for the studio stylist to do it, she wouldn't have time to catch up on the last-minute details that were sure to crop up. She flipped through her Day-Timer and ran her finger down her list of salons. Elegance Day Spa. They were open on Sundays. She picked up the phone to dial.

"You're back." Before Daria got through to the salon, Cynthia stood in her doorway, in pink spandex tights, white hoodie with pink trim, and rhinestone-studded baseball cap, through which her bouncy ponytail swung happily out the back. "Oh," she said. "Sorry. I didn't see you were on the phone."

Daria hung up. "Yes, well, come in." She needed to catch up with Cynthia anyway. She moved her purse from her side chair. "Have a seat."

"Why, thank you." Cynthia, all pink and white and holding a bottle of iced tea, sat on the chair's edge.

Daria pointed to the tea she had pilfered from the kitchenette. "I raided your stash. There was no Evian left."

"No problem. How's your mom?"

"Better, thanks. The damage seems to be minimal. She'll need therapy, but she's tough. My guess is she'll beat the doctor's expectations and then some."

"So that's where your persistence comes from."

"I guess so." Daria had always ascribed her ability to barrel through life to her father, to the ice water he said was in her veins. But it was, after all, Helena who had hung in with Daria, as best she could, and Zack who had left.

"I hope you don't mind," Cynthia started.

Daria braced herself. *She's going to announce she's arranged to move into my office, set up a tent out back for me, all with demographic data, focus group results, and Fisher's enthusiasm to support the change.*

Daria took a drink of tea and grimaced. "What on earth do they sweeten this stuff with?"

"Heaven only knows." Cynthia smiled and shrugged. "I took the liberty," she said, "of asking Mary Catherine to add your mother to the Healing House prayer list."

Daria set down the tea, her tone softening. "That was thoughtful. Thank you."

"Prayer works. But you already know that. How's that yummy Dr. Townsend, by the way?" Cynthia winked conspiratorially.

"Fine." Though when she left T.J. in MacMillan, things had been anything but fine. She wanted a life with him, but leaving the show, exchanging proximity to the City for life in a college town? Forging a new relationship with her mother? She changed the subject, as much to distract herself from all those dangling threads as to keep Cynthia from prying. "What's been going on here?"

"One thing's for sure," Cynthia said, setting her tea on Daria's desk, "we missed you. By the end of the week, I could barely force myself to make it in, what with John hanging around like a lost puppy." She rolled her eyes and lowered her voice. "He's a little on the needy side, do you agree?"

"Needy's one word for him." Daria laughed, then caught herself. Cynthia was setting her up. She was sure of it. For what?

"Anyway, the place didn't hum like it does when you're here. No Daria, no sizzle." Cynthia tilted her head, paused. "I guess it would sound ingratiating to say how much I admire you, but I do. Ever since I saw *Awakenings* for the first time, I've had you on a pedestal."

"So you could knock me off it?" If Cynthia had designs on her job, it was time for Daria to sweep that option off the table.

"Why, I . . . what do you mean?" Cynthia's face deflated.

"Oh, come on, Cynthia. You know and I know you're after my chair on that set."

Cynthia hesitated. "If you mean I wouldn't give anything to be like you, heck, to be you, you're right." Her voice cracked. "But if you mean I'm out to do you in, well, I don't know what to say."

"Cynthia," Daria said, picking up the stack of mail from her inbox, "save the tears for someone who cares. Like John."

Daria untwirled the string on an interoffice envelope to find an innocuous memo from John, outlining the agenda for their Monday morning status meeting. When she crumpled the note, then tossed it into the trash, she caught the dismayed, then hurt look on Cynthia's face.

If Daria had learned nothing the past few months, it was that there was no shame in admitting when she was wrong. Just a couple little words, *I'm sorry,* or, better yet, *I was wrong to say that,* might smooth things over. "Cynthia," she started to say.

But when Cynthia's eyes met Daria's, the ice-water-in-her-veins feeling, familiar yet no longer fitting, took hold of her. That old need to win, to come out on top of the situation, took over. "You can leave now." She turned back to her work, any apology stuck in her throat.

******

Finally, Daria thought as she held the phone to her ear, she had taken her little nemesis down a notch or two.

"You made it back okay?" Frankie asked when she heard Daria's voice.

"Well, I'm back. Whether or not I'm okay is debatable."

"What happened?"

"That little twit was just in here."

"And, by twit, I'm goin' out on a limb and assumin' you mean Cynthia."

"The one and only."

"What did she do now? Have the audacity to tell you how much she missed you?"

"How'd you guess?"

"Just a suspicion."

"You sound just like T.J."

"Guess that means I'm not the only one who thinks she's just doin' what young people do. Butterin' up the boss or the show host or whoever it is that might give 'em a leg up."

"Am I the only one besides Mai Lan who sees what she's up to?" Daria didn't give Frankie time to reply. "Don't answer that. And don't tell me to apologize for making her cry."

"She cried?"

"Tell me you're not feeling sorry for her."

"Didn't you just call me the other day to say how great things went with your mama? What happened to the new, improved, empathetic Daria? Did she swoosh on outta' the sunroof when you crossed the state line into Connecticut?"

"Look, I've gotta go. I'll call you later." Daria hung up, went back to reading Fisher's weekly management report. But after the first three paragraphs of the same drivel she'd been reading for five years, she set it aside. She grabbed the iced tea, took a sip, then screwed the top back on and tossed it to the wastebasket. But when she missed her target, the tea splashed to the floor, and tears formed in her own eyes. She knew why she had lashed out at Cynthia. She was afraid. Again, always, still. Frankie was right. She had learned new lessons with her mother. Why hadn't they stuck? Because, Frankie would say, living the spiritual life took practice.

She had a choice. Another choice. She could try to repair the damage she had done.

She stood, walked to Cynthia's office, and knocked on the door. When she got no response, she reluctantly turned. She wasn't sure she would be able to summon this same willingness to set things right the next day.

But she heard a small and unfamiliar version of Cynthia's voice. "Yes."

When Daria opened the door, Cynthia lowered her eyes, now rimmed with runny mascara and eyeliner.

"May I come in?"

Cynthia sniffed. She nodded.

"I'm sorry I snapped at you."

"I'm sure you're under a lot of stress," Cynthia said. "What with your mother and all."

"No, Cynthia. It's not that. I mean, it is stressful, but she'll be okay."

"Just tell me what I've done." Cynthia's eyes teared again. "I really meant what I said. That things aren't the same when you're not around."

Daria sat in the chair facing Cynthia's desk. "For one thing," she said, "you came into this world a decade and a half after me. That, and the fact that you're beautiful, would be enough." She hesitated. "But you brought things to *Awakenings* I haven't wanted to recognize. Your spirituality, your optimism, your energy. They're what our audience really wants. And they come naturally to you. At least it looks that way." She shook her head. "For me . . . they're still castles in the air. I see them. I want them. But when I reach out to them, they dissipate and float away."

Cynthia looked perplexed.

"What I'm trying to say is, and I don't like admitting this, I feel threatened by you."

"Threatened? By me? Sure, I want to be like you. Learn from you. But threaten you? No."

Cynthia would say that whether or not it was true. Daria knew that. She grasped the arms of her chair, ready to haul herself up and leave the room. She had said too much. Besides, what difference would it make if Cynthia was flattering her? Right now, she just couldn't work up the energy to figure that out.

"Well, if I haven't pushed you too far away, how about coming back into my lion's den of an office? We'll go over next week's notes and see how we can give you some more airtime."

"Really?"

"Better yet," Daria said, "I need a pedicure before tomorrow's show. How about I make an appointment for both of us at Elegance, and we can catch up while we're treated like the local celebrities we are?"

******

Cynthia juggled a stack of files as she climbed into the pink Naugahyde pedicure station.

"Actually," Daria said, taking the chair next to Cynthia's, "give me those." She reached for the paperwork and set it on a chair next to her. "We can get to them later."

The two nail technicians approached, introduced themselves, and massaged the ladies' feet before setting them in the basins of swirling rosewater.

"Ahhhhh," Daria sighed. "I live for this." Then she turned to Cynthia. "When you've been to Healing House, did Mary Catherine mention that they're moving?"

Cynthia bit her lip and nodded. Uncharacteristically, she said nothing.

"And . . ." Daria rolled her hand to prompt a response. "What aren't you telling me?"

"I've been praying, unsuccessfully, I might add, to not badmouth the Healing House board over the whole thing. This is Connecticut, for Pete's sake. Land of milk and honey. People donate tons of money for tax deductions, or to have their names engraved into paving stones at libraries and yes, even churches. It can't be that hard to come up with a million or so to buy the place. It's as if—"

"Is that what it would take?"

"What?"

"A million dollars? To keep Healing House open?"

Cynthia shrugged. "I'm not sure it would cover the whole mortgage. But it would be a great start."

"Mango twist?"

When the nail technician held up a bottle of polish to ask if Daria wanted her usual color, Daria nodded, then turned back to Cynthia. "Have you ever run a fundraiser?"

"I was a Tri Delt in college," she said. "We had bake sales, sponsored walks for juvenile diabetes. Nothing big, though."

"Me either," Daria said. "But I know someone who has."

******

"And here she is," Frankie effused to a woman she had in tow on the Healing House lawn. "Daria, this is Sally Nieman. She's been dyin' to meet y'all. She's a little starstruck, even though I promised y'all are nice as can be. Now, don't make a fibber out of me." Frankie wagged her finger toward Daria.

Daria extended her hand to Sally, expecting Frankie would explain just who Sally Nieman was and how she learned about the HELP HEALING HOUSE HEAL fundraiser. But Frankie was already heading toward the door, calling to another woman—"Bitsy. How are you, darlin'?"—who was seated on a stone garden bench. No doubt Frankie would march her over to Daria, just as she had Sally.

After a few minutes' conversation with Sally, though, Daria excused herself and went to the chair where she sat with Mary Catherine the first time she visited Healing House. She wanted a break, just to take in what was happening. A roomful of women. All shapes, sizes, religious and spiritual persuasions. Some able to pay the thousand-dollar suggested donation. Others, like the women from

Frankie's shelter who were serving as waitresses, contributing their time and talent. The important thing was they were all playing a part in closing in on the fundraiser's goal, thanks mostly to Frankie.

But it wasn't just Frankie and the money being raised that Daria felt grateful for. Since she had returned from Pennsylvania, Daria had been attending Mary Catherine's healing circle. All the members, which now included Frankie, as well as Cynthia and Katrina, had come to the fundraiser.

There were other women too. Many Daria didn't know. She wondered what was going on in their lives, their minds, their hearts. She hoped they knew—or were learning—that a path was being laid for them, that they had choices along the way, and that their stories could help and heal other women.

Chapter Thirty-One
November 1993

Daria shook the rain from her slicker. She adjusted the shoulder strap of her leather tote, balanced it with the sack of herbs and veggies she'd bought at the greengrocer, and the smaller bag of treats from her new friend Lehanna's café. Then she reached inside the mailbox, took out the letters and magazines, and went inside.

After she set the bags and mail on the counter, Daria hung her coat on the rack near the door. When the phone rang, the two-oh-three area code lit up the caller ID. It was Frankie. Familiar Frankie. Daria grabbed the phone.

"I get you off the treadmill?"

"No, why?"

"You sound breathless. Almost anyway."

"No, no. I'm fine."

"Fine. Hmmm. I'm always a little suspect when someone says they're doin' fine. Happy, lonely, depressed, ecstatic. Those I can grab onto. But fine? I never know what to do with fine. So, tell me how you're really doin', sugar."

"Damn it, Frank. Even four hundred miles away I can't hide from you."

"Come out, come out wherever you are."

Daria laughed, then didn't waste another minute. "Okay, first, yes, I'm ever so grateful for the husband of my dreams. And that things are, well, not exactly perfect but better with my mother. The kids are off in Colorado, bonding with T.J.'s boys. Quite nicely, I think."

"So why do I get the feelin' there's a great big, plus-size 'but' at the end there?"

"But MacMillan's not New York. It's not even Fairfield County. I go to a concert at the university and—no matter how earnest or committed the performers are—all I can think of is how much better the Hallelujah Chorus or Mahler's Second would sound in Carnegie Hall. Besides, you're not here. Neither is Mary Catherine or Katrina. Cynthia, even. On the one hand, I miss the buzz. On the other hand, I miss the peace in the midst of crazy I was just beginning to get, thanks to all of you. Here, I don't know. It's so damned quiet and orderly."

"Sorry to interrupt, sugar, but hang on a sec while I grab my violin so I can accompany your sad, sad song. What about those nice girls you met at the book store? The one with the café where you have tea? Didn't that Cheryl actually get you to go to church? And don't give me anything about how much better the homily would have been if you heard it at Saint Patrick's."

"You're right, you're right. Cheryl's great. So is Lehanna. But . . ."

"But nothin', sugar. Just sounds to me like you brought yourself with you."

"Well, of course I did."

"Not just your body, darlin'. Your mindset. Your attitude. Whatever you want to call it. It's like you're still on the lookout for what's gonna fill you up when you've already got a tasty feast on the table right in front of you. But all you want is more, more, more."

"Okay, okay. I guess I just thought after all that time I spent with Katrina and Mary Catherine, and all the talking you and I did, through the experiences with Lizzy and Angela, I just thought, I don't know . . ."

Frankie laughed. "You thought all the work would be over and done? That you and the world were finally the way you wanted and you'd have nothing left to do but sail along on a big, fat cloud of spiritual bliss?"

"I guess I did."

"Remember what Mary Catherine told you about conversion? How it was just about circlin' 'round to where you started from?"

"Umm-hmm."

"Well, guess what?"

"I'm listening."

"Good. 'Cause once you get where you think you're goin', it's time to start all over again."

Daria groaned. "I just hoped it would be different."

"Who didn't? Can you imagine if somebody told us that before we started the work? You think anyone would take it on?"

"Probably not."

"So, what's our choice? Go backwards? I know I can't. And you? You don't have any idea how far you've come. Like Mary Catherine said, that's why we need each other to hold up that big ole' mirror, even when we'd rather not look. Which I might add, happens more and more now that these darn old crow's feet are diggin' in deeper by the day."

"No," Daria said. "Don't go there." She laughed. "You were doing fine when you stuck to the internal work. But the crow's feet, the crepey neck, the sagging . . . well, what isn't sagging? On that happy note, let me get to work, okay?"

"The book, you mean?"

"Yeah."

"Got a title yet?"

"Uh-huh. *At the End of the Storm*."

******

Daria stashed the groceries in the refrigerator, opened a bottle of mineral water, and drank it as she went upstairs. After changing from her rain-soaked jeans to her favorite old sweats, she worked her way through the mail.

First a postcard from Boulder, where Lizzy and Jack and their new stepbrothers were hiking: *Hi Mom. The Rockies are so cool! Needed a new parka and boots, though.* No doubt that was Lizzy's way of warning Daria that her credit card limit was about to be exceeded.

Next an envelope full of photos from Cynthia: *Doesn't Healing House look great?* she wrote in that loopy script of hers. But better than the newly painted building was the image of Mary Catherine and her associates, all smiling as they held up a hand-lettered sign—Thank You, Daria.

Then a note from Katrina, along with a shot of her at a press briefing for her new startup magazine. *Awakened,* it would be called, and it would target the audience Daria, and now Cynthia, cultivated on *Awakenings*.

Finally, a pale blue envelope forwarded from Sound Shore. The name Rush was written in the return address corner. Daria hadn't heard from Angela since their lunch at

Tableau a year earlier. She took a few deep breaths, asking for the ability to accept whatever Angela wrote. Then she reached for her letter opener, sliced through the envelope flap, and lifted out a note and a news clipping.

She read the clipping first. Not much more than a photo and caption. *Angela Rush, Tony Award-winning actress, shown with her son, Jackson.*

Then the note.

Daria—It wasn't long after we met that I found myself pregnant. (An actor who was tending bar at Tableau, the restaurant you and I met at, while he waited for his big break.) At first, I thought BIG MISTAKE. Then I realized I could learn from what you said. How you might do things differently when you were pregnant with me if you knew then what you know now. I kept him. And I can't imagine what life would be like if I hadn't. Jackson's a thousand times better than any Tony. I'm sorry I wasn't able to tell you how important it was for me to meet you. I couldn't then. But I can now.

I'd really like Jackson to know his Nana. Would you like to meet him? If you do, please call. We'd both like that very much.

Angela

Would I like to meet Jackson? Be his Nana? Of course! Daria gathered the picture of Jackson and Angela, Lizzy's postcard, Cynthia's note, the photo of Healing House. She tacked them to her bulletin board, next to the photos of Lizzy's daughter—the Harris's had named her Henley—and the one of Frankie, dressed in a raging red dress, dancing with her live-in lover, Andres.

Before Daria wrote back to Angela, though, she had work to do. She and Cheryl and Lehanna and the others in their writers' group committed that they would write every day and bring ten new pages to their weekly Thursday night workshops.

So far, Daria had written the chapters in her book on surrendering Angela back in the sixties and reuniting with her in the nineties; Nana's stories about Ausrine and the other Lithuanian gods and goddesses; and lessons learned from Jack, Frankie, and Katrina during Lizzy's pregnancy. Last week she finished the chapter on how her relationship with Helena changed once they both divulged their secrets.

This week, she would write about Mary Catherine and the healing circle. It would be the hardest to write—she suspected it would be, anyway—because she was still uncertain about where the light came from that they reflected to one another. Unlike the Magdalene, Daria hadn't yet heard a voice calling her name. But now and again, she found herself looking over her shoulder, wondering when she would.

She sat in her desk chair, then lit a candle. She closed her eyes and waited in silence, just like the women in the healing circle did each Saturday morning. Her thoughts raced. She had no idea where to begin. Besides, she felt certain that when she finally put words on paper, they would sound inconsequential, too small to help someone understand what she wanted to say.

Then, after five or so minutes, Daria's thoughts began to settle. Her doubts dissipated. When she opened her eyes and started to write, the words presented themselves.

Half an hour later, the front door opened. "Daria?"

"I'm in here, honey." Her eyes remained on her manuscript. "Working."

T.J. came to the office door and looked in. "Hi," he said. "How's the light of my life?"

The End

About The Author

Photo by John O'Neil

Marleen Pasch

Marleen Pasch lives and writes in South Florida. Her short fiction, creative nonfiction and articles on health, healing and spirituality appear in numerous periodicals and anthologies. As a workshop facilitator and writing coach, she helps aspiring writers discover their power on the page. Previous to writing full time, she was an award-winning corporate communications consultant. She is a graduate of Cornell University and a member of the Women's National Book Association.

**If You Enjoyed This Book
Visit**

PENMORE PRESS

www.penmorepress.com

All Penmore Press books are available directly through our website.

More books by Penmore Press below.

Carrie Welton

by

Charles Monagan

Eighteen-year-old Carrie Welton is restless, unhappy, and ill-suited to the conventions of nineteenth-century New England. Using her charm and a cunning scheme, she escapes the shadow of a cruel father and wanders into a thrilling series of high-wire adventures. Her travels take her all over the country, putting her in the path of Bohemian painters, poets, singers, social crusaders, opium eaters, violent gang members, and a group of female mountain climbers.

But Carrie's demons return to haunt her, bringing her to the edge of sanity and leading to a fateful expedition onto Longs Peak in Colorado. That's not the end, though. Carrie, being Carrie, sends an astonishing letter back from the grave and thus engineers her final escape—forever into your heart.

PENMORE PRESS
www.penmorepress.com

Mistress Suffragette

by

Diana Forbes

A young woman without prospects at a ball in Gilded Age Newport, Rhode Island is a target for a certain kind of "suitor." At the Memorial Day Ball during the Panic of 1893, impoverished but feisty Penelope Stanton draws the unwanted advances of a villainous millionaire banker who preys on distressed women—the incorrigible Edgar Daggers. Over a series of encounters, he promises Penelope the financial security she craves, but at what cost? Skilled in the art of flirtation, Edgar is not without his charms, and Penelope is attracted to him against her better judgment. Initially, as Penelope grows into her own in the burgeoning early Women's Suffrage Movement, Edgar exerts pressure, promising to use his power and access to help her advance. But can he be trusted, or are his words part of an elaborate mind game played between him and his wife? During a glittering age where a woman's reputation is her most valuable possession, Penelope must decide whether to compromise her principles for love, lust, and the allure of an easier life.

PENMORE PRESS
www.penmorepress.com

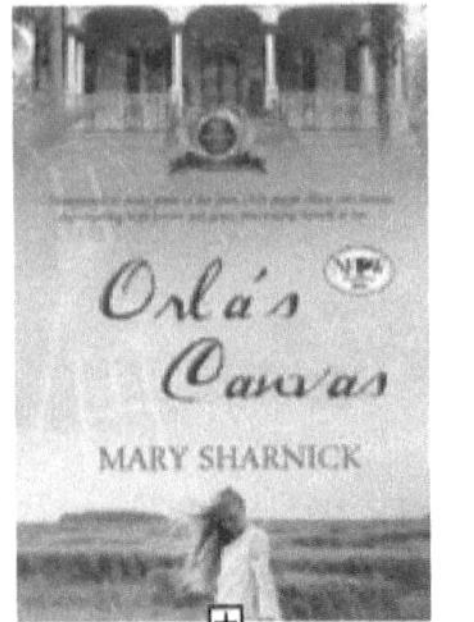

Orla's Canvas

By

Mary Sharnick

Narrated by eleven-year-old Orla Gwen Gleason, Orla's Canvas opens on Easter Sunday, in St. Suplice, Louisiana, a "misspelled town" north of New Orleans, and traces Orla's dawning realization that all is not as it seems in her personal life or in the life of her community. The death of St. Suplice's doyenne, Mrs. Bellefleur Dubois Castleberry, for whom Orla's mother keeps house, reveals Orla's true paternity, shatters her trust in her beloved mother, and exposes her to the harsh realities of class and race in the Civil Rights-era South. When the Klan learns of Mrs. Castleberry's collaboration with the local Negro minister and Archbishop Rummel to integrate the parochial school, violence fractures St. Suplice's vulnerable stability. The brutality Orla witnesses at summer's end awakens her to life's tenuous fragility. Like the South in which she lives, she suffers the turbulence of changing times. Smart, resilient, and fiercely determined to make sense of her pain, Orla paints chaos into beauty, documenting both horror and grace, discovering herself at last through her art.

PENMORE PRESS
www.penmorepress.com

THE LAUNDRY ROOM

BY

LYNDA LIPPMAN-LOCKHART

The Laundry Room dramatizes a fascinating moment in the history of the founding of Israel as a self-ruling nation. Based on actual events, Lynda Lippmann-Lockhart follows the lives of several young Israelis as they found a kibbutz and run a clandestine ammunition factory, which supplied Israeli troops fighting against Arab forces following the end of British occupation in the late 1940s. Under British rule, it was illegal for Israelis to possess firearms, so it was necessary not only to create and stockpile bullets for the coming war, but to do so in secret.

The ingenuity, courage, and sheer audacity displayed by the members of the code-named "Ayalon Institute" as they operated their factory right under the noses of the British military make for an intriguing tale. Lippmann-Lockhart shows readers what it might have been like to be one of the young pioneers whose work shaped the outcome of Israel's fight for independence. The Ayalon Institute remains standing to this day, but the secret hidden under the kibbutz's laundry room was not revealed until the 1970s. It was made a National Historic Site in 1987 and is open to the public every day of the year except Yom Kippur.

PENMORE PRESS
www.penmorepress.com